ALSO BY JAN BURKE

BLOODLINES

AN IRENE KELLY NOVEL

JAN BURKE

SIMON & SCHUSTER
New York   London   Toronto   Sydney

Simon & Schuster
Rockefeller Center
1230 Avenue of the Americas
New York, NY 10020

SIMON & SCHUSTER and colophon are registered trademarks
of Simon & Schuster, Inc.

Designed by Helene Berinsky

Manufactured in the United States of America

ISBN 0-7432-2390-X

In memory of my beloved uncle,
ROBERT M. FLYNN,
reporter for the *Evansville Press*

ACKNOWLEDGMENTS

I am indebted to several members and former members of the Los Angeles County Sheriff's Department for their kind assistance with the research for this book, most especially Detective (Ret.) Ike Sabean, Homicide Bureau Missing/Abducted Children, who was so generous with his time; Detective Elizabeth Smith, Homicide Bureau; and Barry A. J. Fisher, Scientific Services Division.

My thanks also to Edwin L. Jones, Forensic Scientist with the Ventura County Sheriff's Department Forensic Sciences Laboratory, whose awareness of historical crime lab processes, expertise in serology, and willingness to answer my questions was much appreciated. Jim Giddings of Genelex helped me to better understand DNA testing and changes in its applications within forensic science and paternity testing. My thanks to Ed German, CLPE, FFS, for his superb Web pages on fingerprint examination at www.onin.com/fp, including valuable historical information on the development of this field. Additional help was provided by John Mullins, forensic anthropologists Diane France and Marilyn London, and Dr. Ed Dorhing and Dr. Doug Lyle.

Robert M. Flynn, who wrote for the *Evansville* (Indiana) *Press* and was inducted into the Indiana Journalism Hall of Fame in 1992, was undoubtedly the first person to inspire my interest in the world of newspaper work. Many years before this book was completed, I talked to Uncle Bob about the background and story idea, and his reminiscences contributed much to it. I have also received generous and patient help from those he would have referred to as his "ink-stained friends," most especially Debbie Arrington of the *Sacramento Bee;* and a number of authors who were also part of that world for many years, including Charles Champlin, Michael Connelly, Peter O'Donnell, T. Jefferson Parker, Kathy Hogan Trocheck, and Elaine Viets.

My heartfelt gratitude to the staff and management of the *Long Beach Press-Telegram,* most especially to my friend John Futch, Executive News Editor, who gave so much time and assistance, and to Executive Editor Rich Archbold, who allowed me to sit in on meetings and to have access to the paper's newsroom and staff. Veteran reporter and copy editor Richard Stafford was also generous in speaking to me of his experiences.

Librarian Richard Partlow's father was a journalist who was blacklisted in the 1950s, and I thank Richard for helping me to better understand the impact the blacklist had on some reporters' careers.

Rob Bamberger, host of *Hot Jazz Saturday Night* on WAMU, a public radio station covering the Washington, D.C., area, helped me with music research of the kind that only someone with a true appreciation of his field can provide, and his program (accessed via the Internet) gave me great vintage jazz to listen to as I wrote. Thanks also to Dick La Palm, who was Nat King Cole's publicist, and who helped track down information about "Send for Me."

Matthew Godwin of www.earlytelephones.com helped me keep my nickel and dime pay phones straight, and provided other helpful information through his Web site.

Melodie and Greg Shaw, Bill Pratt, and Bob Phibbs not only provided the support of their friendship throughout the writing of the manuscript, they told me about the tunnels that still exist between some of the homes near the Long Beach shore and the bluffs. Bill also helped me with research regarding Rolls-Royces.

James Lincoln Warren, a commander in the U.S. Naval Reserve, took time from writing historical fiction to provide assistance with the scenes off the coast of Las Piernas. If I've run aground in any of those passages, it isn't his fault. Andy Langwiser of Andy's Books in Cypress, California, kindly allowed me to make use of his expertise from his years in major construction work, and O'Malley and his crew are the better for Andy's help. Many thanks to these gracious friends.

The Long Beach Public Library's periodical, local history, photograph, and map collections were used extensively in the research for this book, and I thank the library's excellent staff for their assistance.

Thanks to my family, especially my husband, Tim, and my sister, Sandra, who read nearly every version of this book as it evolved through rewrites. And to my friend S.G., thank you for teaching me a way back to the heart of the matter.

Marysue Rucci helped me find my way to a better manuscript and gave me room to write and rewrite it. Her patient championship made this book possible. To her, and to all of those at Simon & Schuster who lived with changing schedules, my deepest thanks.

PART I

PAPERBOY

Saturday, 11:45 P.M.
January 4, 1958

1

IF THE BLONDE HAD NOT PUT HER HAND ON JACK CORRIGAN'S THIGH, HE might have awakened in his own bed, rather than facedown on the side of a farm road in the middle of the night. Then he would have missed the burial.

Given his condition that night, he might have slept through everything that happened, but a cold wind cut through his clothing, rousing him. He rolled painfully onto his back and found himself looking up dizzily into the rustling, moonlit leaves of tall, thin trees. His perspective was marred by the alcohol in his veins, and the fact that his left eye was nearly swollen shut.

He closed his eyes and tried to recall how he had ended up here. He remembered the party and the blonde . . .

The blonde had smiled and said something to him, then she took another drag from her Lucky Strike.

Corrigan saw her heavily lipsticked red mouth form words, but he couldn't hear what they were. The rock-'n'-roll band was on a break, but someone had turned the radio up, and Jerry Lee Lewis's "Whole Lotta Shakin' Goin' On" was rattling the windowpanes. Conversation in the crowded room competed with the music by notching up the shouting level. An old injury kept him from joining the dancers. No, he admitted—even if his ankle hadn't troubled him, this was not his kind of music. You old fogey, he told himself, and not yet out of your forties.

Not his kind of music, and not his kind of party, which was part of the problem with his mood tonight. He wouldn't have come, but Katy had sent him a note, specifically asking him to be here.

Despite the note, neither Katy nor her mother, Lillian Vanderveer Linworth, had seemed especially friendly when he arrived. That didn't surprise him. Harold Linworth, the birthday girl's father—and Lillian's husband—had politely despised him for years.

Katy's in-laws were there as well, Thelma and Barrett Ducane. Barrett was already hitting the sauce, but Thelma looked almost sober for once. Jack planned to catch up to Barrett as soon as possible.

Thelma let it drop that they had just talked Katy and their son Todd into coming along for an after-hours party on their yacht. A moonlight cruise on their new fifty-foot Chris-Craft Catalina.

"I bought the Sea Dreamer for Thelma for Christmas," Barrett said. "She's quite the sailor, my little gal."

If Thelma was supposed to be the captain of this idiotic voyage, that explained the sobriety. She was careful with her toys. Although the Chris-Craft was by no means the most expensive boat they could afford—pocket change to them, he was sure—Jack thought of how tightfisted they were with their boys, Todd and Warren, and how readily they spent money on themselves. He asked if Warren would be joining them on the boat.

Thelma frowned, openly displeased by the question.

"I told Warren to come along," Barrett said, "but he's off with some of his cronies."

"Surprised to see you here, Jack," Thelma said. "You write for the society pages of the Express now?"

"Should be a nice night for a cruise, almost a full moon," he said, and as he walked away, added, under his breath, "perfect for lunatics like you, Thelma." Going out for a pleasure cruise on a January night. That bitch was nuts. She was probably trying to irritate Lillian, who had once been a close friend, but now had little to do with her. Lillian wouldn't like Katy being pulled away from the party by the Ducanes.

Lillian had always opposed Katy's marriage to Todd Ducane. She had made bigger plans for her daughter, and Jack supposed that after her falling-out with Thelma all those years ago, the idea of Katy marrying Thelma's son had been a bitter pill to swallow.

For once, Jack and Lillian were in agreement. Jack had never liked any of the Ducanes, including Todd. The Toad, as Jack thought of him. But Katy had rebelled. He knew she had since come to see her mistake, but so far, she hadn't rectified it.

Lillian hadn't chosen so well herself, Jack thought, watching as the family gathered for photos. Harold Linworth had little more than his wealth to recommend him. Maybe that had been enough for Lillian. At forty, Lillian was still a looker. But standing next to Katy—Jack smiled to himself. Katy was a little subdued tonight, but still she had that quality, a fire within that drew others to her warmth. Not all of Lily's beauty could match it.

He watched as parents and in-laws stood next to Katy and Todd, the six of them smiling stiffly as a photographer went through the juggling act of focus, shoot, eject the used flashbulb, put a new one in, focus, shoot, and so on.

Why wasn't Warren around? The Ducane brothers were close. He glanced at Thelma and thought he had his answer. He was fairly sure all it would take to keep Warren away would be a demand by Thelma that he attend the party. There was the difference in the two boys—Todd acquiesced to their every demand, hoping to catch crumbs from their table. Warren rebelled. If that was what kept him away tonight, Jack had to admire him for it.

What the hell was he doing here himself?

But Jack had never been able to turn down Katy's requests. Her twenty-first birthday. Katy an adult. What nonsense. She was already a wife and mother. Yet to Jack, she was still a child herself.

Her elegant appearance this evening hadn't changed his thoughts on that—all dressed up in a demure evening gown and long gloves, wearing the Vanderveer family diamonds at her neck. Her dark hair was pinned up in a sophisticated style, her brown eyes emphasized by carefully applied liner.

The overall effect had been spoiled somewhat by the pug. Corrigan hated that damned dog and seeing her holding it tonight angered him. Max, her two-month-old son, left at home—attended to by some stranger, a hired nurse—but the dog in her arms. Maybe that was the sort of family life the Ducanes might like, distanced from their children, but Jack hated to see Katy influenced by Todd in that way.

When Katy greeted him, she leaned forward a little, and the dog squirmed awkwardly between them. She shook Jack's hand, saying, "What an unexpected pleasure." Her sardonic tone would lead any listener to believe he was a party crasher. If she hadn't softly added, for his ear only, "Later," he would have turned on his heel and left.

He did try to leave at one point—even had his hat and coat in hand. Katy had hurried over to him and taken them from him. "Don't be silly," she said, handing the hat to the butler, Hastings, and smoothing the coat into a neatness that didn't seem natural to it.

"Careful, you'll ruin your dress," he said, noticing that he needed to take the coat to the cleaners.

"To hell with the dress," she said, and flung the coat around her shoulders. She smiled at him, eyes bright with mischief. "Now, this is comfort. And it reeks of cigarettes and spilled booze and—what's this?" Pretending to sniff the collar. "Ah, yes, ink. You must have cut yourself."

He laughed.

She took it off again, handing it to Hastings. "Uncle Jack—"

"Does your mother know you still call me that?"

"Never mind her," she said angrily.

"On the outs again, are you? Is that why you've asked to talk to me?"

"No," she said, "no, of course not. Oh, Uncle Jack, please. Please stay until we can talk. You always tell me the truth, and I need—" But she looked up and saw her husband making his way toward them. "Oh damn, here comes Todd."

"Leaving, Jack?" Todd asked hopefully.

"No, just getting my cigarette lighter out of my coat pocket."

"Oh . . . well, excuse us, but there are some people waiting to talk to Kathleen."

Katy leaned closer to Jack and kissed his cheek, then again whispered, "Later," before allowing Todd to steer her away.

Still, she had made no effort to come near him since.

Corrigan was drinking heavily, as usual, but tonight he knew himself for an especially sorry sort of drunk. "Self-pity makes a lousy chaser," he said aloud.

"What?" the blonde shouted back, confused.

"Nothing." He grabbed two martinis from a passing waiter's tray and handed one to the blonde. She smiled. He thought she said thanks.

He looked away from the blonde and scanned the crowd, wondering if he'd catch another glimpse of Lillian or Katy. Unlikely, given the press of humanity between his seat and where Lillian and her daughter were holding court. Trouble with a January party was, most years it was too cold outside on the veranda, so nobody ever had any breathing room. He downed the martini and watched for another waiter.

He would never, so long as he lived, understand the rich. Why had Katy wanted him to be here? A whim, no doubt. She was a bit of a troublemaker, Katy. Kathleen. He was one of the few who ever called her Katy. He smiled, thinking of how it fired her up when he did so. He was a bit of a troublemaker himself.

He thought about that whispered "Later," and about a look he thought he had seen in her eye, something just before Todd the Toad ushered her away from him. It made him wonder why the birthday girl, normally sunny and vivacious, looked so unhappy most of the night. He meant to find out. Curiosity was his besetting sin, and a necessary part of his work as a reporter.

Most of her friends would not believe anything amiss. The smile was still there and as usual a crowd of her admirers near at hand. They didn't know her as well as Jack did.

After a while it was clear that the Toad was on guard and ready to maneuver Jack away from Katy whenever he drew near. The Toad hovered over her tonight—lighting her cigarettes, making sure her half-empty martini glasses were exchanged for full ones, feeding canapés to her dog. Jack decided to bide his time and drink up Lillian and Harold's expensive booze until he could evade their son-in-law.

One of the attentive servants made his way to Corrigan and exchanged the empty glass for a fresh drink.

The party was a success, if you measured such things by the lack of room to move, the sound of raucous laughter, the cloud of smoke hanging thickly in the air. He wondered what Lillian really thought of it. He was surprised at the roughness of some of the characters he saw here tonight. Todd's friends, he supposed. Harold probably hated to see such riffraff crossing the Linworths' Italian marble floors. Not that all of the Linworths' friends and acquaintances were on the up-and-up.

The blonde interrupted his musings with the hand on his thigh. Less than an instant later, he felt a hand on his collar, pulling back hard and cutting off his breath, then yanking him up onto his unsteady feet. A big, fair-haired man with a crewcut was shouting something about keeping his hands off his wife, and before Jack could so much as clench a fist, the giant had landed a blow that knocked him out cold.

Corrigan felt the wind and the chilled earth beneath him and shivered into something like wakefulness. He had passed out again. For how long? He slowly rolled onto his stomach and then pushed himself to his knees. He tried to take inventory. He was sore every damned where. His bad ankle—the one that had doomed his efforts to enlist—hurt like hell. Nothing new there.

He felt along the ground for his hat, but saw no sign of it. He half-hoped the lummox who had attacked him—and yes, at least one other man—had left it with his coat at Lillian's place. If not, it had probably blown away. Corrigan sighed. Young O'Connor told him hats were going out of style, but Corrigan couldn't feel dressed without one.

Still on his knees, he patted his vest, pleased to find the pocket watch still on its chain, not as pleased when the crystal fell out in little pieces. The hour hand was gone. He put the watch back in its pocket, feeling the sore spot where it had been driven into a rib. He had a bruise on his thigh from where something similar had happened with his keys. He eased his cut and swollen fingers into his pants pockets to make sure the keys were still there, and was relieved to find them. A small saint's medal had been lost off the chain, but at least he'd be able to get back into his house without calling O'Connor. And checking his back pocket, he discovered he still had his wallet. He hadn't been robbed.

He rose painfully to his feet, staggering from the double influence of blows and drink.

It was a noisy, shadowy world he had awakened to, one smelling of earth and something medicinal—menthol or camphor. No, he slowly realized, it was eucalyptus. He was standing beneath a eucalyptus, along the outer edge of a narrow grove of the spindly giants, trees probably planted as a windbreak. On the other side of the road, a barbed-wire fence surrounded an empty pasture; in the distance, the tin roof of a dairy barn reflected the moonlight. He was wondering if he could make it that far, maybe sleep it off in the barn, when he heard the sound of an engine starting up somewhere behind him.

Corrigan was seldom a cautious man, but the beating had shaken him, so he stepped back into the moving shadows of the trees, concerned that the giant and his friend might be seeking further amusement at his expense. He frowned at the injustice of it. He hadn't known the woman was accompanied, let alone married, and only the inertia brought on by a forgotten number of martinis had kept him sitting near her as she pressed her attentions on him.

Except for a fleeting image of awakening once in a sedan—a Bel Air? What made him think that? A moment of being propped up against its two-tone paint job? He wasn't sure. He had no certain idea of how they had brought him here. He thought he remembered smelling the woman's perfume coming from somewhere within the car, but he couldn't swear that she had been in the sedan with them.

He watched the road for several minutes before he understood that no car was on it. He moved forward toward the source of the noise, his usual slight limp now a hobbling, uneven gait. He paused at the edge of the grove, peered out from behind one of the wider trees. He could only see from his right eye now, which added to his sense of disorientation.

Before him lay a fallow field. His attention was drawn to an object that sat not far from him: a blue Buick sedan.

The Buick had clearly been in an accident; the front end was crumpled into sharp folds that angled back toward the windshield, so that the car seemed to be forever frozen in a posture of flinching, its metal-toothed grill caught in a buckled grimace. The windshield was darkened and webbed with cracks.

Corrigan steadied himself against the tree, fighting memories of another car accident, long ago. The motor sound drew his attention again. It was not coming from the car, but from somewhere beyond. Not a car motor, but a diesel engine—perhaps a truck or a bus. Where was it? He heard the engine strain as gears shifted.

Suddenly there was light, light from the ground—a beam tilting over the field at a forty-five-degree angle. He watched in disbelief as headlights emerged somewhere behind the car, seemingly from the earth itself. A tractor, coming toward him.

The headlights of the tractor shone through the car from behind, eerily illuminating the Buick's interior, the shattered windshield. Corrigan's stomach lurched as he saw the fractured glass was covered with a brownish red glaze. Bloodstains.

The sight of that blood made Corrigan obey an impulse to hide himself from the driver of the tractor. He moved clumsily farther into the trees and crouched near a low, leafy branch. His head was pounding now, pulsing with the throb of the tractor's motor, refusing to cooperate with his struggle to comprehend what he was seeing.

The tractor circled the car and came to a stop. The gears shifted again and the tractor stood idling as a small, wiry man climbed from the seat. He wore a cap and kept his head down as he marched back to the car, a heavy chain on his shoulder. Corrigan heard more than saw the man attach the chain to the back axle of the Buick.

Soon the driver was back on the tractor, the gears shifting as he pulled the Buick across the field toward the place where the tractor had emerged. Corrigan stepped out from behind the tree, tried to make out the odd shapes of earth and man and machinery across the field. The headlights of the tractor and the moonlight combined to provide just enough light to see an earthen ramp leading down into a shallow pit. Tall piles of loose soil stood at its edges.

The man on the tractor climbed down again, removed the chain, and then maneuvered the tractor so that it pushed the car with a gentle shove, sending the Buick down the ramp and into the pit. Corrigan heard the last loud groan of metal as the car came to a rough halt somewhere against the earth below.

A sharp barking came from the dairy farm across the road, dogs reacting to the unfamiliar noise. The tractor driver turned and saw Corrigan.

Corrigan hobbled back into the trees. He kept moving, tried to stretch his agonizing, clumsy stride as he heard the tractor motor start up again.

It was coming closer now, had crossed the field too fast, much too fast. His ankle was on fire, he couldn't breathe for the ache in his ribs, but he pushed on, held down the bile of fear that rose in his throat. He stayed in the grove, watched the shadows of the tree trunks sharpen as the headlights of the tractor drew closer.

The little sodbuster couldn't come in here with his big damned lummox of a tractor, Corrigan thought, just before he stumbled and took a hard fall into blackness.

2

Gus Ronden ran the washcloth over his arms and chest, then rinsed it out before going to work on his hands. He used a small brush to scrub his nails until the skin at the tips of his fingers bled. He smiled as he washed it down the drain, thinking of his blood mixing with all the other blood.

He had kept the gloves on for most of it, and the boss might have been unhappy to know he had taken them off, even for a moment. But he had never been able to resist the warm, slippery feel of blood, and so he had permitted himself a little barehanded touching. He had been careful, though. The gloves went right back on again.

He would have liked to take a shower, but he didn't want to risk not hearing the door. This had been a busy evening, and he knew the boss was pleased with him. Hinted at a bonus. Well, he wouldn't hear any bitching from Gus if he didn't come through. The truth was, it had all been exciting as hell. He closed his eyes, reliving some of the best parts, then shook himself. He washed down the sink with bleach.

There was still much more to do. He had plenty of time, he was sure, before anyone who was expected would arrive, but he wanted to be ready for the unexpected. That way of doing business had kept him alive.

He had no sooner thought this than he heard a familiar pattern of knocks on the door. Fucking Bo Jergenson! What was the idiot doing back so soon? He quickly gathered the clothing he had stripped out of and stuffed it into the hamper, then grabbed a robe and his .38 automatic. He opened the small metal cover of the speakeasy grill in the door, and seeing that it was indeed Jergenson, called him a dumb fuck to his face before unlocking and opening the door itself.

"Get the hell in here," he said, motioning the trio that stood on his front porch inside, not wanting the neighbors to notice them. "Sit in the living room until I get changed."

He dressed rapidly, mentally cussing out Bo Jergenson all the while.

*   *   *

Bo Jergenson couldn't figure out why Gus Ronden was pissed off all the time. He decided it wasn't worth worrying about. The news he had should cheer up Ronden and the boss. Ronden had just stomped into the room he used as an office and called to Bo to get his ass in there. Bo decided not to take offense. After tonight, he'd have nothing to do with Gus.

"Everything just the way you asked," Bo said, tossing a small, round metal object down on the big desk and taking a seat.

"What the hell is that?" Ronden asked, looking across the desk at him.

"One of them Catholic medals."

"What the hell do I want with some mick's voodoo crap? Those mackerel-eaters are worse than the damned shines with their superstitions. Didn't help him any, did it?"

"Just took it as a little trophy, that's all. Don't mean nothing to me."

"You got back here pretty fast," Gus said, scratching at his black curly hair. Bo, absorbed in watching white flakes of dandruff cascade onto Gus's shoulders, was startled when Gus suddenly asked, "Where did you leave him? It can't be anywhere near here."

"I know. You said so before. So I took him out to the farm."

Gus's face went white, then red. "The farm? You idiot! You damned idiot! Do you know what the boss is going to do to you? Get back out there now!"

Bo was startled at this reaction. "Why should the boss be mad? It will take that gimpy guy forever to walk back here with that bum leg of his."

"Because, you moron, that gimpy guy is a newspaper reporter."

"Reporter!" Bo said, coming to his feet. "Damn it, you didn't tell me anything about that!"

"Well, he is. This could ruin everything. My God." He thought for a moment, then said, "You gotta go back there and take him somewhere else. Then kill him."

Bo shifted his weight. "Kill him? No, no. I didn't sign on for anything like that. You know that's not in my line. Besides, he's out cold."

"You don't know Jack Corrigan. Get him."

"I thought the boss wanted him alive."

"He won't want him alive now—not after this."

"I'm not going to murder nobody, especially not a reporter. They're like the cops—you knock one off, the others come swarming after you. And they don't give up so easy. Just 'cause he's out at the farm don't mean nothing. He don't know what's going on there. He's a city boy."

There was a long silence.

"I'm not going to murder nobody," Bo said again. "Betty or Lew or anybody else squeals on me, I could get the chair. Forget it. And all them people at that party—they seen me have a fight with him." Bo suddenly thought of the butler who had challenged them at the door. He felt relief that he had given the man a phony name.

"All right," Gus said, after a moment. "Since you don't have the guts for it, I'll handle this myself. You'll have to show me exactly where you left him. With luck, he's still there. You come with me—just you and me. The other two will go on to the cabin. We'll collect our pay and we'll be all square."

Bo didn't like it. Even after Gus walked out of the office, Bo stood thinking, trying to figure out how things could go wrong. If Gus did the killing, he should be all right. Bo's vague sense of foreboding didn't lead him to any specific misgivings.

He could hear Gus in the other room, giving directions to Betty and Lew. Lew went right along with Gus's plans, as always, and said, "Tell Bo we'll see him later, then." Betty—what a dame she was!—who had played her part so well at the party, didn't say anything. If she had any questions, she kept them to herself. Bo decided he wouldn't ask any questions, either. Mostly because he wasn't sure what he would ask, anyway.

He started to leave the office, then saw the medal. He picked it up and pocketed it.

Maybe he wasn't as smart as Gus, but he wasn't dumb enough to leave a trophy from a dead man sitting on a desk.

Ezra Mayhope pulled his pickup truck to the side of the dirt road. He opened the thermos and poured a cup of coffee into the cap, then took a long sip.

He didn't need the coffee to stay awake. Dawn was still more than an hour away, but Ezra's day had started two hours ago, when he began loading the pickup truck with the eggs he'd be taking to downtown Las Piernas, to the big hotels there.

The coffee took the chill off the cold, foggy night.

Until a few miles back, his thoughts had been occupied with the subject other local farmers and dairymen were talking about lately—the sprawl of the suburbs over farmland. There were already little enclaves here and there. This housing tract or that one. On the edges of the cities now, but everyone knew what would happen. These new residents would cause taxes to go up, insist on paved roads, drive up the price of water, and bitch about flies and the smell of coops and dairy yards and beets and what have you.

Was a time, Ezra thought now, when no one honked a horn at a tractor. Tractor was the only thing on the road. And nobody was in a big damned rush. Ezra had been forced to go slowly as the road left dairy farms and fields behind and began to skirt the edge of the marshes, where the fog usually hung so thick, you couldn't see much of anything for more than a few yards in any direction. A drive he could have done on any other night, fog or no fog, with hardly a care in the world—but a few miles back, some idiot had driven past him in a hell of hurry, and taking up just about the whole of the road with a fancy city car—a big old Cadillac or Lincoln, maybe. Flew by. Bastard was like to have forced Ezra and his eggs into the soft, salty mire, but somehow they managed to pass each other without a scrape—or anyone landing in the marsh.

In ten years of driving this route, coming from his chicken farm to this intersection, he rarely encountered another vehicle going in the other direction at this time of night. Always scared the bejesus out of him whenever he did, because it was almost always someone from town, not knowing how to drive these narrow roads. He drank his coffee and told himself that was all that unsettled him.

He glanced around and shivered. The marsh was always a creepy place. His kids had begged him to take them to see that monster movie a few years back, *The Creature from the Black Lagoon*. Saw it in 3-D, which gave him a headache, but it was pretty real, all right. It was a bad movie for a man to see if he was someone who had to drive past a marsh in the dark.

The coffee made him feel a little steadier. He'd finish his coffee, then pull out from the intersection onto a slightly wider dirt road, one that would eventually connect him to a paved street that led to Pacific Coast Highway. He'd take Coast Highway to downtown and head over to the Angelus and the other hotels that would be waiting for their deliveries.

He heard a splashing sound and looked to his right. He thought it must have been one of the big seabirds moving through the water, a heron, perhaps. But the sound came again. Then, unmistakably, coughing. Next a sound like retching, then moaning.

"Sweet Lord," Ezra said, watching as a shadowy creature crawled from the marsh. He put the truck in gear and pulled out onto the road, spilling coffee all over the floorboards as he tossed the lid of the thermos down in his haste.

He reached the paved road before his conscience overrode his panic. He was a God-fearing man who read his Bible and he knew the story of the Good Samaritan as well as anybody. The Las Piernas marshes were not the Black Lagoon. That had been a man. A man most likely in trouble. He turned the truck around.

He carefully maneuvered the truck so that the headlights were shining toward the place where he had heard the sound. He immediately saw the form he had seen before. Lying facedown, now, not even all the way out of the water. Soaked in mire.

Ezra got out of the cab of the truck, carrying a flashlight clenched in his fist. He was generally a peaceable man, but stories of the Good Samaritan or no, a fellow had to be careful. What business did anyone have out here this time of night, anyway? What if this fellow was drunk and surly? Never could tell with drunks.

As he approached, though, he saw that the man was shivering hard. Ezra's wariness left him. The man wasn't just shivering, it was a dreadful kind of shaking.

"Hey!" Ezra called. "Hey, you all right?"

The man half-lifted his head and looked at Ezra, although Ezra wasn't sure the man really saw him. The man's face was a horrible sight, bloody and distorted, one eye completely swollen closed. The other eye was open, and Ezra saw that it was a blue eye. The man moaned and dropped his head again. The shaking continued.

Ezra came closer. He had never seen a man who had been so terribly beaten.

Ezra pulled him from the water, then tried to coax him to his feet, but realized the man had passed out. He tried to rouse the man and couldn't. The man's skin was so icy, he was worried that he had not just passed out but died. Ezra lifted him, and the man made a whimpering sound that cut right through Ezra. He had a strange feeling that this was not a man given to making that kind of sound.

He was bigger than Ezra, who struggled to keep his balance as he half-carried, half-dragged the man to the truck. Before long, Ezra was nearly as damp from marsh water as the man. He put him in the passenger side of the cab and closed the door. The man was completely silent now.

He'd take him to St. Mary's, Ezra decided. It would make him late with his deliveries, but he didn't trouble himself too much with that. With any luck, the hotels wouldn't stop buying eggs from him if he told them he had to stop to save a man's life.

That is, he added, looking at the figure slumped against the door, if he had been in time to do any such thing.

3

As they rode in the turquoise and white Chevy Bel Air, Betty Bradford decided that she liked Lew Hacker, liked him plenty. He wasn't much to look at, but still, she liked him. She liked that he was quiet and calm and didn't ask a girl a lot of stupid questions about whether she was a real blonde, or how had she ended up in the life, or could he have a free one?

Lew never talked about any of that with her, although she knew he was as flesh and blood as any other man. Hell, he had a stiffy right now. Hadn't, before she took off her shoes. She turned sideways on the front seat, pulling up her knees so that her feet were on the seat between them, her skirt a tent over her legs. And look who had a tent pole . . .

She pulled a pack of Black Jack gum out of her purse and asked him if he'd like a piece. He laughed a little, getting the joke, which made her like him more. He said he'd always liked Black Jack, even before he was twenty-one, a joke she got right away, which made her feel good, proud of herself.

"We're not going to the cabin, are we, Lew?"

"No."

"So you're passing up all that dough we're supposed to be getting?"

"Supposed to," he repeated. After a moment, he said, "I didn't like Gus's mood."

"I'm with you," Betty said. "What good is the money if you ain't breathing?"

"That's it."

"They didn't tell us everything that was going on tonight, did they?"

"No."

"I mean, okay, someone is owed a beating, that's one thing. Do you know what Gus was up to while we were busy with that guy at the party?"

"No, but I can guess."

She thought this over for a moment, then said, "I'm sticking with you, if that's all right."

"That's more than all right. You're a smart girl."

No one had ever said that to her. Not ever. But it was true. Maybe she wasn't Albert Einstein—okay, she'd be the first to admit that she never did so good in school. Even so, she was able to think for herself, and she had known Gus long enough to have an idea of when he was turning dangerous. That was the first thing a person ought to figure out about anybody, especially in her line of work.

It wasn't always easy. The boss had more than one or two creeps on his payroll, some worse than Gus. She thought about one who no longer worked for him—Bennie Lee Harmon—because he had been sent to San Quentin, sentenced to death for torturing and killing a couple of working girls. The poor kids were just a year or two younger than she was. She shuddered. She never would have guessed it about Bennie. He was good-looking, even seemed kind of meek.

One of the boys said that Gus himself had gone crazy not long ago and cut up a young girl down in Nigger Slough, west of town. One of the others said it happened a long time ago, somewhere else. Until tonight, she hadn't been so sure that it had ever happened at all. Nothing in the paper about it, but they never did write much about things that happened to the coloreds, especially not that ragged bunch down in the slough. Killing a white girl, though! Until tonight, she didn't think Gus would do anything like that.

She had seen that Gus was in a dangerous mood tonight, and he was in one even before Bo went in to talk to him.

Bo. Now, there was a big, sweet dummy. While he went in to talk to Gus, she went into the bathroom and happened to see something she wished to God she had never seen: a laundry hamper with some bloody clothes in it. She figured Gus would never, ever, not in a thousand years, leave something so obvious out where someone could see it. It never would have been there if they hadn't surprised him by coming back so soon. And she figured that if Gus had been happy about them being back so soon, he would have said, "Great, let's go, everybody," and they would have all gone together. But he told Bo to follow him into his office.

She didn't say a word about what she had seen, but Lew went into the bathroom a little later, and she knew he saw it, too. He hadn't said a word all night, but after that, he even *looked* quieter.

She read Gus the minute he walked out and told them to go to the cabin. Saw him look hard at Lew. She didn't think Lew gave anything away, though. He was calm as could be. She wondered if Gus thought Lew was stupid just because he never said anything. Gus was the idiot. Putting Bo in charge of anything wasn't really such a bright idea.

She thought about her car and frowned. Would she ever see it again? Probably not. Not a good idea to go back to Las Piernas, and that's where it was, locked in the garage at Gus's place. The car was a present from a married, rich man who had spoiled her for a time, until he had learned she was two-timing him with Gus. But he let her keep the car, which had special pink carpet installed over the floorboards.

That was the rich guy's little joke, and oh, how she had laughed when she first saw it. She never wore pink dresses, but she adored pink underwear. It gave her a kind of secret pleasure, knowing she wasn't wearing anything drab and white, or too sexy like black or red. Pink was innocent, but a little naughty, too. The fellows she went with always went wild for it—the rich fellow more than any of them. He told her the carpet in the car would be just like her underpants, a little hidden delight that most people wouldn't see until they got close.

She didn't miss the rich guy. She didn't mind leaving Gus. She figured not much good had come to her in Las Piernas, but she surely wished they had her car. She glanced at her purse, thought about the little something in it that she had stolen from the boss's office one night when Gus had been meeting with him out on the farm. That had both thrilled and scared her, but a girl had to look out for herself. Maybe someday it would come in handy, and she could get a new car out of it.

She watched Lew's long brown fingers on the steering wheel of the Bel Air, holding sure and steady as he drove down El Camino Real toward San Diego. She tucked her toes under Lew's thigh. When he looked over at her, she said, "Mind if I keep them warm?"

He shook his head. She saw him swallow hard and she smiled. "Where are we going?"

"Mexico."

"I don't speak Mexican."

"I speak Spanish. We'll be all right."

"You speak two languages? Brother, you don't say much in either one of them."

"*A buen entendedor, pocas palabras,*" he said.

"What does that mean?"

"To she who understands well, few words are needed," he said, and ran a strong hand along her nylon stockings from her heel to the back of her knee, causing her skirt to cascade softly back to her hips, exposing the place where her stockings attached to her garters, and beneath, a glimpse of pink.

4

Eric Yeager shivered and tucked his large hands into the pockets of his peacoat. He waited in darkness behind a rusted iron gate and looked out toward the sea, although the fog was now so thick he couldn't see the ocean, a hundred yards away. He could hear it, though. A storm was coming. If he hadn't heard that on his car radio, he would have known it by the sound of the breakers. He stretched a little, his muscles sore from a hard night's work. There was a painful wound on his forearm that stopped him mid-stretch. He felt a brief flare of anger as he recalled receiving it, then smiled to himself. The wound had, after all, been more than avenged.

He was a young man, strong, and if not precisely handsome, attractive enough to draw women to his side without much effort. He was not foolish enough to doubt that his uncle's millions were part of that magnetism. Everyone in Las Piernas knew that Mitch Yeager and his wife were childless, and doted on Eric and Ian, their nephews, who had lost both parents before they were ten.

He wondered what everyone in Las Piernas would think of Uncle Mitch's latest act of charity. Word wasn't out about the adoption yet, but once it was, would women be so anxious to date Eric and Ian, knowing Uncle Mitch now had a young son?

Uncle Mitch had assured them that he would always take care of them, but Eric was uneasy. Ian, younger and bolder than Eric, had shrugged this off. "We're worse off without Uncle Mitch than we are with him. He didn't have to do shit for us, and look how many nice things he does for us all the time. We owe him some loyalty—think about Aunt Estelle."

Eric didn't have much respect for his aunt, who never stood up to anybody, but he knew that she loved babies and had always been sad about not having one of her own. Maybe, as Ian claimed, Uncle Mitch had decided to take this kid under his roof for her sake.

Eric doubted it.

He knew what Ian would say to that, too. Ian sometimes called him "'Fraidy," as in "'Fraidy Cat." Eric had beat the crap out of him more than once for that, but nobody ever taught Ian anything with a fist. Eric secretly admired him for it, but still wished he would wise up about Uncle Mitch. They couldn't count on him forever. Especially not with this new kid in the picture.

"Uncle Mitch's plans are always good ones," Ian had said. "You know that." He smiled and cuffed Eric on the shoulder. "You aren't jealous of an itty-bitty baby, are you?"

"Just worried about the future, little brother," Eric said. Every now and then he had to rub in the fact that he was older.

"You know what's wrong with you? You need some action. When you aren't doing anything else, you worry."

Eric admitted this was true. Tonight, he hadn't found time to worry at all, until now, when he was sitting here waiting for Ian.

Eric reached into his coat and brought out a pack of cigarettes and a silver monogrammed lighter. Neither the initials nor the lighter were his. He flicked the flint wheel of the lighter and it sparked a flame on the first try. Pleased at this, he closed the lighter with another motion of his wrist and repeated the actions several times before he lit a Pall Mall, something Uncle Mitch would have hated to see him do. Uncle Mitch hated cigarette smoking. A pipe or an occasional cigar would have met with his approval. This, Eric thought, was the kind of crazy shit he had to put up with.

Now, when he was supposed to remain concealed, Uncle Mitch would have especially disliked seeing him smoke or playing with the lighter. He would have knocked the crap out of Eric for stealing the lighter in the first place.

Uncle Mitch didn't like the fact that Eric and Ian liked to read James Bond books. Didn't seem to understand that those were the only books they wanted to read at all. Uncle Mitch was trying to move up in the world, and didn't want them to read paperback novels. So what. Eric had a copy of *From Russia with Love* waiting for him at home.

Every now and again, Eric had to do something that Uncle Mitch wouldn't like.

He reached into his pocket again and felt comforted by the small objects he touched.

Let Uncle Mitch have his baby. Eric would make sure that he and Ian would be all right.

The concrete beneath his feet was as damp as if it had already rained. He looked around him. These old bootleggers' tunnels weren't built for comfort. This one led back to a mansion up on the bluff. The boats would pull ashore on moonless nights, and the rumrunners would bring the booze up from the shore into these tunnels, and then into the cellars of the rich people's houses. If the prohibition agents asked questions, why, the rich people just said they used the tunnels to store their little boats or to get down to the beach to sun-bathe. Nothing the government could do about that.

Eric liked to think he would have made a good bootlegger. His dad, Adam Yeager, had been a rumrunner. Eric barely remembered him, but Uncle Mitch had made sure to tell the boys all about him as they were growing up. Whatever else you might want to say about Uncle Mitch, you had to admit he loved Eric's dad.

His dad had been one wild son of a bitch, but smart, too. The family had lost a lot of money during the Depression. Adam's bootlegging kept them out of poverty. That's what Uncle Mitch always said.

The fog had rolled in sooner than expected, and as the minutes went by, Eric began to wonder if Ian would be able to make it ashore without trouble. Maybe Uncle Mitch didn't always make such great plans after all. In fact, Eric was certain of that.

Eric tended to improvise more than Ian did. Sometimes things happened on the spot, and you had to be able to react, kind of like James Bond might.

Tonight he had been forced to make some decisions, and they were good ones. He hoped Ian had been able to figure out what to do. It was taking him too long to get back here.

If anything had happened to Ian . . .

He heard someone moving across the sand, coming closer. He hesitated, then took another drag.

"Put out that damned cigarette," a voice said from the whiteness beyond. Gradually, Eric could make out the figure in the wet suit. Ian was okay. Everything was going to be okay.

"Try and make me, little brother," he answered, and laughed.

5

MITCH YEAGER HUNG UP THE PHONE AND EXHALED HARSHLY. HE listened, wondering if the call had awakened Estelle and the baby, but upstairs, all was quiet.

He had expected to feel different somehow. So much waiting and planning had gone into this night. Not everything had been done according to his instructions, of course. And there were a few more matters to attend to. His pleasure would have to wait a bit longer.

He could be patient.

The thought made him smile.

Loose ends. That was it. He would feel better once he settled everything to his satisfaction.

At least he knew Eric and Ian were home now. He would have to find some way to reward them. Eric, he thought, needed more assurance. He loved his nephews, but neither of them was all that bright. Took after their late mother in the brains department.

Mitch heard the baby cry, but Estelle rushed in to take care of him, and soon he quieted. Mitch wondered if the boy would be smart. Couldn't really tell yet, of course. If he was, Mitch would teach him to run Yeager Enterprises. Wouldn't that be something? Yes, that would be perfect.

He moved to his desk and picked up a small, framed photograph—a black-and-white image of Mitch and his brother. Adam, about twenty, his arm around Mitch's skinny shoulders. Mitch was fifteen or so. Adam smiling, his eyes full of mischief.

He missed him every day. Every single day.

6

VIEWED FROM THE BACK, THE MAN WHO HAD SPENT THE LAST FEW HOURS keeping a vigil in the hospital room might have been mistaken for a boxer. He was an athletic man in his late twenties: his sturdiness could not be hidden beneath his suit, nor his height disguised by the odd way in which he leaned against the window, both large hands against the glass, one splayed open, the other clenched in a fist; his forehead was bent against the same cold, smooth surface. It was raining, but he seemed unaware of the drops colliding against the other side of the pane, or of his own reflection, the reflection of a man revisiting some too familiar misery.

His hands, their knuckles crosshatched with scars, might have fooled the unobservant into thinking that he made his way in the world with his fists. But a closer look at the right hand, the open one, would reveal black ink stains marring otherwise clean, long fingers.

"O'Connor?"

It was no more than a puzzled whisper, but the younger man's reverie was instantly broken, and he moved to the bedside of the man who had called his name.

"I'm here, Corrigan," he said quickly.

"Should have known," Corrigan murmured, turning his right eye—the one that wasn't bandaged—toward his visitor. Speaking slowly through stitched and swollen lips, he said, "Can't the devil wait 'til I'm dead before he sends his minions?"

"It's worse than that, Jack Corrigan. The bastard made me come here alone, on account of him and the boys below being too busy laying in fuel for the times to come. Claims they've never had to build a fire as hot as the one they'll need for the likes of you."

"I say we make him wait. I'm going to nobody's cold hell."

"Agreed," O'Connor said. He watched as Corrigan tried to take stock of his surroundings. "You're in St. Mary's."

"What time is it?"

"Nine o'clock. Sunday night."

"Sunday night . . ." Corrigan repeated, bewildered.

"You've needed the rest. And need more. Don't worry, just sleep. I'll be here."

Corrigan seemed unable to resist the suggestion, and began to fall asleep again, but then as if suddenly recalling something troubling, he looked up at O'Connor and said, "The car . . ."

O'Connor frowned. Jack hadn't driven a car in more than twenty years—not since the accident that had permanently injured his ankle and caused so many other troubles. O'Connor decided that Corrigan was still in a fog, confused as any man might be after so severe a beating. "Don't let that trouble you now, Jack," he said. "Everything's going to be fine."

Corrigan seemed unsure of this, but lost his struggle to stay awake.

O'Connor felt a sensation of relief run through him from his shoulders to his shoes, and he now looked around the room as if seeing it for the first time. Up to that moment, he had been aware only of his battered and bandaged friend, of his own helplessness and anger, of long-ago memories of the only other time he had seen Jack in a hospital bed. But now Corrigan had awakened and spoken and even joked a bit. There was still plenty to worry over, but O'Connor relaxed enough to acknowledge to himself that he was tired.

O'Connor got the call at five this morning, not long after Jack had been found at the edge of a marsh, soaked to the skin in brackish water. Someone at the hospital had found O'Connor's business card and phone number in Corrigan's water-logged wallet. O'Connor had insisted Jack carry the card, thinking of the nights when Jack might spend his cab fare on booze. *In case of emergency, please notify . . .* he had written on the back of it and added his home number. He had been called more than once. Nothing else the hospital staff had found in the wallet had been readable, but because O'Connor had lived in three different apartments in the last five years, he had used pencil to write his phone number on the card. Pencil didn't run.

Forty dollars had survived the soaking, so O'Connor was fairly sure the reason for the beating hadn't been robbery. God knew what had happened to Jack or why, but O'Connor figured that it was likely the answer would have something to do with a woman. That could wait.

A uniformed officer had stopped by to take as much of a report as he could, which wasn't much of one. O'Connor had asked him to get in touch with Dan Norton, a friend of Jack's who worked as a homicide detective with the Las Piernas police. He hadn't had much hope that the officer would do that, so he was surprised when Norton had come by for a few minutes, at about ten that morning. He was one of half a dozen friends who had visited while Jack was still out cold. O'Connor knew Norton would make sure the case got whatever attention could be spared to it.

O'Connor looked around the room. There was a second patient's bed, empty but neatly made, and after a brief study, he adjusted it almost to a sitting position. He pulled his tie free of his collar, tucked it into his pocket, took off his suit coat and draped it neatly over the back of a chair, removed his shoes and placed them beneath, then climbed onto the bed.

He lay on his side, facing Corrigan, trying to mentally list his enemies. It was a long damned list.

A young nurse came in and shook her head when she saw him, but said nothing.

She took Corrigan's pulse, made a note on a chart, and said, "His color is better. That's a good sign."

"He woke up," O'Connor said.

"When?" she asked, surprised.

"Just now. Talked to me a bit, then fell back to sleep."

"You should have come to get me," she scolded.

"It was me he wanted to talk to," he said.

She rolled her eyes in exasperation, then caught the look of amusement on his face. "You're going to get us in trouble, Mr. O'Connor. Visiting hours were over long ago. If one of the nuns comes in here—"

"One of them has come by already," he said, smiling.

"Look, why don't you just go home and let us—"

The smile disappeared. "Forget it. Until I know who did this to him, I'm not leaving."

"I know, I know. You're going to defend him single-handedly if his attackers make another attempt on his life."

"Do you think I'm not up to the job?" he asked, throwing his long legs over the edge of the bed, sitting up straight.

"Apparently you don't think this hospital is."

"Although the reputation of the Sisters of Mercy is undoubtedly a fierce one," he said, "and while I'm sure many a man has died of cruel injuries sustained from wimples and rosary beads, playing bodyguard is not really in their line of work, now is it?"

"Is it in yours?"

"If need be."

They were reporters, the other nurses said, this man and the patient. She had not imagined that the work was so rough. This one had charmed his way past the end of visiting hours with his smile and that faint echo of Ireland in his speech.

Corrigan moaned and O'Connor was up on his stocking feet and next to the bed in an instant. Together they watched and waited, but there was no other sound from him, save that of his steady breathing.

The nurse studied O'Connor. His hair was dark and thick, a little ruffled. A thin scar cut one of his black brows in half, and his nose had been broken at least once. His blue-gray eyes were bloodshot; there were dark circles beneath them, circles that were not merely the result of this one night of vigilance.

"You need to get some sleep, Mr. O'Connor."

He shook his head, went back to watching Corrigan.

After a moment, she said, "Next time he wakes up, you'll let me know?"

He looked up again. "Right away," he said, crossing his heart in a schoolboy's gesture.

"I wonder what you were like as a child?" she said, glancing at his unmended socks and rumpled hair.

"Ah, my dear," he said, not meeting her eyes, "no, you don't. No, you don't."

He did not want to sleep, and he did not worry that he would. He washed his face with cold water, then lay back down on the bed, watching Corrigan. He spent a number of minutes in the same useless way he had spent earlier hours—speculating on who had done this to Corrigan, and why. Jack had been closemouthed about what he would be doing this evening. Thinking back on it, O'Connor realized that Corrigan had made stronger than usual protests about O'Connor keeping tabs on him.

"Why on earth didn't I know you were up to something then and there?" he murmured to himself. "It's not as if I just met you, is it?"

7

O'CONNOR GOT HIS FIRST PAYING JOB WHEN HE WAS EIGHT YEARS OLD, in 1936. That was the year he began selling the *Express* on the corner of Broadway and Las Piernas Boulevard. At that time, the morning paper in Las Piernas was the *News,* the evening, the *Express.* Although the papers were owned by the same publisher—Mr. Winston Wrigley—and worked out of the same building, the two staffs were fiercely competitive, paperboys included. The star reporter of the *News* was a woman named Helen Swan; on the *Express,* young Jack Corrigan was making a name for himself.

Every day, O'Connor hurried from school to the paper, never failing to admire the big ornate building itself ("Grand as a palace," he'd told his sister Maureen) or to feel important as he stood on his corner, shouting headlines, calling out the words *"Ex-press* here!" in a manner that caught the ears of bustling businessmen and shoppers on their way home. He quickly learned how to charm his customers, how to make sure they bought their papers from him and no one else. He promoted the star reporter of his paper, smiling and singing out, "Jack Corrigan! Jack Corrigan! Only in the *Exxxx-press."*

One day, as he was extolling Corrigan's work he heard a woman laugh. He turned to see a beautiful young lady—blond, blue-eyed, and bow-lipped, dressed in a fur coat and walking arm in arm with none other than his champion. She laughed again and said, "I suppose you'll be hurt if I don't buy one from him, Jack."

Jack winked at O'Connor, then said, "No, Lil, I'll be hurt if you don't give him a tip as well." So she had given him a silver dollar for a paper that cost a nickel, and when she had refused the change, or to take twenty copies, he had been so astonished that for a time he just stood looking at the coin.

"What's your name, kid?" Corrigan asked.

"O'Connor, sir."

"Hmm. Got a first name?"

O'Connor felt his cheeks turn red, but answered, "Connor."

"Connor O'Connor? That's a little redundant, isn't it?" the woman said, laughing again.

But Corrigan took his arm from hers then and hunkered down so that he was eye level with the boy. "No, it's not. It's a name passed down from a king. Do you know about him?"

"Conn of the Hundred Battles," O'Connor answered.

Corrigan smiled. "So, Conn of the Hundred Battles, what's the best corner in Las Piernas?"

"For selling the evening edition? Corner of Broadway and Magnolia."

Corrigan peered down the street. "Ah, yes. Southwest corner, I suppose. A courthouse, office buildings, two busy restaurants, and a bus stop."

"Yes, sir."

"Jack . . ." the woman said impatiently.

"In a minute, darling. This is my fellow newspaperman. We're talking business. Besides, my father would rise from his grave to haunt me if I didn't show respect for one of his countrymen." He stood and tipped his hat. "Thank you for the conversation, Mr. O'Connor," he said, and tossed a nickel to the boy.

"I already paid for the paper!" the woman said.

"No, my dear," Corrigan replied. "I paid for the paper, but you tipped him, remember? A dollar. You're the soul of generosity."

"And you're the soul of bunk," she said, making him laugh as they walked off.

At home that night, Maureen explained that "redundant" meant exactly what he had guessed it meant, but O'Connor was too excited about the silver dollar (which he had shown only to Maureen) to feel any harm from the rich woman's words. He was convinced it was a lucky dollar, and perhaps it was, because when he went to work the next day, the boss told him he was being given the corner at Broadway and Magnolia.

Several weeks later, he was making a heated protest to Geoffrey, the night security man, who was perhaps not ten years older than the paperboy.

"But Jack Corrigan's my *friend* and it's important!"

"O'Connor, please be reasonable," Geoff was saying in a low voice. "I let you stay here after the other boys have all gone home, and I could get in trouble for that. Mr. Corrigan is a busy man. He's working on his story about the trial and I'm not going to disturb him."

"Just try. Please!"

Geoffrey sighed, then lifted his phone. "Mr. Corrigan? Sorry to disturb you, but there's a paperboy here who . . . No, sir, I haven't taken leave of my senses, but . . ."

O'Connor, desperate, pulled out his lucky dollar. "Send this up to him!"

Geoff said, "I don't think he can be bribed for a silver dollar, kid."

Corrigan must have heard the exchange, though, because in the next moment Geoff was listening again, and his expression changed to one of disbelief. "Yes, sir," he said. He turned to O'Connor. "Let me get somebody to watch the desk. I'll take you up there myself."

"No," O'Connor said, "he should come down here."

"Oh, for goodness' sakes—"

"May I please speak to him on the phone?"

Geoff handed the phone over with a "be my guest" gesture.

"Mr. Corrigan?"

"Hello, kid. Come on up, I'll show you the newsroom."

The temptation was mighty and he nearly gave in, but he said, "Sir, I've talked this over with my big sister and—"

"Your big sister? Listen, old pal, you've been holding out on me. How old is she?"

"Maureen? Eleven."

"Hmm. A little young, even for me. Nevertheless, what did the glorious Maureen advise?"

He thought hard, trying to remember the exact words Maureen had told him to use. "I saw something today that seems important. It's about the trial. But if I come up there to the newsroom, people from the *News* are going to know where you heard about this, and if they do, they'll want me to be their . . . their . . ."

"Paperboy?" Corrigan supplied.

"Unidentified source," O'Connor said, finally remembering the rest of the speech.

There was the slightest hesitation before he said, "Put Geoff back on the line, kid."

It was not O'Connor's first defeat, but it was bitter all the same, and as he handed the phone back to Geoff and turned away from the desk, he found himself unable to meet the security guard's look of sympathy. He put on his cap and was pushing the big front door open when Geoff called, "Hey, kid! Don't leave."

When O'Connor turned back, Geoff said, "He wants to know if you've had supper yet."

O'Connor shook his head.

"Then wait for him over at Big Sarah's, down the street. He'll hear your story there."

O'Connor grinned and thanked Geoff as he hurried out the great brass doors.

Big Sarah's was an all-night diner two doors down from the paper. It wasn't a fancy place, but O'Connor had never eaten a meal that his mother or one of his sisters hadn't cooked—unless you counted an apple or two from a street vendor—so he was nearly as much in awe of Big Sarah's as he was of the Wrigley Building. His breath frosted the window as he peered in and saw that the place was nearly empty, just one old man drinking coffee at the counter.

It was a little cold out, but he was sure he would be thrown out of the place if he stepped inside, so he stood just outside the diner's entrance. He took off his cap and was combing his hair with his hand, when the roundest woman he had ever seen caught his eye and motioned him inside with a wave.

She greeted him with a warm smile and said, "You must be Mr. O'Connor. I'm Big Sarah. Come on in, right this way, honey. Handsome Jack hisself called and told me you'd be coming. Do you need to wash up?"

"Yes, thank you, ma'am," he said.

"What fine manners! The gents is straight back there, near the phone."

In the men's room, he took off his thin jacket and washed his hands and arms up to the elbows, carefully avoiding one place on his left arm. Fascinated by a cloth towel that was dry when you pulled on it, even though it seemed to be just one towel looped on a continuous roller, he considered trying to pull on it until the wet side showed up again. But it made such a noise, he stopped after three tries. He used a little more water to finish combing his hair, then—remembering to be on his best manners, and certain that Big Sarah would check up on him—thought to wipe down the sink. But here the towel mechanism was found to have a shortcoming—the towel couldn't reach the sink. He used his handkerchief instead.

When O'Connor stepped out of the washroom, Corrigan was standing next to Big Sarah, who was laughing at some joke he had just made. The only other customer in the place had left. Corrigan noticed O'Connor and smiled.

"Let's get some food in him, Sarah."

"Two specials, comin' right up," she said. "You like fried chicken, Mr. O'Connor?"

"Yes, ma'am," he answered.

They sat in a booth, and it was all O'Connor could do not to run his hands over everything, to feel the smooth leather of the seats or the shiny tabletop. He followed Corrigan's example with the napkin, resisted the temptation to keep straightening his flatware.

Big Sarah brought Jack a cup of coffee and O'Connor a glass of milk. He didn't take a sip of it until Jack took a sip of his coffee.

O'Connor thought that Jack would want to hear his secret information right away, but instead Jack asked, "Won't your mother wonder where you are?"

O'Connor shook his head. "No, sir."

Jack looked skeptical.

"She's working tonight. She does for a lady—cooking and cleaning and sometimes minding the lady's little girls. They're just babies, the girls."

"You've been to this house?"

"Oh no, sir." But he blushed.

"Hmm. But you might have taken an unofficial look at the place, maybe followed her to work one day, just to see if it was a good place for her to work?"

Looking at the table, he said, "Might have."

Corrigan smiled. "And your father? Does he work nights, too?"

Eyes still averted, O'Connor said, "No, sir."

Corrigan took out a cigarette and lit it. He watched the boy balance his fork on its edge, then put it down flat, then pull his hands away from the table. Jack waited.

"He was a roughneck," O'Connor said, meeting his eyes at last.

"Your father worked in the oilfields?"

O'Connor began to repeat the story as he had heard Maureen tell it so many times. "My da came from Ireland to Las Piernas to be a roughneck. Before I was born. Before Maureen was born. When Dermot was two."

"And how old is Dermot now?"

"Seventeen."

"So your father must have been here at the beginning of the boom."

O'Connor nodded. "Pat—his cousin—got him signed on with one of the big oil companies on Signal Hill. Pat works up in Bakersfield now."

"And you help out by working for the paper."

He shrugged. "A little."

Big Sarah brought the chicken dinners. It was more hot food than he'd had on his plate in a long time, but O'Connor, just having thought of his family, suddenly felt as if eating it would be a selfish act.

Sensing the problem, Corrigan said, "Sarah's feelings will be terribly hurt if you don't finish every bite."

O'Connor nodded, and after a few bites, tucked into the meal in earnest. The boy finished his supper before Corrigan was halfway through his own, so Corrigan handed him a menu and told him to choose a dessert.

"Apple pie," O'Connor said, but continued to read the menu.

"You sure?" Jack asked.

O'Connor nodded. "It's American. So am I."

"Not Irish?"

"Oh, sure, but I'm Irish *American.* Maureen and me—" He could hear her correct him. "I mean, Maureen and I—were born here. The others are Irish. My parents, too."

"You have other brothers and sisters?"

"Yes, sir. There are seven of us, but only the three at home. The other four are all old and married. I think they're even as old as you."

Corrigan laughed.

O'Connor went back to perusing the menu. He couldn't help but notice that the chicken dinner special cost forty cents, and hoped that Mr. Corrigan had plenty of money on him. Then he remembered that he had the silver dollar with him and relaxed. It was lucky, but if Jack Corrigan needed it to pay for the meal, O'Connor would spend it.

"Changing your mind?"

"No, sir," he said, setting the menu back in its holder. "I just like to read."

"An admirable trait, Mr. O'Connor."

It was only after the pie had been eaten that Jack said, "Now, I haven't forgotten that you called this meeting on account of some very important business." He looked around the empty diner with the air of a conspirator. "Is it safe to discuss it here?"

"Yes, sir. I believe so. It's about the Mitch Yeager trial. The one you've been covering down at the courthouse."

"Hmm," said Jack, lighting another cigarette. "Mitch Yeager just might beat that rap. His older brother, Adam, is serving hard time, but Mitch did his bootlegging with some big names in town—not old enough to drink the stuff, and he was running rum. Now that bootlegging is out of style, young Mitch has found other pursuits—just as illegal, though. Even if he does tell everyone that he's simply a businessman being harassed by the *Express*."

"I know. I've been reading your stories."

"You have? At ten years old?"

"No, sir. I'm eight."

"Eight." He digested this fact for a moment, then said, "I thought we didn't hire paperboys younger than ten."

O'Connor shifted in his seat, then said, "I'm tall for my age, so I fibbed to get the job. I'll be nine soon. Are you going to peach on me?"

Jack rubbed his chin. "No. Go on."

"Well, I wanted to see Yeager for myself, so I asked Duffy if I could just take a peek from the balcony."

"Duffy?"

"He's one of the guards at the courthouse. He buys his papers from me."

"I should have known. We'll skip the matter of truancy for the moment. This Duffy agreed to let you 'peek' at a real, live mobster on trial?"

"Yes, sir. Only I couldn't see Yeager so good—so well. I saw you—at least, I saw the back of your head."

"How could you possibly know it was the back of *my* head?"

O'Connor blushed again. "I saw the lady with the fur coat sitting next to you."

"Ah, yes, your benefactress." When O'Connor looked puzzled, Corrigan said, "The lady who gave you the big tip."

"Yes, sir. What was that other word, please?"

"Benefactress." Corrigan waited while the boy repeated it to himself several times, then prompted, "You were saying?"

"Oh. Well, mostly I could see the jury. I could see all of them. This one lady kept glancing up at the balcony, and it seemed to me that something was making her nervous."

"What makes you say that?"

"She would twist her handkerchief. Not all the time, just after she glanced at the balcony."

Corrigan looked away, blew out a mouthful of smoke. O'Connor watched him stub out his cigarette and grind the butt into the glass ashtray. He smiled ruefully at O'Connor. "I suppose I'm going to have to ask Lillian to stay home. Apparently she's too much of a distraction."

"Lillian is my benefactress?"

He pronounced it perfectly, Corrigan noticed. "Yes. Miss Lillian Vanderveer. Of *the* Vanderveers, you understand."

"Oh."

"So go on, Mr. O'Connor."

"I figured out that the nervous lady was looking at the men sitting next to me. A big fellow and a little fellow."

Big Sarah came by and refilled Jack's coffee. O'Connor covered a big yawn beneath a small hand. Jack took out his pocket watch. "Holy—it's ten o'clock, kid." He tucked the watch away. "Let me give you a ride home."

"Wait! I haven't told you the most important part."

Jack stopped in the act of pulling out his wallet.

"I kept looking at the little fellow and at the lady juror, and I realized that they might just be what my da calls me and Maureen—two glasses poured from the same bottle. They look alike."

Jack frowned. "As much alike as you and Maureen?"

"More. I think he's the lady's brother—she's pale and skinny and has frizzy red hair and freckles and a kind of pointy nose. So does he."

Jack put his wallet back and took out his notebook. "Describe these people to me—the big man, the juror, the little fellow."

Fifteen minutes later, he was shaking his head in wonder. He knew exactly which juror the kid was talking about and was fairly sure he knew which of Yeager's men had been sitting up in the balcony. The kid was a natural.

"I had to leave before court was over," O'Connor was saying. "I had to go get my papers. But I did see one other thing."

"Much more of this, kid, and I'll have to trade jobs with you."

O'Connor pushed up the left sleeve of his jacket—a jacket that had once been Dermot's. Jack stared at his forearm. "His license number," O'Connor said proudly. "I saw the big man leave the courthouse with the brother. They got into a black two-door Plymouth sedan."

Jack was still staring.

"I didn't have any paper—I mean, I only had my copies of the *Express,* and I had to sell those. So I wrote it on my arm."

Corrigan reached over slowly and gently took the boy's hand in his. "The bruises. Who gave you these bruises?"

O'Connor tried to yank his hand back, but Corrigan held on.

"It's nothing."

Corrigan waited.

"A kid at school," the boy murmured.

"Bigger than you?"

O'Connor nodded.

"You fight back?" Corrigan asked, releasing him.

O'Connor squirmed a bit, then lifted one shoulder. "I tried. But I'm no good at it."

"What's wrong with your old man that he hasn't taught you to defend yourself?"

"It's not his fault," O'Connor said quickly, and looked down at the table, avoiding Corrigan's gaze.

O'Connor's view of the tabletop began to blur. He scrunched his eyes shut, only to feel hot tears rolling down his face. A baby, he thought. Always acting like a baby. And he was crying in front of Jack Corrigan, of all people.

"Conn," Jack said quietly. "Conn of a Hundred-and-one Battles."

"My father got hurt," the boy said softly, speaking down at the table. "He'd been hurt before, even lost a finger, but this last time—it's his back. He can't stand up straight. Can't even be on his feet for more than a minute or two before the pain . . . well, anyway, he can't work." He pulled out his handkerchief, realized it was still damp from the sink and put it away again.

After a moment, O'Connor heard Corrigan writing in his notebook and looked up. Without glancing up, Corrigan reached into his breast pocket and pulled out a clean white handkerchief and offered it across the table.

O'Connor took it and loudly blew his nose into it. He heard Big Sarah walk out of the kitchen, but saw Corrigan wave her back.

"Fine," she called over her shoulder, "but the shifts are going to be changin' and fellers are gonna be showin' up here any minute. I ain't turnin' away business, even for you, Handsome Jack."

Jack smiled. "Wash your face, kid, and we'll get out of here before those spies from the *News* can figure out what's up."

Jack made a phone call while O'Connor washed up. When O'Connor came back out, Jack was saying, "No surprise, is it? Yes, I'll be by later tonight. Hell no, I won't disclose my source, and shame on you for asking."

He hung up and smiled at Conn. "A detective friend of mine. Turns out that Plymouth is registered to one Mitch Yeager. Good work, kid."

O'Connor thanked both Corrigan and Big Sarah before they left. She told him to come in and see her again soon. Jack seemed preoccupied; hands in his coat pockets, he didn't speak as they walked back to the paper.

Jack insisted on driving him home, although O'Connor protested more than once that he didn't live so very far away and could walk. O'Connor didn't often ride in cars, and under other circumstances, the offer of even the shortest trip in Jack's Model A would have been snapped up in a minute. Instead,

O'Connor was busy seeking the intervention of all the saints and angels, praying that his father had downed enough cheap whiskey to fall asleep, and that Jack Corrigan would let him off at the curb and drive off before seeing the hovel where they lived.

The small apartment building wasn't far from downtown. O'Connor hated the place. He was glad Corrigan was seeing it at night—when he might not notice that its dull pink paint was peeling, that the lawn was brown, that the walkway was choked with weeds. As Jack, in defiance of heaven, not only pulled over to the curb but turned off the motor, O'Connor thought that even in darkness, everything about the place said no one would live there unless he couldn't do any better for himself.

Corrigan was watching him, though, and not the building. "Would it help if I went in with you, explained—"

"No," O'Connor said quickly, for though the place was kept neat and tidy, his father did not allow strangers past the door, would not let anyone who was not a priest or a family member see what he had become. "No, thank you. I'll be all right."

Corrigan put a hand on his shoulder. "All right, then, kid. Maybe you know best. If I can make something of what you've told me about the juror, I'm in your debt."

"I could be your secret agent," O'Connor said quickly, voicing the hidden, impossible hope that he had held all afternoon and evening.

To his credit, Corrigan managed not to laugh or smile. "It's an idea worth considering," he said. "But listen to me, Conn. Mitch Yeager's not someone to play games with. This is serious business, and if you're going to be my secret agent, you can't take risks like following gangsters' cars and writing down their license numbers while you're standing in the middle of the sidewalk."

"I didn't," the boy said. "I memorized it, then went into the rest room to write it down."

Jack stared at him, then started laughing. "Oh, forgive me, kid." He grew quiet, then said, "Conn, if there's one mistake repeated by generation after generation of men, it's that they underestimate their boys." He looked toward the dimly lit porch of the apartment building. "You be careful all the same, kid. Be careful all the same."

Jack Corrigan's stories on jury tampering in the Mitch Yeager trial sold a lot of copies of the *Express* over the next few weeks. This made Winston Wrigley happy, which meant that both Corrigan's and O'Connor's bosses were happy. This happiness extended to almost everyone who worked in the Wrigley Building, except, of course, the staff of the *News*—most especially its star reporter, the woman who came to the corner of Broadway and Magnolia one afternoon and stood watching O'Connor for fifteen nearly unbearable minutes.

The newsboy felt more nervous than the day he had seen Corrigan jostled on the street by one of Yeager's men, not long after Jack had stopped by to talk to him. A policeman had seen that and prevented a fight. He didn't think a copper would defend him against Helen Swan.

This wasn't the first day she had watched him, but this time, to his horror, she was walking straight toward him. With great effort, he prevented himself from making the Sign of the Cross as she approached.

He had asked Jack about her, and Jack had laughed and said, "Swanie? Brother, when they made the first pair of trousers, they had Swanie try 'em on to make sure they'd be tough enough for any man." Then Jack winked at him and said, "She's the daughter of a suffragist, you know."

It was a word O'Connor didn't know the precise meaning of, but thought it probably meant her mother made people suffer. Helen Swan didn't exactly look mean, O'Connor thought as she moved closer. All the same, he had stopped calling out the headlines of the *Express* and found himself just standing there, waiting for her. He decided there was something about Helen Swan that made you give her your attention when she wanted it. She was a brunette with big brown eyes that he couldn't look away from. She was not exactly beautiful, not in the way Lillian Vanderveer was, but she had an unmistakable style all her own. O'Connor thought she carried herself as if everyone who hadn't bowed or curtsied to her yet soon would.

"O'Connor, isn't it?" she said in a low, melodic voice.

He swallowed and nodded.

She smiled. "Jack Corrigan seems to know a lot about what goes on near this corner lately."

"He's a fine reporter," O'Connor said loyally.

Helen Swan gave a soft, husky laugh. "Yes, he is. Utterly shameless, but a fine reporter." She began to walk off, then turned and said, "Be sure to tell Jack I said hello."

It was late that evening before O'Connor saw Corrigan again, and under the circumstances, he considered not conveying Miss Swan's regards. Jack was sitting in a booth at the back of Big Sarah's; two women sat across from him. One was known to O'Connor—Lillian Vanderveer.

The other was a woman O'Connor had never met before. She was also a blonde, but her eyes were beer-bottle brown. Her cheeks were flushed and she was laughing hard at some remark Jack had made.

Big Sarah caught O'Connor's eye and shook her head. O'Connor was about to leave, but Jack called out to him.

"Mr. O'Connor! Don't rush off."

"Oh, for crying out loud," Lillian said. "I'm beginning to feel like I'm going steady with a little kid."

"You are," Big Sarah answered, causing Jack and the other woman to laugh again.

Corrigan had been drinking, O'Connor realized. He accepted this without great upset; over the last few years, since the accident on the oil rig, his own father was often in this state. He gauged Jack's mood to be jovial, not surly or mean. Nevertheless, he had long ago learned to be wary of men in this condition, knowing their moods could change without warning. So it was that when he approached the booth, he stopped an arm's distance from Jack's side of the table.

Corrigan didn't fail to notice this distance. The reporter said nothing, but rubbed his chin thoughtfully. O'Connor glanced at the women, who had fallen silent.

"Mr. O'Connor," Corrigan said, without a trace of the drunkenness Conn had seen just a moment before, "allow me to introduce you to Mrs. Ducane, a good friend of Miss Vanderveer's."

"How do you do?" O'Connor said.

"Hiya, kid," the woman said, smiling. "Call me Thelma. You must be the little hooligan who's driving Lil crazy."

"Thelma!" Lil said sharply, but Thelma only laughed.

"I didn't mean anything by it. You know that—right, kid?"

Before he could answer, Jack said, "Mrs. Ducane and Miss Vanderveer were just leaving."

Thelma's laugh brayed again, but Lillian gave Jack a cool look. "First the trial," she said, "and now this. Maybe I'll do as Daddy suggests and go out with Harold Linworth again. "

Jack smiled. "Capital idea. And capital is what it would be, right? Aiding the cash flow at Ducane-Vanderveer?"

"That is a despicable suggestion—"

"Speaking of despicable, I suppose Daddy wouldn't want you to start seeing your first love again. Oh, wait, that's right—"

"Don't say another word, damn you!"

"C'mon, Lil," Thelma said, rising to her feet with a wobble. "This is getting boring. Let's go play with the big boys."

Lillian hesitated, giving Jack an opportunity he did not take. She stood and walked out without a backward glance. As the diner door closed behind them, O'Connor heard Big Sarah mutter, "Good riddance."

"How about a cup of coffee, Sarah?" Jack said. He motioned to O'Connor. "Have a seat."

O'Connor slid into the other side of the booth, which was still fragrant with a mixture of the women's perfume, smoke, alcohol, and the congealing remains of a banana split. Jack saw him studying the dessert dish and said, "Booze gives Thelma a sweet tooth."

"I don't like her," O'Connor blurted.

"Thelma?"

He nodded.

"I don't like her much, either," Jack said. "But her father is in business with Lillian's father, so the two girls have been close friends for several years now. I think Thelma managed to introduce Lil to some bad company." He paused and said, "But that's no story for a kid's ears." He shook his head in disgust with himself. "Ungentlemanly of me to even bring it up."

Big Sarah came over with a cup of hot, black coffee and set it in front of Jack. O'Connor stayed silent while she took the dirty dishes from the table. She gave him a wink and said, "Want anything?"

"No, thank you, ma'am."

She left them to wait on two men who were sitting at the counter.

O'Connor figured he might as well tell Jack the bad news now and get it over with. "Something happened at the corner today."

Jack paused in the act of lifting the cup of coffee.

"Miss Swan came up to me. I'm pretty sure she knows I talk to you."

The cup rattled against the saucer as Jack set it down and started laughing. "Swanie? Swanie figured it out already?" He laughed again. "Helen Swan is smarter than any man in that building—including Old Man Wrigley. My hat's off to her, by God!"

O'Connor was puzzled. "You aren't upset?"

"No, why should I be? This is great. She's got to be jealous as all get out." He paused. "She scare you?"

O'Connor shrugged. "A little. At first."

"And now?"

"There's something about her—I don't know."

"And you want to be a reporter?" Jack scoffed. "You'll have to do better than that. What's this 'something'?"

The boy's brows drew together. "All right, then. She puts me in mind of a queen."

Corrigan grinned. "Ah, yes. She does have that effect on gentlemen of all ages. And the next thing you know, they're giving her their utter loyalty and devotion, rushing off to do her bidding."

"Not me," O'Connor declared. "I'm loyal to the *Express*, one hundred percent!"

"I never doubted it, Mr. O'Connor."

They talked for a time about O'Connor's day at school and the stories Jack was working on. Jack drank another cup of coffee, then suggested they go for a long walk together. "Not quite ready to call it a night, are you?" he asked.

No, O'Connor wasn't.

The double bill at the downtown movie house was letting out just as they neared the theater, and Jack took O'Connor's hand as they made their way across that crowded section of sidewalk. Perhaps because Jack was recognized or perhaps because there were no other children nearby, some of the men and women leaving the theater watched Jack and O'Connor. The women usually smiled at them—Jack would nod or touch his hat brim.

For those moments, O'Connor ignored the fact that Jack was not much older than his oldest brother and fantasized that he was Jack Corrigan's son; that his father, Jack Corrigan, had taken him to see *The Texas Rangers* and *China Clipper*, that he was the son of the best reporter in the world and everyone knew it, that his father was proud of him and thought him the finest of young men, and then . . . and then they had walked beyond the edge of the crowd and Jack released his hand.

As his hand dropped free of Corrigan's, O'Connor thought of his real father, Kieran O'Connor, and felt ashamed of himself. The small pleasure of the fantasy was forgotten.

Corrigan was asking him something. "I'm sorry," O'Connor said, "I was thinking so loud, I didn't hear you."

"I was asking if anyone had ever taught you how to box."

"No, sir. Dermot tried once, but it didn't take. If I did the right thing with my hands, I did the wrong thing with my feet."

"A common problem," Corrigan said, "even among the pros."

They had reached the shore by then and Corrigan stopped to take off his shoes. "C'mon," he said, "take yours off, too. Easier to learn on the sand."

O'Connor followed suit, then shivered as his bare feet hit the cold beach. "You'll be warmed up in a minute," Jack said.

The moon shone bright over the water and sand. Jack began to show O'Connor how to hold his fists, how to throw his weight into a punch, how to protect himself from a counterpunch. The sand both braced and slowed his feet, and twice when he overstepped, it cushioned his falls. Some of Dermot's lessons came back to him, but now made more sense.

Jack rolled up his pants legs and dropped to his knees, held both hands up. "Okay," he said, "come at me. Hard as you like."

After a few hesitant punches, Jack said, "Harder."

O'Connor punched a little harder.

"Harder," Jack said again. "Pretend I've been mean to Maureen."

O'Connor began walloping Jack's open palms.

After a few minutes of punishment, Jack yelled, "Okay, okay! Truce! Uncle! Hell, I'm not going to be able to hold a pen tomorrow." At O'Connor's look of horror, he said, "Just a joke, kid. Just a joke. I'm fine. How are you?"

O'Connor was breathing hard, and as Jack had predicted, he felt warm from his exertions. But the breeze off the water was cooling him, the sand was soft beneath his feet, and he knew he had boxed better this time than he ever had with Dermot. He smiled. "I'm fine."

Jack stood and brushed off his legs and feet. "We'll have another lesson tomorrow."

"Do you mean it?" O'Connor asked.

"Sure. But don't try this out on anybody until you've had a chance to really learn what you're doing."

"Oh, I don't aim to start fights."

"Kid," Jack said as they began to put on their socks and shoes, "if I thought you were aiming to start fights, I wouldn't have taught you anything about boxing."

"Who taught you?"

"My father."

O'Connor was silent, suddenly seeming to need all his concentration for his shoelaces.

"Your dad ever teach you anything?" Corrigan asked.

O'Connor looked up. "Oh, sure. Lots of things. When I was little, he taught me how to tie my shoes. And when I get big enough to shave, I'll know how, 'cause he used to let me watch him do that. And he used to sing, so I learned a lot of songs from him."

Corrigan was quiet as they began to walk back to the Wrigley Building, heading up American Avenue. Nearby to the north, eerily silhouetted in the moonlight, were hills so crowded with oil derricks they seemed cloaked in a strange black forest of identical leafless trees. "That's where my dad worked," O'Connor said, pointing. "He built some of those wells."

"Roughnecking—that's some of the hardest work anywhere," Jack said.

O'Connor nodded. "My dad likes hard work. Maureen remembers him better than I do—from before the accident, I mean. He never drank in those days. Not a drop. And even now, I know . . . I know it's not what he really likes. Do you know what I mean?"

"I think so, yes."

"I keep praying that the Lord will cure him. I don't understand why he doesn't. I mean, Jesus suffered on the cross, but he didn't stay up there for years at a time, now, did he?"

"I'm not the man to teach you about religion, Conn. I'll be a poor enough boxing coach."

Jack saw that the boy was making some earnest reply, but just at that moment, a Red Car came by, rumbling its way down the rails to the next stop.

"What did you say?"

"I said, never mind boxing—I mean, I won't mind learning it. But what I really want you to teach me, Mr. Jack Corrigan, is how to be a newspaper-man."

8

THE NURSE CAME BACK TO CHECK ON CORRIGAN, BREAKING THE SPELL reminiscence had cast on O'Connor. She attempted another round of banter with O'Connor, but after his third one-word reply gave it up and left him to brood over Corrigan alone.

He watched Jack, still filled with wonder that the man had taken an eight-year-old boy's ambitions so seriously. Jack had told O'Connor to begin by keeping a diary, to note what he had seen and heard each day, and his thoughts on any matter that struck his fancy. "That will be private," he said. "So I'm going to trust you to do that on your own. I'll give you assignments to turn in to me."

O'Connor had borrowed paper from Maureen that evening and wrote, "Jack Corrigan told me this will help me learn how to be a newspaper reporter. I hope he is right. P.S.: He gave me a boxing lesson, too." A week later, Maureen presented him with a gift, a small cloth-bound diary with gilt-edged pages and a lock and key. She had earned the money doing mending for the lady their mother worked for, and O'Connor knew it must have taken the whole of her earnings to buy it. When he wanted to pay her back with his lucky silver dollar, she said, "Oh no—never give away your luck. Besides, this is an investment on my part. I want to be able to brag that my brother is the famous newspaper reporter Conn O'Connor, whose name is on the front page of the *Express*. So you do what Mr. Corrigan tells you and fill up this diary."

Several months later, another visitor had stopped near his corner.

Mitch Yeager stood eyeing him for long, nerve-wracking moments before he approached O'Connor. O'Connor knew that Yeager had managed to weasel his way out of the jury-tampering charges, a subject Jack had discussed bitterly and at length with his protégé. Yeager had power and powerful friends. He even had influence over Old Mr. Wrigley, according to Jack, because Old Mr. Wrigley—under pressure from advertisers who were Mitch

Yeager's business partners—had forbidden Jack to write any more stories about Yeager. That made O'Connor angry, but it also made him believe that Mitch Yeager was someone to fear.

Not much older than Dermot, O'Connor thought, watching him come closer. But Yeager's youth didn't soften anything about the man.

He stood staring at the boy. Conn swallowed hard and said, "Paper, mister?"

He heard laughter behind him and saw Yeager look up with a scowl. He turned to see Jack Corrigan.

"Picking on schoolkids now, Mitch?" Jack said. "You start bullying Wrigley's paperboys, he might be willing to let the ink flow again."

"The kid would have been better off going to school instead of hanging out in a courtroom," Yeager said. He looked back at O'Connor. "A kid can get in trouble playing hooky."

Jack put a hand on O'Connor's shoulder. Conn was ashamed to feel himself shaking beneath that hand.

"He's a smart kid," Jack said. "Why don't you be smart, too, Mitch?"

Yeager gave a small nod. "Sure. A smart man can wait for what he wants. Someday you'll find out just how smart I can be, Jack Corrigan."

He turned and walked away.

"Who told him?" Conn asked, his mouth dry.

"I don't know, Conn," Jack said. "Could have been someone on the paper, or a cop, or someone in the D.A.'s office . . ." He frowned, then sighed. "No, it's probably my fault."

"Your fault? No!" he said fiercely. "You never would have peached on me to the likes of Mitch Yeager!"

Jack smiled ruefully. "Appreciate the faith, kid, but my guess would be that Lillian told Mitch just to spite me. She's a little irritated at me."

"What does she care? She's married now. To that rich Linworth fellow."

Jack didn't say anything.

"She wanted to marry you," O'Connor said, deciding to get something that had been troubling him out in the open, "but she doesn't like me. I made her mad at you."

"No, kid. No, that's not true. As far as Lily was concerned, I was just fun and games. Hobnobbing with the hoi polloi, that's all. She flirted with men like me and Mitch because it was exciting to her, but she was always going to marry money. When you're older, you'll understand."

"Does it make you sad?"

"Hell, no," Jack said.

After a moment, O'Connor ventured to say, "I'm glad you didn't marry her."

Jack laughed. "So am I. She's got one hell of temper, and she's probably mad at both of us. At Mitch, too. Probably told him that a kid caught him at his game—kind of thing she'd do, just to piss him off."

The memories of those early days with Corrigan were bittersweet to O'Connor. The years had brought many changes in his life, some good, some bad. Jack Corrigan's friendship had remained a constant.

"Through the best of times, and the worst of times," he said softly to himself.

Some of the worst came quickly to mind. Jack's near-fatal car accident, which left him with the limp that kept him out of the service. A dozen other dark days, but without any hesitation he could name the worst of these: April 6, 1945.

Maureen and his mother had both found high-paying jobs at one of the war plants—Mercury Aircraft. It had allowed the family to move into a nicer place. Maureen worked days, then took care of their father in the evenings while their mother worked second shift. O'Connor worked part-time, from six to eleven, four evenings a week at the *Express*—by then he was a copyboy, and had even sold a few stories to the paper. Despite the late nights, he did well in school and was close to graduating.

He remained devoted to his sister, and protective of her. Every evening, when Maureen's shift ended at five, he was there at the gates of Mercury Aircraft, waiting to walk her home. Often, a neighbor who worked at the plant would join them on this walk, but he liked it best when it was just the two of them, away from their neighbor and away from their parents, able to talk and dream of the future. They did that more often in those early days of April. The war was coming to an end, it seemed—the Allies had crossed the Rhine.

O'Connor knew the end of the war meant that men would be coming home and taking their jobs back, and that Maureen and his mother might lose their jobs, but he couldn't be sorry about it. Who could think of that after all these years of war? When you saw Gold Stars hanging in windows of those who'd lost loved ones, who didn't wish for every mother's son to come back home safely? One of his older sisters was a war widow. O'Connor's only regret was that it looked as if it would all be over before he was old enough to enlist.

If the war didn't end soon, though, he feared Maureen would end up an old maid, taking care of their parents until she was past the age of marrying. He was seventeen, and felt sure that Maureen was nearly at a nuptial deadline—that she only had until she was about twenty-two to find a husband. His mother and older sisters had all been married before the age of nineteen.

It was just the two of them still at home, Conn and Maureen. Dermot had moved out to a place of his own years ago. Most of the care of their father had fallen to Maureen and his mother, although O'Connor shaved him. He also took on many of the household tasks that might have otherwise been his father's.

O'Connor had been glad when Maureen took the job in the factory, thinking she'd meet more fellows. She had a job in purchasing, so she got to wear a dress to work—his mother had a higher-paying job, on the line, and wore slacks, which had nearly thrown Da into a fit until he saw the check she brought home.

Dresses or no, he lost hope for Maureen—he soon realized that with the war on, it was nothing but women and old men there at the aircraft plant, anyway. She hadn't a chance of meeting a man who was near her age, unless he had some problem that made him 4-F. She told him that he was judging them too harshly, and that if he didn't stop standing by the gates of Mercury Aircraft, scowling at every man who talked to her after work, she'd never meet anyone.

Once, when he complained that one of her dates was 4-F, she reminded him that Jack was 4-F because of his ankle—but the moment she said it, she apologized. They both knew how hard it was for Jack not to be able to enlist. After that, O'Connor never used a man's handicap to as a reason for Maureen not to date him. Since he was good at finding information on people, it wasn't too difficult for him to find other reasons to criticize a would-be suitor.

He began to suspect that she had stopped telling him about the men she was interested in. Lately, he noticed she wore a heart-shaped locket, hidden beneath her blouse, but he saw it fall free of its hiding place when she bent to pick up a paper she had dropped. He questioned her about it, and she told him she had purchased it herself to keep men from annoying her—told them she had a steady beau. "Who's annoying you?" he wanted to know, firing up.

"You are!" she told him.

That Friday night in April, he didn't meet her after work. He had a night off from his job at the *Express*, and he had a date. For months now, he had been one of the many young men who sought the attention of another high school senior, Ethel Gibbs, and she had finally agreed to go out with O'Connor, surely the shyest member of her court. Maureen had been more excited about the prospect of her brother going on a date than perhaps he had been himself. A vicarious bit of pleasure for her, he thought, since she seldom dated.

Looking back on it now, he could not remember where he had planned to take Ethel. He hardly remembered why he had wanted to date her, what it was that had seemed so attractive about her. He could only vaguely recall her face.

He could, however, recall perfectly that moment when her mother opened the front door and looked in a puzzled way at the young man who stood before her, wearing his best clothes, smelling of his father's cologne. He remembered Mrs. Gibbs's blushes as she stammered confused apologies on her daughter's behalf. Ethel had left an hour ago, she said in dismay, with—but she halted mid-sentence, not naming O'Connor's rival. O'Connor had felt his own face redden and only managed to murmur, "My mistake, I'm sure."

He had delayed going back home, had wandered around the streets of downtown Las Piernas for a couple of hours before deciding that he might as well swallow his shame and let Maureen know that Ethel had stood him up. Going up the steps of the porch, he wondered how she would take it. Probably be more disappointed than he was, really.

As he opened the front door, he saw that although there was no blackout ordered that night, the house was nearly in total darkness. He heard his father shout frantically, "Maureen! Maureen! Is that you?"

"No, Da, it's me, Conn," he called back, turning on the lights as he went toward the back room that had been adapted for his father's use.

A small lamp near the bedside cast the only light in the room. His father had moved himself to a sitting position—an act that he could barely manage on his own, and only by enduring tremendous pain. Kieran O'Connor's hair was silver, but that night, looking at his father in the light of that single lamp, was the first time that O'Connor found himself thinking, He's become an old man.

"Conn!" his father said sharply. "Conn, listen to me—your sister—she's not come home."

"Not come home?" O'Connor repeated blankly. "Maureen, not come home?"

His father's face twisted in agony.

"Da, lie back down now. I'll get you something to eat."

"To hell with that!" his father roared. "It's your sister I'm worried about, not my damned belly!" And to O'Connor's shock, the older man burst into tears.

"Da," he said, coming to his side, easing him back on the bed. "Da, don't now. Don't. It might not be anything—maybe she had to work overtime. I'll call the factory . . ."

"I've already called," his father said, quickly wiping a hand across his face. "There's been no overtime since February."

O'Connor felt a coldness in the pit of his stomach. Maureen was dedicated to taking care of their father. She would never leave him, not even for a few moments, without arranging for someone to care for him.

"Conn," his father said, "never mind me, now. You've got to go look for her. You know she always comes straight home to me. Something's wrong. What if she's—if she's been in an accident?"

"I'll find her. I promise."

He began by calling the neighbor who often walked with them. She was surprised at his questions—Maureen had walked as far as the corner of their street with her, before turning to walk toward home. Maureen had mentioned no other plans. The neighbor hadn't noticed anyone else nearby.

O'Connor left the house carrying a flashlight, feeling more worried now. He retraced the path between the corner and the house, looking at first for Maureen herself, and then on the ground for some sign of her having passed this way, a lost earring, a footprint, anything. He knocked on every door of every house that had any view of the corner, or of the street, but no one had seen her or noticed anything out of the ordinary.

It was growing late now. He went back to the house and told his father that he'd had no luck. He called the police. He also called his mother, who got permission to leave work.

A patrolman came to the house. O'Connor guessed him to be about fifty. He took a report, acting no more excited than if O'Connor had told him a car had been stolen. Less so. He said, "I'll file this with Missing Persons."

"What do you mean, file it?" O'Connor asked, struggling to keep his temper.

"Most adult disappearances are voluntary, sir."

"No—this isn't voluntary. Someone has taken her. She takes care of my father. She'd never leave him. This is a crime . . . for God's sake, she's in danger!"

The officer shrugged. "People get tired of responsibilities. But we'll keep an eye out for her."

O'Connor said, "I work for the *Express*." He didn't tell him that he was only a copyboy.

The patrolman paused, then said, "Look, it's not up to me. You call Detective Riley first thing tomorrow."

"Tomorrow! By then she could be God knows where! He could have . . ." But the thought of what could be happening to her so distressed him, he couldn't say it aloud.

The officer patted him on the shoulder. "Don't worry, son. I'll be on the radio, asking all our patrol cars to keep an eye out for her. You just wait—I'll bet she'll come back a little later this evening. Ninety-nine percent of the time, if an adult disappears, it's because they forgot to tell someone their plans or they don't want to be found."

"She's in that one percent then," O'Connor said angrily.

"If so, we'll be a little more sure of it tomorrow."

"That one percent," O'Connor said. "They aren't numbers, you know. Those are human beings. A young woman, in this case. Someone who is loved and who has a job and a home and who has never said a cross word to anyone in her life . . . a good girl."

"Call Riley in the morning," he said, and left.

Instead, O'Connor called Jack Corrigan. Corrigan listened to O'Connor's anxious recital in silence, until O'Connor described what the patrolman had said and done. Jack interrupted him.

"Never mind Riley," he said grimly. "Unfortunately, Missing Persons is the retiring cop's pasture in most police departments around here. Riley—that asshole wasn't any good when he was really on the job, and now he's just sitting around waiting for them to engrave his gold watch. Speaking of which . . . hang on." There was a brief pause. "It's late, and Wrigley might not go for it, but let's give it a try. Listen, Conn, grab the clearest, most recent black-and-white photo of her you can find and meet me down at the *Express*. Bring two or three of them if you can."

O'Connor waited only until his mother arrived to care for his father, a few minutes after he had found three photos of Maureen that he thought the engravers might be able to work with.

Old Man Wrigley had been reached at home. By the time O'Connor got to the paper, Jack was already sitting at a typewriter, writing the lead. Wrigley's son, who was news editor, picked out a photo and told O'Connor to sit next to Jack and answer his questions.

O'Connor listened as Jack called the chief of police and asked if he'd care to comment.

There was a pause, then Jack repeated the story of Maureen's disappearance, and the patrolman's lack of concern. There was another pause, then Jack said, "Yes, sir, the sister of one of our own staff. I know the family personally . . . Exactly, sir . . . No, she wouldn't have abandoned her father." O'Connor saw a kind of triumphant light come into Jack's eyes. "That's what I thought, sir." He began writing notes.

When he hung up, he said, "Chief claims it was all a misunderstanding. You go on home, I'll file this and come by for some follow-up."

Detectives came to the house. Jack came to the house—often over the next few days—and then other reporters, for other reasons. Friends and family, neighbors and curiosity seekers. None of them were of any use.

O'Connor hardly mourned Roosevelt's death the next week, and later had no heart for the victory celebrations at the end of the war. Maureen was missing. God knew what was happening to her. And it was his fault.

Neither of his parents ever said that to him—in fact, once hearing him say it, they protested adamantly that it wasn't so. But he believed that they must, in their heart of hearts, feel it to be true—that perhaps they even said it to each other, and only guilt had made them protest. It hardly mattered—he said it often enough to himself.

For five years, O'Connor and his parents went through the motions of being a family, but Maureen's absence grew nearly to be a stronger force than her presence. His father's interest in life beyond his room, always something Maureen had cajoled from him, began to fail, and what remained of his health failed with it.

O'Connor's eldest sister, Alma, had lost her husband in the war, and now she came to live with them to help his mother. His mother, who, like his father, seemed suddenly to age after that one April evening, was grateful for Alma's help.

Alma was not Maureen, though. O'Connor found himself ill-at-ease with this prim woman, who was seventeen years his senior and all but a stranger to him. In truth, he decided later, the thing that bothered him most was that she was staying in Maureen's room. His mother had packed up Maureen's belongings and placed them in the attic, and she allowed Alma to place her own things on the walls and shelves of Maureen's room. To O'Connor's way of thinking, his mother was giving up on Maureen. Alma was seen by her youngest brother as encroaching and little more than a squatter. Beneath all his resentment of her, he carried the fear that some spiritual connection to Maureen had been broken by these changes in the household, that by moving

Maureen's possessions, they had taken away a place for her to come back to, somehow made it impossible for her to return home.

Jack had been O'Connor's salvation. It was Jack who had talked Mr. Wrigley, the publisher, into promoting his copyboy to general assignment reporter. O'Connor later learned that Jack had support for this idea from an unexpected quarter: Helen Swan.

"I told the old man the truth," she said when O'Connor asked about it. "I told him Jack was giving you writing lessons, and if they turned out not to be good ones, I'd give you better ones myself, because I could see when some half-pint had ink in his veins, even if Wrigley couldn't."

He knew of no one who talked back to Mr. Wrigley the way Helen Swan did. He remained in awe of her.

It had taken him a while to realize that there was a strong friendship beneath the rivalry between Helen and Jack. In the spring of 1936, she left the paper for a little more than a year, not long after Jack's car accident. O'Connor was still a paperboy then, and he began to see that Jack missed her terribly.

O'Connor was convinced that it was her relentless needling that pulled Jack out of the misery he had fallen into when he was hospitalized after the accident. "Get up off your ass," she said the first time she visited him. "I'll let you set it down again in a room across the hall. There's a blind guy in it. He can't see you pity yourself." Jack had winced, and she added in an angry voice, "So you'll have a limp. There are other people around here who've lost more than that."

O'Connor gathered up his courage and told her to leave Jack alone.

Helen stared at him, apparently just realizing he was in the room. "I thought the hospital didn't allow kids under sixteen into patients' rooms."

"They don't," Jack said. "But the doctors ran some tests and figured out that O'Connor has never been younger than forty-two."

"All right," she said, coming to her feet, "bowing to his seniority, I'll do as Conn asks."

"No, don't go, Swanie," Jack pleaded. "Make her stay, Conn."

Conn started to try to convince her, but she raised a hand to cut him off. She sat down again and sighed. "Jack Corrigan, I don't know what you've done to deserve the boy's loyalty."

O'Connor always thought it was the other way around. Looking back, he wondered at the patience Corrigan had shown. More than once, as an adult,

O'Connor had asked Jack what on earth had caused him to all but adopt him from the time he was eight—why he had troubled himself over such a grubby little brat. Corrigan usually laughed and said, "*You* chose *me*. Not the other way around. Same way all stray dogs operate—easier to let you follow me than to keep kicking you away." O'Connor thought there was some truth in the jest—the times when Corrigan roared at him to leave him the hell alone, his scathing criticisms of O'Connor's writing, the bouts of heavier-than-usual drinking when Jack would become quiet and withdrawn—none of these had the power to keep O'Connor away from him for long.

Helen Swan had been right about the writing lessons. All those years ago, when O'Connor asked Jack to teach him to be a newspaperman, Jack had taken him seriously—for reasons O'Connor was never entirely sure of.

Even at eight, O'Connor was reading at a level beyond that of most children his age, and Jack began by giving him assignments—most of which taught him to read the paper with an eye toward the way it was written. Jack asked him now and then if he was still keeping the diary, but never asked to see it. O'Connor asked him once how he knew that O'Connor was really writing in it. "Because I believe you are an honorable young man." That was, O'Connor knew, the highest praise Jack could give anyone, and no reward could have been greater for his work.

And work it was. There were lessons on finding the heart of the story, on writing clean, clear prose to tell it. He learned to notice differences in style. Jack would read to him, and ask him to tell him which reporter wrote the story. Corrigan's and Helen Swan's he began to recognize for their skill. Others, he could often spot because of their weaknesses.

He learned to observe and to describe what he saw. At first, the descriptions were delivered verbally, and sometimes breathlessly during a boxing lesson. Later, he wrote small stories for Jack, who did not spare his feelings when critiquing the results.

So it was that by the time O'Connor was added to the staff of the *Express*, Mr. Wrigley got a reporter who was far from the greenhorn he expected. One day as he stood talking to Helen Swan in the newsroom, Wrigley walked up to them and said to her, "Seems I won't be needing to give you teacher's pay."

She smiled and made O'Connor blush by saying, "Imagine what you'll be getting out of him five years from now. Keep this boy challenged, or you'll be reading his bylines in the *Herald* or the *Times*."

The challenge of reporting for the *Express* was the only thing that kept him from going crazy after Maureen disappeared. He thought at first that Jack might have believed that all he needed was distraction, something to keep him from dwelling on her disappearance.

He had underestimated Corrigan.

Jack had no more given up on the idea of finding Maureen than O'Connor had.

Jack spent time with him in the paper's morgue, going through clipping files on disappearances. O'Connor had been astonished at the number of them.

"Don't jump to conclusions," Jack told him. "There are young runaways mixed in here, and plenty of people who are lost because they don't want to be found. Women whose husbands beat them, men who want to escape debts or responsibilities, teenagers who have cruel parents, parents who—well, of a terrible kind—so terrible the paper can't print the details."

"But there have to be some missing girls who are like Maureen," O'Connor protested. "She wasn't a runaway, no matter what the coppers say."

"I know that and you know that. But after you've read enough of these, you'll understand why detectives are skeptical people."

He read them, and had to admit that in many cases, it was as Jack had said. He found two other stories, though, in which young women near Maureen's age had gone missing in the month of April, although in other years—young women who seemingly had no reason to disappear. Less, he admitted to himself, than Maureen had. Anna Mezire. Lois Arlington. Both twenty years old. The coincidence was too strong to ignore.

"I want to talk to their families," he told Jack.

"Fine, but remember—both of them are old news as far as the *Express* is concerned. Don't try to do anything about it on company time."

The mothers of the missing women, wary at first, became more open with him upon hearing that his own sister had disappeared. He spoke to them separately and learned that they were each unaware of any other cases. Anna had disappeared on April 30, 1943. Lois on April 18, 1941. But neither woman had any more information about her daughter's disappearance than what he had read in the paper. He took down the names of a few of the girls' friends, but he found that the ones who hadn't moved away had little to tell him. "I think about her," one of Anna's friends said. "I think I'm always going to feel sad in April. My brother's a policeman, and he said that Anna's probably dead, and I should just accept that as a fact. But I can't, you know? It would be easier—I hate to say it, but it would be easier to know that she was dead."

O'Connor had been hard put to hide his feelings as she spoke, not to let her see how angry these words made him. He would never give up hope, he thought as he took a streetcar back to the paper. He would never want to learn that Maureen was dead.

But before many months had passed, he decided that anything would be better than not knowing—anything. He could and did imagine so many horrific possibilities for her fate, the notion of her being beyond harm ranked far from the worst of them. *Please, not suffering,* became his evening and morning prayer, his silent plea throughout the day.

One afternoon he learned that Jack—who seemed to have a "pal" in every government office and on every street corner of Las Piernas—was getting calls from a worker in the county coroner's office whenever a Jane Doe was brought in. O'Connor insisted on going with him to view the next body.

"You sure you want to do that?" Jack asked. "It's seldom—well, it's not the sleeping beauty parlor, if you take my meaning."

"Then why do you go?"

"Why do you think I go, kid?"

O'Connor was silent for a moment, then said, "Thanks. But I'll be going with you from now on, if you've no objection."

"None whatsoever."

O'Connor got sick the first time, but Jack still brought him along the next time.

They made these trips for five years.

Each miserable April, O'Connor watched for reports of missing women that might fit the pattern, but there were none.

In April 1949, in San Marino—about thirty miles north of Las Piernas—a three-year-old girl went out to play in a field overgrown with weeds. She fell into an abandoned well—ninety feet down, through a fourteen-inch-wide opening. Her parents heard her crying and called police and firemen. Word of the rescue effort spread, and in Las Piernas the city editor of the *Express* looked up from the wire reports to see who was available to cover it. There was only one unassigned reporter in the newsroom. Young O'Connor. The editor sent him on his way to San Marino.

The scene was already crowded when O'Connor arrived. Heavy equipment, rescue workers, volunteers, neighbors—even diminutive adults who offered to be lowered down the pipe. Well-diggers were urgently excavating a parallel shaft.

"Not a sound out of her since the first hour," a patrolman said to O'Connor. "Jesus, I got a little girl not much older than her."

Next to them, a man from the *Herald* suddenly said, "What the hell is that?" They turned to see trucks laden with odd-shaped equipment approaching the scene.

"Television," a reporter from the *Times* said. "KTLA. Saw them out at the electroplating plant fire over on Pico a couple of years ago. Looks as if they're getting more sophisticated."

The cop and the man from the *Herald* looked amused.

O'Connor didn't. He was thinking about something Jack had given him to read recently, a report on television.

The man from the *Times* was saying, "It's no joke, my friends. Two years ago there were a little over three hundred televisions in Los Angeles. You know how many there are now?"

"About twenty thousand," O'Connor answered.

"Bingo. Trust the cub to know. What paper are you with?"

"The *Express.*"

"The *Express*? You know Jack Corrigan?"

For the rest of the long hours there, the man from the *Times* took him under his wing, introducing him to others, getting him as close as possible to the rescue itself.

After fifty hours of frantic effort, the rescue crew reached the little girl— to the heartbreak of everyone who had worked or watched or waited, they reached her too late. The coroner would later determine that she had died not long after rescue efforts began.

When O'Connor got back to the *Express,* tired, dirty, and thoroughly depressed, the city editor said sourly, "I don't know why you should bother writing it up. Everyone has been watching it on televisions. Twenty-seven hours straight, and people who own sets had their neighbors camped out in their dens. Never seen anything like it. At least Jack has that angle covered."

After O'Connor filed his story, Jack took him drinking.

"It was amazing, Conn," Jack told him. "Everyone huddled around the screen, feeling as if they were right there." He took a pull off a cigarette and exhaled slowly, shaking his head. "The world is not going to be the same place tomorrow morning."

"It never is," O'Connor said absently. "Like it or not."

Jack studied him. "What's on your mind, Conn?"

"I'm just thinking that I'll find out about wells in Las Piernas."

"A follow-up story? Sure. Good idea."

Honesty made O'Connor shake his head. "No, Ames Hart is already work-ing on that one."

"Should have known. Anything that might end up being some kind of reform, Hart's on it."

"I'm only thinking . . . you know, maybe . . . Maureen," O'Connor ended on a whisper.

Ames Hart told O'Connor that a law was going to be passed, mandating the capping of wells. And more gently, he mentioned that none of the abandoned wells in Las Piernas was so wide that an adult woman would have been likely to have fallen down it.

O'Connor waited for another April.

April 1950 was a strange April—colder than most. A fraction of an inch of snow fell in Los Angeles, and in Las Piernas as well. That might have been the biggest local story that April, if work done in an orange grove damaged by frost had not uncovered three bodies.

Maureen O'Connor, Anna Mezire, and Lois Arlington were no longer missing.

9

THE NIGHT AFTER MAUREEN'S FUNERAL, O'CONNOR DRANK HIMSELF into a stupor. He awoke the next morning to find himself lying next to a woman who (he decided) was better-looking than he had any right to expect her to be. He looked around, saw that he was in his own apartment, and stared at the ceiling as memories of the previous evening came back to him—of leaving his parents' home with Corrigan, going to a bar, and drinking steadily. Two women joined them. Jack left with one, he stumbled out with the other.

This one. He remembered the fumbling, desperate way he had taken her, and—worst of all—weeping as he had not wept at the funeral. She had held him and not said a word. He had eventually fallen asleep.

He got out of bed and dressed quietly, his movements slowed more by his shame than by his hangover. He was not one to pick up women in bars and bring them home on any occasion, and he believed that to have done so after his sister's funeral revealed him to be the worst sort of man.

He wondered if the woman was a prostitute, and what he might owe her if she was, or if he had already paid her. He looked in his wallet—hard to tell what he had left at the bar, but he didn't seem to be down much from where he had been the day before.

She came into the kitchen while he was making coffee. She was dressed and was smoking a cigarette. "Good morning," she said, although she appeared to be just as hung over as he was.

"Good morning." He hesitated, then added, "Care for some coffee?"

"Thanks, Conn. I'd love some." She smiled a little crookedly, then said, "Vera, in case you've forgotten."

"Vera. Of course."

The smile widened a little. "Listen, maybe I'll skip that coffee. I should get going."

"It's no trouble," he said.

"That's okay. Do you see my coat? Wait—there it is, by the door." She moved to get it, but he reached it first and held it for her as she put it on. She turned toward him and briefly embraced him. "Nothing to worry about, Conn. Nothing at all."

"I'd like to see you again," he found himself saying.

She shook her head. "I'm leaving town today, remember? Or maybe you don't—anyway, if I come back through here, I'll look you up, all right?"

"Wait—" He hurried back to his wallet, pulled out a business card. "If you should need anything, give me a call."

She took it, gave him a quick kiss, and left.

He hadn't even asked her last name, he realized.

Except to reprimand himself for dishonoring his sister's memory, he forgot about Vera. He concentrated on trying to find some lead in Maureen's murder. The owner of the orange grove was an old woman, nearly blind, who was so upset over the discovery of the remains on her property, her grown children feared for her health. No one had worked in the grove through every year of the disappearances, and police were convinced that none of the workers had any idea of the grave's existence. The other two bodies might not have been identified if O'Connor had not previously brought attention to the similarities in the women's disappearances. Maureen's body was fully clothed. One of the detectives said to O'Connor that he could be relieved about that, because the other two were buried nude.

Corrigan, who had been tipped off about the discovery in the grove before O'Connor, had gone with him to the police department. He had watched O'Connor as the detective told him these and other details. Jack finally told the man to shut the hell up.

A young detective just making his way up through the ranks, Dan Norton, was kindest to him, and kept in touch with him long after others in the department began avoiding him—as the likelihood of solving the cases seemed more and more remote, the less welcome his unanswerable questions were to them.

Norton told O'Connor that he didn't think all three women were necessarily killed by the same person.

"Why do you believe that?"

"The coroner found similar fractures on each of the other women's skeletons—a kind of ritual, you might say, something that indicates they were tortured."

O'Connor went pale.

"Conn, the *other* two. Bad, I know, but at least your sister was spared that, as far as anyone can tell. We didn't find those same fractures on Maureen. She was clothed. There were other differences. Things like that make me wonder. Guesswork on my part, and it still leaves the big question of how killer number two knew about the grave. Seems to me either he saw one of those burials, or killer number one squawked." He paused, and added, "I swear to you I won't let this case go, and you can call me and ask me about it anytime. I like you and I like Jack, but if you're going to keep covering the crime beat, and you don't want to find guys ducking out of here when you walk in the door, forget asking anyone else if they've made any progress on the case. For some of these guys, it's like being handed an 'F' on a report card on a daily basis. Truth is, we don't know much and we may never know much. That's hard to hear, I know, but I'm not going to feed you bullshit just to make myself look good."

It was hard to hear. It was also the beginning of a friendship.

Within two months of Maureen's funeral, O'Connor's father died of a stroke. One day not long after that, O'Connor's mother invited him to come by the house that evening. He saw her as often as possible, worried that all the losses were becoming too much for her to bear. That night she sent Alma off to see a movie and had a quiet dinner with her son, talking to him of his job at the paper. After they had washed the dishes, she sat down next to him, took his hand, and said, "I'm selling the house, Conn, and going home. Alma's said she'll come, too."

He knew that there was only one place she had ever considered to be home, but still, he was shocked by this announcement. "All the way to Ireland? But this is where—"

"This is where *you're* at home. It's a fine place for most, perhaps, but I've lost too much here. I don't blame the whole country for what's happened to us, but I won't live with ghosts. I can't walk past the corner without thinking of Maureen. God knows I can't live in this house without thinking of your poor father and all he suffered." She paused. "That's why I packed up all your sister's things, Connor. I think somehow I knew."

He said nothing.

She sighed. "If you want Maureen's things, lad, you may have them. I'll not be taking them with me."

"Yes, thank you." He took his hand from hers and put his arm around her shoulders. "Lord, I'll miss you so."

She began to cry. "I know there's no sense asking if you'll come with me . . ."

He shook his head. "Not as long as her killer is free."

She pulled a clean handkerchief from the pocket of her dress and wiped her eyes. "Well, you must come to see us, then. And . . . if they should learn anything . . . about Maureen . . ."

"I'll tell you straight away."

A month later he got a call at the paper from Vera. He nearly did not remember who she was, until she said, "We met in April." She named the day of his sister's funeral. "Remember?"

"Yes, I remember," he said quietly.

There was a pause. "Look, I'm living in Las Vegas now. I'm just in Las Piernas for a few days. Let's have lunch together."

He hesitated. "It occurs to me that I don't even know your last name."

"Smith," she said, and laughed. "True fact."

"Look, Miss Smith—"

"It's extremely important that you meet me for lunch, Mr. O'Connor," she said firmly, all the laughter gone from her voice now.

"All right."

They met at Big Sarah's diner. It was a hell of a place, he thought later, to be told you were about to become a father.

"I won't demand you marry me," she said. "It's just that I'd like some help."

He thought of how he had felt on the morning after Maureen's funeral, his feelings of having betrayed his sister's memory by sleeping with this woman. But he also remembered that Vera had comforted him, and until now, she had asked for nothing. *What should I do, Maureen?* he asked silently.

A strange feeling came over him, a feeling he was too Irish to ignore. It was as if everything inside him that had been in turmoil for these past five years grew quiet and calm. At a moment when he had every excuse to feel confused and unsure and panicked, he found instead that he knew exactly what he must do.

He studied Vera for a moment, then said, "I'll marry you."

She looked taken aback. "To tell you the truth, I'd rather you didn't."

"I won't have my son or daughter raised a bastard. If you don't want to live with me, fine. If you think I'm going to ask you for . . . for anything else,

I won't." He paused. "What kind of situation are you in that you can think of living openly as an unmarried woman with a child?"

"I can tell people I'm a widow. The Korean War, I'll say. There aren't so few widows around these days that one more will attract much attention. Besides, suppose you meet some woman you really want to marry, and you're tied to me?"

"I won't."

"You don't know that."

He was silent.

"I can see there's no use trying to talk you out of that prediction. Okay—suppose I meet someone else?"

"Then we can divorce, but if the man you marry has any prejudice against the child, the child will come to live with me."

"Divorce! I thought you were Catholic."

"I am, and I wouldn't like it, but I won't father a child and not give it my name. That would be worse."

They argued for a while. He was sober now and more than able to hold his own in a verbal battle. He found himself admiring her ability to do the same. In the end, after setting down several conditions of her own, she capitulated.

They would meet at city hall the next day, witnesses in tow.

When he got back to the paper, he tried to concentrate on the story he was writing and could barely do so. The newsroom was always a noisy place—a mixture of the clatter of keys being struck, the ching of typewriter bells ringing at the end of each line, the zip of carriage returns. The sounds of pages pulled free, the shuffling of thin layers of carbon paper between sheets of cheap copy paper. Voices calling "Copyboy!" The low chug-chug-chug of the wire service Teletypes. Phones rang on empty desks. Conversations went on everywhere. If not on the phone or writing, men were making wisecracks or arguing or horsing around.

Sound and smell. Cigarette smoke hung thick in the air, along with the scent of the stale remains of takeout lunches. A good number of the room's occupants reeked of booze, and more than a few would be half in the bag by four o'clock. Sometimes, O'Connor thought, the newsroom seemed like a bar with desks and typewriters. The paper did have a phone that, if one picked it up, rang in the Press Club, the bar across the street, to make it easier to summon staff back to the newsroom from their revered watering hole.

This afternoon, most of them were here, trying to finish stories before deadline. Summer and sweat and men under pressure. Men, and Helen Swan, who kept glancing his way. He could swear she could read his thoughts. He kept watching the door.

Corrigan had barely crossed the threshold of the newsroom when O'Connor stood up and hurried over to him. He asked him to step outside with him for a moment. Jack started to protest, but halted mid-sentence and said, "Sure. You look as if you've got something on your mind."

O'Connor nodded and led the way back downstairs.

Outside in the summer heat, he told Jack about his wedding plans, and asked him to be his witness.

Jack called him every name for a fool he could think of. "Conn, how the hell do you even know it's yours?"

"I don't. It could be my child. It might not be."

"If it's not, why on earth—"

"I did something that could have resulted in a child being conceived. I have to own up to that, Jack."

"The hell you do! Wait until it's born and have blood tests. She's just trying to take you for everything you're worth."

"I'm not worth much. Surely she could have done better than a reporter if she was looking to trap someone into keeping her in style."

"Maybe not. You don't know who she's been with."

"No, I don't. It doesn't matter. It's not a trap. She didn't even want to get married."

"The oldest trick in the damned book. They all want to get married, believe me. Hell, it sounds to me as if this broad just wants your money, Conn."

"If all she wanted was money, she would have asked for it from the first night I met her. Look, Jack, you aren't going to talk me out of this one. I'll go back inside and ask Geoff or Helen or one of the others to come with me tomorrow if you won't. I'd like it to be you, though."

"Conn, slow down. Think for a moment. What kind of life is that kid going to have?"

"I'll do what I can."

"What, keep it yourself?" Jack asked incredulously.

"No, she's bound to give it a better life than I could."

"Maybe not. If you find out it's yours, then ask your mother—"

"My mother's going back to Ireland, Jack," he said, struggling to keep his temper. "I won't add to her worries, and I won't keep her here. You're not to mention it to her."

"Not to mention—!"

"No. Not yet. I'll let her know when she's in Ireland. I'll tell her after the baby's born."

Jack shook his head. "You're what now, twenty-two? Conn, you're not thinking straight. A marriage is a legal contract. You have no idea what you're getting into. You're talking about throwing your life away on a whore who—" He broke off, quickly raising his hands to deflect a blow. "Damn it, Conn!"

"You're not to talk of her that way, Jack. Never again."

"All right, all right."

O'Connor subsided.

"What is it?" Jack scoffed. "Love?"

"Not a bit of it."

Jack sighed. "All your hard work, so this—this *dame* can have a chunk of your check?"

O'Connor said nothing.

"I wish I knew why the hell—"

"I've told you. It's the child needs thinking of, Jack. Not me, not Vera. The child."

Jack studied him. "Why do I feel as if this has something to do with Maureen?"

"Don't," O'Connor said, and averted his eyes.

"Conn," Jack said sadly. "Jesus, Conn."

O'Connor looked up again. "Will you do it or not? If the answer's no, I'd best get busy looking for someone else."

"I'll be there—under protest."

"You'll not say a word to her that makes her unhappy," O'Connor warned.

"Oh, not on her wedding day," Jack said sarcastically, and turned and went back into the Wrigley Building.

When the baby was born, Vera sent word to him. A boy, named as they had compromised—Kenneth John O'Connor. He had wanted to call him Kieran, after his own father, in the Irish naming tradition used in his family, and after Jack, but she said the name Kieran was "too foreign" and so he had agreed on the name she had thought closest to it.

True to other agreements they had made, she did not live with him as his wife. He sent money. She occasionally sent a photo. More often, a change of address.

Jack was quick to point out that the boy looked nothing like him. O'Connor nearly knocked him down for that.

"Teaching you to fight was the stupidest thing I've ever done," Jack said when O'Connor had regained his temper, "because you don't know your friends from your enemies." But after that day, Jack never remarked on the child.

In no other matter, O'Connor realized, did he keep his thoughts so guarded from Jack. Whatever they might argue about was argued openly—except for this subject. He knew this was in some part due to the fact that he didn't fully understand his own feelings about Vera and the boy. He only knew that when he thought of Vera, he thought of what had happened in her presence—of her comforting him as he wept, certainly, but even more often of that moment in Big Sarah's, when he felt so calm—and how, for some reason, he never worried about Maureen's ghost feeling disappointed in him after that. He decided that even if Vera had come to him that day to say that she needed help because another man had left her pregnant, his answer would have been the same.

Two years ago, in 1956, she had filed for divorce. He had been surprised to discover how depressed that had made him feel. There had been no request for child support.

Working on a newspaper had taught him all he needed to know about finding information on someone. He had called in a favor or two to learn the name of the man she was marrying and to look into his background. He could find nothing objectionable. Reports were that the man treated Kenneth as his own. O'Connor signed the papers. He hadn't heard a word from Vera since then.

In that same year, Winston Wrigley II, the son of the founder of Wrigley Publications—who was now semiretired—faced up to what publishers all over the country were starting to realize: Americans who used to look forward to reading the evening paper after work now looked forward to watching the news on television. The news was being read aloud to them by men at desks. Newsmen before cameras instead of behind them—Huntley, Brinkley, Cronkite. Circulation for the *Express* was down and he saw no reason to expect it to pick up again.

The *News* and the *Express* would be combined into one morning paper: the *Las Piernas News Express*.

Winston Wrigley II was better liked than his father by the staffs of both papers. Although the family was wealthy, his father had insisted that he learn the business the hard way—moving from paperboy to copyboy to reporter to editor. He gained further respect from the staff by openly discussing the end of the evening edition, keeping as many people employed as possible, and doing all in his power to find jobs for the others. O'Connor remembered evening after evening of farewell parties at the Press Club, the bar across the street from the paper. Helen Swan said it was a wonder that such a sizable herd of drunks could make it back and forth across Broadway without at least a few stragglers being flattened.

O'Connor had been sure that he would lose his job. Winston Wrigley II kept him on. When one of the older reporters groused about this, Wrigley said, "O'Connor's been on our payroll since 1936."

"As a paperboy!" the reporter said, then blushed as he realized his mistake.

"You never know how high a paperboy might rise in the business," Wrigley said calmly. Like his father, he seldom raised his voice.

O'Connor sat up with a start, and realized that despite his resolve, he had dozed off in Jack's hospital room. He glanced at his watch—it was past eleven.

Jack stirred awake again, and this time O'Connor called the nurse, as promised. When she had left, Jack murmured something, and O'Connor came closer to hear him.

"Now that Miss Ass-Full-of-Sunlight has done her duty, tell me the truth."

"Your speech is slurred, but I'm so used to listening to you when you're under full sail, I can understand you."

"Funny. Not that I would mind a drink."

"None for a while, I'm afraid. The worst blows were to your head."

"Thank God. What if they had injured something I use every day?"

"If you can crack jokes with a cracked skull, I suppose you're going to be all right. Eventually, anyway. If I showed you a mirror, you'd scream like a little girl."

"Given how I feel, I may just start screaming on principle."

"Sorry, Jack," O'Connor said, his voice no longer teasing. "It's inhuman, but they can't give you anything for the pain for a little while yet. Something to do with the head injuries."

Jack was silent for a moment, then asked, "What about the eye?"

O'Connor hoped the truth wouldn't lead to some sort of setback, because he had no practice at trying to lie to Jack. "Don't know yet. Old Man Wrigley came by earlier, when you were still out cold. He told me he's going to bring in a specialist for you."

"Kind of him."

"Don't give up hope, Jack. They really don't know."

"Might as well tell me the rest."

"Not sure I should . . ."

"Damn it, Conn! Have I ever, in the last twenty years—"

"All right, all right. Settle down. For God's sake, don't kill yourself just getting pissed off at me. You've three broken ribs, four broken fingers, and plenty of cuts and bruises. The cuts and scrapes wouldn't be so much of a worry if you hadn't decided to go for a swim in a swamp."

"A swamp?" He looked puzzled.

"Okay, not exactly. You were found in one of the marshes by an egg farmer, and you were half-drowned and so cold he wasn't sure you were alive. If you don't become feverish from that, it will be a miracle."

"I remember a farm . . . eucalyptus trees . . . feeling where my damned keys cut me when somebody kicked me."

"Do you remember who did this to you?"

But Jack was caught up in other thoughts. "Listen—this sounds strange, but I swear it's true—someone was burying a car on that farm. In the middle of the night, or sometime after midnight, anyway. Doesn't that sound strange to you?"

"Yes," O'Connor answered truthfully.

"But I'd swear I saw it, Conn. I woke up in a eucalyptus grove, a windbreak, probably. A dairy on the other side of the road. And I saw a farmer burying a car."

"Well, I've always been a city boy, so I couldn't tell you why farmers do what they do in the wee hours of the night or any other time. So let's talk about before the farm."

"You don't believe me."

"I believe you, Jack. I do."

Jack fell silent.

"Who did this to you, Jack?"

He frowned, winced at the pull on his stitches, and said, "Big guy at a party. Never saw him before. Thought I was making time with his floozy and coldcocked me. One punch. Wasn't expecting it."

"How big a man?"

"Three inches shorter than the *Titanic*, if you stood them back to back."

"Hair?"

"Blond. Crewcut. Blue eyes, I think. But that might have been the dame. I'm a little confused about him." He put a hand to his head. "Someone else joined the fun, but I didn't get a good look at him. He was behind me most of the time."

He fell silent again.

O'Connor waited a bit, then tried again. "You were wearing your good suit when you ended up in the marsh. Or what was left of your good suit—"

"Where is it?"

"The ER nurses showed it to me, and told me they'll bring the remains of it up here once it's dry. If I had any fear that you could get out of that bed and put it on, I'd have them burn it. So—you were wearing your good suit. Where'd you go last night?"

"Lillian's place. Katy's birthday."

O'Connor couldn't hide his disbelief. "Katy's birthday party? Lillian invited you?"

"No. Katy did."

He was wearing down, but fighting it, O'Connor thought.

"Conn, something was eating at her. Really bothering her."

"Bothering Katy?"

"Yes . . ." Jack's thoughts seemed to drift, then he looked back at O'Connor. "She kept saying she wanted to talk to me, but she obviously didn't want the family to hear what she had to say. You know she's never serious about much of anything, but tonight . . . I mean, last night . . . she was troubled."

"If you're worried about her, I'll call her tomorrow. Maybe she'll come and visit you."

"Go by their place tonight."

"Tonight? Jack, it's almost midnight."

"She's a night owl."

"And I suppose Todd Ducane won't mind my calling on his wife in the dead of night?"

"Guess again."

"What are you saying?"

"He has a mistress. He's home maybe three nights a week."

"First of all, maybe that's what's troubling Katy. And second, what if I happen to luck into one of the three nights?"

"Katy doesn't care. I offered to pound him so flat she could use him as rug."

"This being when you yourself hadn't been made into a carpet."

Jack ignored him. "She told me not to bother. She doesn't want him. She's known about this for months. Old news."

"Okay, to everyone but me, I guess. All the same, maybe Todd will be a dog in the manger and still not take to my showing up on his doorstep at midnight. People have been shot for less."

"He drives an old heap, it will be parked in the drive."

"Not the garage?"

"No. He likes to irritate the neighbors. Hopes it will get him a gift from Lillian."

"I think I understand. Lillian owns the house, right?"

"Right."

"And his parents won't buy him a new car, so he figures he'll embarrass Lillian into coughing up the dough for something worthy of the neighborhood."

"Yes."

"Why did she marry the Toad?"

"Ask her."

"When I see her tonight."

"Yes."

"And who's going to keep an eye on you? I don't want to risk having someone come in here and finish what they started."

"I'll be fine. See Katy. Go over and find out if she's okay."

"Why don't I just call her from the pay phone downstairs?"

"You'll wake the baby and everyone else."

O'Connor sighed. "It's that important to you?"

"Please."

"I'm on my way," he said, grabbing his coat and hat. He paused as he reached the door. "Jack, where are your hat and coat?"

"I don't know. Lillian's? I'm not sure."

"I'll make a note to ask her about it before Hastings gives it away to charity."

"The butler? He's probably pressing it as we speak."

"Get some sleep."

"Can't seem to avoid it . . . Hey, Conn?"

O'Connor waited.

"Thanks."

"Just rest. I'll let you know what the princess has to say."

*   *   *

O'Connor drove his Nash Rambler through the rain, his window down a crack to keep the windshield from fogging up, allowing the rain to pelt in. He talked to himself over most of the distance, calling himself a sap to do the bidding of someone in Jack's condition, a man who had been beaten so badly, he believed that he saw a car being buried on a farm.

Then again, O'Connor thought, maybe Jack really saw it. O'Connor was inclined to believe he did, but it made so little sense, he had to question Jack's condition at the time. If not dazed by the beating, perhaps by the booze. Jack wasn't usually one to see visions while drinking, but he had been a hard drinker for many years, so perhaps he had reached that stage where he had downed enough martinis to bring on the pink elephants.

O'Connor's thoughts moved quickly to his bigger concern: that someone had been out to murder Jack. This big blond man he spoke of had knocked him out cold with one punch, Jack said. So why did he keep on beating an unconscious man? If he had done anything like that at the party itself, people would have intervened. So he had to have taken Jack away, and in full sight of witnesses. O'Connor began to feel more anxious to talk to Katy—perhaps she'd be able to tell him what had happened. Best of all, she'd know who was at the party.

He turned the corner to the Ducanes' street, and braked hard to avoid hitting a police barricade.

10

THE NASH FISHTAILED ON THE SLICK STREET, BUT HE MANAGED TO BRING it back under control and stop without hitting either of the grim-faced officers who were now shining flashlights through the windshield. They wore slickers, but the wind was gusting, and no ducking or turning of their heads prevented the rain from pelting into their faces. When one of them moved to the driver's side, O'Connor rolled his window down a little more and showed his press pass. Even as the officer took it, O'Connor's attention was drawn to the Ducanes' home. The circular drive held a strange combination of vehicles: a battered black Hudson, which O'Connor took to be Todd's old heap, a dove gray and black Rolls-Royce Silver Cloud, and the coroner's wagon.

O'Connor felt his stomach lurch.

Along the street there were patrol cars as well, and a T-Bird that O'Connor had seen many times before. The T-Bird belonged to an old friend—Detective Dan Norton.

"It don't take you creeps any time at all, does it?" the patrolman said, handing the pass back.

"What's going on, Officer?"

"Why should I tell you?"

"Who is it, Joe?" the other cop asked, walking over to the window. To O'Connor's relief, it was someone he had met before, an officer named Matt Arden.

"A reporter," the man called Joe said. "Only there is no such thing as 'a' reporter. It's like one ant or one cockroach. They just don't come in singles."

"Officer Arden, we've met before," O'Connor said.

Arden peered in and said, "Oh, it's you." He turned to the other officer. "He's okay, Joe."

"He's waiting right here until I get the word. Go up and ask at the house."

"Matt—what's happened here?" O'Connor asked.

"Woman got herself killed," Joe answered, before Matt could reply.

"A woman . . . my God . . ."

"Hey, Conn," Matt said, "you all right?"

"Arden, why are you still here?" Joe said. "I thought I told you to get up to the house."

Matt gave O'Connor a helpless look and hurried away.

"Now, be a good boy," Joe said, "and move this jalopy over to the side of the road, so you can wait out of the way. Go on, move it."

In a daze, O'Connor moved the car, parking beneath a large tree.

Between disbelief and sadness, one thought returned to him again and again:

What am I going to tell Jack?

Jack was in no condition to receive news like this. What might it do to him?

As cool as Lillian had been toward Jack over the years since the accident, she had never prevented Katy from becoming attached to him. That had happened because both Jack and Lillian were friends of Helen Swan.

O'Connor remembered those days. Helen had become angry at Old Man Wrigley not long after Jack's accident, and she left the paper. To Wrigley's chagrin, she went to work for his goddaughter, Lillian Vanderveer Linworth, who did everything she could to keep Helen from caving in to his efforts to recruit her back. Lillian even moved to her ski lodge in Arrowhead for a time and took Helen with her.

Eventually, Lillian returned to Las Piernas. Helen went back to work at the newspaper, but by then she was attached to Katy and would often baby-sit her. Jack got to know Katy through his close friendship with Helen. Even as a toddler, Katy took to Jack.

O'Connor recalled, with a mixture of amusement and shame, that he had felt jealous of Katy when he was a young boy. Maureen had helped him get over it, talking to him about Jack being the sort of person who would only stay attached to those who didn't try to lay claim to him. "Grab on to him too tightly, Conn, and he'll let go of you."

When he saw the truth of this, he asked his sister how she had figured that out about Jack, since she had only met him once or twice. She said, "When you told me what happened that night at the diner, when Lillian Vanderveer complained that Jack was spending too much time with you? She was jealous of you. Showing it was her mistake."

That had sounded like nonsense at the time. It had been many years before he could figure out how Lillian Vanderveer could possibly be jealous of him. But he trusted Maureen and took her advice: he hid his feelings.

Eventually he hid the jealousy of Katy so well it disappeared, perhaps because as he grew a little older he realized he had nothing to fear from her. In time she won him over, as she did almost everyone, and he began to think of her as a lively, if spoiled, younger sister.

For all the wealth of the Linworths, he thought, she might have been better off if she had been part of the O'Connor family. His own mother had never been as reserved as Lillian, and although Kieran had been difficult to live with, O'Connor never doubted his father's love. Harold Linworth was as much an absentee father as he was an absentee husband.

Linworth had kept his distance, but he was one of the few. Katy was beautiful and young and spirited, and if she wasn't rich yet, she was destined to inherit a fortune. So was Todd, although hers would be the larger. O'Connor hadn't seen much of Katy in recent years, and not at all since she had married Todd, a fact that now ladened him with guilt.

A woman got herself killed, the cop said. How? O'Connor knew that the only way he'd find out anything tonight was if Dan Norton would talk to him.

He thought about seeing Todd's battered Hudson parked next to Dan's shiny T-Bird. Was Todd home, then? Was he the one who killed Katy? Had she threatened to divorce him over the mistress?

The wind gusted and the rain drummed against the roof of the car, then subsided back to tapping.

He saw Matt Arden return with a figure who hunched into his raincoat and carried a big umbrella. Dan Norton. O'Connor felt something ease in his shoulders—a tension he hadn't realized he was carrying. Whatever else was going wrong tonight, the best of the best had been assigned to this case. O'Connor put on his hat. He picked up an old newspaper from the seat next to him and sheltered under it as he got out of the car.

Norton smiled and said, "Jesus, O'Connor, they don't even pay you newshounds enough to buy umbrellas?"

"Mine's warm and dry at home, Dan. Haven't been there in almost a day, so . . ."

Dan immediately sobered. "How's Jack?" he asked, moving his umbrella so that O'Connor was a little drier, and he a little more wet.

"He regained consciousness, at least. Too early to say much, but he seems to have his sense of humor."

"Good sign. I guess you've heard what happened here? Although how you did, I'd love to know."

"Jack asked me to check on Katy—Kathleen. Just a feeling he had, I guess. I didn't come here knowing she had been murdered."

"Kathleen? No—Jesus, Conn, who told you that?"

O'Connor stared at him. "But . . ."

Matt Arden said, "I believe he misunderstood something Joe said, sir." He explained what had been said when O'Connor arrived.

"Hell, it's not Kathleen," Norton said. "It's one of the maids. The one that looks after the baby. Nursemaid, I guess they call them. . . . Conn, listen, this is a hell of a mess. Are you here to cover this for the *Express?*"

"No, but—"

"But nothing. If you are, I can't say another word to you."

"Ever?"

"You know what I mean."

"And you know what I mean. If I know something went on here and I don't let the paper know about it, Mr. Wrigley would have every reason to fire me."

"He won't. Not if you mean the old man. He knows what's going on himself and swore he'd cooperate. But I have to make sure—he didn't send you out here to cover it?"

"No. I'm here for the reason I told you."

"All right. Wait here, and as soon as the lab guys finish up, I'll come back and tell you more. Right now I'm a little busy."

"Dan—what's going on?"

He hesitated, then said, "The baby's missing. Little Maxwell Ducane. Kidnapped, looks like. But we don't know where the Ducanes are—any of them."

"What?"

"They went out on the Ducanes' new boat, but haven't come back—they were only supposed to be gone for a couple of hours, but there was fog late last night and this storm came in right behind it, so who knows what they ended up doing? Could be over on Catalina Island, waiting it out. Tried to get them by radio, but no luck. The Coast Guard will look for them, but in this weather—anyway, that's it in a nutshell. Now sit tight, and I'll tell you more when I can."

So O'Connor waited, listening to the rain. He had felt so relieved to learn that it wasn't Katy who was murdered, but hearing the rest of Norton's news so soon after that had brought an end to that relief. Mixed with his anxiety for the child was his frustration at only having bits and pieces of information.

The coroner's van left. Who was she, he wondered, that poor soul who'd been killed just because she worked here?

He caught a glimpse of movement in his rearview mirror, someone coming up the sidewalk. He waited, watching, but no one passed the car. He looked back, but the rear window was fogging up, and between that and the rain, he wondered if he had seen anything more than shadows.

O'Connor stepped out of the car. He tried to see if someone had moved behind the bushes that bordered the walk, tried to peer through the rain, but the wind drove it hard against him. He hurriedly got back inside.

He divided his attention between watching the street and glancing in the rearview mirror, but other than shifting shadows from the windblown branches of the trees, he saw nothing.

Suddenly there was a change in the pattern of the patrolmen's movements. One of the wooden barricades was moved aside as Lillian Vanderveer Linworth's chauffeured Rolls pulled up to it.

The Silver Cloud moved slowly past O'Connor's car, then stopped and backed up, pulling alongside the Nash. He wondered if the police had asked her to come to the house, or if she had decided to see the crime scene for herself. Knowing Lillian, probably the latter—Lillian was never one to be passive. O'Connor didn't blame her for coming here. He had spent a lot of time standing on the corner where Maureen had last been seen.

The chauffeur stepped out of the car, holding a large umbrella. The wind didn't make it of much use to him. He was a young man, younger than O'Connor. He made his way miserably over to the driver's side window of the Nash and waited politely. O'Connor took pity on him and rolled down the window, figuring no one enjoyed standing out in a cold rain.

"Mr. O'Connor? Mrs. Linworth would like a word with you, sir."

"I'm waiting for someone. May I come by the house later on instead?"

The chauffeur hurried back to ask. O'Connor saw one of the windows of the Rolls open a fraction of an inch. He heard Lillian's voice, but couldn't make out what she was saying.

The chauffeur hurried back.

"Yes, sir, she would appreciate that very much. She said not to regard the hour, sir—to come at any time, day or night. I'm to impress upon you—"

"You have," O'Connor said. "Please tell her that I'll try not to make her

wait up too late. And that . . . well, tell her I'm sorry to hear of her troubles."
He saw that the chauffeur was getting soaked, umbrella or no. "Why don't you
go back to the car and try to dry off a bit, now?"

He saw a look of determination on the man's face and wondered at it,
until he heard him say, "Mrs. Linworth asks if you have need of an umbrella."

"Is she offering yours to me?"

"Yes, sir."

"Ah, Lily . . ." He shook his head. "You may tell her, with my compliments,
thanks all the same, but I only use umbrellas when it's raining."

"But, sir, it *is* raining."

O'Connor smiled. "I'm Irish—I don't even see it falling. Go on. Tell her
thanks, but I've got my own with me."

"Thank you, sir." He hesitated, then added, "If I may say so, sir—she
meant well."

"Not a doubt of it."

A few minutes later he saw Norton motioning to him. He reached for the
slightly soggy copy of the *Express* again and held it over his hat as he hurried
toward the barricade.

Norton again shared his umbrella. "Mind your manners in there," he said.
"Not everyone loves the fourth estate as much as I do."

They walked quickly toward the sheltered entryway of the house.

"I saw the T-Bird," O'Connor said. "You don't usually drive it out to a job."

"The department sedan's in the shop. Should have it back tomorrow.
Listen . . . about Jack, I'm damned sorry, O'Connor. Might as well tell you,
they haven't been able to learn a thing about it. Jack have anything to say?"

"Not really. He seems—a little mixed up."

"Strange how that works. Some son of a bitch tries to crack your head
open, you feel confused for a time. Don't let it worry you, Conn. Memories
may come back to him after he's had a little time to recover." Dan closed the
umbrella, shook it, and leaned it up against a wall. He turned to an officer
who stood at the door and said, "Anyone tries to take that, shoot him."

The officer smiled. "Sure thing, Detective Norton—if you'll do the paper-
work on it."

Dan turned to O'Connor. "These days, they give 'em a wise-ass test before
they let them on the force."

O'Connor followed Dan inside. Two other detectives stood in the marble entryway. They nodded at Norton, then frowned at O'Connor, but said nothing as he passed them. O'Connor glanced around but could see no signs of violence.

"You've been here before?" Dan asked, looking back at him.

"Yes," O'Connor said. "I've only been inside once. A party, not long after Katy and Todd were married—a little more than a year ago."

"Katy. I like that better than Kathleen. She owned the house before she married Todd?"

"Far as I know, her mother—Lillian Linworth—still owns it." O'Connor looked around as he spoke. "Katy has lived here for about three years, so yes, she was living here before she married Todd."

"Would have thought they could have afforded a place of their own."

"Together they're in line to inherit something like three fortunes," O'Connor said, "but I don't know that they have any money they could truly call their own—either one of them. Jack has always said that no good could come of that."

"Parents foot all the bills?"

"The Linworths pay most of them."

Dan said, "Why the Linworths and not the Ducanes—the older Ducanes, I mean—Todd's parents?"

"Rumor has it the Ducanes haven't given a penny to either of their children."

"Well, why should they, right? Last I looked, nobody gave you or me a nickel we didn't earn."

Someone gave me a silver dollar once, O'Connor thought.

He recalled comments he had heard others make here and there about the coldness of the Ducanes toward their sons. More than just a matter of withholding money. Even the other swells thought the Ducanes were lousy parents. "You talked to Warren Ducane—Todd's brother?"

"Hasn't returned home yet this evening." He gave O'Connor a speculative look. "But you might know where to find him?"

"Sure, I've a few ideas. I'd like to know what happened to the child first, though."

"Wouldn't we all. But okay, fair is fair. Come upstairs with me," Norton said. "Most of the place appears to be untouched. A back door leading to the kitchen was damaged, that's all. Point of entry, it seems. Fingerprint men are working on all of that area, just in case these assholes got careless. I wouldn't lay any bets on that, though."

"More than one murderer, then?"

"Maybe not. Come and have a look. Don't touch the handrail."

O'Connor followed him up the long, curving marble staircase to the right. As they climbed the stairs, Dan said, "Let's start in the nursery."

The coroner had taken the body of the nursemaid from the house, but O'Connor still found it disturbing to view the room. He could easily imagine the room as it must have been moments before the woman was killed: a white bassinet—stripped of its bedding—with a mobile of stars and a moon hanging near it, colorful Mother Goose figures on the walls. A changing table, diapers folded below. A wooden playpen, soft blue blankets folded over one rail. Everything neat and tidy.

Just as it was now. Except for the blood. Sprayed everywhere, it seemed, in long streaks across the one wall and most of the floor. He could see long, heavy smears where the woman had obviously slipped and fallen in her own blood, bloody handprints on the floor near the bassinet, as if she had tried to crawl to it as she died. There was blood on the bassinet itself, but not much. A dark, wide pool of blood had spread and dried on the floorboards beneath it.

"What was her name?" O'Connor asked quietly.

"Rose Hannon. Thirty-four, widowed, lived in. Pleasant and easygoing, by all accounts. Loved the baby as if it were her own. No family anybody seems to know about." Dan paused, then added, "I think whoever killed her enjoyed watching her die."

O'Connor looked at him.

"Cut her throat, then watched her crawl."

"The baby was in the bassinet?"

"Mrs. Hannon was crawling toward it . . . so yes, I think so."

"The blood—"

"We don't know yet. The lab took the bedding to test it."

"So little Max might not be alive."

"That's a possibility. Especially when infants are taken."

They stood silently for a moment, then O'Connor said, "A living baby would be worth more in ransom than a dead one."

"I only hope they're as smart as you are."

"This happened last night?"

"We think it happened Saturday night, maybe early Sunday."

"Saturday night? While Katy was at her birthday party?"

"Coroner said he'll get back to me on a time of death, but as you know, those time-of-death guesses are never all that accurate. Except on *Perry Mason*. You watch that show?"

O'Connor shook his head. He was still trying to absorb the idea that an infant could have been missing for so long without anyone knowing of it.

"Well, I guess if you've got Corrigan to entertain you, who needs television, right?"

"Last night, and no ransom note yet? No calls?" He felt his hopes sinking.

"We don't know about the calls—no one here to answer them. Got the phone company checking on that. But no notes, no." He put a hand on O'Connor's shoulder. "Don't let that weigh too much with you yet—sometimes these guys want everyone to sweat, so that by the time you get their demands, you're desperate."

"Katy and Todd haven't been seen since the night of the party?"

"That's what we're beginning to believe. The maid—Katy's housemaid this is, not the victim—had the weekend off. She helped Katy get all set to go before the party, but she had to catch a bus, so when she left on Saturday, everyone was still here."

"Where was she all this time?"

"She took off to visit her mother in San Diego. We have that verified. Took the bus back home today, got to the house at about five, and noticed the back door had been jimmied. Came into the house, nothing seemed to be wrong at first. Eventually, she came up the stairs and saw the mess in here."

"She called you?"

"Naw. Went hysterical, the neighbors heard her, and *they* called us. She was out on the front lawn, with one of the neighbors trying to calm her down, when we got here. Took a while to get her to make any sense and even longer to get her to come back into the house with us." He paused and said, "Let's go down the hall."

"Wait—can you tell me, did they take the things they'd need to care for the baby? Blankets and such?"

"I asked the same thing. No—the maid didn't think so, except for one blanket. Probably the one they carried him out in."

O'Connor followed him down the long hallway, moving in the opposite direction of the baby's room, almost to the other end of the house. He couldn't help but think about the distance of the parents' room from the baby's room.

He had a different sort of shock when Norton showed him into the large master bedroom. In contrast to the nursery, the bedroom was pristine. Nothing out of place.

"Did the maid straighten up in here before she walked down the hall?"

"She swears she didn't."

"Did they never come home, then?" O'Connor asked.

Dan smiled. "Anyone ever tell you how Irish you sound when you're upset?"

"Dan . . ."

"No, it doesn't look as if they did. I brought the maid in here, and she says the room looks just the way she left it last night."

He walked over to a door at the other side of the room and beckoned O'Connor to follow. O'Connor did, and found himself in the biggest closet he had ever seen in his life. Two sides held women's clothing, a third, men's. The fourth was set with drawers—full of gloves, socks, shoes, and accessories, Dan said. There was another door on the other side of the closet.

"I live in a place smaller than this," O'Connor said.

"I'm glad to know the force still pays better than the paper. Anyway, I checked the laundry hamper there—nothing in it. I asked the maid, and she says no dress or shirt or any other item of clothing that the Ducanes wore on the night of the party is hanging up in here."

They continued across the closet to a connecting door. Dan opened it. "Now, here's why you shouldn't live in a big house if you want to be happily married. The wife can move out on you without moving out."

O'Connor could smell Katy's favorite perfume even before he saw that this room was more feminine than the other. It was clearly more lived-in than the other. A hi-fi stood in one corner, a television in another. The bed was an old-fashioned canopy bed, with ruffles and frills abounding. To one side of it was a nightstand with books piled high on it, and a second bassinet. O'Connor found himself relieved that little Max Ducane was sometimes allowed in here with his mother, might have even slept near her at night. On the other side of the big bed, he saw a dog's bed—almost as frilly as Katy's bed.

"Where's the dog?" O'Connor asked.

"Well, that's a good question. Presumably, with Mrs. Ducane."

"On a boat? I can't believe that." He thought for a moment. "Where's Katy's car?"

"Katy's little roadster is parked at her in-laws' place."

"And the Ducanes' car?"

"At the marina. Apparently Todd and Katy followed his parents to their place, then took off for the marina in the Ducanes' car. Unlike the Linworths, the Ducanes drive themselves."

"Which is a shame, or someone might have noticed their absence before Katy's maid came back from San Diego."

"True. The Ducanes have fewer servants than the Linworths, though. The cook-housekeeper isn't live-in, and she only comes in Monday through Friday."

"They keep to themselves and they hate to pay anyone a decent wage. Ask the people who work at Ducane Industries. If it hadn't been for the war . . ."

"Cheap, huh?"

"You wouldn't want to wait on their table. Cheap when it comes to labor, yes. But that doesn't mean they don't live well themselves. They'll buy anything that pleases them."

"Like a yacht."

"Exactly."

O'Connor looked around the room again. "Jack tells me Todd has a mistress."

Norton's brows went up. "Oh yeah? Well, I didn't think they had this arrangement of bedroom furniture because he snores. Got a name for the mistress?"

"No. But Jack might be able to tell you more."

"Knowing Handsome Jack, he was there before Todd."

"Not so handsome now. He may need a new nickname."

Norton shook his head. "He'll charm them, no matter what condition that mug of his is in when the bandages come off."

"Maybe so. So nothing else taken from the house? Just little Max?"

"Besides a woman's life? No, nothing, as far as we can tell. Oh—I should probably mention, on the night of the party, Katy's mother gave her some diamonds, a necklace, I guess, a family heirloom of the Vanderveers. No sign of that, either."

"Where would she have put them?"

"What do you mean?"

"Is there a safe in the house? I just can't picture her mother giving her diamonds without being sure that she had a secure place to keep them."

"You know why I like you, Conn? You think of questions most of my fellow detectives don't think of. Fortunately, I thought of that one. There's one in the closet."

"Behind some of the clothes?"

"Right. We got the combination to it from Lillian Linworth herself. She says only she and her daughter knew the combination. Said that Katy had it changed just this week. He smiled. "Mrs. Linworth is something else. Warned me she'd be changing it again."

"So why are you looking in a safe at a private residence? When Katy comes back . . ."

"Her mother can tell her she was curious to see if the diamonds were put away before Katy got aboard the yacht. When Mrs. Linworth opened the safe and the diamonds weren't in there, she said she was sure her daughter did not return to the house after leaving the party—that Katy would have put the diamonds away as soon as she came home."

"And did she discover anything else in it?"

"Papers. A deed to the only property Katy owned—a place up in Arrowhead that Lillian gave her when she turned eighteen."

"Ah, yes. That's where Katy was born. So even if she didn't own this place, she had that one."

"There was also a will. Made out on Friday afternoon."

"A will? On Friday, you say? She spent the day before her twenty-first birthday getting a will made?"

"Interesting, isn't it? Not many people who are that young think to make wills. And guess who she leaves all her worldly possessions to?"

"Her son—Maxwell."

"Surprisingly, no. To one Jack Corrigan."

"Jack?"

"So he never said anything to you about this?"

"No. Not a word. I don't think he knows about it, if that's what you're wondering."

"So why would she leave everything to him? By the way, that's including, should the need arise, guardianship of her son."

"I haven't the slightest idea. Only that he's been something like an uncle to her over the years. She calls him 'Uncle Jack,' in fact. She's fond of him."

"Nothing romantic?"

"Good God, no."

"Hey, I gotta ask, right?"

"What did Lillian say?"

"Exactly what you did—he's Uncle Jack. Seemed shaken up by it, though. I'm actually sorry we allowed Mrs. Linworth to open the safe, because now her daughter's likely to be a little unhappy with me for letting her snoop through her papers."

"Nothing less than you deserve," O'Connor said absently.

"What's on your mind?"

"Just worrying about the child, and Katy and the others. Wondering what I'll tell Jack. And—Dan, why wouldn't they have come back to shore as soon as the weather looked a little rough?"

"I can think of all sorts of reasons. Boats can't always make it to shore right away for one reason or another. Fog early this morning, remember? They set out at midnight, fog started rolling in around two or so. Then this storm got here faster than the weatherman said it would. Maybe they were closer to the harbor at Avalon than the one here. Mrs. Linworth assures me the Ducanes are excellent sailors, but who can really say how well they know how to handle a new boat or navigate?"

O'Connor said nothing.

"Yeah," Dan said, "worries me, too. Hell of a night. Why don't you take me to see Warren Ducane?"

11

D AN NORTON GAVE SOME HURRIED INSTRUCTIONS TO MATT ARDEN AS they passed the barricade. O'Connor waited at the Nash. Much to Norton's disgust, O'Connor had insisted they take his car.

He watched his mirror, until Norton said, "I'm not having you tailed, if that's what you're wondering."

"Good. I'll get us there a little faster, then."

"Why are you being so mysterious?" Norton groused.

"You'll be happy about that later."

"Don't tell me we're going to some dame's place, because I've been waking women up all night on account of this guy. The six ex-girlfriends all lost sleep when I came around looking for him."

"Are you trying to convince me that you minded that? Warren's only twenty, and I don't think he's dated an ugly girl yet."

Norton laughed. "They were lookers."

"To be fair, he's better-looking than five or six of you or me."

"You wouldn't look half bad if you didn't have a habit of finishing every barroom brawl Corrigan starts."

"I wish I could have ended the fight he was just in."

Norton sighed. "Me too."

O'Connor drove up into the hills. When he turned onto a winding private road, Norton said, "Jesus Christ. He's up at Auburn's Stand?"

"Last I saw him. And he seemed to be there for the weekend."

"Last you saw him?"

"I was invited to join the fun this weekend. One of our mutual friends is moving to Paris. Auburn gave him a send-off."

"Oh, ho! Moving up in the world, are you?"

O'Connor shrugged. "Doubt that accounts for it."

"Auburn Sheffield," Dan mused. "Told his old man to go to hell, and built a bigger fortune than any of the rest of the Sheffield clan."

"Yes. That's how the place got its name. Auburn took a stand."

"Quite a bit older than you or Warren, isn't he?"

"Yes, but Auburn's friends are a real mix. Some older, some younger, some straight-laced, some rebels. I admire him for that."

"You consider him a friend?"

O'Connor nodded. "A good man, Auburn."

"Any reason we shouldn't have come here in my car?"

"As I say, he's a friend who invited me to share in his hospitality. I won't return that kindness by bringing five squad cars—"

"Me? In a squad car? Are you—"

"—led by a flashy T-Bird up the road to his home."

Dan eyed him narrowly, then suddenly grinned. "But you didn't call him from Katy Ducane's house, either, or give him a warning."

"You're my friend, too. I wasn't going to give Warren a chance to slip away. Besides, it might prove to be a little embarrassing for all concerned."

"What the hell is going on up here, anyway?"

"Just a house party, but one or two of the married men have been friendly with women who don't look much like their wives."

"Conn—it's a homicide investigation. You think I give a damn about some guy putting his noodle into someone else's soup? You've got to be—"

"One of the married guys is the chief of police."

"Shit," Dan said. "Stop the car."

O'Connor obeyed, then said, "Maybe you'd like to hear my plan."

"Shit," Dan said again, holding his head in his hands.

"It'll be my Nash at the gate, not your T-Bird. You stay in the car, I'll see if Warren is still here, and if so, I'll try to get him to leave with me. That way, if I'm wrong about where he is, you haven't ruffled any feathers."

Norton agreed to it, then said, "Thanks."

The guard at the gate of Auburn's Stand stayed in his shelter, opening the gate with the press of a button, and waving O'Connor in without looking closely at his passenger, or objecting to guests arriving at one in the morning.

"Party's still going on," O'Connor said. "Although it looks as if it has thinned out a bit."

"Thinned out?" Norton asked in disbelief, seeing the wide, sweeping concrete drive crowded with cars.

"Oh sure," O'Connor said, nudging the Nash into a narrow space in a gravel overflow parking area. "If we had come here last night, we would have parked outside the gate."

"When did you leave last night?"

"Not long after midnight, which was a lucky thing, I suppose. I was home and sober by the time the hospital called me this morning."

"Warren was still here at midnight?"

"Yes. Tried to talk me into staying." He glanced up at the house. The mansion's lights were on, although the windows of some of the upper rooms were dark.

"Wait here," O'Connor said. "I'll bring him out to you."

"No argument from me," Norton said, recognizing the chief's Cadillac two cars away. "But I want to be the one to break it to him, Conn. I have to be able to see his reaction. You understand that, don't you?"

"Sure."

O'Connor borrowed Norton's umbrella and walked uphill toward the house. When the wind threatened to turn the umbrella inside out, he closed it. He was soaked by the time he reached the front door.

Auburn's butler welcomed him. Conscious of the muck on his shoes, at first O'Connor declined to come in, but seeing the man would stand there letting the heat out of the place until he crossed the threshold, he stepped just inside the door. He asked for Auburn. "I need to speak with him privately, please."

The butler nodded.

Conn could hear men's and women's voices, soft music and laughter, coming from another room. The click and clatter of billiard balls on a pool table.

Within a few moments, Auburn appeared. He was in his late forties, neatly dressed in a sweater and slacks, and, O'Connor was relieved to see, wide awake and sober.

"Conn? Glad you could rejoin us!"

"I'm afraid I'm here on an errand you might not like, Auburn. Is Warren Ducane here?"

"Yes, in fact we're playing billiards. Is anything wrong?"

"Forgive me, Auburn, but I think it would be best if I talked to Warren himself. Could you ask him to speak with me for a moment—without making anyone else curious about it?"

Auburn looked concerned, but said, "Certainly."

As he began to walk away, O'Connor asked, "Has Warren been here all weekend?"

Auburn turned to him in surprise, but said, "Yes."

"You're certain?"

"Absolutely. Conn, is he in trouble?"

"Not if he's been here the whole time."

"He has, since Friday afternoon. I sent my car to pick him up from his home, and he has remained the entire weekend. I give you my word. And if my word won't do, I'm sure the chief's will."

"Yours will do better than the chief's."

Auburn laughed.

"Don't let Warren know I asked, Auburn."

His brows drew together.

"I'm not trying to make trouble," O'Connor said. "Not for you, and not for Warren."

After a moment he said, "All right, Conn, I won't tell him you asked."

He came back a few minutes later, Warren in tow. Warren looked wary, but curious.

"Conn? What is it?"

"Warren, I'm sorry to bother you, but I need to ask you to come with me for a moment. I've got someone with me who needs to talk to you."

When he hesitated, Conn said, "It will be all right."

Auburn had apparently asked his butler to bring Warren's coat to him, because he came to the foyer carrying it, and assisted Warren in putting it on.

"I—should I get my other things?"

"If necessary, you can come back for them," Auburn said. "Or I can have them brought to you."

They were both rain-drenched by the time they got to O'Connor's car. O'Connor looked back and saw Auburn watching them from the front porch.

Norton got out of the Nash and introduced himself, showing his badge.

"What's this about, Detective?"

"Let's get inside the car, all right? Can't talk out here in the rain." He held the back door open. Warren climbed in. Norton came around and got into the backseat, on the other side, behind Conn. Conn started up the motor and turned on the heater.

"Is your car near here, Mr. Ducane?" Norton asked.

Ducane shook his head. "No. It's in the shop. Auburn sent a car for me on Friday."

"You've been here since then?"

"Yes. What's this about?"

"If you don't mind," Norton said, "I'd rather we spoke at your home. Would that be all right?"

"Sure, but . . . am I in some kind of trouble?"

"No, Mr. Ducane. Not as far as I know."

O'Connor got directions from Warren to his place. He glanced at Warren in the rearview mirror. Ducane looked boyish and scared. His straight, dark hair was sticking up in tufts—a result of his running his hands through it. His blue eyes had dark smudges beneath them—perhaps the result of two nights of partying at Auburn's Stand—and his handsome face was drained of color.

Conn wished Norton would just tell him what was going on. It seemed cruel to make him wait. But this was Norton's case, and he wasn't going to interfere.

They didn't travel far to reach Warren's home—at least not in miles. In situation, the residences were entirely different. Warren Ducane lived in the back house of a "two on one" lot—his was a small house built at the back of a large lot, behind a bigger home, accessed from an alley rather than the street. One of many such places slapped together during the wartime housing shortage.

A uniformed officer stepped out of a patrol car parked in the alley.

"It's all right, Officer Arden," Norton said. In a low voice, he asked Warren if the young man could step inside with them. "I imagine Matt might appreciate a chance to use the bathroom. He's been waiting for you to come back home, and it has been a long shift for the poor guy."

O'Connor knew this wasn't exactly true, but did nothing to give Norton's game away.

Warren was agreeable. They crowded into the small living room of the house, and could see from there that they were in one of four rooms: the house had a kitchen, a bathroom, a bedroom, and a living room. Doors were open to all of them. The bedroom had men's clothing strewn about, and the bed was unmade. Warren quickly pulled the door to it shut. The other rooms were relatively tidy. Warren allowed Arden use of the bathroom, then went to a narrow linen cupboard and brought out three clean, dry towels.

Arden started to go back out, but apparently reading some signal from Norton, stayed inside, near the door.

Warren turned on a small gas heater, then invited O'Connor and Norton into the kitchen, saying it was the largest room in the house. He started the coffee percolator as O'Connor and Norton took seats at the kitchen table. O'Connor heard the cups rattle in their saucers as Warren set them on the counter.

Warren watched the coffeepot for a moment, then sat down with a kind of resignation, as if unable to come up with another way to delay hearing what was about to be said.

"The coffee will take a few minutes. What's this all about?"

"I'm afraid it's about your family, Mr. Ducane."

"My family? My parents? Has something happened to my parents?"

"Your brother and his wife joined your parents on their boat late Saturday night. They haven't returned."

Ducane face went from chalk white to a gray color. "Not . . . not all of them? Not all of them together?"

"Yes . . . Are you all right? Maybe you should put your head down between your knees for a moment."

Warren obeyed, and a little of his color returned to him. But when he sat up again, he still seemed dazed.

The coffee began to percolate, the coffeepot making intermittent burbling sounds.

Ducane sat staring and then asked, "Todd and Kathleen, too?"

It was always like this, O'Connor thought. People in shock thought if they asked the question in a different way, the answer would be different. As if enough questions would bring about an answer they liked, or one that made sense to them.

"Yes," Norton said, perfectly patient. "Your parents and Todd and Kathleen."

Warren trembled. "No . . . there must be some mistake. Yesterday was Kathleen's birthday. There was a party. My parents were going to take their new boat out after the party. On their own. Not with Todd and Kathleen. Todd and Kathleen must be somewhere else."

"Your parents invited them to go with them. Many people at the party have said they were told this, including Kathleen's parents."

For a moment, there was only the arrhythmic hiss and boil of the coffee-pot.

"No," Warren said again. "They didn't take Todd. Not Todd."

Norton said nothing.

Warren's face crumpled, and he made a horrible, wounded sound, one

O'Connor had heard a thousand times and never wanted to hear again. Norton, who had probably heard it a hundred thousand times, put a hand on Warren Ducane's shoulder. Warren covered his face and sobbed in earnest.

The coffee percolator stopped, its red indicator light on, and O'Connor stood and poured the coffee. He placed cups before each of the other men and offered one to Arden, who politely declined. For a time, O'Connor was the only one who drank any of it.

Warren stood up, hastily excused himself, then moved back to the bathroom. They heard him retching, the flush of the toilet, then the sound of water running in the sink. After a while, he came back out.

"Sorry," he said shakily.

He reached for his coffee and drank a little, then pushed it away.

"Are you sure the boat is lost? I mean, couldn't there be a chance they're all right?"

"Yes, of course," Norton said. "We haven't given up hope by any means. The Coast Guard is watching for it. The *Sea Dreamer* could just be blown off course. We've tried raising her on the radio, but so far, no luck. But then, it could just be that there's some problem with the radio on board."

Warren nodded, then fell silent. He looked at O'Connor. "Why are you here, Conn?" he asked, as if it had suddenly dawned on him that Conn was not a policeman.

"Jack Corrigan asked me to stop by Todd and Katy's place tonight."

"Oh." He still seemed confused. "Will he be coming here, too?"

"No. Jack's not feeling well, I'm afraid."

"I'm sorry to hear that," he said. "Tell him I said hello." O'Connor couldn't hear any insincerity in that, just distraction. Warren suddenly hit upon another explanation for Conn's presence. "Are you here to get a description of the boat for the paper? I think I have a snapshot of it. Maybe that will help."

"I'm afraid, Warren, that I'm here—"

"Oh, you just said—because of Kathleen! Jack and Kathleen are friends. Kathleen . . ." Tears welled up in his eyes again. "And the baby? What's going to become of that little boy?"

"Mr. Ducane," Norton said, drawing his attention. "Mr. O'Connor assisted me in finding you. I'm afraid there's more I must tell you."

Warren looked at him wide-eyed, anxious.

"Your nephew Max—Todd's son?"

"The baby! Oh my God! They weren't crazy enough to take an infant on that—"

"No, sir."

"I'll take care of him. I will, somehow. My God, I just can't believe that Todd—"

"Mr. Ducane, I'm sorry. There's no easy way to tell you this, but tonight we've learned that the baby has probably been kidnapped."

"Kidnapped?" he asked. Blank-faced again. Disbelieving.

"The child's nursemaid was murdered."

Warren seemed to sway, and for a moment O'Connor thought he was going to pass out. But he steadied himself and said, "I'm sorry. I'm sorry, I just can't seem to understand. I just—Todd's baby is missing?"

Norton went over it with him at least a half a dozen times. Finally, Warren got past the stage of simply repeating whatever was said to him. Norton kept pouring coffee for him.

"Tell me about your brother," Norton said.

Warren seemed on the verge of tears again. Norton waited while he struggled to regain his composure.

"He's a good man," Warren said in a hoarse voice. "A great brother." Deep breath. "The best. I—I can't think why he would have gone with my parents. It's crazy. They're crazy."

"Your parents?"

He nodded. "But not Todd. Todd's smart. God! I hope it's all some mistake."

But he didn't look as if he believed it could be, O'Connor thought. He looked as if he didn't have any real hope.

"Your brother mention any problems lately?"

Warren seemed surprised at the question. "No, not really."

"I mean," Norton said, "most young couples have problems . . ."

"Oh."

O'Connor could see him hesitate, trying to figure out what he should or should not say.

He sighed heavily. "I think they have a few. Adjusting to life with a new baby in the house, things like that. But nothing they couldn't work out, I'm sure."

"What about outside of his home life?"

"Todd didn't mention anything to me. My God, he's . . . he's . . . he's on a missing boat, and his child has been taken . . . how could any of that be his fault?"

"I'm not saying it is. Not at all. I just wondered who might want to put pressure on him."

"I don't understand."

"Mr. Ducane, I suspect there will be a call or a letter or something of that nature sent to your brother's home, asking for ransom. And I can only believe that this is going to come from someone who doesn't realize that your brother himself is missing."

"I see. Yes. All right. But who could it be?"

"Any enemies?"

"None that I know of."

"Did he mention any strangers coming around, or persons who might have taken an unusual interest in the child?"

Warren shook his head.

"Any work done on the house recently?"

"No . . . at least . . . well, I don't really know. Lillian—Kathleen's mother would have arranged for anything like that." He suddenly sat up straighter. "Lillian! Have you told her . . . ?"

"Yes."

"Poor Lillian. Kathleen's her only child. My God. My God. What has happened?"

Norton continued to question him, about Todd, Todd's friends, Katy, Katy's friends. How the household staff had been hired. In the end, O'Connor wasn't convinced that Norton had learned much, mostly because Warren Ducane didn't seem to know much about his brother's life since marriage.

When O'Connor dropped Norton off at his car, he reminded him that if they had taken the T-Bird, the seats would have been as damp as the ones in the Nash were, since they still hadn't dried out from having three rain-soaked men in the car a few hours earlier.

"Not to mention all the mud on the floorboards," he added.

"I'll keep that in mind. Now you owe me about five thousand favors to one, but who's counting?"

"What about finding Warren Ducane?"

"Four thousand nine-hundred and ninety-nine. But we'll be keeping an eye on him from now on, so don't expect future credit."

"You suspect him of the kidnapping?"

"No, not really. I don't think he faked that reaction. He was genuinely shocked. But . . . I don't know. Something's off with that guy. I've got to try to get in touch with the family lawyer, though, because unless his folks have cut him out completely, it seems to me that instead of being split two or three ways, the Ducanes' fortune will now go to one man." He was quiet for a moment, then added, "You sure he was at Auburn's all weekend?"

"I'll ask again—and try to get more details. But Auburn said he had been there since Friday, and he backs up Warren's story about not having a car up there. Auburn's never been one to lie."

"Well, we'll see. What are your impressions of young Warren?"

"He loves his big brother, is perhaps even fond of Katy, and doesn't give a damn about his parents. Little Max was hardly a person to him, and the nursemaid, Rose Hannon, could have been murdered weeks ago for all he ever noticed of her."

"Hmm. You ask me, the parents didn't seem to give a damn about him, either. And young men usually don't get attached to their nephews until the nephews can talk or throw a ball. I'll bet most maids are invisible to everyone but their employers."

"Oh no. They're often invisible to the employers, too. My mother used to work as a maid before the war came along."

"Don't think we feel the same way about Rose Hannon as Ducane does— some of the other detectives you saw tonight will be making sure we pay attention to Rose's life and not just her death."

12

Warren Ducane was shaking. They were gone—all except the big cop outside.

Why was that cop here? Warren didn't understand any of it.

He was miserable, thinking about Todd. Katy, too, really. He knew Todd thought she was cold, and he felt a little disloyal to Todd for disagreeing with him about that. The fact was, Warren didn't want anything bad to happen to Katy. She had always been nice to him, so he couldn't dislike her the way Todd did.

What had happened?

He thought and thought about this. His parents had never said anything about taking Todd and Katy with them. How like them to be selfish enough to cause the whole family to die because of one of their whims. Warren saw these television shows, with the wise parents who were kind to their children, with the funny little misunderstandings that everyone laughed over at the dinner table, and thought that one day someone ought to tell the truth, write about families like the one he was born into. Selfish fools for parents.

But nothing would be funny about that—he knew that from personal experience.

He felt sick about Todd. Just sick.

And the baby . . . that made no sense at all. Wouldn't kidnappers make sure someone had money before taking his baby? Todd and Katy were almost broke.

What the hell had happened?

A woman murdered at Todd's house. The baby kidnapped, and Todd maybe out in the ocean somewhere. Katy, too.

It was all wrong. Wrong, wrong, wrong. Never should have happened.

He had spent a week wondering if, when the time came, he'd be able to act shocked when he got the news of his parents' deaths.

He hadn't needed to act shocked at all. The shock was genuine.

Todd. Katy. The baby.

What had he done? What had he done? God, help him—

No, no use asking for God's help. Too late for that, if you made deals with the devil.

His fault. All his fault.

He heard himself make a keening sound, and clapped his hand over his mouth.

He wept for a time, wept until he was exhausted. But still, sleep would not come.

What had gone wrong? It should have all been perfect. Dozens of leading citizens could swear he was at Auburn's house all weekend. He had been playing poker with the goddamned chief of police when his parents were supposed to be out on the yacht—how much more perfect could it be?

Not Todd. Not Katy. Not the baby. Just his parents.

He didn't understand any of it, and he no longer trusted the one person who could explain it to him.

Who could help him?

He thought about Auburn. Auburn's kindness to him.

He had used Auburn to some degree. He was not proud of that.

And now, far too late, he realized that he had been used himself. The thought made him furious—and in the next moment, utterly alone and helpless.

They'd left a cop here to guard him, they said. To make sure he was safe.

To imprison him, they meant. To keep an eye on him.

What did the cops suspect?

He looked at the phone. He thought about making a call. Decided not to. Cops were probably listening in. Or they'd get the phone company to tell them whom he had called.

Probably wouldn't get through, anyway. He would have to wait a couple of days, until the devil he had dealt with came back to town.

Then he would make a call. Just to ask, just to learn if it had just been a mistake. If there was still a cop outside on Monday night, he'd say that he needed to walk down to the drugstore for some cigarettes, find a pay phone, and make a call.

And be followed and then . . . no. That wouldn't work.

Besides, he already knew the answer to his questions, didn't he?

He could recall every word of the conversation. The conversation with the devil.

Mitch Yeager.

The offer to loan him money, which—thank God!—he had refused.

The flattery, which of course he fell for—stupid ass!

Then the questions, designed to make him talk more and more about all the things that made him most angry about his parents. Fueled his outrage over long-held grievances that were real enough. Agreed with him that his parents were a pair of selfish drunks. Yeager confiding that his own parents were drunken losers, that he and his brother had saved the family fortunes. Assuring Warren that—just as Warren suspected—Barrett Ducane was ruining the family companies.

"I think you'd do a better job of running them."

"Not me. But Todd could."

"You and Todd together. I could advise you."

"Why would you?"

"I want to invest in your companies." (Your companies! Already making it sound as if he owned them.) *"I see the potential. But not if your father is running them."*

And then later, asking about the new boat, the *Sea Dreamer*—a sore subject for Warren, knowing that Katy and Todd were fighting over money and he himself barely scraping by—and eventually a few questions about where it was docked and when his parents would next be going out on it.

And finally those damning words, the words that made him understand things he wished he didn't have to think of now. The story that Yeager would be going away with his wife and the child they had adopted two months ago, spending some time out of town on a quiet little family vacation, but not too hidden away—some place where people would see them, and note they were there. His reassurance that he would be in touch sometime soon. And the hint—more than a hint, really—that Warren ought to think about being away from home over the weekend, should be somewhere that people could vouch for him.

He had known then, hadn't he?

Of course he did.

He did not have the slightest doubt that if he told the police Mitch Yeager had asked him these things, Mitch Yeager would deny everything. Yeager might even make it sound as if Warren planned it all. And since Warren was supposed to be the one who gained everything, he was the big suspect.

That was why there was a cop outside his door right now.

*   *   *

But what about Max? Why did the kidnapping have to happen now? He wondered if Yeager had done that as well, but it didn't make sense. He couldn't see that Yeager would gain anything by that. People lost at sea in a boating accident, something that couldn't be proved, wouldn't change how people thought of him—that was the sort of thing he would do.

God knows who all was at that party. Maybe someone there learned that Katy and Todd were going on the boat and decided it would be the perfect time to steal Max.

There would be a call. A demand. He just had to be patient.

He was so tired. Maybe he could fall asleep. Fall asleep and wake up, and this would all be over. Todd would be okay, and the police would apologize for their mistake.

If only he could talk to Todd. That thought started him crying again.

13

IT WAS PAST THREE O'CLOCK IN THE MORNING NOW. O'CONNOR WONDERED if Lillian would still be awake and decided there was little possibility she would sleep until she knew Katy's fate. When he drove up to the Linworth mansion, he wasn't surprised to see lights on downstairs.

The rain was letting up. Maybe the Coast Guard would have better luck searching for the *Sea Dreamer*.

He scraped as much mud off his shoes as he could and made his way to the door. Hastings, Lillian's elderly butler, let him in, took his coat, and pretended not to notice how disheveled O'Connor looked. He escorted O'Connor to a library, where a fire burned brightly in a stone fireplace with a bench hearth.

O'Connor took a seat on it, hoping the fire would take some of the chill off and begin to dry his damp clothes.

Not long after Hastings left, Lillian Vanderveer Linworth entered the room. She was looking tired and grief-stricken, he thought, and wondered what possible comfort he could be to her.

Even with the strain of this day showing on her face, though, she was exquisite. He remembered thinking she was beautiful twenty or so years ago, but realized he had been mistaken. She had been pretty and petulant then, and was beautiful and in command of herself now—assured and elegant in a way she never could have been at twenty or even thirty. Tonight her skin was paler than usual, the area around her eyes a little swollen. He knew better than to expect to see tears from her—those would be saved for moments alone.

He rose to greet her, but she motioned him to be seated, saying, "I'd offer you a change of clothes, but you're larger than Harold, or any other man in this house."

"Brobdingnagian, that's me," he said, still waiting for her to be seated first.

She halted, mid-stride, halfway across the room, smiled a little to herself, then came forward, sitting down in the leather chair closest to him. *"Gulliver's Travels."*

"Yes. How are you, Lily?"

"More than any other of my friends and acquaintances," she said, "you must have an idea of how I am, Conn."

"It's never the same for anyone, is it? Maureen was my sister. I don't like to think how I'd feel about losing a child, or a child's child."

"And yet you've never seen your own boy, have you?"

"Not in person, no. I think it would only confuse him to have another 'daddy' in the picture at his age. But I know that Kenny is loved and well cared for—spoiled, if anything."

O'Connor also knew that Lillian's attitude toward him had changed when she learned of his child. He knew that she had long been involved in charitable projects for caring for unwed mothers and their children. Shortly after Jack had complained to her about O'Connor's "foolish marriage," she had contacted O'Connor to say that if he or Vera needed her help, she would gladly give it. O'Connor never took her up on it, but Lillian seemed to look at him differently from then on. Helen Swan had told him that he ought to stop thinking of Lillian as the brat she was at nineteen, that life had knocked her around a little since then, and he had realized that was true. He thought perhaps Helen had influenced Lillian's attitude toward him as well. Over the last seven years, O'Connor and Lillian had become close friends, even as she continued to become less and less friendly with Jack.

She asked about Jack now, though, and he knew he couldn't keep putting her off.

"Too early to say much with any certainty," he told her.

He turned at the sound of the library door opening. The butler entered with a bottle of expensive single malt scotch and two glasses.

"Thank you, Hastings," she said, and the butler nodded and left.

"Past Hastings's bedtime, isn't it?" O'Connor asked.

She poured the scotch and handed one to him. "Do you honestly believe he would retire for the evening if I asked him to? If I'm awake, Hastings is awake."

"Is that a blessing or a curse?"

"Mostly a blessing, although I never felt that to be the case when I was younger. But having a truly loyal person in your life is nothing to take for granted, so I'm more appreciative of him now."

"Just one?"

"There are others. If you are wondering if I doubt Jack's loyalty, stop wondering." She laughed softly. "Perhaps not faithful, but loyal."

"And you to him, in your way."

"Yes, always in *my* way, isn't it? Except now. Are you going to tell me the truth about what's happened to him?"

He sipped the scotch, felt its smoothness on his tongue.

"Harold doesn't mind you staying up all hours, drinking scotch with reporters?"

"Harold is supposedly in Dallas tonight, getting a good night's sleep before meetings. He took his private plane to Las Vegas early Sunday, to meet 'an associate'—or so he told me, which shows you just how dumb Harold thinks I am. At some point, someone may be able to discover which Nevada whorehouse he's in, and tell him his daughter is missing and his grandson has been kidnapped. It will be interesting to see how long it takes him to come home. He will come home for appearance's sake, of course. That will only make this all the more unbearable."

He said nothing. She sighed and said, "And you still haven't told me about Jack. The truth, Conn."

Talking to her about Jack was a tricky business even when things were going well. He had never believed that Lillian was really in love with Jack all those years ago, but he had faith in the adage about women scorned, and he had no doubt that Jack had hurt her pride. Jack thought this was nonsense, and told him so.

Helen Swan complicated the picture, because Lillian and Helen were the closest of friends, and no one who liked Helen could avoid Jack, so Lillian had never managed to sever all ties to him. And Katy's devotion to Jack was, Conn suspected, something Lillian envied.

And yet now, unmistakably, Lillian was worried about Jack. He wondered if he was too tired to have this conversation with her and remain aware of the pitfalls. He decided to risk it.

"I wish I knew the truth about what happened to Jack on Saturday night. He's beat all to hell. You know how many fights the two of us have come out of together, but this—no matter what you or Old Man Wrigley may think, this was not the result of a brief brawl at a party. Someone tried to kill him, Lily."

"What?" She set her scotch down with a thump. "What are you saying?"

"Just that. Someone literally tried to murder him. And there's still a good possibility that their attempt will succeed, because he's not a sure bet to survive this by any means. They beat him so badly he may lose an eye, left him in the marsh, and . . ." He took a deep breath, slowed himself down. "He was unconscious for a long time." Think of the good things, he told himself, the signs that he's not lost. "But this evening, he woke up a couple of times. He spoke. He's still got his temper and his sense of humor, so I'm hoping that means . . ."

". . . that he'll recover without permanent brain damage." Lillian finished the sentence for him. She averted her eyes from his, looked into the fire. "Does he know who did this to him?"

O'Connor shook his head. "No, and I'm hoping you might help me find out."

"Me?" She looked back at him, surprised.

"Did you see Jack leave—the people who took him?"

"I'm afraid I was a little distracted at that moment. It was just as Katy and Todd were getting ready to leave with Thelma and Barrett. I tried one last time to talk Katy into staying. Useless. I blame Thelma. Thelma, damn her, enjoys spiting me, so she was going to make sure my party for Katy ended early. Thelma put pressure on Todd, Todd put pressure on Katy." She looked away for a moment, then said, "I only caught a glimpse of Jack being carried out. I didn't realize there had been a fight. Frankly, I thought he was drunk."

"Who invited the men who carried him off?"

"I don't know. I didn't invite them. Harold claims they weren't invited at all. However, Hastings tells me otherwise."

"Oh?"

"Hastings said he wanted to shut the door in their faces, but that the big blond man had an invitation card, probably one of the ones we gave the Ducanes. Thelma insisted on having three dozen or so to extend to their friends."

"Did Hastings recall his name?"

She hesitated, looking toward the library door, then said softly, "I worry that he may be getting a little deaf. It's such a ridiculous name, he can't have heard it correctly: Bob Gherkin. Like the pickle."

O'Connor rubbed his chin.

"Do you know that name?" Lillian asked.

"No. But it makes sense that I wouldn't."

"What do you mean?"

"I haven't had time to really do any digging, but the way I figure it, what happened to Jack probably came about because one of the stories he's written in the last few months has angered someone. Jack works the crime beat, and he makes plenty of enemies. At the same time, because he works that beat, he's aware of almost every small-time hood in Las Piernas—sooner or later, most of them have been in a jail or a courtroom, if not both. Those are people I'd probably know, too, given the number of stories we work on together. But the networks these fellows establish can reach beyond the city limits, so if someone wanted to set Jack up, they'd use people he's never seen before—otherwise he'd know who to connect them to, or smell a setup from the start."

"But how could it be a setup? *Jack* wasn't invited."

"Yes, he was."

"By whom?"

"Katy."

Lily fell silent.

"Was something troubling her?" O'Connor asked.

"Many things," Lily said. "She told me she wanted to divorce Todd." In a bitter voice, she added, "Jack's advice. I told her to try to work it out, for the baby's sake. If she had divorced Todd, they never would have gone sailing . . ."

"Lily . . . you can't blame yourself."

"You're wrong, Conn," she said. "Indeed I can. Not just for this, either."

"What are you talking about?"

She picked up her scotch and began sipping it. He thought she might not answer him, but then she said, "How much do you know about Jack's car accident? The one in 'thirty-six."

"I was just a kid. I didn't know much."

She laughed at that. "Right. You were the smartest little kid I had ever been around. You scared me. But I scared easily in those days, too easily."

"You never acted scared."

"Maybe a young boy couldn't see that kind of scared for what it was. Jack could. But that's not the point."

"You were in the car, I know that much. I don't think he would have told me you were, but I was such a shadow to him in those days, I suspected he was going to get together with you. So I came out here and waited over in your neighbor's yard and saw you leave the house and get in the car with him."

She smiled. "You were born to this business, weren't you?"

"That or a job in espionage. Jack didn't like my spying, but he also knew I wouldn't talk about his personal life to anyone else. He told me I was never to mention that you were with him that night. He felt terrible, and knows you've never really forgiven him for getting in that wreck—that much I know."

"Forgiven him? Conn . . . I caused the accident."

He frowned.

"Not the way Jack tells the story?" she asked.

"No. He said he had been drinking."

"A safe claim to make, I suppose. No, it was my fault. I threw a temper tantrum, grabbed the wheel, and we crashed into a tree. Jack couldn't walk, was bleeding and in pain, but did I stay to help him? No."

"He said you were hurt, too."

"Treated at home. Discreetly." She stared into the fire for a long moment, then said, "No injuries I couldn't survive, obviously. I was young and stupid and so afraid that the report would leak out that the relatively new Mrs. Harold Linworth—whose husband had just gone to Europe, preparing to make more money out of the war—was involved in an automobile accident. The driver a single man, former lover—I think you see what I mean. I got out of the car and left him there. Went to a pay phone and called Hastings. He, at least, had the good sense to report the accident, so that Jack got help before he bled to death."

"Jack has never held anything about that night against you, you know."

"Of course I do. That's part of what makes it so unbearable. His damned forgiveness."

She went back to staring at the fire.

After a moment, O'Connor said, " 'If you forgive people enough, you belong to them, and they to you, whether each person likes it or not . . .' "

She looked back at him and smiled softly. "Another of your quotations? Whose is it?"

"James Hilton."

"*Good-bye, Mr. Chips?*"

He shook his head. "*Time and Time Again.*"

"Ah. I've not read that one yet. Let me guess—Jack told you to memorize passages of books that struck your fancy, to have these quotations handy for stories."

"Maureen. To have them handy for life, I suppose."

"Maureen. Your sister. I wish I had met her."

He didn't say anything. Maureen had been gone from his life for over ten years now, and still he missed her. Missing, he thought, meant exactly that—gone like a piece of you, carved right out of you, missing from you.

"I hope they find both of them," he said suddenly. "All of them, I mean, but for your sake, I hope they find Katy and Max."

"I so want to believe they will . . ." she said in a hoarse voice, then waited until she had control of herself again. "I so want to believe it, I can't let myself think that they won't find them."

"Norton, the detective who's in charge of the kidnapping case?"

She nodded. He could see the strain showing again, her struggle to keep back tears.

"The best there is. Trust him."

She nodded again, then suddenly stood up and moved toward one of the windows.

O'Connor stood, too, watching her roughly pull back the heavy draperies, clutching the velvet material in one hand.

"Damn this rain," she said.

14

DAWN WAS A LITTLE MORE THAN AN HOUR AWAY WHEN LORENZO Albettini, the captain of the fishing vessel *Nomadic Maiden*, told his crew of four to haul in the nets. His younger brother Giovanni was one of those four, and Lorenzo watched him with pride. Gio already had his captain's papers, and soon they would buy a second boat and catch more fish for the booming population that now lived along this coast.

The rain had let up over the last few hours, giving way to mist an hour or so ago, and the swells were not nearly as heavy as they had been. Lorenzo was still using fog signals to let any other vessels that might be passing this way know of the *Maiden*'s presence.

Gio and the others had just pulled the last of the haul aboard when Lorenzo saw the other boat come out of the mist, drifting straight toward the *Maiden*'s bow. A large pleasure boat, dead in the water: no lights, no motor, not making way. Crabbing a bit with the current. Lorenzo cursed, sure this was a matter of the storm setting some rich man's expensive new toy adrift. He called to Gio to rig the fenders and picked up his megaphone. He hailed the pleasure craft, which he could now see was a beauty—teak decks and a sleek white hull. A Chris-Craft—fifty-footer, he would guess.

He was not entirely surprised that he received no reply from it.

Lorenzo was a good pilot, and he easily maneuvered the *Maiden* alongside the drifting yacht. The *Sea Dreamer*, he could now see.

He called the Coast Guard. The radio operator interrupted him to ask his position. This was a little embarrassing for him. He was able to take the *Nomadic Maiden* in and out of a crowded harbor with ease, but he was not a navigator. He knew the coast—its lights, forms, and buildings—and stayed within sight of these markers. "South of Catalina Island, north of San Clemente Island."

"We'll find you. Over," the operator said. When Lorenzo named the vessel he had found, he heard a sudden change in the radio operator's voice.

"The *Sea Dreamer*? Any survivors? Over."

Survivors? Lorenzo was taken aback. He had been sure that this was just another of the many pleasure boats that had probably slipped free of their moorings and ended up adrift at sea last night—a common occurrence after a storm. "I don't see anyone on deck or at the helm."

"*Nomadic Maiden,*" the Coast Guard operator said, "the *Sea Dreamer* had four adults aboard. Over."

"Four?"

"Two males, two females—and a small dog. Please ascertain as soon as possible if there are survivors belowdecks, and if so, if they are in need of medical attention. Over."

So he called Gio to take the helm of the *Maiden,* and taking a lantern flashlight with him, Lorenzo lowered himself onto the *Sea Dreamer.* He secured her to the *Maiden* with a tow line. Gio, he saw, was watching around them, keeping his eyes moving, as he should.

Lorenzo called out again, a hopeful picture in his mind's eye of four adults, exhausted and sleeping below, but safe.

There was no reply.

His gut feeling, having heard the stories so many times over the years, produced another picture: someone going overboard, someone else jumping into the water to save him, both lost, the others not knowing how to operate the boat or the radio, perhaps washed overboard as well.

Not so easy to go overboard on a yacht this size, the hopeful Lorenzo thought. He called out again.

Silence.

Lorenzo took another moment to get the feel of the vessel, to listen.

Nothing but the creaking of the pull on the line, the lapping of the sea at the hull.

To all appearances the *Sea Dreamer* was seaworthy, but there might have been engine trouble. He would check that later. He used the flashlight to glance around the upper deck and helm station, casting its beam over the surfaces of the bridge.

He hurried down the companionway. He flashed his light in the salon area. Empty. In fact, except for taking on a little water—not enough to do more than wet the bottoms of a rich man's deck shoes—the *Sea Dreamer* seemed pristine, with everything secured just as it should be. He frowned, wondering at it. Galley the same. Dinette folded away and secured. No one in the head. He checked the two stacked berths in the midship cabin. Empty. The two in the forepeak were empty as well.

He began to feel uneasy and told himself not to get spooked over nothing. But the hair on the back of his neck stood on end as he made his way carefully to the aft stateroom's double berth.

Empty.

Not a sign of life.

Nowhere on the yacht did he find any sign of occupants. He climbed back to the upper deck and called to Gio.

"Tell the Coast Guard, no one aboard."

Word quickly came back that they should stay where they were, that a Coast Guard helicopter and cutter were on the way.

Lorenzo moved back to the helm of the *Sea Dreamer.* The sky was lighter. Usually, he loved this time of day, watching the dawn. Usually, he spent a moment or two thinking of what the new day would bring, and of his plans for the future of the Albettini Brothers Fishing Company. Now he looked out at the sea and thought of two men, two women, and a small dog.

He was going to try the engines, but there was no key. He could have started it without one if he had to, but he didn't have to. Just as well. Probably get in trouble with the Coast Guard. He turned the radio on to see if it worked. It did.

He heard the sound of a helicopter in the distance and turned the radio off.

The *Sea Dreamer* and its emptiness were the Coast Guard's problem now.

When O'Connor returned to the hospital, he was carrying Jack's hat and coat, entrusted to him by Hastings. Jack was showing the first signs of fever, and it was clear to O'Connor that the nurses were keeping a closer watch on their patient. O'Connor napped in a chair, waking to hear Jack muttering in delirium about the burial of the car. He began to grow more certain that Jack had actually seen such a thing—no fleeting hallucination could become such a persistent idea.

Helen Swan walked in at six o'clock.

"I'll stay with him this morning," she said. "I've cleared it with Wrigley. Go home and shower and shave and sleep a little if you can. He doesn't expect you before ten."

"What would Jack do without you, Swanie?" he asked, giving her cheek a kiss as he put on his coat.

"He tries to find out on a regular basis, Conn, so please don't ask that question when he's back on his feet."

* * *

He fell asleep but woke at eight-thirty when the neighbor in the apartment next to his began singing *"O Sole Mio"* at a volume that could have been heard down at the opera house. He lay in bed, remembering his interrupted dream: of Katy when she was a toddler. In the dream Maureen laughed and played with her, which had never happened in real life—his sister had never met Katy. Everyone in the dream was happy, but now, as he awakened from it, it made him feel sad. He got out of bed, but the feeling of the dream stayed with him even after he left the house.

In the newsroom, as O'Connor made his way to his desk, the other newsmen asked about Jack and said how sorry they were to hear that he had been hurt so badly. O'Connor figured three out of five meant it. In this business, those odds indicated great regard. Jack was the object of more than a little envy, but he knew how to live with that and still form friendships with most of his coworkers.

O'Connor was drinking his first cup of strong black coffee of the day, quietly listening to other newsmen make wild conjectures about the kidnapping of the Ducane baby—now apparently no longer a secret—when Winston Wrigley II called him into his office.

"Have a seat," Wrigley said.

O'Connor obeyed.

Wrigley wasted no time on small talk. "They've found the *Sea Dreamer.* No one aboard. The Coast Guard is searching the waters between here and where the boat was found, but they don't hold out much hope for finding survivors."

Over the last few hours, he had more than once thought that Katy might be dead, but now, perhaps because of the dream, he said, "Did anyone actually see Katy and Todd get on that boat?"

"O'Connor," Wrigley said in a gently chiding tone.

O'Connor looked away. There was no use talking to anyone about an idea like that, he thought. You went out and found out if there was any possible truth to it, or you gave it up on your own, but pitching it to an editor was a stupid idea. "Sorry."

"An insincere apology if I've ever heard one."

"Then here's a sincere one—I meant no disrespect to you, Mr. Wrigley."

"All right, fine. I want to send you to talk to the captain of the fishing boat that found the *Sea Dreamer.* I want you to get whatever you can from him, write it, and then go home. I've got other people covering other aspects of this—stories on those who are missing and so on."

"But there's so much more . . ."

"Undoubtedly. Once you have the fisherman's story written, go home. Not to the hospital, but home. You look like hell. I can tell that you aren't thinking straight. And I know why. But unless you're going to leave newspaper work and become a male nurse, you've got to leave Jack's care to the medical profession and help me prove to someone that I'm not crazy."

"I don't understand . . ."

"Jack's laid up in the hospital. I've got to have someone take over covering the crime beat."

"Sir, I . . ."

"You don't know what to say, and you don't want to cut Jack out of his job. Right. My father tells me this should go to one of the older men. That's because he's such an old man, people in their—how old are you now?"

"I'll be thirty next—"

"—people in their late twenties seem like children to him. He forgets that you have more years on the job than many of those men. He also forgets that he's retired."

"But, sir, Jack will be back."

"Yes, he will. And I can think of only one man who will sincerely welcome his return if that means handing the crime beat back to him—that's you."

"You couldn't get me to keep it."

"I know. So do as I say. I wouldn't have you working at all today, but with all hell breaking loose and Jack gone, we're stretched thin."

O'Connor could see that Lorenzo Albettini was tired of answering questions. But one of O'Connor's brothers was a commercial fisherman, so he was able to converse just enough on the topic dearest to Lorenzo's heart to win him over.

"Why didn't you go into business with your brother?" Lorenzo asked, using a can opener to punch two triangular openings in the top of a Coca-Cola.

"He has six sons."

Lorenzo smiled and took a sip of Coke. "That explains it."

"My brother tells me that the day after I work so hard to write a story, someone wraps one of his fish in it. Not true, though—he lives in San Francisco. Someone wraps one of his fish in the *Examiner*."

"If he comes this way, you must introduce us."

"I'm sure he'd like that. You work with your brother, right?"

And in this way O'Connor began to hear the story of the yacht that came out of the mist.

"I don't believe it, though," Lorenzo said, tossing the empty Coke can into a wire trash container.

"Don't believe what?"

"That anyone went overboard."

"Why?" O'Connor asked, surprised.

"First," Lorenzo said, counting off on a finger, "the yacht is too neat and clean, too tidy. Everything stowed away. Let me ask you this. If you invited friends over to celebrate a young woman's birthday, you would probably raise a toast, or something of that nature. Am I right?"

"Yes. So, you saw no glasses, no champagne . . ."

"Nothing—nothing. People are enjoying themselves, and someone gets swept overboard—if you are one of the others, you don't wash up the glasses and put them away. You leave things where they are and rush to that person's aid."

"But if the storm comes up and you want to make the ship safer?"

Lorenzo counted off finger number two. "You put on your life vests. Problem number two—the life vests are stowed, none are missing."

"Yes," O'Connor said, seeing it. "If you didn't put them on the moment you came aboard, you put them on when the seas turned rough. Especially if you haven't been out on the water much. What else?"

Lorenzo touched the third finger. "No key."

"In the ignition?"

"Exactly. Why would you take the key out of the ignition? Who turned it off and took the key with them? Wouldn't you want to have the ability to move under power?"

"Number four?"

Lorenzo smiled. "You need more?"

"You obviously have a sharp eye, Mr. Albettini. Does the list stop at three?"

"Call me Lorenzo, please. All right. Four—the dog. You know what a frightened dog does? But perhaps all of that washed overboard. Better than the dog is number five. The radio. I can turn it on when I come aboard. It was not on before I arrived."

"Perhaps the people left aboard didn't know how to use it."

"Think about that for a moment. Put yourself on that yacht."

O'Connor tried to picture the scene. "Four people on a yacht. One or two go overboard, or one goes over and another tries to save him. The people still onboard are terrified."

"Yes! You begin to see it."

"They've already lost half of the people aboard, they're in the middle of a storm, they can't see the shore."

"Yes. They are very, very alone. Nothing in this world can make a person feel as alone as the sea, even when she is calm. When she is raging? Ten, twenty times worse."

"You'd do whatever you could to get someone to help you. Was the radio on an emergency channel?"

"No," Lorenzo said, then waved a hand in dismissal. "It didn't need to be. If someone has been to see any movie that has so much as a toy boat in a bathtub in it, they know what to do."

"They flip switches until the radio lights up, and yell, 'Mayday,' into the mike."

"Exactly. And if they don't hear voices on the channel they are on, they search for a channel where they hear voices. They're desperate. They try to get someone, anyone, to help them." He was silent for a moment, then added, "Sometimes you hear these cries, and they cannot tell you where they are. Not in time." He sighed.

"But sometimes you do find them."

"Yes, yes. And the Coast Guard never gives up. Never."

"No one heard a call from the *Sea Dreamer*."

"No—and the Coast Guard was trying to call the *Sea Dreamer,* because of the child."

O'Connor sat back and thought over all that Lorenzo had said. Had anyone been on that boat at all? Or was it merely set adrift?

"Strange, isn't it?" he said aloud. "The parents and two grandparents of that child disappear on the same night the child is taken."

"Very strange," Lorenzo agreed.

"Something a human might arrange, even if there was no storm."

"In fact, I don't believe the ocean is to blame. The sea is not the one who did this, and neither is the sky."

15

O'CONNOR TALKED TO SEVERAL MEMBERS OF THE COAST GUARD TO GET an opinion of Lorenzo's theories. All but one said, in one way or another, that Lorenzo was full of hooey. The one who hesitated was in charge of the investigation. He said, "If Mr. Albettini had seen as many of these situations as I have, he might not have come to those conclusions. But perhaps I've seen so many, things that aren't alike begin to look alike—so I will certainly consider his points."

The others explained Lorenzo's questions away without much trouble: The group aboard the *Sea Dreamer* had been wearing expensive evening clothes, and therefore probably didn't bother with life jackets. They could have all been washed overboard with one wave, before anyone had a chance to use a radio. The key could have been lost overboard as well, or, if two or three of the members of the party went overboard, someone who was inexperienced, panicking at the thought of leaving them behind, might have tried to stop the boat by turning the engine off and taking the key out of the ignition. If that individual was also lost overboard, the key would have gone with him.

O'Connor went back to the Nash, made some notes, then found himself cursing his tiredness, because he had missed asking a question. He went back to the investigating officer and asked, "When did the storm arrive here?"

"Not until about five on Sunday morning."

"If they were only out on a pleasure cruise . . ."

"It was preceded by fog and heavy swells," he added.

"When?"

"The fog? It started rolling in around one, and by two o'clock, visibility between here and Santa Catalina Island was less than one hundred feet."

O'Connor thanked him and went back to the car.

O'Connor was not a man who simply did as he was told, but exhaustion was setting in, and so he obeyed Wrigley's orders. He wrote the story, handed it to a copyboy, and walked next door to the deli that had replaced Big Sarah's diner when she retired. He picked up a couple of ham sandwiches, then went home without going back into the building, not waiting for what he was sure were bound to be fireworks. He had a phone. They could call him.

Thinking about this, when he got home, he took it off the hook. He pulled the 45 RPM adapter off the spindle of his record player and switched the speed to 78. He set a small stack of records on the spindle, brought the changing arm over, and settled it gently over the 78s. He listened to them while he ate—until Nat King Cole's "Send for Me" began to play. By the second verse he found the lyrics too close to home, and he turned the phonograph off. His appetite lost, he cleaned up, put the phone back on the hook and undressed, then fell asleep.

The phone rang an hour later. He lifted the receiver, heard Mr. Wrigley say, "Your pet theory has been cut. I didn't want you to find out when you opened the paper tomorrow, so there it is. Get some sleep."

"I was," O'Connor answered, and hung up.

He tried to resist falling asleep again, but could not.

At two that afternoon, he was dressed again and on his way out to his car. Just as he fished his keys out of his pocket, he heard the familiar whistle of a Helms Bakery truck. He stopped the light yellow van and bought a doughnut, which he ate as he drove to the hospital.

Jack was asleep. Helen motioned to O'Connor to step into the corridor.

"He sleeps most of the time," she said, "and when he's awake, he's not coherent. Mostly he talks about that damned car."

"Did they bring his clothes up? The ones he was wearing when he was admitted?"

Her eyes widened. "You're not thinking of dressing him and taking him out of here?"

"No. I just need to see the clothes."

They went back into the room, and she opened a cupboard. "Here, take them," she said, handing him a large paper bag. "Hold your nose when you open it. They reek to high heaven."

He moved back outside to the corridor, Helen following him. He opened the bag, caught a whiff of its contents, then said, "Have you got a coat with you? Better to do this outside. I'll meet you on the patio."

A few minutes later, they had spread a bloodied set of men's clothing out on the patio.

"Good God," Helen said, lighting a cigarette. "Do you think he's got any blood left in him?"

"Sure. He took hits to the nose and mouth," he said absently. "They bleed easily." He had been looking at the soles of Jack's shoes. He set the shoes down and began turning Jack's pockets inside out. In the pocket of Jack's suit coat, he found a long, thin, damp leaf.

"I'll be damned," he said.

"Don't expect me to bet against the chance of that happening. What have you got?"

"A eucalyptus leaf."

She took a drag on the cigarette. "I'm going to guess that you haven't suddenly developed a mania for botany."

"Jack saw the car being buried. He really saw it."

"I should have known. Whenever anyone carries a leaf in his pocket, this is the sort of thing that happens. And all these years, drink has taken the blame for it."

"He told me that when he came to from the beating, he was in a eucalyptus grove, a windbreak." He thought back on what Jack had said. "A dairy nearby—I think he said it was across the road from the farm."

He searched through Jack's other pockets, but found nothing. He frowned. "His keys."

"What?"

"The hospital staff found his wallet, his broken watch, but there aren't any keys. Jack said his keys cut into him when someone kicked him."

Helen paused halfway in the act of bringing the cigarette to her mouth and said, "Maybe they fell out of his pocket during the fight."

"The beating, you mean. Jack didn't get to counter any blows."

"But his hands—"

"Stepped on."

"Jesus."

"I've got to find that farm."

She stubbed out the cigarette and said, "Conn, it's just one leaf. Eucalyptus trees are everywhere."

"Not in newsrooms or swamps or even inside the mansion where the party—oh hell." He ran a hand over his face. "Wrigley was right, I'm not thinking. Poor Lily. I haven't even called to tell her how sorry I am."

"For what?"

"About Katy. Don't you know?"

She went very pale, and he suddenly realized how clumsy he had been, his mistake in not mentioning this to her as soon as he saw her. She had been here all day, with Jack, and didn't know. Of course she didn't know. And she thought the world of Katy.

"Tell me," she said, in a hoarse voice. "Tell me."

He stood. "They found the yacht. No one aboard. The Coast Guard is looking . . ."

"Katy . . ." Helen's eyes filled with tears.

It shocked him. In over twenty years, he had never known her to cry.

"Oh, Swanie, I'm so sorry. That was no way to tell you. I'm such an oaf. I know you love her dearly and you deserve a better messenger than you got. Can you ever forgive me?"

The tears spilled over, and he put an arm around her shoulders. She cried harder, and he pulled her closer.

He thought of telling her that he didn't think Katy had ever been on that yacht, but recalled the reactions of the Coast Guard and Mr. Wrigley. If they were right and he was wrong, it would be cruel to raise false hope.

And he wasn't really sure that his ideas were ones that should provide hope. If Katy and the others didn't get on the yacht, were they alive and missing? Or murdered?

He thought of those years of missing Maureen. He would wait, he decided. And talk to Dan Norton.

He gave Helen his handkerchief. He heard her murmur, "She should have left that fucking idiot Todd the Toad a long time ago. I kept telling her . . . Oh, damn the Ducanes! Because she married into a family of asinine show-offs, she's dead."

He was relieved. She was feeling better if she could swear like that.

She stood up straight, thanked him, and said she'd better get back to Jack. "Don't tell him, Conn. Not yet."

"I've no intention of doing so. I'm sorry I—"

"No, please, I'm glad you were the one to tell me." She wiped her face with the handkerchief and said, "And if you ever tell any of those knuckle-walking simians in the newsroom that you saw me cry . . ."

"Never."

"Thank you." She sighed. "Who knows how long I'll last there, anyway. I get tired of it every now and then and have to do something else." Her eyes clouded again, but she took a resolute breath and shook her head. "We'll see. For now, I want to be with Jack."

"I'm going to take a look at the place where he was found, and then I'm going to try to find that farm. I know you don't think I'll succeed, but I'm going to look, anyway. I can't just sit around."

"No, I don't suppose you've ever been able to do that."

Dan Norton had given something more like directions rather than an address to the Mayhope egg ranch. As O'Connor drove out to it, he was struck by how different this world was, for all its closeness to downtown Las Piernas. Dairy farms, horse ranches, citrus groves, and long, low rows of plants. Mile after mile of roads lined with eucalyptus trees. He found himself curious about what might be growing in the fields he passed. In both Las Piernas and Orange Counties, these farms were becoming endangered. Subdivisions were beginning to merge. What would the people in those houses eat, he wondered, once all this rich farmland was covered in cul-de-sacs?

Ezra Mayhope was pleased to hear that Jack had regained consciousness. O'Connor found him to be a friendly man, eager to be of help. He learned that Mayhope was a widower, struggling but getting by.

Mayhope showed him about where along the road he had encountered the speeding car. When O'Connor asked him what kind of car it was, Ezra said he was sorry, he hadn't had a very good look at it, but thought it was a big, fancy car—definitely a city car.

"Something new and dark-colored. Because of the fog, I didn't see much of anything until he was just a few yards ahead of me, and then he about run me over. He was driving like a bat out of hell. Awfully fast for that road and the fog. I think I scared him as much as he scared me."

"Driver a man?"

"Just caught a glimpse of him, too, but yes."

"What race?"

"White. Had dark hair. But he could come up to me tomorrow and I doubt I'd know him. Didn't really see much of him."

"Alone?"

"I couldn't swear to it, but I think so."

Ezra showed him the intersection near the place where he found Jack, and pointed out the very spot where he had dragged Jack from the marsh—which wasn't hard to see, because the reeds and grasses were flattened there.

O'Connor took Mayhope back home. He thanked Ezra and offered to reward him for his time. The thanks were bashfully accepted, the offer flatly refused. O'Connor bought two dozen eggs.

Before he left, O'Connor asked Ezra if he could think of a place nearby that matched the description given by Jack—a eucalyptus windbreak, farm on one side, dairy across the road. He added that he assumed the field he was looking for was fallow or just recently plowed. Ezra grinned and told him that described about a hundred places.

He drove around for a while, discovered that what Ezra said was true. Eucalyptus trees were a common windbreak, as ubiquitous as another import—palm trees—were in cities. Farms and dairy farms were often located across the road from one another. He wasn't getting anywhere in his search.

He drove back to the place where Jack had been found. Only an hour or so of daylight remained, and he hoped that in that hour he might discover if those who injured Jack had left other clues.

Even before he stepped outside the car, he was struck by the rank odor of the marsh. It wasn't always this strong, he knew, and there were many places along the marshland where it wouldn't have been bad at all. He hated to think of Jack lying in this fetid water. Small wonder Jack was feverish.

He thought of the time frame. Jack had been taken from the party before midnight, taken out to the farm, and then moved from there to this marsh. Found near here an hour or so before dawn on Sunday, about thirty-six hours ago. Rain had fallen on Sunday, but not until a few hours after Jack had been found. Even before the rain, the ground here would be soft and damp.

A group of noisy gulls scolded O'Connor, then went back to their interest in something a little farther away.

O'Connor saw footprints in the muddy earth as he approached the edge of the water. He carefully avoided them. He had a feeling that no one from the police had bothered to come out here, or if they had, no one from the crime lab had been with them. He couldn't say that he blamed them. The rain had undoubtedly disturbed almost any kind of evidence that might have been here.

He saw one set of rain-filled footprints that he thought must be Ezra's, because they were close to the marks left where Jack had obviously lain on the grasses, and because as they headed back to the road they seemed deeper, since Ezra had dragged Jack's weight along with him. When he thought of the muddy mess Jack must have been, it was small wonder Ezra might have mistaken him for a movie monster.

That's where Jack had come out of the water. Where did he go in? From everything O'Connor had been told, and what he had seen of Jack's condition, he didn't think Jack would have been able to move far.

He saw more crushed reeds near where the seagulls were so busy. It was muddier there, and slippery, so he had to walk slowly and carefully as he moved along the edge of the marsh, glancing between the water and the road.

He came across tire prints. They were mostly washed away, but he could see the furrow of the deep tracks stopping just a couple of yards short of the water. A few more feet, and the car might have been stuck in the mire.

He saw footprints, one set very large and deep. The other, smaller set was on the other side of the tire tracks and seemed to show that someone merely stood there.

O'Connor tried to picture it. The car didn't turn around. From what he could tell from the tire tracks, the car had probably backed toward the water from the road, so that if the two men needed to leave in a hurry, they could do so. Risky with the mud, though—he could see where the mud had built as the rear tires spun to move the car forward again.

The big man—the giant who had beaten Jack?—walked to the back of the car and stood near the center of the tire tracks, but slightly back, closer to the water. To open the trunk? The footprints of this man were huge and deep as they moved away from the tire tracks toward the water.

He followed the path of the footprints. It was only when he reached the water that he saw the shoes among the grasses. He knew, even before he thought of the scavenger nature of seagulls. He shouted and waved his arms, and for a moment they flew away, long enough for him to see the body, bloated and unmoving, fully clothed, face unrecognizable. He knew who it was.

Jack had outlived the blond giant.

16

Hastings entered the library with quiet steps, but Lillian had heard the phone ring and expected him. She left her contemplation of the fire and looked up. She received a mild shock and wondered if her own face bore as many marks of grief as the butler's. Poor Hastings. Doing his best to hide it.

"Mr. Yeager on the telephone, madam," Hastings said.

Lillian sighed.

"No one would blame you for not taking calls at a time like this," Hastings said.

Lillian nearly took this offer to be shielded, then thought, as she knew a corporate wife must always think, of the implications for her husband's company. Since the war years, under Harold's less-than-stellar leadership, Vanderveer-Linworth had moved from the position of nearly owning Yeager Enterprises to nearly being owned by it. If Lillian hadn't taken a hand in matters, it might well have come to pass. She shook her head and said, "Harold does far too much business with Mr. Yeager for me to snub him in any way. And knowing Mitch, he'll come to the house if I don't speak to him on the phone. I'll take it in here, thank you."

"May I bring you anything? Coffee? Tea?"

"Tea would be lovely," she said, not really wanting it, but knowing he would feel better if occupied.

She picked up the phone, heard Hastings drop the extension into its cradle, and said, "This is Lillian."

"Lillian, I'm so damned sorry. I can't believe it."

"Thank you, Mitch. I'm not sure I've really taken it in myself. And I admit, I still hope they will find her. Kathleen would have put on a life vest."

"Of course she would have! She was—she *is*—a smart girl. Takes after her mother."

Lillian couldn't speak.

"I feel especially bad because thanks to you, I'm a parent now."

"Thanks to me?" she said, bewildered.

"Didn't Harold tell you? We adopted a few weeks ago! Two months ago today, in fact."

She could hear the joy in his voice, the exuberance. She wasn't sure she could bear anyone's joy right now. "No . . . no, he didn't mention it."

"A little boy. You know my wife has wanted a child, but—well, I won't go into all the details, but Estelle is barren."

Lillian was shocked that he would disclose such a thing to her, and felt embarrassed on Estelle's behalf. She had been friends with Estelle in high school and had always liked her. She was pretty and sweet and generous, one of those girls who could be lively without being a cat—a trick Lillian would admit that she herself had not mastered. But since Estelle's marriage to Mitch, Lillian had more often pitied than admired Estelle.

"You're always in the papers," Mitch said, reclaiming her attention, "because of the work you do for those girls and adoption. And I decided, well, we should go ahead and adopt. Give one of those poor kids a chance, a better life. And I have to tell you, Lillian, Mitch Junior has made a big softie out of me already. I can't help it."

"That's . . . that's wonderful, Mitch. I'm happy for Estelle."

"Sorry, now's not the time to be talking to you about babies, either, is it? I'm a bas— Uh, I'm a fool. Forgive me. I would have talked to Harold but the butler said he isn't around."

"No, he hasn't returned yet. He's away on business."

"But he knows, of course."

"Yes. We reached him early this afternoon."

"Is there going to be some kind of memorial or something?"

She held on to her temper by the thinnest of threads. "If we make any plans, Mitch, I'm sure Harold will tell you of them."

"Aw, I've upset you again. I'm sorry. Forgive me?"

"Nothing to forgive. Good-bye, Mitch."

She hung up, and sat back down on the sofa before the fire. Oddly, she reflected, Mitch's phone call had helped her. Getting angry helped.

Mitch Yeager seemed to forget how well she once knew him. Still knew him, though not at all in the same way. Knew him well enough to doubt that he was sorry for anything he had ever said or done. She also doubted that the phone call was intended to be an act of kindness. Whether because Katy had angered Mitch just two days ago, or because Lillian had refused to marry him more than twenty years ago, she was sure he had intended to hurt her. Mitch Yeager never forgot a slight.

She told herself that she must call Estelle soon. She had so little to do with the Yeagers these days, she hated the thought of doing anything to encourage them to renew the friendship that had been forced upon her by Harold's business relationship with Mitch. To hell with Harold, she thought. If she overlooked Mitch's cruelty, it would be for Estelle's sake.

Perhaps Estelle would be happier, caring for a child. She had seemed so withdrawn in recent years. Lillian found herself wondering if Mitch beat his wife.

Lillian knew that Mitch wouldn't allow any harm to come to the child he had adopted. He'd want to show the world that he took care of his family. He would, in fact, raise the child like a prince.

She found that she could move her self-pity and grief aside enough to feel sorry for that little boy.

On Tuesday afternoon, Warren Ducane drove up the long drive to Auburn's Stand, the hilltop home of Auburn Sheffield. The other Sheffields made a fortune in the ice cream business. Auburn, who had long ago broken off communication with the rest of the family, made a fortune in money.

This displeased his late father, an overbearing man who had wanted him to be the next emperor of ice cream. Auburn's Stand was named so by locals who saw him take his stand against his family. He heard of it, was pleased, and adopted the name for his home.

Auburn made more money in the stock market and other investments than anyone Warren could think of. Rumor had it that he did this to spite his father. After Warren became acquainted with Auburn and spent time listening to him talk about the joys of investing, Warren believed Auburn made money because he just couldn't stop himself. No more than Warren seemed to be able to stop himself from losing money.

He had called Auburn this morning, and Auburn, with ready sympathy, had invited him to come up to the Stand. Auburn, who disliked Warren's parents and their friends, had applauded Warren's independence from the Ducanes and said that he would always be willing to advise him.

Auburn was bidding good-bye to another guest, but introduced him to Warren as Zeke Brennan, a young attorney who had been doing work for Auburn. Warren asked for Brennan's card before he left.

Auburn poured Warren a glass of fine scotch and spent some time expressing further sympathy. After the two men had made small talk for some minutes more, Auburn said, "You came to me for a reason. What can I do for you, Warren?"

"Take all my money."

"What?"

"I mean, it's not mine yet, but it will be at some point. Maybe not for a while, because they have to be declared dead. My parents' attorney called not long after the yacht was found. If Todd is dead, too, everything comes to me. I—I keep hoping that's not the case, and that someone finds them, but they tell me it isn't likely."

Auburn studied him for a moment, then said, "Yes, I suppose you will eventually inherit a large fortune."

"I'll pay you to keep me from turning it into a small one. Stop me from spending it all, Auburn. Help me to tie it up somehow so that I can't run myself into the red in a year or so. I do want to learn about money, Auburn, but I can't do that overnight. I'd be happy to just be able to live comfortably— not like a king, or buying things just for pleasure, but comfortably. I want to save the rest. And I'll tell you why."

"The child."

"Yes. My nephew. Mostly that, yes. But that's not the only reason." He stood up and paced. He had rehearsed how he would explain this, but now he found he had difficulty actually saying it. "There are those," he began, and stopped, "There are those who might ask me for money, and I don't want to be able to give it to them."

Auburn studied him, then said, "I noticed that a police patrol car is parked at the bottom of the hill. The guard tells me it followed you here. Are you in trouble with the law, Warren?"

He shook his head. "No. It's just that they think someone might try to harm me. Because of the murder at Todd's house."

Auburn was silent for a moment, then said, "These people who might ask you for money—do you owe money to them?"

"No, not a dime."

"But they might extort it from you?"

"I don't know. I just don't want them to be able to do it if they try."

Auburn moved to a window and stood at it for some moments. Warren watched him anxiously.

"I provided you with quite an alibi, didn't I, Warren?" Auburn asked.

"Have the police bothered you? I'm sorry. I never intended to cause trouble for you."

Auburn smiled to himself, but said nothing in response.

"You believe that, don't you?"

"Yes. But I doubt your intentions mattered much this weekend."

Warren winced, then said, "I'm sorry. I'm so damned sorry about—about everything. I never should have come here today. I'll go."

"No," Auburn said, relenting, "have a seat."

"I wish I were dead," Warren whispered.

"And what good would that do your nephew, if someone wants a ransom?"

Warren looked up at him. "That's the only thing . . . Look, the truth is, I hardly paid any attention to the kid. I mean, it was great for Todd and Katy and everything, but—"

Auburn smiled. "But he's an infant."

"Yes. A baby, that's all. I thought I'd get to know him when he was a little older. But now—" He drew a ragged breath. "Now this is the only thing I can do for Todd. Take care of Max. I might not be able to do anything at all for Max, he might . . . he might not even be alive. But I have to try."

"I'm going to ask you a very rude and direct question, Warren. I promise you I will keep your answer confidential. But I must know this before I agree to help you. Did you pay someone to have your parents killed?"

"No. I—I hated them. But I didn't hire a killer."

Auburn paced again.

"I'm not saying I'm without blame," Warren added.

Auburn looked at him, but Warren didn't see condemnation in the look. It was almost as if Auburn had been hoping he would say that. Warren couldn't meet his gaze, and looked away.

"Well, you have that business card Zeke Brennan gave you before he left," Auburn said.

"Yes."

"Do you wish to continue to use the Ducane family attorney?"

"No. I don't want anything to do with my father's cronies." He paused, then added with some vehemence, "None of them."

"Sensible. Then call Brennan. Tell him everything you've told me. More if you like. He'll know how to proceed. When the time comes for me to help you with my own expertise, I'll do so."

"You can charge a fee—"

"I don't want one."

"I don't want to take advantage—further advantage—of you."

"You won't be. Let's not worry about that now."

Later, as they walked toward the front door, Warren asked, "Why did you decide to help me?"

"Oh, a number of reasons. When I look back on how angry I was with my own father at your age . . . the things I considered doing to find some relief from his control . . . but no, it's not entirely that. Let's just say I hate to see lives wasted, and that atonement interests me more than punishment."

Warren wasn't sure he understood what Auburn meant, but he thanked him, and when Auburn made him promise to call him the next day, on Wednesday, he agreed to it. As he was about to go, Auburn said, "And promise me you won't kill yourself."

Warren shook his head and said, "I can't promise that," even as something within him eased, just to hear this spoken of so directly.

"All right then, promise me you won't kill yourself before Thursday."

He smiled a little. "All right. I won't kill myself before Thursday."

As Warren drove down the hill, he saw the ocean stretching out to the horizon from the shore. The sun was setting. On any other day, he might have thought it beautiful. Now, he could only think of darkness, and endless, cold, deep water.

"Todd," he whispered. "Forgive me."

Then he saw the patrol car waiting to follow him home. He wondered how long this hell would last.

Until Thursday, at least.

17

It took twenty minutes of searching, but finally O'Connor saw a public phone sign on a restaurant on the edge of town and pulled into its lot. He fished a handful of coins from his glove compartment, found the phone booth, went into it, sat down, and shut the glass door. He found his hands were shaking. He took a deep breath, picked up the receiver, and deposited a dime, listening to the small bell chime twice as the dime rolled through the mechanism.

The operator would have put him through to the police department without charge, but he had decided to call Norton directly. Dan said it would take him about forty-five minutes to make some calls and get out there, but O'Connor should go back and wait for him at the scene.

O'Connor called Wrigley next.

"I thought I told you to sleep," Wrigley said, but when O'Connor told him why he had called, there was a long silence. Then he said, "You mean to tell me Jack killed the man who fought him?"

"No. The man was shot. Jack doesn't carry a gun. And he didn't fight Jack, he beat him. There's a difference."

"Agreed. You sure he's the guy?"

"No, but how many blond, crewcut giants might have died not far from where Jack was found?"

"Right. Listen, I'm not sure I've got anyone I can spare at the moment. What a damnable few days this has been. To make matters worse, Harvey quit."

Harvey was one of their best. He had been a top war correspondent who, when he was wounded overseas, recuperated in Las Piernas and decided he wanted to stay. Wrigley had always considered his hiring a coup.

"Harvey? Why?"

"Some newsroom joker pulled the old cap gun prank today."

O'Connor knew the trick. There were a couple of typewriters with the usual sandwich layers of paper and carbon paper already loaded in, ready to go for a man on a hot story. You didn't sit at that typewriter unless you were under pressure to begin with. If someone also placed a layer of caps from a cap gun just behind that first sheet of paper, the hapless reporter who rushed to write his lead had the caps explode with a bang as he typed.

"Harvey thought he was back on Guam?"

"Exactly. Wouldn't admit that, of course. Really shook him up and then he was embarrassed. Think you can talk him into coming back? He's a friend of Jack's, I know, but you get along with him, too, right?"

"Sure, but don't count on me to persuade him to do anything. I'll call him but he's his own man."

Harvey was reluctant to talk at first, but thawed a little as O'Connor told him how Jack was doing and moved on to tell him about finding the floating giant.

Then O'Connor said, "Here's the problem, Harv. You know how it works. I can't be the guy who found the body and the guy who writes the story. Wrigley's lost his best man for the job, because you quit—you had every right to, of course. But what that means is that this story gets lost. And if someone in town knows this man in the marsh, we might learn why this giant was paid to beat the living hell out of Jack."

"And why the giant was shot," Harvey said slowly.

Hooked, and O'Connor knew it. "And who paid for any and all of that."

There was a silence, then Harvey said, "Wrigley put you up to this?"

"I told him you'd make up your own mind."

After another long silence, he said, "Tell me how to find this place in the marsh."

It was dark by the time O'Connor got back to the marsh, and for a few moments, he wasn't sure he'd be able to find the body again. He did, though, and waited in the cold darkness for Norton and the others to arrive.

Once he had shown them the body, he was asked to wait in his car. He didn't mind getting out of the cold and away from the stink. And he didn't especially want to watch the poor bastards who'd have to fish the giant out of the muck and mire going about their business. So he went back to the Nash.

Harvey had to tap on the car window to wake him up when he arrived. O'Connor talked to him a while, then Harvey talked to Norton. Eventually he got enough for a story and left quickly, hoping to get something in before deadline. Before he went he told O'Connor that the dead man was presumed to be one Bo Jergenson. "Ever hear of him?"

"As a matter of fact, yes. Or something close to it. The Linworths' slightly deaf butler told Lillian that a tall gent who showed up at her daughter's birthday party was named Bob Gherkin. Close enough, wouldn't you say? He's the one who attacked Corrigan."

O'Connor hoped Harvey would check the typewriter before he sat down to write the story.

After the coroner's wagon left, Norton motioned O'Connor to come over to where he was talking to a crime lab worker. A second worker was trying to make a cast of one of the drier sections of tread marks.

"You said Jack's keys were missing?"

"Yes. Did you find them?"

"Describe them. Key chain, too."

O'Connor thought for a moment, then said, "Three keys on a plain metal key ring. Nickel-colored. A key to his front door—Yale lock, I think. A key to my place, and a key to the back entrance to the Wrigley Building." He pulled out his own keys and showed them what those last two keys looked like. "Hardly ever use the one for the paper, because the door is rarely locked. He also had a little saint's medal on the ring, brass or maybe even gold—yellow metal anyway. Gift from a priest he helped out once. It's a little worse for wear, has a little nick in it, but Jack won't be without it."

"Which saint?"

"Patron saint of reporters—St. Francis of Sales."

Norton nodded to the crime scene investigator and the man held up a cellophane envelope. "Don't touch it," Norton warned O'Connor. "Take a look and tell me if that looks like it."

There was a gold-colored medal in the envelope, bent near the top, where it had apparently been pulled by force off the key ring. O'Connor saw a small nick near the bottom.

"That's Jack's—not a doubt in my mind. He caught it in a metal desk drawer at work a few weeks ago and jammed the drawer. I can see the nick that was left on it when he finally worked it free. You found it on Jergenson?"

"In his trousers pocket."

"No keys with it?"

"No, and if they aren't in the marsh, then maybe someone is using them to try to get into Jack's place. I've got an undercover car keeping an eye on it, just in case our friends stop by, but I won't be able to do that for long. You think you can swing by there just to make sure the place hasn't been turned upside down?"

"Sure. But—listen, Dan, there are some things I want to talk to you about—about Katy."

"Tell you what. There's a steak place not far from Jack's. Let's go by his house, take a quick look, grab his teddy bear or whatever the hell else he may need at the hospital—other than a bottle of rye—and leave. Then you can tell me all your troubles over dinner. And I can get the hell away from the stench of this place."

Jack's house was locked up and showed no sign of disturbance. O'Connor called the hospital from the home of one of Jack's neighbors and learned that Jack was awake—and that Helen had told him what had happened to Katy and the baby. O'Connor asked to talk to him, and asked him where the spare key was hidden, and if he minded if Dan Norton entered the house with him.

Jack sounded listless, but he told O'Connor that the latest hiding place was in part of a window air conditioner at the back of the house, and that he didn't care what Dan Norton did. But at the end of this dull recital, he said, "Come by later, if you get a minute, Conn."

"I'll definitely be there," O'Connor assured him.

"For a drunk," Norton said, looking around the tiny living room, "Corrigan leads an orderly existence."

O'Connor didn't reply to him. Norton watched as he walked through the small home. In the bedroom, James Joyce's *The Dubliners* was on the nightstand. O'Connor took it with him. As nearly as he could tell, nothing in the house had been disturbed.

"Going to bring him a bottle?" Norton asked.

"No. I don't want to kill him."

"Kind of surprised you had to call him to find out where the spare key was. Surprised you don't have a key to this place yourself. After all, he's got one to your place, right?"

"He looks after my place when I travel. Helen looks after Jack's place when he goes somewhere. She lives nearer than I do, and I guess they got into the habit years ago. I didn't know where the spare was because Jack never leaves it in one place all the time, but I've never known him to forget where he's hidden it, drunk or sober."

"You finished here?"

"Yes."

Over dinner, O'Connor told Norton his theories about the *Sea Dreamer.*

"I don't believe all hell just accidentally broke loose among four sets of people who were as connected to each other as were Katy and Todd, Katy's in-laws, Katy's child and his nurse, and Katy's good friend Jack Corrigan. And for starters, I don't think the Ducanes were ever on that yacht." He went over all the points Lorenzo had made to him. "He's not a homicide investigator, but he knows boats."

Norton didn't say anything for a long while, then shrugged. "A possibility. Until I know what happened to the bodies, couldn't say one way or another. I know the chief isn't going to stand for anything other than the simplest explanation. He won't want to hear about boats that didn't really have anybody on them. But if the bodies are on land, we'll find them easier than if they're in the ocean."

"I've been thinking about the car, the one Jack saw the farmer bury."

"Maybe saw. Maybe didn't. He'd had a skinful—as usual—and so many blows to his head, it's a wonder it's still attached to his neck."

"I believe him." O'Connor told him about the leaf.

"So the part about the eucalyptus grove could be real," Norton acknowledged. "If you said to me, 'Jack claims he was in a eucalyptus grove,' that would be one thing. So many of those trees around, it wouldn't be hard to believe. But seeing a farmer bury a car in the middle of the night? Makes no sense."

O'Connor brooded in silence.

"Look, Conn, he's my friend, too—but I have a job to do here, so I can't let that count with me when I take a look at his story. What I can count is the number of times I've been around him lately when he was absolutely sober. I can do that without having to call Einstein to help me do the math."

"He remembers things, even when he's been drinking. Like the key."

"This is bigger than a key, and in less familiar territory."

"I think he saw it," O'Connor said, "if for no other reason than this: it's too strange a thing for him to talk about, unless he did see it. You ever hear him talk about hallucinations before now?"

"No," Norton admitted. "But I've heard him talk when I knew he was confused by the booze. Add the whacks he took on his skull . . . he could easily be mixing up separate memories, combining them into one." He held his hands up in a gesture of helplessness. "It would be hard for me to call this a lead."

O'Connor decided he might as well let it drop.

Norton must have seen this in his face. He said, "All right, all right. Tell you what—if the bodies don't wash ashore within the next week or so, I'll get someone to canvass the farms near the marsh, ask if anyone has seen anything odd going on around there."

"Anything else going on in the investigation?"

"We're checking again for fingerprints at the Ducane house and in the boat and in the car that was left behind at the marina. We've got that new ninhydrin method now—we can sometimes find prints on paper."

O'Connor tried to appear as if he was encouraged by this news, but he knew that until a suspect was in custody, the likelihood of matching the prints to a criminal was not good. He had seen the rows and rows of metal cabinets that housed the department's thousands of fingerprint cards. Although a fingerprint expert would be able to narrow the search somewhat, it was still a long and tedious task that would only bear fruit if the Las Piernas Police Department had at some point taken the criminal into custody.

For the next two days, O'Connor was kept so busy between his work at the paper and keeping Jack's spirits up, he had little time to look for answers to the many questions he had about the night Jack was injured. Jack's fever subsided, but his memories of the attack did not grow clearer. Since he had learned about Katy and the others, and about the kidnapping, Jack hadn't seemed to care about much of anything. O'Connor thought the news about Katy had damaged Jack more than the man who had used his fists on him.

One of the worst moments came when Jack asked him to look in his coat pockets, to see if his keys were there. "I might have left them in my coat at Lillian's."

"You probably had them taken from you. Remember? We found the saint's medal on the giant. Besides, you told me the keys were still in your pocket when you woke up in the grove."

"I might have been mistaken."

"You have a cut and key-shaped bruise on your thigh."

"Maybe the giant cut me with his own."

O'Connor decided to humor him and searched his pockets. "Nothing, just this note."

"What note? Read it."

O'Connor opened it. "It says . . ."

"What? What's wrong?"

"It's nonsense, that's all."

"Give it to me, Conn."

Reluctantly, O'Connor did as he was bid, but the injuries to Jack's hands left his fingers too clumsy to open it. "It's Katy's handwriting. Must have slipped it to me at the party. Open it and tell me what it says," he demanded impatiently.

O'Connor took a deep breath, let it out slowly. "It says, 'Is it true that Mitch Yeager is my father? You're the only one who will tell me the truth. Call me.'"

"Damn it!" Jack said, covering his eyes with his hand. "Damn it!"

O'Connor waited, and when Jack said nothing more, he put the note back into the coat and carefully hung it up again.

Jack kept his eyes covered, his bruised and swollen fingers over the bandaged one, the palm of his hand covering the less injured one.

"Oh God. She died thinking that son of a bitch might be her father," he said. "Who the hell would put a sick idea like that into her head?"

"The husband who was about to be divorced?"

Jack let his hand fall and looked at O'Connor. "Probably." He considered this grimly for a moment, then said, "That bastard wouldn't let her talk alone with me for five minutes, and that's probably why. God damn it! What a cruel damned thing to tell her."

Worried that getting this upset would harm him, O'Connor said, "Jack, it doesn't matter now."

"I think of her being out there . . . lost in the sea, in darkness. Of her being cold. And alone. And afraid."

"No, Jack. Katy wasn't ever afraid of anything."

Jack smiled a little. "No, she wasn't."

They sat in silence for a time. Jack said, "Don't tell anyone about that note, Conn."

"If you're going to insult me, Jack Corrigan, I'll leave."

Jack laughed softly and said, "I was wondering what it would take to get you to leave me the hell alone."

"Just for that, I'll stay." And then he thought to tell Jack the story of Harv and the caps, and Jack laughed and immediately guessed who had done the trick, and the two of them considered various ways in which Harvey could be avenged.

On Wednesday evening, as he made his way across the hospital parking lot, O'Connor felt the sensation of being watched. He turned and looked behind him, but saw no one. He scanned the lot, but saw only one familiar car— Norton's T-Bird. Norton wasn't in it. Shrugging, he went into the building.

As he stepped out of the elevator, he saw Norton leaving Jack's room.

"Hiya, Conn," Dan said wearily.

"Hello, Dan. You look beat. Have you slept since Sunday?"

"Not much. Thought I'd stop by to see how Jack was doing, though." He shook his head. "I've seen worse, but that doesn't make it any easier to see a friend in that kind of shape."

"I keep thinking that if a guy delivering some eggs hadn't come along and helped him, you and I might be at Jack's funeral right now. If he doesn't cheer up, we may be yet."

Dan looked uneasy. "Listen—I didn't realize how down he was feeling. If I had known, I wouldn't have said anything to him about it at all."

"About what?"

"They found the Ducanes."

Although he had known it might come to this, O'Connor now realized that in some corner of his mind he had harbored hope that they would be found alive. He felt the grief well up in him, and close on its heels, a fear for Jack's recovery.

"Not all of them," Dan quickly amended.

"Who, then?"

"This is off the record—and not really official yet, anyway. Thelma and Barrett. Not exactly together. Her body washed up south of here. Clothing and jewelry told them who it was, because . . . well, you know how it is with floaters."

O'Connor nodded.

"Barrett was in worse shape. Ruined the romantic stroll taken by the couple who discovered him."

"But no sign of Todd or Katy?"

"No. Conn, we're lucky to get two of them, and you know it."

"You've told Warren?"

"Yes. He asked about Todd and Katy, too."

"So you're sure they drowned?"

"Nothing's certain until the coroner does the autopsy—not even the iden-tifications. But we really don't have any reason to doubt that they drowned at this point."

"Any word on the child?"

"Not a peep. Not a good sign."

O'Connor looked down the hallway.

"Go on," Dan said, "I'll catch up with you later."

O'Connor entered the room quietly. Jack was staring out the window. When Jack turned to him, he was surprised to see not grief, but a look of calm res-olution on his face.

"Get out your notebook," Jack ordered. "I'm going to give you a list of lowlifes. You've met most of them. I'll tell you where you're most likely to find the others. You've got to go looking for them tonight. By daylight, most of them will be back under their rocks."

"Why?" O'Connor asked. "You think they might know who did this to you?"

"Who gives a rat's ass about that? I want to narrow down the list of thugs who know how to sail."

18

As he drove out of the hospital parking lot, O'Connor saw a beat-up old Ford leave as well. Before long, he was convinced the gray car was following him. The driver was a white male, but he couldn't tell much more than that.

Instead of going home, he turned onto Pacific Coast Highway. At a light at the edge of downtown Las Piernas, a couple of hot rodders idled behind him, then peeled out as the signal changed, racing past the Nash. The Ford continued to follow at a distance. He considered losing his tail, then decided he'd rather learn who it was.

He drove to Gabriel's, a bar near the beach, and took the only open spot at the curb in front of it. He walked in quickly, pausing at the doorway just long enough to see the Ford pulling into the bar's small parking lot. On a Wednesday night, he knew, there was little chance the driver would find a parking space there.

Wednesday night was poetry night. The place would be packed.

Gabe, the owner and bartender, was doing his best to cater to the Beat Generation these days.

The interior was dark, save for a few candles on tables, and a spotlight on a small stage near the back—a young, bearded man dressed in black was reading poetry while someone else played a set of bongo drums. Layered within a haze of cigarette smoke, the air in the bar carried an odd mixture of other scents: strong coffee, spilled booze, and faux bohemians. There weren't too many of the genuine articles in Las Piernas, O'Connor thought, at least not on a permanent basis. He wondered if poetry night at Gabriel's might change that.

O'Connor saw Gabe, who nodded toward him.

O'Connor made his way toward the back door, where a redhead named Nancy, who had moved up in the world of Gabriel's from cigarette girl to waitress, stepped into his path. She was drenched in Evening in Paris perfume. "What's your hurry, Conn?" she asked in a whisper.

"I've got company coming," he said softly, slipping her a five. "And I don't want to disturb the poet. Delay my shadow a little, then let me back in?"

She sighed. "Don't get hurt out there. You aren't the first one to leave by this door tonight. Probably smoking reefers out there."

He smiled. "We who are strictly squaresville have certain advantages over the cool."

"You're crazy. And I don't mean that in a good way."

He watched as a skinny man entered the bar. The man seemed familiar to O'Connor, but between the smoke and the poor lighting, he couldn't make out his features. He seemed frail, not up to whatever job he had taken on. It made O'Connor feel more wary, not less—if the man wasn't strong, he might be carrying a weapon to even the odds.

No use delaying, though, he thought.

When he was sure the man had seen him, he stepped outside and stood so that the door itself would hide his presence when it opened again. He was now in the alley behind the bar. There was a strange scent that he had smelled only a few times before, but recognized nonetheless—Nancy was right, someone was smoking marijuana nearby. He heard giggling and the sound of voices, then a young man knocked over a metal trash can as he and his girlfriend stumbled away. O'Connor ignored them, concentrating on the door. A single lightbulb burned beneath a green metal shade over the door—otherwise, the alley was in darkness. He had to stop the man as he came outside.

A moment later the door opened cautiously. He waited until the man had stepped into the alley, then tackled him from behind.

The man fell hard. An "umphh" of breath came out of him as he hit the ground. He lay so still that for a moment O'Connor wondered if he had been knocked unconscious. Pinning the man's arms, he said, "If you wanted to see me, all you had to do was come by the newspaper."

"No I couldn't," rasped a familiar voice.

"Ames?" O'Connor said, startled.

"Yes. For God's sake, Conn, you're crushing me. Get off."

O'Connor stood and helped Ames Hart to his feet, apologizing as he brushed off Ames's clothing. Hart stood on shaky legs, his hands on his thighs, trying to catch his breath in the way a runner might after a hard sprint. Thank God, O'Connor thought, that he hadn't thrown a punch at him or hit him over the head or taken any of the other measures he had considered.

O'Connor hadn't seen Ames Hart for some time. Known to the staff of the *Express* as Red Hart—though seldom to his face—Ames had covered the follow-up story of the little girl in the well, the legislation that required abandoned wells to be capped. That was less than ten years ago, but Hart looked as if he had aged thirty years since then.

Hart had been one of their best reporters, a muckraker who turned in one daring story after another—until Old Man Wrigley heard a rumor that Hart had once been a member of the Communist Party and asked Hart to deny it. Hart told Wrigley he had no right to ask the question, and Wrigley fired him, saying that when he had an answer—the correct answer—he could have a job.

Hart had remained stubbornly silent on the matter. Jack had argued with Wrigley on Hart's behalf—and nearly lost his own job.

It wasn't a good time to lose a job, but for Hart, matters got worse. He had been blacklisted. No other paper would touch him. He lost his home and barely managed to keep himself clothed and fed. Jack had become worried—not long before, a friend on one of the L.A. papers had committed suicide after being blacklisted. Jack eventually found a job for Hart with a small radio station in Los Angeles, where Ames worked off-air and under a different name. It required all Jack's charm to talk Hart's widowed sister into letting her "pinko" brother sleep in a spare room until he got back on his feet, but once Ames was under her roof, she became fiercely protective of him. Hart had managed to get a place of his own since then, but seeing the condition of his suit and the wear on his shoes, O'Connor thought he must still be struggling to get by.

"Why the hell were you following me?" O'Connor asked, his guilt making his tone abrupt.

"Trying to see you in private," Ames said, wheezing breaths between each word. "You know what would happen if anyone saw you talking to me?"

"It's not like that anymore," O'Connor said. "You saw the crowd in the bar. This generation won't follow in Old Man Wrigley's footsteps. I'll bet his son would hire you."

Ames gave a small laugh. "O'Connor, I don't know which is more charming, your naïveté or your optimism." He sniffed the air and frowned. "Perhaps not so naïve . . . were you out here smoking tea?"

"No, a pair of lovebirds before me, but thanks for thinking so highly of me."

"I do think highly of you, and Jack as well. You know I'm doing news writing for the station I work for?"

"Yes."

"So I've built up some sources. And I've heard something that might be of interest to you."

"Go on." O'Connor shifted on his feet, feeling impatient with Hart's drama.

"I've heard that a thug with connections in my neighborhood in Los Angeles was hired to beat up a newspaper reporter on the *Express*. Thug's name is—"

"—Jergenson. Bo Jergenson."

"Yeah," Hart said, and looked so dejected O'Connor regretted interrupting his act.

"Ames, look—"

"I guess you don't need me."

"Jergenson's dead, Ames, and not from natural causes. Someone put a bullet through his forehead and left him not far from where Jack was found. That's the only reason I know his name."

"No fooling?" He became animated again. "A bullet, huh? Well, I guess it could still be the dame, right?"

"What dame?"

"Blonde by the name of Betty. Hooker, but she's not as strung out or worn down as most. She's the mistress of a guy named Gus Ronden."

"Any last name?"

"Hell if I know it. You can bet it isn't ever going to be Ronden. But that's probably lucky for her."

"What do you know about him?"

"Not too much. Reputation for being a little psycho. You might have seen him around the pool hall—the one down at the corner near the paper?"

O'Connor shook his head.

"Go by there, you might run into him."

"What's his line?"

"Pimping, mostly. Word is, he rents out high-dollar girls like Betty by the hour, but I have a feeling he doesn't own the stable. He's probably mob-connected. Always manages to keep himself out of the hoosegow."

"What does he drive?"

Ames shrugged. "I don't know. Ask around at the pool hall."

"Thanks, I will. Sorry about knocking you down."

Ames smiled. "Not the first time that's happened to me. As long as I can get back up again, I guess I'll be all right."

Thursday morning began badly: He learned that Jack was unlikely to regain sight in the injured eye. Jack laughed about it, said he was going to buy a patch so that he could look like the mysterious man in *Brenda Starr*, and maybe then some gorgeous woman reporter would fall in love with him. Helen said she guessed that let her out of the running. They teased each other back and forth until O'Connor decided all the bravery was admirable but unbearable in these moments when he himself felt nothing but murderous rage, so he quickly excused himself to go to work.

At the newspaper, O'Connor tried the simple way first: looking up Ronden in the phone book. He didn't find a listing. He looked at the clock, pulled out a story he had nearly finished last week, and worked like crazy to turn it in before the pool hall opened at ten. He got over there by ten-thirty.

He spent the next few hours hiding his billiards skills, usually letting others win. During this process, he learned that Gus Ronden hadn't been seen since the Friday before Katy's birthday party. Nobody seemed to miss him much.

O'Connor softened up the bartender at the pool hall by telling stories and jokes, leaving good-sized tips, and aiding in the forcible removal of a rowdy patron or two. By the time he got around to asking him about Ronden, the bartender was in a confiding mood.

"He's no good," the bartender said. "Give you an example—cut up a colored girl in Stockton. Bragged about it, and about how he hired some slick lawyer and weaseled out of going to jail. He made out like the local coppers up there didn't care, because she was a Negro. I think that's all eyewash—they must have made it hot for him there, because he moved down this way. Probably figured if he'd do that to a black girl, next he'd do it to a white."

"Any idea where I could find him?"

"Don't go looking for him, kid. You'll just be looking for trouble."

"I like to find trouble before it finds me."

"So that's how it is. Sorry I can't be of more help, then—he has a house, somewhere over here on the west side of town."

"Kind of surprised to hear he could afford one."

"Oh, Gus is never short of money. Squeezes a penny until Abe Lincoln has bruises, but somehow I don't think that's the secret of his wealth."

"Know who he works for?"

"The devil, for all I know."

So he drove to the county offices and looked through property records to learn where Ronden lived, and then went back to the paper, where he used the crisscross phone directory to look up the phone number, which was listed as that of Elizabeth Bradford. Betty. He called repeatedly, but got no answer.

It was late afternoon by the time he got to Ronden's place. He knew it was a bad time to allow himself to go calling on anyone connected to Jack's beating. He knew he didn't have his own temper in hand, but he couldn't keep himself from hunting Ronden.

The house wasn't much of a place, nothing more than a rundown wood-frame. Most of the houses on the street were in poor repair—torn screens, weedy gardens, peeling paint. Directly across from Ronden's was one of a few exceptions: a white picket fence guarded a home with a green lawn and neat flowerbeds. Nice for Ronden to look out his window and see that, O'Connor thought dryly. The view this neighbor had was not nearly so pleasant. Ronden's house was a graying white, with a lawn that was a mongrel collection of weeds.

He watched Ronden's house for a time before getting out of the car. There was no movement or sound of any kind coming from the house. He wasn't exactly sure what he was going to do if Ronden was home.

Punch him, the way Jack had been punched? Literally take an eye for an eye?

Beat the hell out of him, then turn him over to Norton?

Pretend to be a salesman for the Fuller Brush Company, walk off peaceably, then call Norton?

He wasn't sure which of these ideas he'd stick with, he only knew that he couldn't sit in the car, staring at the dump Ronden called home.

As he walked up the porch steps, one creaked loudly. He paused, wondering if he was a fool not to have brought a weapon. But he had no real experience with guns, not much more than Dan Norton taking him to a firing range a few times. With Dan's tutelage, he'd managed to hit a paper target fairly consistently, but he knew that men were not likely to act like paper targets, and thought himself little match for someone who truly knew what he was doing with a gun.

He knocked hard on the door, half in anger, half in fear. He kept his fist clenched. But after a while, it was clear no one would be coming to the door. He listened for the sound of movement within the house for a long time, and became convinced that Ronden wasn't home.

He walked up the rutted dirt driveway toward a dilapidated garage, one that looked old enough to have housed a Model T at some point, if not a carriage. A short fence between the house and the garage enclosed a small backyard. He was surprised to see pink roses growing along the back wall. They seemed well tended—the only thing about the place that was.

He turned back to the garage. There was no lock on the latch that held the double doors closed, so he opened it and pulled on the one on the right. It swung out toward him with a loud creaking. If Ronden was in the house and hadn't heard him yet, the man was deaf.

The scents of oil and dust greeted him, but no car occupied the garage. A few rusty garden tools and a push mower stood against one wall, a workbench on the other. He opened both doors and stepped inside to get a closer look, taking care to avoid stepping on the oily tire marks on the concrete floor. Big tires, set wide apart. A big car.

He pulled a string hanging next to a bare lightbulb overhead, but nothing happened. Either the bulb was burned out or the electricity was off. Had Ronden abandoned his home after killing Bo Jergenson?

He looked more closely at the workbench, but it appeared that little work was done on it. There were no tools on or near it. He saw a rusting footlocker beneath it, though, and bent to open it. He had just released the latch when a gruff voice said, "What are you doing in here?"

Startled, O'Connor banged the back of his head on the underside of the bench.

"Jesus!" he said, wincing. He straightened, and saw a man in his sixties pointing a shotgun at him. He raised the hand that wasn't rubbing his head.

"I'll thank you not to use the Lord's name in vain."

"I'm sorry."

"What are you doing in here?" the man asked again.

"My name's O'Connor. I'm with the newspaper. Put the gun down and I'll show you my press credentials."

"You've got that vicey-versy. You show me your credentials, nice and slow, and then maybe I'll put down the gun."

O'Connor did as he asked.

After taking a look at his press pass, the man lowered the gun and said, "I would think the world would be mighty tired of reading about the likes of Gus Ronden."

"You own the place across the street?"

The man nodded. "Name's Ed Franklin. Doesn't seem to me that being a reporter gives a man a right to trespass on another man's property, Mr. O'Connor."

"It doesn't." O'Connor made a quick decision. "Let's step out into what's left of the sunlight, Mr. Franklin. I'll tell you why I'm here."

He told Franklin what had happened to Jack, and of his suspicion that Gus Ronden had murdered Bo Jergenson. "Jack Corrigan is like a brother to me," he ended.

Franklin drew a deep breath and exhaled slowly. At some point during the story he had broken the shotgun open, and now cradled it with the business end pointing at the ground. "I'm sorry but not surprised to hear that Miss Bradford involved herself in this. I had hoped . . . no, I will *still* hope and pray that she will someday abandon this way of life."

"You planted the roses for her, didn't you?"

He nodded. "She admired the flowers at my place. She told me she's fond of pink." He blushed to a fiery red, then added in a low voice, "You'd not believe how she proposed to thank me."

"I would," O'Connor said. "When did you last see them here?"

"She has a place of her own, she tells me. An apartment near the ocean. But she is here quite often. I last saw her here on Saturday. She was with a dark-haired man and a big blond fellow. Not that the dark one was little. He was good-sized, too, but next to the other one, anyone would look short. Might be part Mex, but I couldn't say for sure. They're the ones who attacked your friend, I suppose."

"And Ronden?"

"All sorts of comings and goings around here on Saturday. I kept an eye out. One of his creepy friends came over early on. Young guy. Dressed sharp, has some money I would guess. I didn't see them leave, but everybody was gone by around ten, because Gus left at about that time." He grinned. "I can always hear this garage open."

"I don't doubt everyone on the street can hear it. What does Gus drive?"

"Dark blue Chrysler Imperial—almost looks black. He has some fancy name for the color, but I don't know what it is. Brand new, a 1958, but he bought it late last year. Push-button transmission, power steering, purple dash lights. Electric everything. It's a beauty. Takes better care of it than he does the house or his girlfriend."

"Leaking oil, though?"

"No, that's from Betty's car. She hasn't been allowed to park it in the garage very often since he bought the Imperial, though."

"When did he get back on Saturday night?"

"He came back around midnight, I think. Then not much later, Betty and those two I mentioned came over—the blond giant and the Mex."

"Not the sharp-dressed man?"

"No, he didn't show up again. Heard Gus yelling at somebody. Betty left with the dark one. The blond one drove off with Gus."

"You remember what the other car was? The one Betty and the dark-haired man were in?"

"A Chevy Bel Air. Turquoise and white."

"You have any idea where Gus might be now?"

He shook his head. "He came back in the wee hours, then left again in a big hurry." He thought for a moment, then added, "Betty told me that Gus has a place up in the mountains. I don't know which mountains, though. To be honest, he's never struck me as the outdoors type."

"That helps, Mr. Franklin. I have one more favor to ask." He took out his notebook, wrote down Dan Norton's name and phone number, then tore out the page and gave it to Franklin. "Call that number, please. Tell Detective Norton that I was over here, and that I took care not to step on a nice set of tire tracks in the garage. Tell him that I said Gus Ronden killed the giant, and I'll fill him in on anything else I learn a little later."

"You sure you don't want to call him from my place?"

"He's going to be a little perturbed with me as it is, and he might find a way to make me wait around here a little longer than I'd like."

At home, O'Connor made six peanut butter and jelly sandwiches and packed them in a hamper with a thermos full of hot coffee. He packed a few things for an overnight trip, as well as some warm clothing—gloves, sweater, thick socks, hat, and warm jacket—and drove the Nash to San Bernardino. He found a cheap motor lodge and rented a room. He was so tired by that time, neither the music from a honky-tonk next door nor the lumpy mattress could keep him from a good night's sleep.

The next morning he was waiting outside the property records office. To his relief, he found a cabin belonging to one Augustus Ronden listed not far from Lake Arrowhead. He had been worried that the cabin might end up being in the Sierras rather than the San Bernardinos, or listed in another county, perhaps as far away as Tahoe.

He began the drive up into the mountains, taking the narrow cliffside highway that wound its way up from the foothills. He wore the warm clothing he had packed the night before. He was less than two hours away from Las Piernas, but there was a marked difference in the climate. The weather front that had dumped rain on Las Piernas had left snowdrifts here.

O'Connor had never lived in a place where it snowed, and had no experience of driving on icy roads. He was glad the two-lane highway had been plowed earlier in the week. The road was dry, the air crisp and laden with the scent of pine.

When he reached Lake Arrowhead, he stopped in a real estate office to get directions to the lane leading to Ronden's place. Once the salesman determined that he was not a potential buyer or renter of a cabin or ski lodge, he sent him on his way with a local map.

He drove on plowed roads until he got to the private drive that led to Ronden's cabin. The road was higher than the cabin, which sat on the downslope, in a small hollow. He could see a glimpse of it from here, but not much more. He was sure he had the right one, though, because a big, midnight blue Chrysler Imperial was parked at the end of the drive, surrounded by snow. Ronden hadn't been able to get down the drive, either, although there were snow chains around the Imperial's tires. Ronden would need to take them off and do some shoveling to get the car free if he planned on leaving the cabin. O'Connor saw this as an advantage. If he needed to leave in a hurry, he'd be halfway down the mountain before Gus Ronden could move his car an inch.

He walked up to the Imperial, which was unlocked, and pushed snow away so that he could open the door. He pulled down the visor to look at the vehicle registration—like most people, Gus Ronden kept this in a plastic and leather holder, held onto the visor by thin springs. The name and address were Ronden's. O'Connor reached to open the glove compartment. It contained a few maps and receipts and a pint of gin. He backed out of the car and stooped next to the driver's seat, moving his hand carefully beneath it. Even through his gloves, he could feel the cold steel of a gun. He pulled the revolver free, emptied it of bullets, and returned it to its hiding place. He pocketed the ammunition and began to walk carefully down the drive.

He quickly realized that he had not planned carefully enough. He needed boots. Within a short time, his shoes, socks, and pants legs were uncomfortably wet with slushy snow, and more than once he nearly lost his balance.

He followed a bend in the drive and stepped into a clearing. A small cabin stood before him. The snow was disturbed in front of it, and behind a shredded screen door, the wooden front door was open. He stepped back among the trees. Was Ronden inside the cabin, or somewhere in the surrounding forest? He shook his head at the sight of the screen. Why didn't the man take care of his property? He supposed insects wouldn't be much of a problem in winter.

Within a few seconds he heard the sound of something scraping against a wooden floor, followed by a loud crash. He watched uneasily, teeth chattering with cold, asking himself why he wasn't coming up with any big ideas now. He wasn't going to approach without any place to take cover, not when Ronden might easily poke the barrel of a gun through that torn screen and shoot him on sight.

Suddenly, the screen door flew back on its hinges, and a black bear came out of the cabin. It paused, sniffed, and stared toward him, then scampered off to the left, moving much faster than O'Connor had ever imagined such a large animal could travel.

When his heart rate slowed enough to allow him to stop praying in thanks for near misses with potentially dangerous wild creatures, he moved toward the cabin. He could believe any number of things about Gus Ronden, but not that he was a bear tamer in the off-season.

He mounted the porch steps, pulled open the broken screen—probably the bear's version of ringing a doorbell—then stood on the threshold of the cabin, looking at chaos. The bear had been having a grand time of it in the front room, which housed a kitchen, dining area, and sitting room. The kitchen was a shambles—the refrigerator stood open, its meager contents spilled on the floor. A set of Melmac plastic dishes had survived a fall from a cupboard, but a copper canister of sugar had been bent into an unusable shape. The floor near the door was damp, and it seemed colder in the cabin than outdoors.

O'Connor looked in the other rooms and found them unoccupied. The bed was made, the closet empty, the bathroom clean. He walked out to the front room again and looked around. Other than the open door and the bear's mess, he didn't see signs that anyone had been here lately. The fireplace held ashes, but there was no telling how long they had been there.

This last made him think about the lack of footprints. If Ronden drove up here early on Sunday, the first of the snow would have fallen here before he arrived. He had chains on his tires, so there was some snow, at least at these higher elevations. If he walked to the cabin from the car, new snow would have covered his tracks. But it was nearly a week later now, and there was no sign that he was living here. O'Connor wasn't sure if a bear could open a door, especially a locked door. He looked at the door again. Unlike the screen, it hadn't suffered damage.

Why had the door been left unlocked? He heard a vehicle and looked back toward the road. There wasn't a clear view of the lane from here, but with the screen door open, he could hear any cars that went by. Had someone else waited for Ronden here? Perhaps they had then driven off somewhere together. But why leave the door open? Maybe the second man—or woman—hadn't latched it properly, and the wind had done the rest.

He made the trip back to the cars. Got back into the Nash, started the car, and turned on the heater.

Where could Ronden be? Had he left voluntarily, or was he lying dead somewhere in the woods, buried by snow? O'Connor wondered if he had nearly stepped on him, coming down the drive.

O'Connor shivered. He looked out the windshield at the Imperial as he tried to warm up. The car's big, sweeping fins and distinctive trunk design, with the spare tire shape on it, gave the Imperial a kind of space-age look that the Nash would never have.

He thought of changing clothes before he headed back to Lake Arrowhead. He'd look for a pay phone there and call Norton. The thought of dry clothing was appealing, but the thought of getting out of the car to get his overnight bag out of the trunk . . .

The trunk. He stared ahead at the trunk of the Imperial. Ronden would have brought a change of clothes up here too. If Ronden's suitcase was still in the trunk of the Imperial, then he hadn't left the cabin voluntarily, and was probably dead. If it wasn't, he had met someone here and left, and the chances of finding him were slim.

O'Connor put his gloves back on again and forced himself to leave the warmth of the Nash. Just as he reached the Imperial, he heard cars coming up the lane. He pushed the button lock and the trunk opened.

A San Bernardino County Sheriff's Department patrol car and Dan Norton's T-Bird pulled up, but O'Connor scarcely spared them a glance. He didn't even notice the set of keys, the ones he would later identify as Jack's. All he knew was that he had found Gus Ronden, curled up in the space-age trunk, frozen solid and not bleeding from the bullet hole through his left eye.

PART II

THE BURIED

May 1978

19

"MY HERO IS AN ASSHOLE."

"Irene . . ." Lydia said in mild protest.

I said it sadly, not as a declaration of pride. I did not deliberately choose an asshole to be my hero. I discovered he was one in the way most of us make such discoveries: I got to know him.

Lydia, a friend since childhood, knew that I spoke of none other than Connor O'Connor.

At a distance, over years of reading my morning newspaper, I had come to admire O'Connor more than any other journalist, and that included Mr. Woodward and Mr. Bernstein. I was in J-school during the Watergate years, so that's saying a lot.

Both Lydia and I wanted to become reporters long before Watergate, and there was never any doubt in my mind that the newspaper I most wanted to work for was the *Las Piernas News Express*. The *Express* was the first newspaper I read—my father read its funny pages to me before I learned to read, then helped me with the big words when I started reading the articles themselves. By the end of grade school, I began looking for stories written by O'Connor, because I knew they would be good ones. I wanted to be like him.

When Lydia and I were in the fourth grade, we cajoled our neighbors into buying subscriptions to a self-produced newspaper that lasted one issue—Sister Mary Michael, catching us in the act of surreptitiously using the school's ditto machine for edition number two, suspended publication.

We were on the school newspaper together in junior high, high school, and college. She was often an editor. That was fine with me. I just wanted to be a reporter, to write like the man who had inspired this dream, whose words had lured me into my career. O'Connor.

The asshole.

"He's not, really," Lydia said.

I just shook my head.

"Well, I will admit you have a reason to be upset," she said.

Of course I had a reason to be upset. The legendary O'Connor had just stabbed me in the back.

"Would you be happier over in features?" Lydia asked.

I glared at her.

"No," she said. "Stupid thing to ask."

"You should be working in news, and we both know it."

"I don't want to have to deal with what you're putting up with," she said.

She meant the hazing I was experiencing in the newsroom.

My first job after college didn't take me to the *Express*. The *Express* only had openings in features, not news. My first question on any job interview was, "Do women cover hard news for this paper?" The answer was seldom an unqualified "Yes." At the *Express*, the answer was, "Once upon a time we did, but not now. Maybe someday, if we like your work in features, we'll give you a shot at it."

Someday wasn't soon enough, so I went to Bakersfield, where there was an opening in news on the *Californian*. As an added benefit, I could get away from the embarrassment I felt when I was dumped by a creep I had dated in college—the number-one inductee in my Dating Hall of Shame.

Lydia stayed in Las Piernas and took a job in features. Not so many years earlier, the features section was known as the "women's pages." Lydia wrote about cooking. The editor of the food section left the paper about eighteen months later, and the next thing you know, Lydia was promoted.

I'd been gone from Las Piernas for two years. Now I was back, and thanks in part to Lydia's help, I was able to land a job at the *Express*, too.

The first day I walked into the newsroom, I discovered with no surprise whatsoever that its occupants were almost all white (the sole exception: Mark Baker, who is black) and almost all old (I counted four who were under forty, and Mark was one of them). H.G., the city editor, was pushing sixty. He was a quiet, cynical man who smoked cheap cigars and whose rugged face seemed to have only two expressions: one indicated his usual state of unflappable, contemplative calm and the other mild, private amusement. He led me to my desk wearing the former and walked away wearing the latter. The cause of the change might have been the shock on the faces of his fellow newsmen. The leading caveman, who I later learned was known as Wildman Billy Winters, came up to me and said, "Honey, you're in the wrong room. Women write for features—down the hall."

I was ready to reply when the publisher, Mr. Winston Wrigley II, strode out of his office and said, "She's in the right room, Bill. And she's not the first woman to work here. Ask O'Connor—Helen Swan was one of his mentors. Ms. Kelly was taught by Helen—and Jack, too. That's more than good enough for me."

It took me a moment to recall that Helen Corrigan had been Helen Swan before she married. The journalism program at the college had three or four former staffers from the *Express* on the faculty. Helen was easily my favorite instructor at Las Piernas College.

Another favorite was Jack Corrigan, who had taught there, too. He had died of a stroke six months before I started working at the *Express,* while I was still up in Bakersfield. I hadn't learned of his death until after the funeral. Hardly able to talk for crying, I'd called Helen. She told me it was quick, that he had been among those he loved when it happened.

"Every morning after he turned fifty, the first thing Jack would say was, 'What a pleasant surprise,'" she said. "I suppose that was because he believed that anyone who had lived as hard as he did shouldn't take any new day for granted."

Thinking of her that first day in the newsroom of the *Express,* I vowed to find time to visit her.

My first weeks in the newsroom of the *Express* weren't especially happy ones. About a third of the men were openly hostile or patronizing. I heard the word "honey" more times than a beekeeper. Some, like Bill Winters, treated me as an occupying force, my desk a beachhead taken by the enemy. Others tried to pretend I was invisible. A few didn't seem to have any problem with it. Like H.G. and the news editor, John Walters, they were content to watch events unfold, and neither helped nor hindered me. That was fine. I figured anyone who didn't hinder me provided all the help I needed.

Then there were those who thought Winston Wrigley II had hired me to "improve the decor," as one of them put it—inveterate oglers, and generally the most repulsive guys in the building.

I wasn't held dear by most of the women staffers, either. I saw them every time I wanted to use the bathroom, because the newsroom of the *Express* had no women's room nearby. You didn't even need to step out into the hall to find a men's room. There was one right off the newsroom.

There were three women's bathrooms in the entire building: one downstairs, near classified advertising, where the staff taking calls for ads was entirely female; one upstairs, near the executive and business offices of the paper (where the typing pool and payroll clerks were female); a third on the same floor I worked on. Same floor, but reached through a maze of hallways, and at the far end of the large open room that housed the features department. It was as if whoever designed the building wanted to make sure that no one ever brought a tampon anywhere *near* the newsroom.

So I had to allow time for the hike when nature called, and it was easy to see that I was as much an outsider among the women in the features department as I was among the men in the newsroom. Whenever I entered this domain, there was a noticeable pause in the clatter of IBM Selectric typewriters all across the room. The faster a features reporter went back to typing, the more likely I thought we'd get along once the novelty of my situation wore off. Lydia was there, of course, but in those early days we went out of our way not to spend time together at the paper, so that we wouldn't be accused of being unprofessional or wasting company time. We seldom spoke more than a word or two of greeting to each other until after work. Later I learned that some of these women—most of whom had worked for the paper for several years—had previously tried to move over to the news side. They had been turned down. One more reason I was so popular.

I could have eased some of this, I'm sure, if I had gone drinking after work with the staff, or out to dinner with "the girls." The minute I was finished with work, though, I had to hurry home to my father.

I almost hadn't taken the job in the first place. I half-hoped Mr. Wrigley would tell me that he still didn't have a job opening for a woman in news, so that I could come back home to my dad and say, "I gave it my best shot, and it didn't work out, so I'm going to stay home and take care of you." But I'm not sure twenty-four hours a day of his rebellious daughter would have given my father much peace of mind, and my whole reason for coming back to Las Piernas—leaving behind a job I liked and a man I wanted to get to know better—was to make life easier for my father, to have time with him while I could. It did not seem likely that much time was left in that life.

My problems with O'Connor began on a Thursday, the day before I decided he was an asshole. Before then, he had merely been grim-faced and standoffish, but he was that way with everyone.

That Thursday, I had received permission from my city editor, H.G., to take a couple of hours off to take my dad to a doctor's appointment—a follow-up visit after his first major cancer surgery. Part of Dad's stomach was gone now, and he was weak and thin, but we were relieved: if the cancer had been worse, they would have taken the whole thing. He couldn't eat much, he got sick a lot. He slept most of the day.

He was alive. Recovering. I said this to myself whenever some insistent fear for him pushed its way into my thoughts. I said this to myself a lot.

I had an assignment that day, too, to cover a school board meeting. There are not many assignments that are lower level than school board meetings.

Despite delays at the doctor's office, I managed to get my dad back home before I needed to leave for the meeting. But the woman we had hired to care for him while I was at work called in sick. It wasn't the first time, and I wondered if I should just tell her not to bother coming back. The thought of going through the interviewing and hiring process again was so daunting, I put off making any plan of action for seeking a replacement for her.

I called my older sister, Barbara. She wasn't home. I reached her answering service—she has a business as an interior decorator. I left a message.

My father's voice, once so strong, able to command anything, called to me as not much more than a whisper. I hurried to his bedside.

"Barbara won't come here," he said. "It's because of your mother."

"Mom died twelve years ago. That's not much of an excuse for Barbara."

"Your mother died of cancer. Barbara's scared. Don't judge her so harshly."

"You think I'm not scared?"

"Oh, you are," he said softly. "And I'm sorry for that."

"Dad— I didn't mean to say . . ."

"Hush. You've got more Kelly in you," he said, taking my hand, "so I know you'll be all right. That's why I called you."

We sat in silence. Probably nothing else in this life had cost my father's pride more than asking me to come back home from Bakersfield. That gave me some idea of how frightened he was himself. I swore a silent oath: I would stop bitching about Barbara to him.

"I'm just going to sleep," he said. "Don't worry about me. You go on to work."

"Dad, it's only a school board meeting—"

"It's your job. Go."

Able to command anything, even at a whisper.

"Call the paper if you need to reach me," I said.

"I will. I promise."

But just before I left, he got sick to his stomach again. He had managed to get out of bed, so the bedding was okay. I helped him change into new pajamas and cleaned up the floor. I didn't want to go, but he insisted that the next time he was sick he wouldn't be such a damned fool, and he'd use the plastic basin on his nightstand instead of trying to get up.

"Go on, now," he said, "do your work. I'll die of guilt if you stay here."

"Don't talk about dying. Not from anything," I said.

"Go."

So I hurried to the meeting. I will admit that it did not hold my interest. My thoughts wandered to my own worries. I did manage to grasp the main issues under discussion. I rushed back to the paper.

I thought of calling my dad, but if he was asleep, I didn't want to wake him.

I called Barbara. I got the answering service again.

My father and I knew that Barbara would be fairly useless in this sort of crisis. Neither of us had expected her to develop an ability to vanish that would be the envy of a magician.

I wrote the story about the school board as quickly as I could. I got it in just before deadline. I went home.

My father was sick all night long. I dozed off on a chair in his room sometime before dawn.

Barbara never returned my calls, but just as I finished dressing, I heard a car pull up in the drive. I looked out the window, expecting to see her Cadillac.

Instead, I saw a cherry red '68 Mustang convertible. The woman who got out of it looked with disdain at the car next to hers in the drive—my Karmann Ghia. Her long gray hair was plaited into a thick braid. She wore blue jeans and an embroidered denim shirt.

My father's aunt, Mary Kelly. I felt myself smile.

I opened the door and said, "What's a night owl like you doing out and about so early?"

"Why haven't you come by to see me? Never mind—I know the answer to that. Are you late to work?"

"Not yet."

"Patrick called me last night, told me his helper was sick. I thought he meant you. Glad to hear it was just that other one. I don't think she was good for him, anyway. Why don't I take over for her?"

"Mary, that's generous of you, but—"

"But nothing." She looked me directly in the eye and said, "I want the time with my nephew. Patrick is dear to me."

"I know he is," I said, returning the look. "But you argue with him."

"Of course I do. He needs someone to argue with—he's a Kelly."

"Not now he doesn't."

"Irene. Are you going to stand there and tell me that in the weeks you've been home, you haven't argued with him once?"

She had me there.

She smiled and said, "Thought so. You can trust me not to do him harm, Irene. You know that."

"Yes, I do. Thanks, Mary. If it's okay with Dad, I'd certainly appreciate it. It would be—a great relief."

"Prissy Pants isn't anywhere to be seen, I suppose."

"I do fear that one day you'll slip up and call Barbara that to her face."

There was a certain glint in Mary's eye that made me quickly add, "That was not a dare."

Mary laughed and said, "Go on to work, I'll mind things here."

As on many another occasion, I prematurely felt pleased to finally be out of the woods. The woods are surrounded by quicksand.

Knowing that Mary would not abandon my father, I set to work on the next story assigned to me—an increase in the fees for dog licenses—with more enthusiasm than I had felt in some time. It wasn't that the story itself was anything glorious. The difference was that I could concentrate on what I was doing without worrying too much about the care my father was receiving.

I got some good quotes from dog owners, went back to the newsroom, ignored everyone there, and went to work. I had a story. I knew how I was going to tell it. Nothing else mattered. It felt good.

The newsroom was all but empty by the time I finished. Most of the men had gone across the street for the traditional happy hour at the Press Club. I filed my story with H.G.

Now that the story was in, I realized that I had been putting off going to the bathroom. I'd never make it to the women's room in time. I glanced around. No one was looking toward me. I ducked into the men's room. Fortunately, no one was in there.

I went into a stall and closed the door. I wasn't in there for more than the most important minute when I heard the bathroom door open and the voices of two men. Mortified, I pulled my feet up, not wanting to betray my presence.

I recognized the voices—O'Connor and Mark Baker. My first fears were allayed when neither of them tried the stall door. Then I realized what they were talking about.

"Why are you so down on her?" Mark Baker said.

"Because she's not much of a reporter."

"Man, that's cold."

"I'm going to ask Helen if she ever really taught her."

"You think she lied in her interview?"

There was a pause, then O'Connor said, "No, I doubt that. But you'll never convince me that Helen had much influence on anyone who turned in a half-assed story like the one Kelly turned in yesterday. And that wasn't the first weak piece she's filed. She doesn't put any effort into anything. She just does the minimum. The worst part is, she's giving every man who thinks we ought to have an all-male newsroom all the ammunition he needs for his arguments. She's a sorry excuse for a reporter, and she's going to make it more difficult for any other woman who wants the job."

"I think you're being too hard on her." Mark laughed, a little uneasily. "C'mon, man, you have to at least admire her guts. She's been taking shit from almost every dude in the newsroom."

"And giving it back," O'Connor said as they moved toward the door. "What a mouth she has on her. Who knows? Maybe Wrigley asked her to talk dirty to him . . ."

The door swung shut and I couldn't hear any of his other complaints or innuendoes.

I waited until I stopped shaking, or at least didn't shake quite so much. I went to the sink and washed my hands and face. At that point, I didn't care if Wrigley himself walked in on me.

Just about anyone else on the news staff could have said the same things about me, and I would have shrugged it off. But O'Connor, the man whose work made me want to be a reporter, thought I was lazy, foul-mouthed, and had slept my way into a job.

I lived past the initial few seconds when I felt an urge to cry. That, I decided, would really undermine any chance I had at surviving in the newsroom.

Close on the heels of this devastation was rage.

I took a deep breath, turned around, and marched out of the men's room. In retrospect, I'm glad only two people saw me at that moment, and that of any two it could have been, it happened to be Mark Baker and O'Connor.

I considered letting O'Connor hear just how foul-mouthed I could be, and telling him I learned all those words from his mother. Instead, I walked up to them, looked only at Mark, and said, "Thank you." Out of the corner of my eye, I saw O'Connor's suddenly bright red face. I heard him call my name as I strolled out of the newsroom. I kept walking.

The moment I was sure I was out of sight, I scurried like a rabbit through the warren of corridors to features. Lydia was still there, signing off on the last of her pages for Sunday's paper, which would be printed on Friday.

"Come with me into the women's room," I said. "Hurry."

She looked puzzled, but followed.

"Are you okay?" she asked. "You're kind of pale."

"I need a favor," I said.

"Okay, what?"

"Would you please get my purse from my desk? I just made a grand exit, and going back after it will ruin the effect."

"You quit?" she asked in dismay.

"No. Not yet. Get the purse and I'll buy you a drink. . . . Not at the Press Club," I added hastily. "How about the Stowaway?"

"All right." She started to leave, then said, "Why did you drag me into the women's room to ask me this?"

"I might go into the men's room, but I don't think O'Connor will go into the ladies'."

"What?"

"Long story, which I'll tell you over that drink."

We made our escape. The Stowaway is a small place, a quiet little restaurant with an ocean view. I called Mary from the pay phone when we got there, and found she didn't mind if I got back a little late.

I told Lydia my story over dinner and drinks. And declared my hero an asshole.

"And you know what the worst part of it is? He's right."

She tried to argue with me.

"Okay, so I'm not about to stop swearing for his sake, and I didn't sleep with anyone to get the job. But he's right about my work being half-assed."

"Irene, with everything that's going on . . ."

"No excuses, Lydia. None. You stuck your neck out to get me hired at the *Express,* and I've let you down."

"Baloney." For Lydia, that was red-hot cursing.

We sat in silence for a few minutes.

"What are you going to do?" she asked.

"Prove him wrong," I said.

20

O'CONNOR PACED ACROSS HELEN CORRIGAN'S LIVING ROOM FLOOR AS he listed his many grievances against Irene Kelly. Every now and then he found himself starting to address his complaints to an empty, overstuffed chair—the one that had been Jack's favorite. The loss of Jack somehow further fueled his ire. Everywhere he turned, there were sharp reminders of him here. Even the air itself—although Helen had quit smoking years ago, Jack hadn't, and the room still carried the scent of his cigarettes.

He wouldn't—and couldn't—talk of Jack. But he had a good deal to say about Ms. Kelly.

Helen patiently listened to it all.

"In the men's room!" he said, still not quite believing it himself. "And never a word to let us know she was in there. She should be ashamed of herself."

Helen smiled. "While you feel just dandy about your own behavior."

He sat down on the sofa beside her, suddenly tired. "No, of course not."

"Have you apologized to her?"

"I've tried. Twice. You may remember that I rarely work on the weekends—I made a special trip in today to try to talk to her."

"And?"

"I'm a mute version of the invisible man, as far as she's concerned."

"Honestly, Conn. Where's that famous persistence of yours?"

"The last of the O'Connors to beg on bended knee died in the fifteenth century."

"I'd love to ask all those generations of Mrs. O'Connors if that's true."

He laughed, then shook his head. "I don't know why Ms. Kelly irritates me so."

"I have some idea."

"She irritated you when she was your student?"

"Not at all. She and her friend Lydia were two of the best I've had in the last decade."

"Really? I'll grant you that her writing is all right, but we both know that's wasted on someone who won't do the work. In fact, it makes it worse—a waste of talent."

"Now, perhaps we're getting closer to at least one of the reasons she angers you. You already know she has talent."

"So what? Nothing I've read of hers indicates she's capable of really going after a story."

"Oh?" Helen reached for a copy of the *Express*. O'Connor recognized it as today's paper. He had a story on page one, but Helen flipped past that to a story on page five. She held it out to him.

"What?"

"Read the story about the dog license fee increase."

He did, then looked up at her in disbelief. "This isn't hers."

"If I were a gambler, I could make some money right now. Is it a good story?"

"Yes. But—"

"It's hers. No byline, naturally, on a story like this by a new general assignment reporter. She's not handling the sort of A-one stories you are."

"She hasn't earned that."

"No, I imagine she feels lucky that Wrigley the Second hasn't assigned her to the society pages. But that story is hers. I'd know her style anywhere."

He frowned as he reread the article. "May I use your phone?"

She handed it to him.

He dialed the newsroom and asked for the city desk.

Helen listened in amusement as he confirmed that the story had been written by Irene Kelly.

"I don't understand it," he said, hanging up.

"No, you don't."

"What's that supposed to mean?"

"Conn, how old were you when Jack took you under his wing?"

He thought of the day Lillian Vanderveer had given him a silver dollar. "Eight."

"Don't you think it's past time you paid that back?"

For a moment, he thought she might have read his thoughts.

Seeing his puzzled looked, she said, "You're a generous man, Conn. I could name a dozen examples of that generosity without having to work at it. And raising Kenny—"

"Kenny was fourteen when he came to live with me, Helen. I can hardly be said to have raised him."

"We'll argue about that another time. I'm not talking about your home life now. I'm talking about your professional life. As a newsman, whom have you helped along the way?"

He considered this in silence for some time, uncomfortable with the realization that while he had worked hard to be worthy of the lessons Jack had given him, he had never taken the time to show the ropes to less experienced reporters—something Jack had done not only with him but with others. He could look around the newsroom and see any number of men who had been helped by Jack—H.G., Mark Baker, and John Walters among them.

Jack had shared his expertise throughout his career, had been a teacher long before he joined the faculty at the college—as Helen had been, too. Neither of them had been much older than Ms. Kelly was now when they first encouraged O'Connor to write. That thought brought a sour reflection in its wake.

"Ms. Kelly doesn't want help from the likes of me. Especially not after she eavesdropped yesterday."

"I never knew you to be fainthearted before now, Conn. Show some spine."

"It's not a matter of being afraid of her."

"I'll tell you what," she said. "You're a good Catholic boy in need of some penance. I'm going to be your priest." She laughed her husky laugh. "You've sinned against Irene by opening your yap about her to another member of the staff. You agree?"

"Readily, but . . ."

"So, for that sin, your penance is to help her even if she doesn't want you to do so. Even if she never says, 'Thank you, oh wise and wonderful Mr. O'Connor'—help her."

"Look, Helen . . ."

"And for your far worse sin of showing rather sexist prejudice against her—something I never thought I'd see from you, Conn—you must learn everything you can about her. You claim she isn't working at being a reporter—do some digging. Find out why the hell not."

He was taken aback. "Do you think she's in some kind of trouble?"

"She may not be in trouble, but with only one story from her like this, I feel fairly sure that something's going wrong somewhere in her life."

"What do you suppose her problem is, then?" he asked irritably.

"Conn, I'd tell you if I knew. Hell, I haven't seen her since she left for Bakersfield. She called after Jack died, but I was too damned distracted with my own troubles to ask her about any of hers."

He looked again toward Jack's chair. He felt a tightening in his chest.

"Conn?"

"All right, Swanie," he said. "I'll try to help her."

21

WARREN DUCANE GLANCED AT HIS WATCH. THE YOUNG MAN HE HOPED to introduce to the others was a little late to the meeting, but Warren did not doubt that he would arrive. If the others would be patient, all would be well. Warren was in no hurry—he had waited for this moment for sixteen years.

He looked at the faces of those gathered around the long table in Zeke Brennan's law office. Zeke, Auburn Sheffield, and Lillian Vanderveer Linworth. So good of her to come. He had worried she wouldn't show, that the strain between their families might have endured even after his mother's death. He was pleased to discover that she didn't seem to feel animosity toward him.

The first five years after Todd was lost at sea had been the most hellish time of Warren's life, but he had managed to get through them without doing either of the two things that seemed most likely to him: killing himself or confessing to the authorities. Warren believed it was his cowardice and not his courage that had prevented either. That, and Auburn's friendship. Auburn had extracted weekly promises from him not to commit suicide, until a day when Warren finally promised not to try it without notifying Auburn first.

Warren's life had changed. He no longer attended social events. Once a man who could seldom tolerate being alone, he now found himself seldom able to tolerate the company of others. His reclusiveness was seen by others as an indication of his grief—after all, others would say, the man had lost most of his family in one evening. That much was true.

One person, however, could command his presence at any gathering: Mitch Yeager. He realized that Yeager was monitoring his moods, as well as making sure that Warren knew where things stood. He wasn't sure what Mitch Yeager had planned for him. Yeager, once confronted, said Warren had nothing to worry over, provided he wasn't overwhelmed by an urge to make accusations that couldn't be proved.

Yeager surprised him unpleasantly one day by telling him of a recording. The tape, Yeager said, made clear that Warren desired his parents' deaths and wanted to take over his father's company. Warren was assured that on the tape, Yeager would be heard adamantly refusing to be a part of any murder plot and advising him to seek psychiatric help.

Warren, reflecting on the work that had been done recently on the Nixon tapes, now wondered if specialists could determine that the tape Yeager secretly made of their conversation had been altered. And he was beginning to suspect that such a tape could not be used as evidence against him.

But no one in this room knew any of that.

Instead, he told Lillian what he had told Zeke and Auburn sixteen years ago, about the event that had led to this gathering. How it happened that Warren, leaving the Las Piernas Country Club after a luncheon engagement with Auburn, literally bumped into Yeager's wife Estelle, who was not too steady on her pins. He was surprised to see her in that condition. He later learned that on the days when her adopted son was in preschool, it was not unusual for her to polish off three martinis in the country club bar.

She smiled up at Warren and asked him if he could help her figure out where she had parked. He gave her his arm and guided her to her car. He offered to give her a lift back to her house, but she shuddered and said, "Mitch wouldn't like that much."

Perhaps because of the booze, or perhaps because she hadn't realized that Warren wasn't truly a friend of the family, before she settled herself into her BMW, Estelle invited Warren to her young son's fifth birthday party. Believing this was another appearance commanded by her husband, Warren accepted the invitation.

"I'd be pleased to come. I don't think I've ever met Mitch Junior, have I?" he had said.

"Oh, probably not—I try to keep him out of the way when Mitch has his friends over. And he's not Mitch Junior. We decided to call him Kyle. That was Adam's middle name. Did you know Adam—Mitch's brother?"

Warren shook his head.

"Oh. Well, he's been gone for some years now," she said uneasily, and looked away.

"I like the name Kyle," Warren said, mostly to distract her from what were obviously unhappy thoughts.

She smiled. "Me too. Besides, I could only cope with one Mitch in the house at a time." She blushed, then said, "Please don't ever tell Mitch I said that."

"I promise I won't," he said. She thanked him and hurried off, as if afraid of making further unguarded remarks.

Yeager had smiled tightly when Warren arrived at the party, his eyes glinting as he turned to his wife—who was perfectly sober on this occasion. Warren, correctly guessing that Yeager neither expected nor wanted him to be there, saw the color drain from Estelle's face, and hurriedly spoke before Yeager could lash out at her. "I hope you don't mind my only coming by for a few minutes—I can't stay long. Just wanted to wish your son a happy birthday."

Warren had by this time learned to hide his emotions, behind a bland look perceived by Yeager as a mixture of stupidity and meekness.

Yeager laughed and said, "What could be more important than my son's birthday? Come in and stay as long as you can."

Warren saw Estelle's relief and smiled.

He moved into a room crowded with adults. On the back lawn, a clown entertained a half dozen young children. Two young men were shooed away from raiding a table of hors d'oeuvres—Mitch's nephews, Eric and Ian, he later learned—then they sat pinching and lightly punching each other whenever their harassed Aunt Estelle wasn't looking. He thought they were probably in their twenties—too old to be acting so childishly.

Warren carefully set the wrapped gift he had purchased—a Tonka dump truck—at the base of a great pyramid of birthday plunder. He heard familiar laughter and turned toward it, smiling.

Todd! Todd's laughter. In the next instant, he told himself that was not possible, was it? But the memory of that laugh was so clear . . .

The sound came again, and he realized it was a child's laugh. He could not control the disappointment he felt, even as he chided himself for reacting as he did. The laughter of one boy as he ran from another, that was all. The laughing boy came to stand before Warren. A dark-haired, dark-eyed child.

The boy studied him, then glanced at the package Warren had added to the pile of gifts. "Did you bring that for me?"

"Are you Kyle?"

"Yes."

Warren wondered how the child had managed to take note of one among so many, but he said, "Yes, that's for you. Happy birthday, Kyle."

"What is it?"

"Something I hope you'll like."

"Me too," he said, and ran off to join the other children.

"Me too," a voice said behind Warren, startling him. He turned to see Mitch Yeager.

He wondered how long Yeager had been standing there. He managed to say, "You'll have to let me know if he does."

"Come and sit down—you look as if you've seen a ghost."

Warren laughed. "Thanks, but I'm fine. Just don't like to be in crowds anymore." It was something Yeager knew to be true of him. He saw Yeager's expression clear, so he added, "I really can't stay."

"No? Why is that?"

"I've got to meet with Auburn Sheffield this afternoon."

Yeager frowned. Mention of Warren's arrangements with Auburn never failed to irritate—and distract him. "I'll never understand what made you give that old geezer so much control of your money. I could have helped you do much better with it, and you wouldn't have to live like some beggar in the meantime. You sure you can't get out of that deal?"

"Not a chance," Warren said. Zeke Brennan had made sure that Yeager could never pry him out of the agreement. Warren shrugged helplessly, and again used the truth to distract Yeager. "I never was smart about money. That's why I went to Sheffield. And you said . . . I knew you didn't want contact with me."

Yeager looked quickly around him, then said in a low, angry voice, "Watch what you say and where you say it, Warren."

"Sorry."

"Try not to be such a stupid ass all the time."

Warren was pleased to make his escape shortly after receiving that bit of advice.

Warren had cleaned that part of the story up a bit when telling it today. His mother had once hinted to him that Lillian Vanderveer Linworth had run wild as a young woman, but you'd never believe it now. Now she was the picture of sophistication and restraint. He wondered if Katy would have matured in the same way. Somehow, he couldn't imagine it.

She heard him out, then said, "Do I understand you to say that you believe Kyle Yeager is Todd and Katy's son—that he is really Max Ducane?"

"Yes."

"Warren, that's impossible. He was adopted before Max was taken."

Warren looked over to Auburn.

"I was as skeptical as you, Lillian," Auburn said, "at first."

"At first . . . ?"

"The adoption records are sealed, of course," Zeke Brennan said, "and discreet inquiries by an investigator who works for us have led me to believe there is little chance of proving any of Mr. Ducane's suspicions in a court of law." He paused. "All the same, we were able to learn a few things."

"Things that led me to believe Warren hadn't just been imagining a resemblance to Todd," Auburn said. "One was that the judge who approved the adoption had long been suspected of being—let's say, indebted to Mitch Yeager and his associates. Another was that no one—absolutely no one—other than a few of Mitch Yeager's closest henchmen claims to have seen the child until after Max was taken. Strangely, all of the Yeagers' servants were given a paid leave of two months—something Yeager had never done in the past. Yeager claimed it was to allow time for his new family to become acquainted, but rumor has it that when the servants returned, there were plenty of adjustments still going on."

"Even natural parents may need more than two months to adjust to a new infant in the house," Lillian said.

"Yes," Auburn agreed. "But Mrs. Yeager, who had supposedly taken care of the child during those months, suddenly did not know how to manage his care—a nursemaid was hired in January."

"Forgive me, I don't like to speak ill of the dead, especially of someone who was once a friend. But the truth is, Estelle was one of the biggest lushes in town. It could be that Mitch finally had to accept the fact that a drunk shouldn't be the only one caring for his son."

"You misremember that bit of history, I think," Auburn said. "If you think back, I believe you'll realize that Estelle was just starting to drink around the time when Kyle started preschool."

Lillian shrugged. "It makes no difference to anyone now."

"Have you ever met Kyle Yeager?" Warren asked.

"No, I don't know the boy."

"It isn't surprising that you haven't met him," Auburn said. "Mitch has never introduced his adopted son into local society. He was sent away to boarding school at the age of nine, and the moment he graduated, packed off to New Hampshire—to Dartmouth. He wasn't brought home for holidays or vacations. I know a few people who met him briefly at Estelle's funeral—he was only eleven when she died. Why did Mitch hide him away?"

"Mitch started a new family not long after that," Lillian said reasonably.

"Not everyone can manage to make a new wife comfortable with the children of a first marriage."

"Mitch and his son have been at odds for years now, Lillian."

"Where have you been, Auburn? It's called the generation gap. 'Don't trust anyone over thirty,' remember? Even that's a little dated, I suppose. Now it's the Alliance for Survival telling them to 'question authority.' "

"Perhaps that's all it is. Perhaps it's the natural set of differences between child and parent. However, when you see Kyle, I think you'll better understand why Warren and Zeke and I feel as we do."

"Does he really look so much like Todd?"

"No. Nor does he look exactly like a male version of Katy. But there is something of each of them in him, I'd say."

"Auburn," she said, her voice a shade more brittle than before, "what you have offered as proof is hardly enough to justify the sort of accusation that goes hand in hand with this . . . this notion of Warren's. You're saying, then, that Mitch arranged the murder of the nursemaid? That he kidnapped my grandchild? It makes no sense. Why would he do such a thing? He has the resources to adopt any number of children. Why would he go to such lengths?"

"You will forgive me for asking this, Lillian, but isn't it true that you were once close to Mitch?"

"Yes," she said, without hesitation. "Shall I name a few of your youthful follies now, Auburn?"

He raised a hand, in the gesture of a fencer acknowledging a hit. "That won't be necessary—we haven't got all day."

"Indeed not. Now . . ."

"Your pardon, Lillian. I only bring up your ties to Mitch Yeager because I know that he never forgives anything he perceives to be an injury or an insult."

"I'm fully aware of Mitch's ability to hold a grudge."

For a moment, Warren saw what he thought was another small change in her composure—as if she had briefly reminisced and found the reminiscence unpleasant.

Then she looked directly at Warren and said, "Auburn is right, Mitch doesn't forgive easily. Mitch had a high school crush on me. I don't think I meant much to him at all—certainly not enough to bring him to murder anyone or kidnap a child decades after our little teenage romance had soured. Your accusations, however, were they to become known, would displease him to a degree that might lead him to respond in ways . . . well, in ways I don't like to contemplate."

"By the time he learns of my plans," Warren said, "I'll be beyond his reach."

She studied him for a moment, then said, "And so your plans include leaving me here to deal with his wrath? He's very touchy about his reputation these days."

"No. I'm not asking you to be involved in this in any way. I just wanted you to know . . . in advance. I didn't want my plans to come as a shock to you."

"Exactly what are your plans, Warren?"

But before he could answer, the intercom in the conference room buzzed. Zeke Brennan answered it and said, "Yes, please show Mr. Yeager in."

22

AUBURN SHEFFIELD HEARD THE SOFT, SUDDEN INTAKE OF LILLIAN'S BREATH as a young man wearing a suit and tie entered the room. Her reaction to Kyle Yeager was unhidden for only the briefest moment, as (knowing Lillian) Auburn had anticipated it would be. He looked down at the stack of papers on the table before him to hide a smile while the introductions were made.

When he looked up again, Kyle was saying, "Yes, of course we've met. Good afternoon, Mr. Sheffield."

He was tall and had an almost military bearing, shoulders and back straight. Equally unusual in young men of his age, his dark hair was cut short. His brown eyes reminded Auburn of Katy, although he could not imagine that hers were ever so solemn. He could not say that the rest of his features strongly resembled those of either parent—or as Auburn reminded himself, of the people he assumed were Kyle's parents—but he had not known Todd well. Warren believed Kyle's smile was nearly identical to Todd's. Auburn wondered if Warren had seen that smile since Kyle was five.

Kyle waited politely for Lillian to be seated before he took a seat himself.

Zeke Brennan spoke first. He thanked Kyle for coming and asked if he had been able to find the time to read the photocopied newspaper articles he had been given when Auburn visited him in Hanover.

"Yes, sir." He glanced uneasily at Lillian and Warren. "I'm sorry," he said. "That must have been a horrible time for both of you."

Warren looked away, but Lillian said, "Thank you. Yes, it was terrible."

"About sixteen years ago," Zeke said, "Mr. Ducane set up a trust. The trust came about in a rather unusual way, and its conditions are also unusual." Zeke paused. "At that time, Mr. Ducane met a young boy whom he believed to be his nephew, Max Ducane."

"Sixteen years ago? Oh." He looked hopefully toward Lillian. "So—the kidnapper was caught?"

"It's not quite so simple, I'm afraid," Lillian said kindly.

Warren started to speak, but Zeke intervened, motioning to him to wait. "At the time he saw the boy, it was, for various reasons, impossible for him to prove his belief that the boy was his missing nephew. But he made arrangements so that when the boy reached adulthood, he would be eligible to receive a substantial sum of money. There would be two conditions that the boy—now a young man—would need to meet. He would be required to sever ties with his adopted family and to legally change his name to Maxwell Ducane."

Auburn watched Lillian and saw her surprise. Kyle, however, seemed no more than politely interested, and waited for Zeke to go on. But it was Warren who broke the silence.

"The boy I met was you, Kyle," he said.

"Me?" He laughed uneasily. "No . . ."

"Yes. You are my nephew." He said it with sureness.

"Mr. Ducane, I . . . I'm sorry, I don't mean to upset you, but I don't really understand how that can be possible. My adoptive father and mother told me many times that . . ." He lowered his head, then murmured, "They both told me many times that my mother was a prostitute. My father was one of her customers. So unless your brother . . ." He glanced up at Lillian, blushed, and turned to Zeke as he said, "No, I'm sure he didn't. There are adoption papers. I have always felt grateful, because if I hadn't been adopted by the Yeagers, I probably wouldn't have survived. My birth mother died two months after I was born, and I probably would have died with her. Instead, I was raised by a wealthy couple, had the love of my adoptive mother, and received privileges no person of my birth could have dreamed of having."

"Are you fond of Mitch Yeager?" Auburn asked.

Kyle gave him a fierce look, then answered, "What does that have to do with anything? He took me in. Fed and clothed me. Paid for my education."

"My God," Lillian said softly.

"I don't claim that there is any affection between us," Kyle said. "I am sure I was adopted because my mother—Estelle, I mean—wanted a child so badly. I loved her, and I have no doubt that she loved me."

"Mitch Yeager abused her," Auburn said. "And before Estelle had been dead a month, he married a woman thirty years his junior and soon fathered three children with his new wife. He did all he could to forget your existence. You don't owe anything to Mitch, not on your own behalf, and certainly not on Estelle's."

Kyle looked as if he would object, then seemed to change his mind. His fists clenched, then opened. He said, "Whatever you may know or not know about my mother—I respect her memory, so I'm not going to share gossip about her or her husband with you."

"I meant no disrespect to her," Auburn said. "But I do know that she felt trapped in her marriage. She didn't believe she had the means to escape it, but I think she might have been pleased to know that someone offered you a chance to separate yourself from Mitch Yeager. And twenty million dollars ought to allow you to cut the ties."

"Twenty million!"

"That's part of it," Warren said. "Twenty million, as well as some real property worth—"

But he had recovered his composure. "As . . . as tempting as that offer is . . . and as sorry as I am that your nephew was taken from you, I'm afraid I'll say no."

"Kyle . . ."

"No, Mr. Ducane," he said angrily. "My birth mother may have been for sale, but I'm not." He stood up and said to Lillian, "If you'll excuse me, ma'am—"

"Kyle," she said, "are you in a hurry to return to Hanover?"

"No, but . . ."

"I take it you aren't staying with Mitch?"

"No. Mr. Brennan arranged a hotel room for me here in town."

"I wonder if you might have dinner with me this evening, at my home."

"If you're trying to convince me—"

"No, I knew no more about any of this than you did. But I am planning a small dinner party—nothing fancy, mind you—and would love to get to know you a little better before you head back home again. And I have a few photographs of Estelle that I would like to give to you. But if you have other plans . . ."

"No, I don't." He studied her for a moment, then said, "Forgive me for asking, but do you really have photos of her?"

"Yes. We went to school together."

He looked around the room. "Are these gentlemen invited as well?"

"Only if they promise not to say a word to you about Warren's offer."

Warren raised a hand as if taking an oath. "Not a word."

"And they must agree to allow us time to ourselves."

"A promise," Auburn said.

"Forgive me, Mrs. Linworth," Zeke Brennan said, "but I'm afraid I have a previous engagement."

"Another time, then, Mr. Brennan. And you, Kyle?"

"All right," Kyle said. "Yes, thank you—what time shall I be there?"

"Let's say seven. No need to dress up—would that be all right with you?"

"Yes, ma'am."

"Fine. Auburn can give you a lift from your hotel, and I'll have my driver bring you home whenever you decide to leave. I'll see you all at seven."

She rose, and the men did as well. She left the room.

Kyle stared after her.

Auburn laughed. "Lillian has always been a force to be reckoned with, Kyle."

Kyle smiled. "I can see that." He turned to Warren and said, "I'm sorry, I didn't mean to be so rude to you. Your offer is very generous, but I'm just not comfortable taking it."

Warren shrugged. "I won't force it on you, but I'd appreciate it if you'd give yourself a few days to decide anything definite." He raised his hands, palms out, as if in surrender. "I won't say more about it unless you tell me you want to talk about it again."

"All right. I'll think about it, but I don't want you to get your hopes up. Deal?"

"Deal. See you this evening."

Zeke Brennan showed Kyle out.

When they had left the room, Warren sat down with a sigh. "Thank God Lillian was here, or I don't think he'd have anything more to do with us."

"Yes," Auburn said. "And if I were you, Warren, I'd search through your mother's scrapbooks to see if she took any photos of Estelle. It won't hurt for you to have a few offerings of your own."

The moment she was home, Lillian called Helen Corrigan.

"Swanie, it's Lil. Look, I have an emergency on my hands and I need your help."

"What's wrong?"

"Nothing's wrong, I just need you to see someone. Long story, which I'll tell you this evening. You're coming to dinner here at seven—dress casually. And bring Conn—warn him this is not for the newspaper, all right?"

"Okay, Miss Mysterious."

"Miss—oh! Helen, you're a genius."

"I am, am I?"

"Well, I think so. Know a good-looking single young woman who might be able to join us? No hussies—someone sharp, who has the ability to converse. You must have met someone with half a brain during all those years of teaching."

Helen laughed. "Good grief, Lil."

"I'm serious."

"All right. Let's see . . ." There was another laugh, and she said, "If she can make it, I've got the perfect candidate."

"Swanie, I've known you too long. I know that laugh. You're up to mischief."

"I just want to give Conn a challenge. But don't worry. I'm bringing someone you'll adore. But you have to be the one to invite Conn, and don't tell him that I'm bringing anyone else along with me, all right?"

"Helen . . ."

"Lillian, I promise I'll keep these two pups of mine in line."

"Is she a newspaperwoman?"

"Yes."

Lillian sighed. "And she won't write about this evening?"

"No. Have I ever let you down?"

Lillian's voice softened. "Oh, Helen, forgive me—I'm in a tizzy. No, you've never let me down, which is why I always end up coming to you when I'm in a fix. See you at seven."

23

E VEN BEFORE THE DINNER DEBACLE, THE OLD FART WAS MAKING ME crazy.

Dinner Debacle. Men's Room Incident. Byline Blowup. I was starting to think of my life in the newsroom as a series of B-movie titles.

On the Monday after the great Men's Room Incident, O'Connor walked by my desk and said in an overly loud voice, "Great story about the dogs, Kelly."

Kelly. Not Ms. Kelly or Miss Kelly. This probably isn't something a lot of people would even notice, but it seems to me the naming business is part of deciding who is on the team and who isn't. Last name only, you're on.

I was still angry with him, though, and decided I was going to ignore him, but he ignored me first. He kept walking.

Later, he waited until Mark Baker was standing near my desk, walked up to him, and said, "What I said the other day was crap. I'd appreciate it if you would forget every word of it."

"No problem," Mark said, and looked at me.

I pointedly turned my attention back to the black IBM Selectric on my desk. I was writing a story on Las Piernas High School's astounding success in a drill team competition. Not a story that would win a Pulitzer, but I wasn't ashamed of it, either. I had found a quotable kid who made all the difference.

Lydia told me that O'Connor had been asking her a lot of questions about me. That bothered me. It bothered me even more that she had answered most of them. I asked myself why I cared and couldn't come up with a good answer.

Then came the Byline Blowup.

A week after the Men's Room Incident, I was working on a story about art supplies. I hit upon this one by accident—I was waiting for my father to finish his latest round of chemo, when Aunt Mary became irritated with my anxiousness and told me to take a walk. So I strolled down toward the emergency room. Sure enough, there was someone there with bigger problems than mine: the mother of a teenager who had started hallucinating in art class, then passed out. So far, he hadn't regained consciousness.

"He doesn't use drugs," she said. "I don't know what caused this."

At first I chalked this up to the "not my Johnny" syndrome—no love is so blind as parental love.

But some of his friends came by to wait with her, and after talking to them for a while, I became convinced that her son might be the clean-and-sober type after all. I got a few details from his classmates about what had been going on just before he started freaking out.

I took down the mother's name, address, and phone number. When the doctor came out to talk to her, she let me listen in. I asked him if chemicals in use in the art class could cause that reaction.

"Conceivably," he answered. "We won't know the answer to that until his blood work comes back from the lab."

When I got back to the paper that afternoon, I contacted a woman in the purchasing department of the school district. I had been trying to build trust with her; she had been a minor source whom I had hoped to go to for more in the future. I hadn't really planned on hitting her with anything big so soon, and at first I feared that asking for a list of art supplies purchased for one of the local high schools might be more than she was willing to risk. The records were ones I could demand to see, but I preferred not to do that—taking that approach only builds future resistance.

When I told her about the episode in the emergency room, though, she asked me to meet her at a coffee shop in forty minutes. When she arrived, she was carrying a big stack of photocopied invoices.

"I have a son that age," she said, and left without anything more than my thanks.

I don't know how O'Connor learned I was working on that one, but he did. I found a note on my desk in his odd, nearly indecipherable scrawl: the name and phone number for the Center for Occupational Safety in New York, an organization that could give me information about the hazards associated with art supplies.

I marched over to his desk and said, "Do you think I'm so helpless, I can't do my own research?"

"No," he answered.

I was trying to come up with something truly disagreeable to say to him about not being able to buy me off with little favors, when, as if reading my mind, he added, "I know you have no intention of accepting an apology from me, but we do have to work together here. Just use that information if you can, toss it if you can't. I'm sure you'll do what's best for the story."

So I used it. I felt proud of the result of my work: a story that revealed that a local high school was using dangerous chemicals in art classes with poor supervision and inadequate ventilation, and had come close to causing one student's death.

H.G. praised me. John Walters praised me. Wrigley II praised me. This last had me all puffed up with pride until Wrigley also handed off the story to O'Connor for a rewrite and basically took it away from me.

To my further irritation, O'Connor complained about that before I could, then he went on to make it a much stronger story, discovering that a teacher at another school in the district was out on permanent disability, probably as a result of exposure to the same chemicals. I hadn't dug deep enough, or in enough directions.

I felt angry with myself over that, and had just decided that he deserved all the glory anyway, when I learned about his next campaign on my behalf. Before the shouting between O'Connor and Wrigley was over, everyone in the newsroom knew exactly who had made sure I'd get my first byline in the *Express*.

When Lydia asked me—in front of O'Connor—how it felt to have that byline, I told her that I would find it less embarrassing and painful to fall flat on my ass while crossing a busy street.

My only comfort was seeing the frown that remark brought to O'Connor's face.

Lydia frowned, too, as she watched him walk away. "What's wrong with you?" she asked.

"He's way too involved in my career, thank you. I want to earn my bylines on my own. And I don't want to share them with that jerk."

"He's not. You ask me, you're the one who's being a jerk. He said something out of line, and he knows it, and besides, that was before he knew about your dad."

I felt as if I had swallowed a block of ice. "What?"

She had the look on her face that a person gets when he or she suddenly figures out that a really good idea was actually a really bad idea. Shouldn't fill blimps with hydrogen. Shouldn't dive headfirst into unknown waters. Shouldn't tell everyone at work about the health problems of your best friend's father. She broke eye contact.

"You told him about my dad?" I asked, horrified.

"Not much . . ." she said faintly.

Translation: too much.

I tried to explain that although I knew her intentions were good, I'd rather that details about my personal life—and my father's health—did not become the property of newsroom gossips. When she insisted that O'Connor wasn't the type to spread gossip, I reminded her about the Men's Room Incident.

"Are you ever going to let that go?" she said.

The real problem was that I would have preferred O'Connor's respect rather than his pity.

That was a Monday. The next day, I came into the newsroom and went to my desk without hearing one double entendre, without a single "honey," without so much as a sour look. In fact, the whole room became quiet, then everyone managed to be really busy all of a sudden. Shades of the features department. I felt uneasy, and that unease only increased when I happened to surprise a look of sympathy on Wildman Billy Winters's face.

O'Connor had told them.

Over the next few hours I received several offers of help, compliments on the art supply story, and friendly reporting advice from veteran newsmen who had wanted nothing to do with me for weeks. I managed to get through the day without letting my temper get the better of me, mostly because I was afraid that if I started to express my true feelings about their sudden solicitousness, my brief career in journalism would be over.

On Thursday, while I was out grocery shopping, Aunt Mary took a phone call. Helen Swan, calling to ask if I'd come to dinner with her at Lillian Vanderveer Linworth's palace. Mary said she knew I'd be delighted, and asked what I should wear.

To say that she then forced me to go would be unjust. I didn't really want to see Helen at a party at some Lady Bountiful's mansion, but I surrendered when Mary told me she had decided I must accept the invitation. I knew what sort of contest of wills I was in for if I resisted Mary, and at that moment I didn't have that much fight left in me.

* * *

Helen greeted me warmly when I picked her up at her home. It was the first time I had been there since Jack had died, and I found I could feel his presence—or maybe the lack of it. She talked cheerily as she gathered up her purse and turned off lights, but I found myself staring at an old chair, thinking of Jack Corrigan telling a story at one of the parties they had held for the staff of the college paper.

We stayed only long enough for her to grab her keys and lock up the house. That we didn't linger was okay with me.

On the way to the Linworth mansion, she stressed that no matter what happened or what I heard, we were at a social event at the invitation of one of her good friends, and writing about it was strictly forbidden.

As soon as Lillian Linworth's decrepit butler opened the door to the royal library, I saw O'Connor. I almost turned on my heel and went right back out. The only thing that kept me from doing so was seeing that he was as shocked as I. We both looked at Helen. She was smiling and saying, "Conn, what a pleasant surprise . . ."

His brows lowered, and his mouth made a flat line. Then he said, "I doubt it is either a surprise to you or pleasant for Ms. Kelly to find me here."

Mrs. Linworth seemed deaf to all of that, and introduced herself to me as Lily.

I was supposed to call her majesty by her nickname?

Then she said, "Conn, would you please serve as bartender this evening? What will you have, Ms. Kelly?"

I asked for a vodka and soda on the light side. I thanked O'Connor when he handed my drink to me, sipped it and found that it was about four times as strong as I would have made it myself.

He was drinking scotch on the rocks. While Helen and Lillian chatted across the room, he stood next to me in awkward silence. He made the ice in his glass swirl rhythmically with a slight motion of his wrist, and studied the cubes as if they might roll over like the goodie inside an eight-ball toy, the answer to some problem printed on one side. There was something in his face that either hadn't been there before or which I hadn't perceived. Not anger or frustration . . . I had seen plenty of each of those in the last few weeks. Sadness, maybe? Maybe he was missing Jack.

I found myself feeling guilty for continually snubbing him, and thinking that I ought to apologize to him for being such a pain in the ass, but before I could say anything to him, three more people were ushered into the room, and O'Connor moved forward to greet them.

We were introduced to Auburn Sheffield, Warren Ducane, and Kyle Yeager. I went straight toward the one who interested me most: Auburn Sheffield.

Not that the others weren't interesting. Kyle Yeager was cute in a Clark Kent kind of way, and Warren Ducane struck me as one of those men who find themselves adrift in their middle age. But Auburn—not every day you get a chance to talk to a guy like him.

I had grown up hearing the story of his rebellion against his family. His home was named in honor of it, after all. In fact, there was a scenic turnoff in the road leading up to Auburn's Stand that was known to anyone who had spent his or her adolescence in Las Piernas. Local make-out hot spot. Not that anybody ever took this Catholic girl up there.

Within a few moments, Auburn was regaling me with little-known facts about Las Piernas history, including plenty of great dirt on the Sheffields—his uncle Hector was apparently a dangerous lunatic. The Sheffield name was on a street, a subdivision, a library, an elementary school, and a number of buildings downtown. They had made a fortune selling ice cream, and, he said, stayed cold and rich ever since. Auburn had to be seventy or eighty years old, but I've encountered plenty of people half his age with less life in them.

Warren Ducane was deep in conversation with O'Connor, who was making drinks for the new arrivals, and Helen was talking to Lily, so it wasn't too surprising that Kyle Yeager joined us. Auburn pulled him into the conversation.

"Kyle just graduated from Dartmouth, Irene," Auburn said, with so much pride, I thought maybe this was his godson.

"Congratulations," I said. "What did you major in?"

I heard a familiar voice say, "Now, *that's* an original question."

O'Connor had brought their drinks over, and handed them off as he said this.

I felt my face turn red.

"But a natural question," Kyle Yeager said quickly. He smiled at me. "I'll answer it, even though you're going to think I'm a nerd when I tell you. I majored in computer science, with a minor in geography. If it had been up to me . . ."

"He's being modest," Auburn said. "He didn't tell you that he has also been accepted into Dartmouth's prestigious business school, Tuck."

"Must make your old man proud, Kyle," O'Connor said, in a tone I'd never heard him use before. "Preparing to take the reins of Yeager Enterprises?"

I saw a quick flash of anger on Kyle's face, then he smiled. "I'm surprised to discover a man in your profession who knows so little town gossip," he said to O'Connor—calmly, if you ignored a certain martial light in his eyes. "I'm a bastard, so I have no idea if my 'old man' would be proud, ashamed, or even if he's alive to hear what's become of me."

"I meant no offense—"

"Of course you meant offense," Kyle said, his tone just as pleasant as before. "As did I. Although I'm a little better informed than you, it seems—I know you're a reporter for the *Express*, and that you've never liked my adoptive father much. But just in case you are preparing a story—ownership of Yeager Enterprises will be handed over to Mitch Yeager's own children, not to me."

O'Connor smiled, too, more genuinely than Kyle had, I thought. "Well, now, that only proves that Mitch is as big a fool as I've always thought him. No, no—no need to get fired up again. Ms. Kelly is already angry at me, and I can't take on the whole of your generation. But just so you know, tonight is off the record—Helen's retired, and Irene and I have promised our hostess that neither of us will be writing about anything we hear this evening, Mr. Yeager." He then excused himself and moved over to where the others were standing.

Helen was staring at Kyle with an odd look on her face, Warren looked as if he were about to be ill, and Lily seemed bemused. When I glanced at Auburn, I thought the two of them might be in on some private joke. This seemed even more likely when he said, "Excuse me, I need to speak to our hostess," and moved away.

Next to me, Kyle said, "I'm sorry—I didn't know you were a reporter."

"According to some people here, I'm not much of one," I murmured.

"Who? O'Connor?" he said, "Well, why should his opinion matter so much? It doesn't to me."

I should have felt comforted by this ready championship, but I heard some echo of my own indignation in his words and found I didn't really like the way it sounded.

I glanced over at Helen, who seemed to be watching us more than listening to those who stood near her.

"You know what, Kyle? I shouldn't have said that. The truth is, it does matter to me. He's a great reporter, someone I've admired forever. I guess that's why it bothered me when he criticized my work. But I deserved a lot of what he said, and he's apologized more than once, so I suppose I shouldn't keep harping on it. I need to move on, let it go."

"That's not always easy."

"No," I laughed. "But I'm making an enemy out of him for no real reason. I'm sorry if he's written something negative about your dad—"

"Don't be. Since we're being honest about things, I'm not my dad's biggest fan. And O'Connor never wrote anything untruthful about him, as far as I can tell. Listen—is it true that you aren't here as a reporter?"

"Yes."

He seemed to brood over something.

"Why geography?" I asked.

"Pardon?" he said, coming out of his reverie.

"I know why computer science is a hot major, but why the minor in geography?"

He smiled. "Professor George Demko. I took his class just because it fit my schedule in my freshman year. Contagious enthusiasm, I guess. My two fields of study aren't as far apart as you'd think."

For the next few minutes, he talked to me about navigation and Polaris submarines and atomic clocks and the launch of something called a GPS satellite, which he said would someday be able to prevent anyone from ever being lost. Eventually he lost me—or noticed he had lost me—and laughed and said, "Sorry—now you do think I'm a nerd."

"Not at all. Why apologize for being intelligent? I'm just sorry I couldn't keep up with you."

"I suppose I got on to GPS because I've been thinking about the Ducanes. Do you know their story?"

"Warren's family?" I shook my head.

"His father, mother, and his brother—Todd—were all lost at sea."

"That's awful," I said, looking over to where Warren stood, staring up in a melancholy way at a portrait above the mantel, a painting of a beautiful young woman who somehow looked familiar.

"That's Kathleen," Kyle said of the portrait. "Katy, I think they called her. Mrs. Linworth's daughter, who died in the same boating accident. Her daughter was married to Todd Ducane. Do you really not know this story?"

"No."

"Well, I didn't, either, until Mr. Sheffield gave me some articles to read. Actually, O'Connor and your friend Helen wrote many of them. A sad story."

He told me about the night the *Sea Dreamer*'s passengers and crew disappeared, and Max Ducane was kidnapped.

Standing in the same room with members of both families, seeing the portrait of a vivacious young woman who was near my same age when she died, knowing the reporters who wrote many of the stories—for a few moments, I was simply stunned, and overwhelmed with sympathy for Lily Linworth—who was transformed in my mind from "her highness" to a mother who had lost both child and grandchild—and for Warren Ducane, whose air of being a lost soul was now perfectly understandable. So much devastation wrought all at once would have been difficult for any family to cope with. Twenty years had passed, but they were twenty years without loved ones. Life would not, could not, have been the same after that night.

Within a few moments, though, my reporter's instinct began to give me an itch. "Kind of strange, don't you think?" I said to Kyle. "I mean, the kidnapping taking place on the same night?"

"You don't know how strange it gets," he said with feeling.

We were called in to dinner before he could say more. Helen sat between Auburn and O'Connor, while I was placed between Kyle and Warren, and Lily presided at the head of the table.

There was only small talk while we ate the meal—leg of lamb, which I must admit was gloriously prepared. We had just been served a dessert of fresh strawberries and whipped cream flavored with a hint of Grand Marnier when Kyle said to Lily, "Irene is too young, of course, but did Mrs. Corrigan and Mr. O'Connor know your son-in-law and daughter well?"

All the clatter of silverware ceased abruptly.

Lily said, "They knew Kathleen very well, yes. I haven't broken my promise to you, though. I'm sure they're wondering why you mention her."

"Because he resembles her," Helen said, openly staring at him now. "Especially when you get angry, Kyle. Or—I don't know—seem especially determined."

"What is this all about?" O'Connor said irritably.

"Mr. Ducane has a theory that I am his lost nephew," Kyle said. "He's such a believer in this theory, he offered me a substantial financial incentive to start calling myself Max Ducane."

This announcement caused an argument to break out between O'Connor and Warren Ducane, consisting mostly of O'Connor calling Warren a fool and Warren calling O'Connor a busybody who had no say in the matter. It hadn't gone very far when Lillian Linworth said, "I won't say I'm without my doubts, Conn, but I'm inclined now to think that there is at least a possibility that Warren may be right."

"Lily," O'Connor said, in a far more gentle tone than the one he had been using with Warren, "I can see why you would *want* it to be true, but that doesn't mean it is."

"I'm enjoying being present while you refer to me as if I'm not," Kyle said. "But I should point out to Mr. O'Connor that I haven't said I'd accept Mr. Ducane's offer."

"He said no to us," Auburn said.

"How coy," O'Connor said.

"Lily, if you don't mind," Helen said, "I'll ask Irene to take me home now. I'm—I'm not feeling well."

"Oh, Helen, I'm so sorry," Lily said. "I never meant for you to be upset by this, or to—"

"I know, dear. I know. Irene? Do you mind terribly if I cut this evening short?"

"Not at all—"

"I'll take you, Helen," O'Connor said. "I wouldn't want Miss Kelly to miss any opportunities."

"What are you saying?" I said.

" 'Substantial financial incentive'—isn't that the way you put it, Mr. Yeager? Or is it now Mr. Ducane?"

I stood up, grabbed my bowl of strawberries and whipped cream, and pitched it at his face. He managed to get an arm up, which deflected the bowl enough to keep it from hitting him, but its contents kept sailing and reached the target. The bowl broke.

O'Connor didn't say a word. He just stood up and left the table. I was horrified, but tried to keep my voice steady as I said, "Let me know how much that bowl cost," to Lily, which for some reason made Warren and Kyle laugh and applaud.

"Ms. Kelly, I'd be pleased to replace that bowl," Auburn said.

"No, really—I—and his suit. Oh God. His suit."

"You leave these small problems to me," he said. "It will give me pleasure to be of service to you. Just worry about getting Helen home, all right?"

Before I fled, Kyle asked for my number. I gave him my number at work.

As I drove Helen home, I began feeling worse and worse. She didn't say anything until I pulled up in her driveway.

"It's Jack, you know," she said then.

For a moment, I thought she was hallucinating, seeing the ghost of her dead husband.

She looked at me and said, "Conn's problem is Jack."

"I don't understand . . ."

"He's not angry with you, Irene. He's just angry and upset because Jack died. They were . . . oh, theirs was some wild combination of relationships. Father and son, older and younger brother, mentor and protégé, friends, coworkers, drinking partners . . . and a real pair of hell-raisers. They used to back each other up in brawls—Jack would start the fight and Conn would finish it. Barbarian, some would say, but uncivilized or no, it was just one more part of the bond between them. Jack did a lot for Conn, but it's just as true—perhaps truer—that Conn looked after Jack. Conn was one of the people with us when Jack had the stroke. I don't think Conn has known what to do with himself since that moment. It has made him surly as hell. I've never seen him behave in the way he's behaved lately. I'm worried about him."

We sat in silence.

"What can I do, Helen?"

"Try to be patient with him. He'll probably make that as hard as possible. But, Irene—oh, what he can teach you if you'll let him! More than Jack or I could ever teach you. He's got the gift. Lately, though . . . his writing is never poor, mind you, but his writing hasn't been at its best since Jack died—except once."

"The art story."

"Yes. When he worked with you."

"Not exactly *with* me . . ."

"Don't quibble."

"I keep insulting him. I . . . I don't think he brings out the best in me."

"Why are your stories better lately?"

I laughed. "Okay, you've made your point."

We fell silent again, then I said, "Helen, what about Warren Ducane's claim?"

She sighed. "I don't know. Lily is right, but a few facial features and expressions hardly prove he's Max. Still, there's something . . . something about him that truly does remind me of Katy. Wishful thinking, probably. If Lily and Warren both accept him as their heir, he'll be the richest young man who ever asked you for your phone number."

"Aren't there blood tests or something that can be done?"

"If Katy or Todd were alive, they might be able to show something—although I believe those tests can only exclude people who aren't parents, not prove that a person is the parent. In any case, it doesn't matter—Katy and Todd are dead."

"Kyle said their bodies were never found."

"No, they weren't. But believe me, the world would have heard from Katy by now if she were alive."

Early the next morning, a press release was issued by the office of an attorney named Zeke Brennan. Kyle Yeager was legally changing his name to Maxwell Ducane, and would instantly become the wealthiest young man in Las Piernas. The release stated that he would not be available for interviews.

O'Connor tried calling his hotel. He had checked out.

Lillian Vanderveer Linworth would only say that she looked forward to getting to know the young man better, but had no plans at present to change her will. Mitch Yeager refused to comment.

Kyle—or Max—didn't call me.

Twenty-four hours after the announcement, O'Connor filed a story noting the disappearance of Warren Ducane.

24

"WHAT ARE YOU DOING?" SONYA YEAGER asked her husband. "ARE you cooking?"

Mitch Yeager looked at her with disfavor. "No, I'm standing here in my robe and slippers at the stove, holding onto a pan, because I lost my way to the bathroom."

"Mitch, I really get that you're angry."

He clenched his teeth. She had gone to one of those est seminars a year or so ago and hadn't been able to talk right since. *I get. I get.* Werner Erhard was the only one who got—he got a lot of money for telling people that they couldn't leave the room to take a leak while he insulted them. Now, there was a racket. A fucking cult. Mitch had let Sonya go to get her out of his hair for the weekend. When she wanted to keep enrolling in other courses, though, he refused—he didn't want his kids talking like she did now.

"A man gets up to make a glass of warm milk for himself," he said. "What's it to you?"

"We have a cook. It doesn't look right for you to do stuff like this yourself."

"Who the hell is looking? And who the hell cares if they do?"

"I get that," she said, nodding her pretty blond head. "But I could have done that for you. All you had to do was ask."

"I didn't want to trouble you," he lied. He suppressed an impulse to tell her that she'd be better off spending her time with the peroxide bottle, because her dark roots were showing. She took comments about her hair to heart, and he didn't want to have to deal with one of her crying jags.

"It wouldn't have been any trouble, Mitch. I like doing things for you."

Problem is, you only do one thing well, he thought to himself. Aloud he said, "Go to bed, Sonya. I'm fine."

"Okay, I get that you want to be alone."

"Right." Well, if Werner could teach the bimbo that much, maybe the money hadn't been wasted after all.

He poured the milk from the pan into a glass and took it into the larger of his two studies. He flipped a control on the Lionel train set that occupied most of the center of the room and idly sipped his milk as he watched the black steam locomotive make its way around the elaborate circuit laid out for it.

He had bought this train for that little shit who was now calling himself Max Ducane.

He tightened his fist in anger, thinking of the boy giving up the name he had given him. He had bestowed his brother Adam's middle name on him, and now he rejected it. Rejected the Yeager name, too.

Mitch sat down in an overstuffed chair, took another sip of milk.

Some of his earliest memories were of Adam, warming a pan of milk in the small, sloping kitchen of the tiny ramshackle house downwind of the San Pedro canneries, a rented home in an area that reeked of fish processing (to this day, Mitch could not eat a tuna fish sandwich), a few blocks from the wharves where fishing boats were anchored. His father worked on boats if matters grew desperate, but mostly made a few dollars playing cards with sailors and longshoremen.

When Mitch had been a toddler and troubled with sleeplessness, Adam used to prepare warm milk for him. Warm milk was one of Mitch's few pleasant memories from those days.

It was typical of Adam, who was seven years his senior, to act as both mother and father to Mitch, although both parents were living at that time. Their mother spent the hours she wasn't drinking passed out on the sofa or floor. Their father, Horace Yeager, avoided the house as much as possible.

Horace had hoped that eloping with Myra Granville, the only child of his wealthy employer, would earn him advancement in the company, if not a life of luxury and leisure. Instead, the old man fired him.

Horace then sent his wife in to plead their case—she was informed that her father would not speak to her unless she was no longer living with Horace Yeager. The birth of a grandchild—thought by Mr. Yeager to be a surefire way to soften his father-in-law's heart—only brought about a notice from an attorney, informing his wife that she would not inherit a penny.

By the time Mitch began school, Horace Yeager was living in another house with another drunken woman in another part of the country. Mitch's mother told other people Horace was dead. Within a year, this was true—he was killed by an unknown assailant after he had won a large amount of money in a card game. The money was missing.

Not long after their father abandoned the family, a remarkable person appeared at their door. Mitch remembered looking in awe at the long black car that pulled up in front of the house. A liveried chauffeur came to the door and offered to take Adam, Mitch, and their mother "home." Mitch was six years old. Adam, at thirteen, was less impressed, but no less eager to live at the mansion so often pointed out to him by their father.

Their mother's response to this olive branch was to reply that the chauffeur could tell her father to go fuck himself. The man's startled expression indicated that he was more surprised to hear a woman use such language than the boys were, but he said nothing back to her. He pulled a white envelope from his vest, placed it on the kitchen table, and left.

The envelope was embossed with their grandfather's monogram. His mother stared at it, then said to Adam, "Open it and read it to me. I don't want to touch the damned thing."

There was not, as expected, a letter. There was nothing in the envelope but money.

Their mother was more than happy to touch the money. Mitch saw Adam palm five dollars out of it before he handed it to her. Adam used the five dollars to make sure they ate. The rest, their mother spent on booze.

The chauffeur continued to come by once every two weeks, always bringing an envelope. He always handed it directly to Adam. Adam and Mitch, forbidden to mention their grandfather, began referring to him as "the chief" and spent every night before the chauffeur was due worrying that the old man might change his mind about supplying money to boys he did not know and a woman who despised him.

Adam once took a greater share of the cash for their household expenses, and their mother beat the tar out of him for it. Mitch tried to help Adam fight her off, and got a black eye for his trouble.

Adam repaid her by walking to the landlord's house and tipping him off about the chauffeur's schedule. The landlord learned to come by the house to demand the rent within minutes after the chauffeur appeared.

Adam contrived in this way to keep a roof over their heads and food on the table. Mitch gathered scrap wood for the fireplace, the sole source of heat for the house. That winter, it wasn't enough—Mitch came down with a horrible cough. Fearing pneumonia or tuberculosis, Adam used the five dollars to pay the doctor to come to the house, and to buy the medicine he prescribed for bronchitis.

As he lay recovering, Mitch worried over the burden he had placed on his brother. Somehow Adam still managed to feed them, even if it was an odd assortment of foods that now graced their table. They seemed to have a whole case of tomato soup, and a crate of oranges. To Mitch's surprise, a week later there were two chickens and a rooster in a pen at the back of the house.

When asked about it, Adam said, "Chickens make eggs. Makes more sense to own chickens than buy eggs, right?"

"But how can we afford them?"

Adam winked and said, "I got Ma to let go of some of the chief's wampum."

Mitch always suspected the story of his mother's generosity was untrue. Adam was leaving the house late at night and not getting back home in time for school. When he arrived just before dawn with a new blanket for Mitch's bed, Mitch knew Adam had stolen it.

Adam eventually admitted it, and that he had stolen food as well.

"And don't be mad at me, kid," he said. "We gotta stay alive, don't we?"

Despite a few close calls, Adam was able to avoid being caught. All the same, Mitch lived in constant fear that Adam would be sent to jail. He didn't know what he would do if his big brother wasn't there to help him.

Over the next three years, Adam's thievery changed how they lived. It also changed Adam. Mitch saw him become tougher, more sure of himself. Always big for his age, at sixteen he looked as if he were twenty. He led a gang of other boys now, a group Mitch longed to join. "When you're a little older," Adam would promise. "But I'm going to need me a guy with an education to help out, and you won't be getting up for school if you're out all night with me and my boys."

"You're smart," Mitch said. "And you don't go to school."

"There's different kinds of smart. You stay in school."

His mother would occasionally sober up enough to complain that she wasn't going to have a pack of thieves living under her roof. Adam, now taller and stronger than the child she had beaten, no longer hid his contempt for her. He told her that he didn't want to live with a drunken old whore, either, but they'd have to make do. If she didn't want to live with a thief under her roof, she could damn well move.

One day she seemed to take him at his word. She told Mitch to pack up his belongings, that they were going to find another place to live. He saw that she already had an old valise half-filled with her own clothing.

"What about Adam?"

"We're leaving Adam. That's what."

"I'm not going anywhere with you. I want to stay with Adam."

She slapped him. "Now, you get in there and pack, or I'll persuade you in a way you won't like."

To her dismay, Adam walked in the door just then. "Persuade him to do what?"

Mitch told him.

Adam looked furious for a moment, then said, "You need a drink to steady your nerves."

He poured a glass of rye and stood by and watched as she downed it, then poured another. When she hesitated, he pushed the glass closer to her. She began crying, but drank it.

When she had downed three drinks, Adam said, "Mitch, you go into her room and unpack her bag. I'm going to take a walk with Ma and talk things over."

Two days later, Mitch came home from school to find a policeman talking to Adam on the front porch, and felt certain that his worst fears had come to pass. He wondered if his mother, who had been sulking, had reported her own son to the police. He felt a surge of rage at the thought, rage that allowed him to overcome his dread and approach them.

The policeman's face was sorrowful, though, and Mitch noticed that Adam seemed solemn as well.

"It's Ma," Adam said. "She's dead."

"What happened?" Mitch asked, working hard to hide what he felt—a vast relief.

"She was in an accident," the policeman said gently.

"She was hit by a streetcar," Adam said. "She tripped and fell right in front of it. Nothing the conductor could do."

"Were you there?" Mitch asked.

"No," Adam said, watching him carefully.

Mitch thought he was trying to convey some message to him. He tried to read the look and asked, "Was she drunk?"

"Now, sonny, that's no way to think about her," the policeman said.

Adam said, "Of course she was."

"What's going to happen to us now?" Mitch asked.

The policeman, not knowing his real fear, said, "You'll be fine now. Don't you worry."

"Grandfather is on his way," Adam said. "We're going to live at his place."

"Together?" Mitch asked.

"Always," Adam said, ruffling his hair. "I'm not ever going to let anyone keep me away from my little brother."

Their grandfather, Theodore Granville, proved to be a shrewd man, but not, so far as his grandsons were concerned, an unkind one. He was amused to learn that the boys referred to him as "the chief" and preferred they call him that rather than Grandfather. He had made most of his money in oil, and later in real estate, and had interests now in a variety of concerns. He was by no means a blue blood—a self-made man who had worked his own way out of poverty as a wildcatter in the oil fields, he was, Mitch came to see, not above using any means he could to gain an advantage over a rival.

For the most part, during those early years, he did not want to be troubled too often with his grandsons, an arrangement that suited the boys well. Adam cautioned Mitch that they had to do whatever the old man asked, because this good fortune could be lost as easily as it was gained. Mitch thought the chief had taken too strong a liking to Adam to kick them out, but he heeded Adam's warnings all the same.

So they met the chief's requirements that they be clean and well dressed and quickly learned any rule of etiquette he asked them to adhere to, and did not interrupt any gathering he held or cross the paths of his guests. He more than met their needs for food, clothing, and shelter. He provided them a generous allowance.

Adam, more easily bored than Mitch, soon involved himself in bolder adventures outside the house. Having learned that he had a knack for theft and leading toughs, he was unable to give up either pursuit. He managed to talk his grandfather into buying him a sleek boat. Later, his grandfather served as Adam's business partner, sharing in Adam's profits as a rumrunner.

His grandfather suffered setbacks during the Depression, but kept up appearances as much as possible. While still a teenager, Mitch learned that Adam and his grandfather had a number of shared businesses, not all of them legitimate, and each began to prepare Mitch to take his place in these concerns.

Mitch moved in higher social circles than his brother, and even gained entry to households where his grandfather had been snubbed. Not every door was open, of course. He drew the eye of Lillian Vanderveer, whose parents disapproved of him, and did their best to keep them apart.

Adam married a girl who had more looks than sense. At the chief's insistence, Adam and his wife continued to live in the mansion. Two sons were born to them—Eric in 1934, and a year later, Ian. Mitch doted on them as if they were his own. Life seemed good.

Then, in late 1935, Adam's luck ran out—he was arrested.

The chief used all his power, but to no avail. The papers made hay out of Adam's arrest and trial. The old man was heartbroken. He died on New Year's Day, 1936, and it later seemed to Mitch that he should have taken that as a sign of how terrible the year would be.

The milk was tepid now, and Mitch set the glass aside. He shut the train off and moved toward his desk. He stood for a while looking at two of the framed photos there. One was of his brother, Adam, at about the age of twenty—smiling, looking cocky as always. The other was of Mitch's adopted son, taken when he was nine—the boy who was calling himself Max Ducane now, the boy who had so recently and so publicly renounced his ties to the Yeagers.

He reached for the photo of Kyle and stared at it.

Why had he ever given him any name at all? What did the little son of a bitch think would have happened to him if he hadn't been adopted? Instead of letting him suffer the fate he deserved, he had given the brat his own name, and his brother's name, and his family name, and much more. More than he himself had ever had as a boy. Put the little asshole through college—Ivy League, too. That wasn't cheap.

He spent a moment wishing his own kids were half as bright as Kyle, but unfortunately they got their brains from their mother.

That didn't make him feel any better about Kyle. He had, of course, always had his own reasons for anything he did on his adopted son's behalf, but what did that matter?

The kid had betrayed him, plain and simple. Fuck him, and fuck Warren Ducane, too.

He placed the photo in a desk drawer, facedown.

He picked up the phone and dialed a number.

"Have you found him yet?" he asked.

He did not get the answer he wanted.

Nothing would help him sleep tonight.

25

O'CONNOR MANAGED TO AVOID ME FOR A WEEK. I DIDN'T DO ANYTHING to make that difficult for him. He was covering Warren Ducane's disappearance—thought to be voluntary—and the Max Ducane story, so he wasn't in the newsroom much.

He found time to interview Bennie Lee Harmon, who had been convicted of killing two Las Piernas prostitutes back in the late 1950s. Harmon's death penalty conviction, along with those of about a hundred other prisoners, had been commuted to life with the possibility of parole by a Supreme Court decision in 1972, and now the state parole board had set this "model prisoner" free. O'Connor did his best to get someone to give a damn about the killer's release, but most of the people who had investigated the case were no longer living, nobody from the hookers' families showed up at the parole hearing, and apparently Harmon didn't plan to return to Las Piernas, so the story quickly made the journey to the back pages and then faded completely.

I faded, too. I was back to being the reporter's equivalent of an errand boy.

That mindless sort of work was all right with me, because the weekend had been a bad one for my father. That occupied my thoughts and my time far more than any need to smooth things over with O'Connor and took away any urge I might have had to turn in the best story anyone had ever seen on the new style of parking meters being installed downtown. Dad was doing better by Wednesday, though, and I was able to start focusing on my work again.

I drove out to the southeastern edge of the city on Friday morning for what I was sure would be my biggest job challenge yet—making an interesting story out of a "grip and grin" piece. My red-hot assignment was the groundbreaking ceremony for a shopping center.

"You're a girl, you should be able to write it the way the ladies want to read it," said Pierce, one of the old codgers. He thought he was being encouraging.

By Las Piernas standards, it was going to be a big mall, taking over one of the only remaining stretches of farmland in the city. I had dreamed of coming up with a more interesting angle—something about the last farmer in southeastern Las Piernas County watching sadly as his way of life was paved over by a parking lot. Not quite the loss of paradise in the old Joni Mitchell song, but close.

Unfortunately, the previous owner, a guy named Griffin Baer, had been dead for a few years, and according to the lawyer who had handled the sale for his heirs, Baer hadn't lived on or personally farmed the land. In fact, Baer had been living miles away—in an oceanfront mansion—when he died. The last of the noble farmers had turned out to be a rich absentee landowner, and the sale of the land to developers nothing more glamorous than the end of a family squabble over the inheritance.

There went my angle.

The ribbon cutting when the completed mall opened next year would be a bigger story. I was just on hand to watch a few businessmen and politicians pretend to use a shovel.

The ground was actually already "broken"—rough grading had been done, and stakes here and there indicated where the next phase would begin. I found the construction supervisor, a gent by the name of Brian O'Malley, who in the course of introductions mentioned to me that he knew a Patrick Kelly.

"That's my dad's name."

"Did your father go to St. Francis High School?"

"Yes, he did. You, too?"

"Yes. And you've something of the look of him. How is Patrick these days?"

"Fine," I lied.

He wrote a phone number on the back of his business card. "That's my home number. Have your old man give me a call."

"I'll do that," I said.

He made sure I had a good seat for the ceremony. The event went the way every groundbreaking ceremony went. Speeches promising everyone that building a mall would lead to prosperity for the community. Guys in suits who hadn't had their hands on so much as a gardening trowel in decades taking turns posing with a "golden" ceremonial shovel.

The paper hadn't bothered sending a photographer, so I had to take the photos myself. I did the best I could, but I doubted any of the subjects would be asking if they could buy prints.

I interviewed the city council members, the mayor, the developer, the district manager for one of the department store chains. Not one of them said anything original.

I hung around long after the "show" was over—mostly, I admitted to myself, to avoid going back to the newsroom. While I dawdled, the suits drove off and the actual construction crew started to go to work. An idea struck me, and I approached Mr. O'Malley again.

"Mind if I talk to some of the real 'groundbreakers'?" I asked.

He laughed and said, "That would be a first." He studied me for a moment and said, "They'll tease you unmercifully and their language isn't fit for a lady, but I suppose a lady reporter is used to such things."

"I'll be all right."

"I'll bet you will." He started introducing me to the crew.

They asked to see my credentials to prove I was a real reporter, and one asked me if Las Piernas was so hard up for high society that guys in hardhats now qualified. Others immediately and accurately accused me of playing hooky from the office and gave me some good-natured razzing, asking if I really couldn't think of anything better to do than pester them when they were trying to get some work done. But when they saw I was serious about writing about them, they began to tell me more about their work, their equipment, and best of all, themselves.

A backhoe operator was showing me the accuracy with which he could scrape a layer of earth, when there was a screeching sound that was something like an amplified version of fingernails on a blackboard. It made my shoulders bunch up.

We turned toward the source of the sound—a giant bulldozer excavating an area a few yards away. I heard O'Malley shout for him to hold up.

By the time I walked over, the bulldozer had backed away.

"It's a car," O'Malley said.

"I thought this was farmland," I said, snapping a photo. "It wasn't a junkyard, was it?"

"No, but back before all these environmental laws started being passed, people buried their trash all the time."

"Have you found a lot of other buried trash out here today?"

He frowned, then called the backhoe man over. Before long, an old, smashed-up blue Buick was uncovered. "From the fifties at least," one of the men said.

"We've delayed enough," Brian O'Malley said. "Let's get the damned thing out of here."

One of the men had moved to the trunk and had been working at opening it. When he heard Brian's order, he said, "Wait, maybe there's a briefcase full of money in here." He managed to free the latch, but as he opened the trunk, his face went white. "Holy shit, Brian . . ."

We moved to take a look.

"People," I said, staring in disbelief at the pile of bones and dried sinew before me. Two loose hollow-eyed skulls stared back from within.

"Fuck me, there goes the schedule," Brian said in disgust. Then remembering my presence, said, "Don't you dare tell your father I said that in front of you."

26

THE BODIES WERE SORT OF MUMMIFIED—DRIED OUT, YELLOWISH-BROWN sinew clinging to bone. Both skulls damaged. A man and a woman, judging from the long, stained dress and the man's suit and knot of what looked like it had been a tie near one skull. Piled on top of each other, woman below. And small shiny objects glistened here and there. I took a deep breath and forced myself to take a few more photos before Brian slammed the lid of the trunk closed.

"That's it for now, my girl. . . ."

I know that a true newshound should have been begging him to open it again, but I was really kind of relieved to have the bodies out of sight. I felt a little shaky.

"Doug!" he called to one of the burliest men. "You make sure no one else touches this thing, all right?"

"Sure, boss."

Brian walked back toward his trailer, and I followed him, struggling to keep up with his long-legged stride.

"Did you see what was in there?" I asked.

"You're kidding, right?"

"I mean, besides the remains."

He stopped walking.

"Diamonds scattered over the floor of the trunk," I said.

"Or cut glass," he said, but he didn't believe that any more than I did.

I was ready to fight H.G. for the right to keep covering the story, had my arguments all lined up, and figured I'd have to take them to John Walters—the news editor—and Wrigley as well. But H.G. surprised me. He heard me out as I told him the basics of the situation, then, after a moment's silence, he said, "I'm going to let you stay on this on your own for now. But you are going to have to make some promises to me right here and now—you're not going to hold information back from me, and you're going to call for help if you need it."

I readily promised. "Actually, if I'm staying here to watch what goes on— do you think I could ask for help from someone who might be able to learn more about the property's past? Someone who won't try to take the story from me?"

He laughed. "Sure. Have anyone in mind?"

"Lydia Ames."

"She's in features."

"Trust me. We did a story in our college paper about the university annexing some property—Lydia did all the county record work." I gave him the details I had on Griffin Baer, which weren't many. "The car looks as if it's from the 1950s, but maybe it wasn't new when it was buried. Lydia can find out how long Baer owned the property, and talk to the heirs to learn who lived out here if he didn't."

"If features can spare her from her work there, okay. If not, I'll find someone else and make him keep his mitts off your story."

I reassured him that I had a roll of dimes and that I'd call back if I needed any other help, then hurried back out to the pit that held the car.

Most of the outside of the car was so dirty, you couldn't see much inside. I doubted that absolutely clean car windows would have helped much, because the front windshield had collapsed, and most of the passenger area of the car was filled with dirt, too. The grill was smashed in, making it look as if the car had been in an accident, but maybe that happened during the burial process. There were no license plates on the car.

The police arrived, ending my snooping. Uniformed officers, and not much later, two guys in suits. One of the suits was a broad-shouldered, gray-haired man I guessed to be in his fifties, with a pleasant, easygoing manner. He introduced himself as Detective Matt Arden. He ignored my presence almost immediately and focused his attention on Brian and the workmen.

His partner was tall and slender and far more reserved. He was younger than Arden, probably about forty. No one would have called him handsome. His features were harsh, but he had big, beautiful, intense brown eyes. He looked over the group of us who stood near the car, taking note of everything and everyone. Eventually he was looking at me. I could almost hear him singing to himself, "One of these things is not like the others . . ."

"Irene Kelly," I said, holding out a hand. *Las Piernas News Express.*"

His face kept its oh-so-serious expression, but he shook my hand—nice, firm handshake. "Philip Lefebvre, Las Piernas Police Department."

I heard the mimicry of the form of my introduction and smiled. Taking care with the pronunciation of his last name, I said, "Detective Lefebvre, you can't do much for the folks in the trunk of the car, but you can save a life today."

"Yours?" he said, and smiled. He had a chipped front tooth. For some reason, I found it endearing.

"Oh yes. I was sent out here to cover the groundbreaking of a shopping center. I don't suppose I need to tell you how much this changes things."

"These victims are giving you a career opportunity, then?"

I don't think I flinched—outwardly, anyway. "Don't pretend they might not do the same for you."

He gave a Gallic shrug. "We don't even know if this is a homicide yet."

"I suppose they could have crawled into the trunk of a car, closed it, and even completed their murder-suicide pact inside the trunk, but I don't know how they got the gun out of the car, or buried the car while they were in it, for that matter. Especially not in their evening clothes. Hell, I don't even know how they got their arms back down at their sides after they shot themselves."

"How could you know they were shot?" he asked, then noticed the camera in my hand. "Have you been taking photographs of the car and its contents?"

"Yes. And I don't know for certain about the shooting, or even if that was the cause of death, but they do have wounds on their heads that look like bullet entry and exit wounds."

He sighed. "Are we bargaining here, Ms. Kelly?"

"Irene. And let's not make it any more sordid than it already is—Phil."

That won a laugh from him. I saw Matt Arden look over at us in surprise.

"Look," I said. "I'll make double prints and give you a copy if you promise not to pass them around to other members of the media. But please don't make me stand a thousand miles away from whatever is said and done here."

"All right," he said, "but you won't be in the middle of things, either. You don't try to eavesdrop when I talk to my partner, and you don't touch *anything*—have you been touching the car?"

"No. The only ones who have touched it are a few of the guys on the crew, and most of them were wearing work gloves. I can point out the ones who did make contact with the car, if you'd like."

"Thanks."

He spent time talking to the people I indicated, leaving me to watch—with a uniformed officer at my side—from nearby, but not close enough to overhear his questions or the crew's answers.

A crime lab technician arrived, and a few minutes later, the coroner's wagon pulled up. The police had some photos of their own taken. I began to wonder if mine would be of any value to Lefebvre after all.

After the technician was finished with his initial work on the trunk, there was the tricky job of removing the bodies. I heard Lefebvre speak sharply to one of the coroner's assistants. I caught one word of what he said: "Three."

Three bodies? I was fairly sure I had only seen two, but I hadn't really been able to study the contents of the trunk in the way the police investigators did.

The assistant brought out a small body bag. A child's bones?

Other media started arriving just as the car itself was placed on a flatbed tow truck. Eventually, a lieutenant from the Las Piernas Police Department arrived, and after conferring with Arden and Lefebvre, made a brief statement to the press—remains thought to be human had been found, an investigation into the matter was now under way, but no further comments would be made until the coroner's office had been given a chance to study the remains. Lots of questions were shouted at him, but he didn't answer any of them.

I glanced at my watch. I had a deadline to make and lots of questions to ask, too, but now that the lieutenant was on the scene, Lefebvre might not be able to answer any of them. I wondered if any ID had been found on the bodies. If not, I wanted to get back to the morgue at the newspaper—where articles and photographs and past issues of the paper were kept on file—to see if I could find out who disappeared during the years when that Buick was new.

I found myself thinking about O'Connor. Every year, he wrote about missing persons. He had been writing these stories since 1956. A Jane Doe had been found beneath the Las Piernas fishing pier the year before—and never identified. Someone had nicknamed that woman "Hannah." O'Connor covered the story of the discovery of her body in 1955, then on the anniversary of the day they found her, wrote the first of his "Who is Hannah?" articles. They were some of the most powerful stories I had ever read.

They weren't just about her, but about all the John and Jane Does—and about the other side of the equation, missing persons cases. Now, more than twenty years later, Hannah's case was still unsolved, but O'Connor had helped police to close a number of other cases through that column. If anyone in Las Piernas knew who was still missing, it was O'Connor.

Wrigley would probably give this story to him.

I told myself it could go to worse hands than O'Connor's. If he got it instead of Wildman or Pierce, at least it would be given the care it deserved.

I still didn't like the idea of losing it to anyone, though.

Maybe if I showed O'Connor a little respect, we could start over. I had nothing to gain from being at odds with him, and a lot to lose. For one thing, the paper wouldn't keep me on if I continued to make life miserable for one of its stars.

I looked at my watch again and sighed. A badly thrown bowl of strawberries had probably screwed up my chances of seeing this story through.

27

O'CONNOR GLANCED AT HIS WATCH. SHE HAD ALREADY BEEN AT THE scene on her own for several hours now. Would he be able to convince Wrigley before deadline brought her back here?

Wrigley tapped a pencil against his desk as he looked at the cardboard box O'Connor had set on it. Written in felt pen, in a hand few others could decipher, was a single word, a name: Jack.

Wrigley had thought it said "jerk."

O'Connor was watching the pencil, not the box. He had learned, over the years, that he could anticipate the outcome of any meeting with the publisher of the *Express* by gauging the speed of this tapping. Slow tapping, he was inclined to favor your proposal. Rapid tapping, you were doomed.

This was somewhere in between. Outcome uncertain.

"Tell me, Conn—do you happen to remember shouting—*shouting*, mind you—at me a few weeks ago?"

"Well—"

"Loud enough for the entire newsroom to hear you?"

"Yes, sir."

"Sir, is it? I believe I was Win not five minutes ago."

O'Connor said nothing.

"What were you shouting at me about?"

"You wanted to give Ms. Kelly a skirt on that school chemicals story."

"A generous mention, noting her contribution, at the end of a story you had reworked and greatly expanded. That seemed wrong to you."

"She deserved a byline. Her enterprise brought the paper's attention to the matter. That's all I was saying."

"Oh no, that wasn't all. I remember it almost word for word, Conn, because I may catch an earful from Wildman once in a while, but you don't tend to be a shouter. That impressed me. Made me see the error of my ways.

You told me it was clear that H.G. and John and I were 'wasting her talents'—wasn't that it?"

With a sinking feeling in the pit of his stomach, O'Connor nodded.

"Yes. And you said she could handle tougher assignments than the ones we were giving her, and let me see, now . . . what was it?" He faked concentration, then opened his eyes wide. "Oh yes! How could I have forgotten?"

"How indeed," O'Connor murmured.

"Yes, this was one of my favorites—you said that 'the next time Kelly stumbles onto something big'—that was a little insulting to her, wasn't it, Conn? Stumbled? But you said that if she stumbled onto something big, we ought to let her run with it. Well, Conn, she has stumbled onto something huge."

O'Connor leaned over and picked up the box.

"Put it down," Wrigley said. When O'Connor hesitated, he said in a gentler tone, "If you don't mind listening to me for a few more moments, put it down, please."

O'Connor set it back on Wrigley's desk.

"Despite all that lecturing, you want me to give you the story she's working on now. Is that it, Conn?"

"You know how hard I've tried to find out what happened that night. How hard, all those years ago, I looked for some sign of that car. Prayed I'd find it. Two decades, Win."

"Yes, I do. And if I doubted there was a God, this alone would restore my faith, Conn. Because not only has it been found but the green reporter I've kept hoping you'd take under your wing was right there when it was discovered."

"Proof of the devil, more like." He frowned. "I think I've just heard an echo, though. Have you been talking to Helen Swan?"

"So what if I have? She's an old and dear friend of mine."

"Look, it's my own fault, I admit it, but—Kelly won't have a thing to do with me."

"I wonder if that's true."

"It's true. She can't stand me, and lately . . ."

"You can't stand yourself."

O'Connor looked away.

"I'll give you a choice," Wrigley said after a moment. "You go out to the site and ask for her permission to involve you in this one—or wait until she comes back and let me ask for you."

"Win—"

"Take it or leave it, Conn."

O'Connor stood. "I'll be on my way to talk to her, then."

Wrigley smiled. "Don't forget your box."

"I haven't, Win. Not for a long time."

She was talking to Lefebvre.

That alone was nearly enough to send him back to the car. It had taken him months to establish rapport with Lefebvre, who was an ace detective, but known as a loner in the department and not overly fond of the media. And Lefebvre was *smiling* at her. Jesus. She didn't need his help.

Here he was, overly warm in his suit, his shoes and trousers covered with dirt from hiking in the long way, holding a cardboard box under one arm—looking like a peddler, and for what? To tell her that Jack had seen the car buried? Might as well leave her a note.

He was about to turn back when she saw him. Lefebvre saw him, too. Lefebvre's smile quickly went to a frown.

He watched her face, could swear that for just a moment she looked dismayed—maybe even hurt? No, that couldn't be. And then she was smiling and beckoning to him.

A brave sort of smile. Lefebvre, far from a fool, was looking between them now.

O'Connor thought about the box, about Jack, and put on one of his own brave smiles as he trudged forward in the soft dusty earth to where they stood.

"Phil," Irene said, "you must already know the best reporter on the *Express*. O'Connor will be taking over from here. Thanks for everything."

"Wait!" O'Connor and Lefebvre protested in unison. (Had she, some part of O'Connor's mind wondered, really called Lefebvre *Phil?*)

"I'm not taking over a thing," O'Connor said. "It's your story. I'm just here to ask if I might be of help."

Lefebvre was looking at the box. "Why are you carrying a box with the word 'jerk' written on it?"

"It doesn't say 'jerk,'" Irene said. "It says 'Jack,' right?"

"Yes, but I think you're the first person to read it correctly."

"All right," Lefebvre said, "why are you carrying a box with the name 'Jack' written on it?"

"Because, Detective Lefebvre, on behalf of a fellow named Jack, I've been looking for that buried car for twenty years."

28

B RIAN O'MALLEY LET US BORROW HIS OFFICE. THE CONSTRUCTION TRAILER was roomy, but the tension between O'Connor and Lefebvre seemed to shrink it.

O'Connor set his dusty cardboard box down next to me, but instead of sitting, he leaned against the dark paneling on one of the office walls. I was itching to open up the box and have a look through its contents.

Lefebvre relaxed a little when we agreed that anything he told us about the scene—anything I hadn't seen myself—would, for the time being, be off the record.

"What did you see?" O'Connor asked me.

I described the remains. O'Connor's face lost all color about halfway through my account. When I said the couple appeared to be in evening clothes of some sort, his attention suddenly sharpened. When I added that I thought I had seen a few diamonds on the floor of the trunk, he suddenly sat down on the other side of the box and buried his face in his hands.

I stopped talking and looked at Phil Lefebvre.

Lefebvre looked at me, then back to O'Connor.

"You know who they are," Lefebvre said.

O'Connor nodded. Without raising his head, he said in a strained voice, "Lillian Vanderveer Linworth's daughter, Katy. Katy Ducane and her husband, Todd. My God . . ."

"They drowned twenty years ago," I said, baffled. "That's what Kyle said, anyway."

"Kyle?" Lefebvre asked.

"Kyle Yeager. He's called Max Ducane now," I said quickly, seeing O'Connor look up and afraid that we were going to end up arguing about Kyle.

"Ah, yes," Lefebvre said. "The new multimillionaire. I've read the stories in the *Express* about the . . . missing heir. As I recall, the bodies of the Ducanes— the younger Ducanes—were never found, right?"

"Not until now," O'Connor said, his voice still unsteady.

"You're so sure?"

So O'Connor told us the story of the night Corrigan saw the car buried, of going through the murder scene at the Ducanes' mansion with Detective Norton, and learning that Lillian had given Katy the Vanderveer diamonds that night. Of finding a body in a swamp, and another in the mountains. "Eventually Dan Norton admitted that even if the Ducanes drowned by acci-dent—which I never believed—Jack's beating was connected to the disap-pearance of the child and the murder of the maid."

"You were bothered by something other than the timing?" Lefebvre asked.

"Yes, because we were able to connect Bo Jergenson, the giant, with Gus Ronden, whose body we found in the mountains. And when Norton and his men looked through Ronden's house here in Las Piernas, they found blood on clothes in his laundry hamper that matched the blood type of Rose Hannon, the murdered maid. And he found the knife Ronden presumably used."

"But since Ronden also ended up murdered," Lefebvre said, "Norton wasn't able to track down others who might have been involved?"

"We had some theories, we both followed every lead we could—to nothing but a dead end."

"Norton is retired now," Lefebvre said, "but I'll get in touch with him about this." He hesitated, then added, "I truly appreciate the help you've given us today. The remains may or may not be those of the Ducanes, but at least we will have a starting place to try a comparison of dental records and so on. That alone may save us a great many hours."

I wondered if O'Connor was going to pressure him for a return favor, but O'Connor waited in silence, and I followed his lead.

Lefebvre smiled, almost in appreciation, I thought. Then he said, "I can tell you something more, but I must stress that it is not yet for publication— I would caution you against mentioning it to anyone, especially Mrs. Linworth."

He waited until we both nodded our agreement.

"There were small bone fragments wrapped in a blanket, crushed, it seemed, beneath the weight of the remains of the adults."

"The baby?" O'Connor said. If I had expected him to feel some triumph because he had doubted that Kyle was Max Ducane, I was wrong. He seemed more upset than before.

Lefebvre held up his hands, palms out, in a halting motion. "Do not, I beg of you, jump to conclusions. The coroner's office will be able to tell us more.

I'm giving you this information as a favor—only so that you can, let's say, be ready for any announcement that may come from Dr. Woolsey."

"Will he be able to tell who the baby's bones belong to?" I asked. "I mean, there won't be any dental records, right?"

"No, but if the adults are the Ducanes, it is unlikely that any other infant would have been with them."

O'Connor never opened the cardboard box while we spoke with Lefebvre, and I began to feel as curious about it as Pandora once felt about another. Before I could mention it, O'Connor said something about deadlines, and we thanked Lefebvre, then O'Malley and his crew, and left.

We walked to my car, so that I could drive O'Connor over to the distant place where he had parked his. He explained to me that he had been avoiding the television vans.

The Karmann Ghia's passenger seat barely provided room for a man his size, and he further crowded himself by holding the box on his lap. He was holding on to it in a way that made me decide not to offer to put it in the trunk.

"I didn't know Jack lost his eye because of a beating," I said with a shiver.

"No?"

"No. I never asked him about it myself, because I noticed that when other people did, he came up with some outlandish tale about it. Never the same tale twice."

O'Connor smiled and smoothed his fingers over the box.

I started the car. I had forgotten that I had left the radio on—"Miss You" blasted at us for a moment. I turned it off and apologized.

"I like music," he said. "Including the Stones."

Right, I thought, trying to imagine anyone over forty listening to the Rolling Stones. I left the radio off.

He asked me if I would be willing to stop by the coroner's office to try to learn when they'd be scheduling the autopsies.

"You want me to take you there now?" I asked.

"No—what I meant was, would you go there alone? Before you head back to the paper? I'd go myself, but I think you'll have a better chance of getting information out of Woolsey."

"Because I'm a woman?"

"Because he dislikes me."

"Why?"

He shrugged, then said, "Maybe it's the Hannah articles. I'm told he thinks they make his office look bad."

"Because he fails to come up with an identification once in a while?"

"More than once in a while. He's especially bothered that I bring up the case of Hannah herself—sees me as the one who brings up an old failure year after year."

"I love those articles. They're important—and, I don't know, something in the way you write them really makes the reader feel for the families."

He seemed a little uncomfortable with the praise, but he said, "Thanks."

I handed him the roll of film I had shot. "The first few are of the ceremony, and then there are some of the crew. I know the paper won't publish the most graphic ones of the car, but I'd like to see prints anyway. They might help me . . . or someone else . . . with writing the story."

"I'll ask them to get to work on these first thing. With luck, they'll be printed by the time you get back to the paper, or not long after."

I began to wonder if he was sending me on an errand to the coroner's office as a way of helping me save face, so that I wouldn't have to sit in the newsroom while he wrote the story. I had never written about a murder case, old or new.

When we reached his car, he said, "About this story we're working on now—what would you like me to do next?"

"What would I . . . ? You're kidding, right?"

"No. It's still yours."

I didn't answer right away. I had a feeling my answer wouldn't just determine what happened on this one story. I could have some really fine payback out of this, make him miserable, and test his sincerity about working together. Or I could let him know what I had meant to tell him all along, if we had managed to get off to a better start.

"I want to work together," I said, "but not as equals."

"As I said, you're the boss."

"No. I mean, work together, but you help me to do this right. I covered crime in Bakersfield, but never a murder—just small-time police blotter stuff. Auto thefts and burglaries. Things like that. Never a high-profile case. And I've only been on the job for two years, and you've been on it for . . ."

"I've worked for the *Express* for forty-two years."

"Forty-two! You aren't *that* old!"

He smiled. "I started at eight, as a paperboy." He glanced down at the box, then gazed out at something beyond the windshield. I looked, but there was no view to speak of, just an empty side street and the cinder-block wall of a suburban housing tract, edging up to the fields that would soon become a shopping mall. I watched his face, saw him wince as if some ache troubled him. He turned toward me again and said, "I was a copyboy after that. I didn't sell a story until I was fourteen."

"Gee, so you've only been a reporter for a lousy thirty-six years . . . I've been one for two. So for the good of the story, I think we'd be better off if you called the shots."

"Wrigley wouldn't hear of it."

"That's right, he won't."

"That's not what I mean, and you know it. Don't be afraid to give this a try. I promise I'll speak my mind if I think you've missed something or gone in a wrong direction."

I glanced at my watch. "We haven't got time to argue."

"As a first decision, that's a good one."

Have it your way, I thought. "Tell me what's in the box."

"Notes and a few photos I took years ago. Nothing that will need to go into the story today, but I'll go over them with you after we get this first one in."

"All right. When you get to the paper, talk to Lydia Ames."

"The food editor?" he asked, raising his brows.

"You know exactly who she is, because you've been pumping her for information about me. Wrigley's wasting her talent in features, but never mind that now. She's been looking up the history of the ownership of the mall property—the farm. Is the name Griffin Baer familiar to you?"

"No . . . I don't think so."

"Well, maybe she'll find out that the owner in 1958 was someone else. You're more likely than I am to recognize that name."

"Okay. Anything else?"

"The back story on the disappearance of the Ducanes. Can you write about that?"

"Sure."

He got out of the car, taking his box with him. He closed the door, then leaned his big frame down and spoke through the open window. "Maybe it would be better if I went to the coroner's office, Irene. It's not . . . pleasant."

"Don't worry about me. I'm not afraid of the dead."

"You should be. They sometimes cause more trouble than the living," he said, and walked away.

29

I WAS LOCKING UP THE KARMANN GHIA IN THE CORONER'S OFFICE PARKING lot when my attention was drawn to a long black car. One of the tinted back windows was rolled down a few inches. At first glance, I thought it was a hearse, but hearses don't pull up to the front parking lot of a coroner's office, and in general, the occupant of the back half of a hearse doesn't need fresh air. As I looked closer, I saw that it was a limo. One big enough to spit in the eye of the energy crisis, sitting there with its engine running.

A big, well-dressed man I guessed to be in his late thirties or early forties came out of the coroner's office and headed for the limo. He was tall and broad-shouldered and his muscular build stretched the fabric of his suit. His eyes were hidden behind mirrored sunglasses. He had dark hair except for a white streak near his forehead—not so prominent that he couldn't have hidden it, but he had apparently parted his hair in such a way as to make sure that it showed.

The tinted window slid down, and a silver-haired man looked out, and they exchanged a few words I couldn't hear. The tinted window rolled up, and the big man went around to the other side of the car and stepped in. As it drove off, I caught a glimpse of its blue and gold vanity plates: YEAGER.

It dawned on me that the old man must be Kyle's adoptive father: Mitch Yeager.

I walked into the coroner's office with a dozen new questions in mind.

The dragon at the front desk did not believe that the *Express* would hire a woman reporter, even after I produced my press credentials. If Lefebvre hadn't walked into the building around that time, she might have sold me to a circus before I had a chance to talk to the coroner.

He took in the situation at once and said, "It's all right. Ms. Kelly can come back with me."

Something in his voice or demeanor subdued her. Still, she made him wait until she had pinned a visitor's badge on me.

"Thanks, Phil," I said to him when we were on the other side of a door leading into a wide hallway.

"She's a pain in the ass. But she's a favorite with the coroner, Dr. Woolsey. And I should warn you—unlike most people in his profession, he has absolutely no sense of humor."

I noticed Lefebvre was carrying a big envelope. "The case file on the Ducanes?" I asked.

"No, just their dental X rays. We've had them since just after they disappeared."

"You found that old file pretty fast."

He smiled. "I knew where to look."

I made an educated guess. "Norton had it at home."

He gave a soft laugh. "And how would you know something like that?"

"In Bakersfield, I got to know a few of the guys on the PD. I heard stories of things like this happening—not just there, but in lots of departments. A detective gets haunted by a case, latches on to it in a personal way. He takes things home. Sometimes, the files end up in an attic or a storage locker."

"Yes. If we're lucky, we get the files back before his widow throws them out. You dated someone in that department?"

"No," I said, surprised into answering. I started to say more, thought better of it, and kept my mouth shut. A simple "no" was the truth, after all.

Lefebvre didn't comment. I didn't fool myself into thinking he hadn't read something in my body language or on my face.

"About the file," I said, trying to steer the conversation to safer topics. "This case bothered Norton?"

"Oh yes. Just like it bothered O'Connor. Norton said O'Connor and Corrigan never let up on him about this one. Luckily for me, the stories about Max Ducane—the recent ones—had spurred Dan's interest, and he had already pulled the old file out again."

Matt Arden stepped into the hallway. He didn't hide his surprise when he saw us together, but came forward. "You have the X rays?" he asked Lefebvre.

"Yes."

Matt held a hand out, but Lefebvre didn't give the envelope to him.

"Ms. Kelly would like to speak with Dr. Woolsey," Lefebvre told him.

"I'm sure she would," Arden said irritably. "But he's busy checking up on the guy doing the X rays on the remains."

"Really, Detective Arden?" I said. "I thought he was busy talking to Mr. Yeager."

I had the satisfaction of seeing that I had now surprised Matt Arden twice in less than five minutes.

Lefebvre frowned. "Mitch Yeager is here?"

"No, just one of his nephews," Arden said. "Was. He left a few minutes ago. The younger one."

"Ian," Lefebvre said.

"You two know his kids by name?" I asked.

Lefebvre hesitated, then said, "Neither of them has criminal records, if that's what you're asking."

"It's not what I'm asking—"

"Well, that's all I'm telling."

"Whatever," Arden said impatiently. "But how Miss Kelly knows he was here—"

"Mitch Yeager was here, too," I said. "I saw him out front. He waited in his limo while his nephew came in."

"What were they doing here?" Lefebvre asked.

"You think Woolsey told me?" Arden snapped. "You know what he's like."

Lefebvre's gaze became distant, as if he was puzzling out a problem.

"I don't like it, either," said Arden. "But I can't keep the coroner from meeting with a citizen."

"If the child's remains you found in that blanket are those of Max Ducane," I asked, "the supposedly kidnapped baby, I mean—does that change what happens to Kyle Yeager?"

"That will depend on the terms of the trust," Lefebvre said.

A door opened and a gray-haired man wearing a dark blue suit stepped into the hallway.

Lefebvre turned toward him. "Dr. Woolsey, let me introduce you to—"

"Yes, Irene Kelly," he said abruptly. "My receptionist tracked me down to say you were bringing a reporter back here."

"I suspect she said he was bringing a *woman* reporter back here," I said, extending a hand.

Despite Lefebvre's warning about his sense of humor, he smiled and shook my hand. "Yes, but she didn't mention that he'd be bringing such a pretty one. What can I do for you, Miss Kelly?"

I inwardly cringed, but I'm fairly sure I kept my reaction to the comment on my looks to myself. I smiled back at him and said, "I'm hoping to learn whatever I can about the remains that were found in the car today. I was there when they were found, so—"

"Ahh. What a relief. I'm pleased to know Detective Lefebvre hasn't lost all sense of what we ought to be revealing to the press."

"Without Ms. Kelly's help, we wouldn't have suspected that these might be the Ducanes," Lefebvre said.

"Detective Lefebvre hasn't discussed anything I didn't see for myself," I said quickly. "I'm hoping you can tell me more."

Woolsey smiled at me again. "We're in the early stages of our proceedings, I'm afraid. I really have nothing definite to say about the three individuals at this point."

"You're sure there are three?"

"Oh yes—well, that much I can say. An adult female, an adult male, and an infant. Now, if you'll excuse us, I need to speak with the detectives—"

"Just one other question," I said. "What is the interest of the Yeager family in this matter?"

He shot an angry look at Matt Arden, who said, "Don't blame me. She saw Mitch Yeager outside."

Woolsey glanced uneasily at Lefebvre, then studied me for a moment before saying, "I suppose I should simply ask you to talk to Mr. Yeager himself. His visit was out of concern for his adopted son, Kyle. But I was unable to give the Yeager family any more information than I've given you."

I thought about the lack of rapport between Woolsey and O'Connor, whose nickname for the coroner was Old Sheep Dip, and decided this was not the time to play hardball. One of us needed to be able to talk to him. "When will more information be available?"

"I have the Ducanes' dental records for you," Lefebvre said.

"In that case . . ." Woolsey took out a card and handed it to me. "Call my office in three hours."

"It will take three hours to compare the X rays?"

"If the remains are those of the Ducanes, we will need time to notify the families. Now, if Detective Lefebvre will hand me those X rays, he can escort you back out of the building. And I'll speak to you later, Miss Kelly."

Lefebvre didn't argue. The moment we were outside, I said, "I don't trust him."

"Woolsey?"

"Yes. He lied about the Yeagers."

"What makes you think so?"

"At the press conference, your lieutenant never mentioned how many bodies were found, or whether they were those of children or adults. So how did the Yeagers know about a child's remains being found?"

"I've been wondering about that myself."

I glanced at my watch. "I'd better get back to the paper." I took out one of my business cards and handed it to him. "I should have done this earlier. If there's anything you can let me know . . ."

"Sure." He handed me one of his own cards. "And vice versa, all right?"

"Fair is fair," I agreed.

He started to walk away, then turned back. "Irene . . ."

"Yes?"

"Be careful."

30

WHEN I GOT BACK TO THE PAPER, THE NEWSROOM HAD DEVELOPED ITS usual late-afternoon haze of cigarette smoke. The place was full of noise. In addition to the usual clamor of ringing phones, the snatches of heated conversations, the chatter of the Teletypes, and the shunk-shunk-shunk of electric typewriters, I could hear—and feel—the rumble of the presses. They were in the basement, but they could be heard throughout the building when they ran, beginning as a low hum and increasing to a muffled roar as their speed increased. This was also the hour when bottles started coming out of desk drawers.

O'Connor beckoned me toward his desk—one of the messiest in the newsroom. "Your friend left to interview someone about the farm property. She's supposed to be back here any minute." He pointed to a stack of folders filled with clippings and photos. "I've just come back from the morgue," he said, referring to the archives of the *Express*. "This is what I found on a quick search, enough to give us a start today."

He seemed depressed. I thought it might be the clippings themselves, since he knew the victims. That brought another thought in its wake. "Did you call Helen?" I asked.

His look of surprise was a good one—for a fake. "Helen? Why?"

"Because Lillian Linworth might need a friend over at her place this afternoon when the coroner calls."

"Yes," he said. "I called her. But I didn't give her any details—"

"I didn't think you would. And it must have been hard to keep your promise to Lefebvre."

"It was," he admitted.

I filled him in on what had happened at the coroner's office. "Something weird is going on there. Yeager wouldn't be asking about something that might affect his adopted son unless he had word that a child's bones had been found. Even then, why would he assume the adult bodies were those of the Ducanes? I thought everyone but you believed they were lost at sea."

O'Connor stared at me a moment.

"What's that look for?"

"Nothing . . ." he said, then smiled. "I'm only thinking that you've asked an excellent question about Yeager. What are your guesses about who leaked the information to him?"

"The only people who could have said anything about the child's body are the two of us, Phil Lefebvre, Matt Arden, or someone in the coroner's office."

"Perhaps a member of the construction crew . . ."

"Maybe," I conceded. "But that's not what my gut tells me. Not the crew, certainly not us, and not Lefebvre. And I don't think it was Arden, either. Not unless he's a damned fine actor."

"Homicide detectives often are, I've found. It helps them in their line of work. But you're probably right. Woolsey would be my first bet." He reached for one of two big Rolodexes that sat on his desk near his manual type-writer—one of the few remaining manuals in the room—and turned the dial on its side until it stopped at the T's. He thumbed through that section—I noticed that many of the cards had no names on them, only initials or nota-tions in what was apparently some kind of code. He pulled one of these no-name cards free. The only thing on it was a lower-case "t" and a number. "I'll see what I can find out," he said, picking up his phone.

While he was making the call, I saw Lydia enter the newsroom. Her move-ments were tentative and seemed to become even more hesitant after she looked toward my desk and didn't see me there. She was blushing like a teenaged girl who had just been pushed into an overcrowded boys' locker room. I realized that she felt as if she were trespassing.

Right at that moment, more than any time before it, I was sure that I was right where I belonged.

O'Connor had hung up and was watching her, too. He waved her over. She regained her composure by the time she reached his desk.

"What did you find out about the property?" I asked her.

She pulled out her notes. "As you know, the farm was sold to the develop-ers by the heirs of Griffin Baer. Baer died five years ago, at the age of seventy-seven."

"He was the last one to live there?"

"Well, yes, but he hadn't lived there since 1926. From what I could learn from one of the heirs, Baer had a house down near the shore, and most of the fighting in the family was over that property, not the farm. According to this grandson, Baer used to do nothing but work on the farm, then he sold some mineral rights for a fantastic sum and used the money to build his dream home down by the ocean. He always paid someone else to do the farming after that."

"And the person who cared for the farmland didn't live on it as a tenant?" I asked.

"The grandson said there was a house out there until sometime in the 1960s, but it wasn't really occupied—most of the time, Baer used it as a place to drink with his friends."

"What happened in the 1960s?"

"He said that after his grandmother died—about fifteen years ago—his grandfather didn't feel the need to escape to the house so often, and tore the old place down."

"So when was it sold to the current owners?"

"Two years ago. According to the grandson, Baer's will was vaguely worded, and there was a huge fight within the family—like I said, mostly over the beach property. But eventually, the heirs settled things, and the offer by the developer was generous enough to get everyone to agree to it."

"Did you question him about the bodies in the car?" O'Connor asked.

"No—didn't want to step on anything the two of you might be doing later."

"Good work," he said. "You learned a lot about that property in a short amount of time—thanks."

Lydia left us, glowing from his praise. I asked O'Connor if he had learned anything from his phone call.

"Not yet," he said. He relented a little, though, and said, "I called someone who works in the coroner's office."

"Oh, so that's a cross, like a graveyard cross, and not a 't' on that card? I guess that system makes it harder on the newsroom snoops."

He looked surprised—genuinely, this time—then laughed and told me to stay the hell away from his Rolodexes.

I glanced at my watch and called home, and once again begged Mary's help. She told me not to worry, that my father had slept most of the day and would probably be up and wanting to talk to me when I got home. "So it's you who'll have the long day," she said. "Not me."

O'Connor and I went to work on the story itself. We divided it along the lines of old and new—he would write the background material on the Ducane murders, and I would cover events at the construction site today.

I called Woolsey's office every half hour. The receptionist wouldn't put the first few calls through, and told me to give up and call back at the time Dr. Woolsey specified. I didn't give up, and two and a half hours after I had left his office, Woolsey gave a preliminary confirmation of the identities of the bodies as those of Kathleen and Todd Ducane, and their infant son, Maxwell.

I was still on that call when H.G. told O'Connor that he was wanted in Wrigley's office.

When he came back, about twenty minutes later, he said that Mr. Wrigley had known Katy Ducane, too, and was a friend of Lillian Linworth. "This may seem strange to you, but . . . even though we've believed for years that Katy and Todd were dead, this is hard on everyone who knew them."

"That doesn't seem strange to me at all."

He was silent.

"Katy was only twenty-one, right?"

"Yes. Younger than you are now," he said wonderingly.

I did the math. "Weird, isn't it? She'd be some middle-aged lady now, if she had lived."

He smiled in an odd way, but said, "Yes."

"She seems to have been someone who made an impression on people."

"Spoiled rotten. Headstrong. Alive as anyone I've ever known. Jack and Helen adored her. Her husband—well, none of us were fond of Todd, but perhaps he would have matured into a better man. We'll never know."

"You wish you were with Lillian and Helen instead of here?"

He thought for a moment, then said, "No, Kelly, I'm where I need to be. This is what I do. And in all honesty, I'd be nothing but miserable anywhere else."

I understood that, although I had far less time in as a reporter. The thought of his abilities and years of experience made me feel all the greener. A couple of hours later, with some trepidation, I handed him what I had written so far, and took a look at his own pages.

31

S HE SURPRISED HIM.

He had worried that writing together would be a trying, exasperating experience, one that would require twice as much effort to produce a story, and that he would need to constantly beware of offending her.

But when she came back from the coroner's office, full of observations and questions about the Yeagers, he began to admire the way her mind worked, that she hadn't taken Woolsey at face value. Hell, she hadn't taken *him* at face value.

Perhaps because they were focused on the story, or perhaps because she was better at this than he had expected, it had gone smoothly. Even when she told him—brassy little bitch that she was—that he had missed something in his first draft.

"What?" he had asked.

"Katy. I don't see her in here—not the way you described her to me. Not that girl in the portrait at Lillian's house."

He silently damned her for being right and went back to work.

He found himself pushing himself a little harder than he had been lately, concentrating on his own work in a way he had not done in the last few months, wanting to set an example—and aware of her scrutiny. A little unnerving, this new responsibility, but stimulating as well.

She made a few mistakes, but didn't bridle at his suggested changes. If anything, she seemed eager to learn from him.

They wrote quickly—once he went back to work on it, the story didn't need coaxing along—and finished in time to keep John Walters from losing a bet with H.G. that they'd make deadline.

She had looked so pleased when she handed it off to the copy desk, he smiled thinking of it.

The blend of their styles hadn't been as jarring as he had worried it would be, either. In the most basic ways, hers was not so different from his own. He made a remark about this, and she said it wasn't surprising. "Your writing has been a part of my life since I was seven or eight."

That had taken him aback for a moment. The daily grind of putting out the paper made a man think about days from deadline to deadline, and not in terms of years.

She was younger than his son. He had been writing for the paper for several years by the time Kenny was born.

He wondered if her father worried about her, working in this business, seeing the hard side of the world, encountering lowlifes every day. He looked around him and frowned. Lowlifes in the newsroom as well. He resolved to have a word with the Wildman.

"Tomorrow, will you show me what's in that box?" she asked.

"Sure. Tonight if you'd like."

"Tempting, but I need to get home to my dad."

They walked out to the parking lot together, not saying anything. He reached his car first and stood next to it, watching her walk to the little Karmann Ghia, seeing her fumble through her purse for her keys.

From the corner of his eye, he caught a movement near the fence of the Wrigley Building parking lot. The light in the lot was dim, and beyond it he could see little more than shadows, but he couldn't shake a feeling that someone was there. He watched for another sign of movement, listened for a footstep.

He heard Kelly say, "Good night, O'Connor. Thanks again."

He turned to her and saw, for the briefest moment, the image of a very different young woman, a sister lost to him one long-ago evening. On her way home from work to a waiting father.

"Let me see you home safe," he said to her. "I'll follow you in my car, all right?"

She smiled. "I'll be all right."

"It's late. Humor an old man. It will make me feel better."

He was convinced that she wanted to refuse, but after a moment of studying him, she shrugged and said, "If you can afford the gas and you and that old Nash can keep up with me, fine." She laughed and said, "You probably hear that old 'Beep Beep' song as often as I hear 'Goodnight, Irene.'"

"Not so often these days," he admitted. "I'm surprised someone your age knows that old song."

"Then we're even," she said, getting into the car. "I'm still amazed that you listen to the Stones."

He had no trouble keeping up with the noisy convertible. As it pulled out of the parking lot of the *Express,* he saw another car's headlights come on. A BMW. Not the kind of car one usually saw parked in the alley near the paper. The fellow in the shadows? he wondered. It seemed to move forward as she made the turn, then stopped as O'Connor's car followed hers.

He watched for several blocks, but he didn't see the Beemer again.

O'Connor followed her to a quiet suburban tract, one of the ones built in the postwar boom. Her street was lined with modest homes and well-kept lawns. The grass was a little long in the yard of the house where she pulled in, parking next to a red Mustang. The house itself looked neat and well cared for, so that he thought the neglect of the yard was recent. Lights were on, and as he rolled down his window to wave good night to her, he could hear the sound of laughter.

She waved back to him from her front porch, but still he waited until she had gone in.

He went to a pay phone and called Helen. She wasn't home.

He thought of calling Lillian, decided against it, and drove back to the paper. He looked down the alley and saw, as expected, that the BMW was gone. He drove to a small Irish bar he liked, a place about five miles from the paper, and hoped that no one from the *Express* would trouble to travel that far to drink tonight.

No one from the *Express* was there, but he saw a familiar figure sitting at the bar.

"Have a seat," Lefebvre said to him, motioning to an empty bar stool next to him. "I'll buy you a drink."

"Am I supposed to believe you're here by luck?"

He shook his head. "No. I asked Norton where you liked to drink."

O'Connor laughed. "And of a dozen places you picked this one?"

"I asked him where you liked to drink when you wanted to get away from reporters. He named three of them. I checked them out and took a chance that it might be this one."

"You frighten me, Detective. And if I hadn't shown up?"

"I'd have a drink, go home, and think of another way to find a chance to talk to you."

O'Connor ordered a pint of Guinness on tap. "All right, Lefebvre. The luck was with you. What can I do for you?"

"It's been a bad night for you, I imagine."

"Not entirely."

"Ah. Miss Kelly."

"Now just a minute—"

"Relax. She's a nice kid, but she's too young for me, O'Connor. And for you, too, I assume."

"Definitely."

"I'm concerned about her—the Yeagers might have taken notice of her visit to the coroner's office today. And she made Woolsey nervous."

O'Connor smiled. "Good for her," he said, hiding his own worry.

He took a long drink, and another. Lefebvre didn't say anything, but the silence between them was comfortable. When O'Connor had drained the pint, Lefebvre ordered another one. O'Connor noticed Lefebvre wasn't drinking much himself. That didn't bother him. O'Connor knew his own head to be a damned hard one.

"You can tell me about them," Lefebvre said. "It will help."

"Whom?"

"Todd and Katy Ducane."

"I mean, whom will it help?"

"It will help me find their killer, I hope."

"Read the paper."

"I will," Lefebvre said. And waited.

O'Connor took a drink of stout and said, "You've been a pain in my ass for five years now."

"That bad? I apologize."

"No," O'Connor admitted in fairness. "Not that bad. You've never lied to me or intentionally sent me off on a false trail. You're just far less willing to talk to me than most. Are you offering to help us out now?"

"Not to an extent that will allow a murderer to escape prosecution. But otherwise, yes. And you have a reputation for being trustworthy. Norton swears you will keep a confidence."

"No kidding. But somehow I think you already knew that. So why the change of heart about talking to me?"

"Thank one of your fans."

"Norton?" O'Connor said, and laughed.

"No, Ms. Kelly."

"She didn't talk to you about me."

"No. I watched how you treated her. That's all."

O'Connor took another drink and thought about the fact that if Lefebvre had seen him at a dinner party a few nights ago, he probably would have wanted to knock him off the bar stool.

He stayed quiet, but Lefebvre didn't move, just bought him another round. He began to admire Lefebvre's patience.

What the hell, he thought. I owe something to those bastards for Katy and for Jack. And the child. The poor child.

"Norton said Todd Ducane was a lady's man," Lefebvre said.

O'Connor looked over at the detective. "Jack always called him 'the Toad' ..."

32

T WO THINGS KEPT ME FROM GETTING MUCH SLEEP THAT NIGHT—THINKING about what I had seen in the trunk of a buried car, and reading Anne Rice's *Interview with the Vampire*. I was close to the end of the book, and until that evening, it had been scaring the bejesus out of me in a delicious kind of way. It was due back to the library the next day, and I had planned to try to finish it that night, but finding the remains kind of put me off reading about dead people. I decided I'd turn it back in and buy the paperback and read it when I could handle the idea again.

The living person named Max Ducane—or Kyle Yeager, take your pick— called me at work the next morning. He asked if he could meet me for lunch.

"I'm not even sure what to call you," I said.

He sighed. "Max. Legally, it's my name now."

"Max it is, then."

O'Connor came over to my desk, carrying his "Jack" box. I motioned him to take a seat. He was looking a little bleary-eyed.

Into the phone, I said, "So why, exactly, do you want to meet me for lunch?"

"I don't suppose you're allowed to date anyone you might be writing about?"

"No," I said. I could see O'Connor watching me more closely now, shamelessly eavesdropping. I held the receiver a little closer to my ear.

"Okay," Max said. "Not a date. I'll tell you more about what's going on when I see you—if I can see you?"

"All right. When and where?"

"How about if I meet you in the lobby there at noon?"

"Okay. See you then."

I hung up and wondered if I was making a mistake.

"Who was that?" O'Connor said.

"He says his name is Max Ducane."

"Oh, the former Kyle Yeager, is it? Well, I hope he's nothing like his adoptive father, or you had better take a bodyguard."

"You've met him—I think I'll be fine, don't you? Or do you want to come along?"

He seemed to space out for a moment when I asked—seemed so distracted I wondered if he had heard my question. But then he said, "Thanks, but no. I've already got lunch plans today."

"When you said I should have a bodyguard—did you mean I'd better take a chaperone?"

"No. I meant bodyguard, but forget it. Kyle Yeager isn't much like Mitch."

"You think I'd need a bodyguard with an old man like Mitch Yeager? He's a just a rich businessman."

"That's what he'd love for everyone to believe, isn't it?" O'Connor said bitterly.

I stared at him. Clearly I'd struck some nerve.

"There is more than one way of doing business," he said. "People complain of politicians being crooked? They've got nothing on certain members of the business community."

"So why don't you write about him?"

O'Connor glanced toward Wrigley's office. "I did now and again, as your friend Max noted, but not nearly as much as I would have liked to have written."

"This about advertising dollars?" I asked.

"Mr. Yeager and some of the friends who had invested in his companies made it clear to the first Mr. Wrigley that they'd never buy another inch of advertising if the *Express* continued its 'campaign' against Mr. Yeager. That was forty years ago, and if you think Yeager is a weak old man now, you're wrong."

"You really hate him."

"Hate him?" He looked surprised. "No. But I dislike his way of doing things. He likes to intimidate people. He tried it with me when I was no more than a child." He smiled. "I'm happy to say I had caused a bit of trouble for him even then."

He made something of a show of looking at his watch, then said, "Wrigley's letting me use one of the meeting rooms to go over some background of the Ducane story with you. You've already heard it in bits and pieces, but . . ."

"Sure. Let's go."

I followed him to one of the conference rooms.

He closed the door behind us and shut the curtains to the windows that looked out onto the newsroom—and through which most of the newsroom had been looking in—then set the box on the wooden table at the center of the room. I leaned against a credenza with a phone on it and watched while he put on a pair of cheaters, opened the box, and began taking items out of it, looking at each through the bifocals, then peering over the top of the lenses as he arranged the items on the table.

I strolled around the table as he worked. Some of the materials were photographs, some newspaper clippings. Most were reporter's notebooks and loose, indecipherable notes. With effort, I could make out the handwriting— but like the cards in his Rolodexes, the notes were apparently written in some sort of private code.

I had supposed the contents of the box were disorganized—O'Connor's desk always looked as if someone had busted a piñata full of pink telephone message slips and scraps of paper over it, so it wouldn't have surprised me if he had simply tossed items into the box over the years. I was wrong about that, though—there was a method to the way in which he was laying things on the table. He wasn't sorting them as they came out of the box. They were already in an order of some kind.

The photographs ranged from curling black-and-white glossies to the slick squares of 1950s color photographs—the too vivid reds, yellows, and blues of the film processing of the time.

"Technicolor," I said.

He glanced up, said, "Something like that," and went back to work on unloading the box.

I began studying some of the photos more closely. There was a stack of photos of Katy as a child, often with Jack or Helen, others of her as a teenager. Most of the time, she was smiling or laughing. She was a beautiful girl, not favoring either of her parents, although Lillian had obviously been a looker, too. Katy had a great smile, one that reached her eyes and made you want to smile back at her. I had that response to a black-and-white image; in person she must have been a real live wire.

In one of the photos, I saw that she was holding a cigarette.

"She smoked?" I asked.

"Yes," he said, his brows drawing together. "Every now and then. I don't remember her being a chain smoker. Smoking was thought to be sexy then, you know."

"Do you remember her brand?"

"No, but Lillian might."

He reluctantly gave me Lillian's number, which he knew by heart, and I used the phone in the conference room to call her. She was understandably upset by the news of the past twenty-four hours, but seemed, if anything, grateful to me. I was surprised by this, until she explained that she had spent the last twenty years not really knowing what had happened to Katy. "Perhaps someday her killers will be punished. Conn tells me this Detective Lefebvre is very good."

I agreed that he was and gradually worked my way around to asking about the cigarette brand. "Chesterfields," she answered without hesitation.

Another thought struck me. "Did she use a lighter or matches?"

"She had a special lighter. A gift from Jack. Gold, and it had a Celtic design on it—rather unusual then."

"Her initials on it?"

"Just the letter K, surrounded by a Celtic knot."

After I hung up, I told O'Connor what she said and went back to the photos of Katy. I found myself wondering who she might have become if she had been allowed to live. She would have been in her forties now. Would she have aged well? Become a snooty socialite? A bitter divorcée? A pillar of the community?

O'Connor had written that she had been somewhat spoiled and headstrong, but all the same a lively, energetic person, someone who had made others laugh or smile—and really, if she hadn't gone on to do anything more than that for the rest of her life, we had all been robbed by whoever killed her.

I moved to another stack. These seemed to have been taken in the 1940s and 1950s, and some were obviously taken without the subject's awareness. Men and women dressed in the styles of the time. Twenty years changes nothing so much as cosmetics and hairstyles. I didn't recognize anyone in the photos.

O'Connor had finished by then and called me over to where he stood. He had spent some time that morning at the public library and started with a photocopy of a map he had found there. It was a map of Las Piernas and surrounding areas, dated 1955.

"This is the closest I could find to the time," he said. "But it will help us."

It was hard not to get caught up in the novelty of seeing what the city looked like then. For one thing, about half the current streets were missing—the housing tracts of the 1960s and 1970s hadn't been built yet. O'Connor also laid out two more current maps, one of Las Piernas, the other of Southern California.

" 'All things must change to something new, to something strange,' " he said.

I looked up at him.

"Longfellow," he said.

"Oh."

He seemed disappointed that I couldn't quote the poet back at him. "Did you study poetry a lot when you were in college?" I asked.

"Never went to college," he said. Without another word on poets or education, he used the old map to point out the place in the marshes where Jack Corrigan had been found, and where later, not far away, O'Connor had found the body of Bo Jergenson, one of the men who had attacked Jack. "Helen and Jack and I questioned a lot of small-time hoods, and so did Dan Norton, with the police. We slowly put together a list of people who might have been hanging around with Gus Ronden in those days. Jack's memories of events that night were jumbled, but we learned that he was taken away from the party in a Bel Air. Based on descriptions I got from one of Gus's neighbors, and comments made by others, I learned that one of Gus's cronies was named Lew Hacker, a Hispanic man who drove a Bel Air."

"He's one of the ones who beat up Jack?"

"I doubt he had to do anything at all," O'Connor said, "other than hold Jack while this lummox went to work on him." He showed me a photo of Jergenson, who indeed looked like a giant.

O'Connor marked a place on the map that was roughly in the area where the car had been buried.

"No wonder you couldn't figure out where Jack had seen the car. The farm is nowhere near the marsh, and there's nothing around that spot for miles."

"Back then, the whole of that area was farming," he said. "But I wish I had looked a little harder. If I had found the place then . . ."

"Then you probably would have been buried with the car, too," I said. "Will the DMV have records of the car registration?"

He shook his head. "Not going back that far."

I thought about what he had written in the article. "Katy didn't drive a Buick, right? She drove a little roadster?"

"Right. It was found at Thelma and Barrett Ducane's home. And the elder Ducanes' car was at the marina. Todd drove an old Hudson that was in the driveway at his own house. I saw it there that night."

"So among all the people who might be connected in some way, who owned a Buick?"

He frowned. "I don't know."

I pointed to the stack from which he had taken the photo of Jergenson. "Who are these people?"

"Gus Ronden and friends, if you can call them that. I learned who most of them were in the weeks after Jack was attacked."

He also showed me a couple of photos of Gus Ronden—including a set of mug shots. "I know you said his gun was in the Imperial, and was the one used to kill Jergenson. Was his gun found in the trunk, with his body?"

"No, under the front seat. It wasn't used to kill Gus—the weapon that was used to kill him hasn't been found."

I started looking through the photos. "Some of these look as if they were taken with a telephoto lens."

"Yes. Anytime I learned of anyone who had been known to hang around Gus Ronden, I tried to get a photo. Some photos I took myself, but the telephotos were ones I talked a former staff photographer into taking. There are some here that were given to me by friends of the subjects, or their families, because that was the only way to get a picture of them at all."

"What do you mean?"

"The Ducanes weren't the only ones who disappeared that night. A number of the people in these photos seemed to vanish from Las Piernas—although I think most of them left voluntarily and with money in their pockets."

"Show me the ones you couldn't find."

He sorted a few out of the stack.

"Who made them disappear?" I asked as I looked through them.

"I can't say with any certainty."

I looked up. "But you have a guess."

"Let's just say that around this time, Mitch Yeager seemed to distance himself from some of his former friends. But I haven't a shred of evidence to connect him to anything that went on that night. He himself wasn't in town that weekend."

I moved on to a photo of the yacht. "Do you think the Ducanes were ever out on the *Sea Dreamer*?"

"What do you mean?"

"I mean, what you wrote was that the yacht was abandoned, but there was no sign of violence on it, right?"

"Right."

I looked up. "So whoever attacked them—let's call them the pirates—would have to overpower four adults. One with an infant. Okay, that's possible, I suppose, assuming they came aboard with weapons. But the pirates would have to control the *Sea Dreamer*, and the Ducanes, and whatever boat the pirates returned to shore on. The pirates had to get the two elder Ducanes overboard, then take Katy and Todd and the baby with them on the getaway boat—no, that's not right. The infant wasn't with them. The baby was taken from the house by Ronden. Wait, how does Baby Max Ducane get from the house to the Buick?"

"Maybe Ronden met these pirates somewhere, after he left Todd and Katy's house," O'Connor guessed. "Katy and Todd might have been dead already."

I frowned. "That seems so odd—kidnapping a child just to bury it in the trunk of a car with its parents?"

He shrugged. "Can't argue with the fact that his remains were found there, and that before he was killed, he was home with the nurse."

"Okay, so let's look at what happened to the adults. Let's say the pirates begin by sending Thelma and Barrett Ducane overboard, too far out to sea on a stormy night for them to swim safely ashore."

"Okay, I'm with you so far."

"Then they force Katy and Todd aboard the pirates' boat. They abandon the *Sea Dreamer*."

"So now we have better odds for the pirates, and the reason there's no blood on the *Sea Dreamer*."

"Right."

"The sailor or sailors kill Katy and Todd, put them in the trunk of the Buick, and meet Ronden, who has killed the baby, and toss the baby's body in the trunk with his dead parents." I shuddered. "I think I'm glad Ronden got killed a long time ago."

"Except that whoever planned all of this is still around."

I went back to the photos and came across one of a young blonde with her arm around a much older man. She was a pretty woman, but there was a certain hardness in her face that kept her from being more than that.

"The woman who was at the party with the giant?"

"Yes. Betty Bradford. When I showed that photo to Jack, he recognized her as the blonde who put her paws on him just before he got knocked out by Jergenson. She hasn't been seen by anyone since the night of Katy's birthday party."

"You think she's dead?"

"She was Gus Ronden's mistress, and she was obviously at the party to set Jack up for a beating or worse. Given what happened to Jergenson and Ronden, I wouldn't be surprised to hear she was dead, but I don't know what became of her, Lew Hacker, or a couple of the others."

"Who's with her in this photo?"

"Her sugar daddy before Ronden. She must have been something, too. He'd call me every once in a while, wondering if I had learned what happened to her. He was crazy about her. The old fart even gave her a car." A mischievous light came into his eyes. "Told me he had pink carpet installed on the floorboards because Betty here liked to wear pink underwear."

I laughed, then suddenly sobered. "What kind of car did he buy her?"

He looked at his notes. "I don't think he told me." He frowned. "And stupidly, I didn't ask."

"Is Don Juan here still alive?"

O'Connor shook his head. "Died of a heart attack a few years after I met him."

"Yesterday, when you were telling me about Gus Ronden, you said you went over to his house here in Las Piernas, right?"

"Yes."

"His Imperial was gone—was there another car there, one that might have been hers?"

"No."

"And you said Lew Hacker drove a Bel Air, right?"

He thumbed through his notes. "A turquoise and white Chevy Bel Air. It had been seen over at Gus Ronden's place late that night—maybe sometime after the murders. Neither Hacker nor the car has been seen since then."

I went toward the phone.

"What are you doing?" he asked.

"Calling Lefebvre."

He didn't stop me, but I could tell it was killing him not to. When Lefebvre answered, I said, "Phil, did you find any other bodies in the Buick?"

"Three not enough for you?"

"Plenty. Listen—was the carpet on the car's floorboards pink?"

There was a long silence.

"Phil, you should have said, 'What lunatic would have pink carpet in a car?' or something like that, because you've just given me my answer."

"Damn it to hell, if someone in the lab—"

"Not the lab's fault. Listen, we know who owned that Buick before it was buried."

O'Connor motioned me to shut up.

"We?" Lefebvre asked.

"O'Connor and I know," I went on, picking up the phone and dodging O'Connor as he tried to hit the switch hook, "but the *Express* is going to have to be the first to tell the public who the owner is—understood?"

"And what if it's not a good idea for the public to know that name just now?"

"Detective Lefebvre, do you want to read the name in tomorrow's *Express,* or would you like it now?"

"I have a feeling that I am going to have to grant a favor to hear it."

"Oh no. I'd just like our . . . spirit of openness and honesty to continue."

"That's what I was afraid of. All right."

So I told him about Betty Bradford and her boyfriends. "If you hear from her or anyone who might know what became of her, you know where to reach me," I added.

"I haven't known you twenty-four hours, and already you are a nuisance."

I didn't say anything.

"Thanks," he said.

"You're welcome," I replied, and hung up.

"What did he say?" O'Connor asked.

"That I'm a nuisance."

O'Connor wholeheartedly agreed with this, and for about ten minutes— while I basically ignored him and thought about cars—he gave me shit about spilling my guts to a cop and promising to hold back a story, at which point I stopped him by saying, "Ronden's body was the one you found near Lake Arrowhead, right?"

"Yes."

"I'm looking at these photos, and I have to tell you, Gus Ronden looks like a city boy to me. Why the cabin?"

"A meeting place, I'm fairly sure. Somewhere out of the public eye."

"I wonder. You check to see who Ronden's neighbors were in Arrowhead?"

"Yes."

"Anyone from Las Piernas?"

"A few. Thelma and Barrett Ducane had a place. Lillian had two places. One that she and Harold bought. The other . . ." His voice caught, but he tried to go on. "Lillian had a . . ." He halted and looked away from me. After a moment he said, "She had a big place up there that had been in her family since the early 1920s. She gave that one to Katy—Katy was born there, so Lillian wanted her to have it for her young family. Katy willed it to Jack." He told me the story of the will in Katy's safe.

"Hmm. We'll have to get back to that. Any other locals?"

He studied his notes, and after a few minutes of tense silence—during which I wasn't sure if he was looking at the notes or just trying to get past the thought of Lillian's lost hopes—he suddenly said, "I'll be damned."

"Griffin Baer, the guy who planted the Buick on his farm," I said.

O'Connor nodded slowly, then asked, "How did you know?"

"A guess based on your reaction. If it had been a name that was familiar to you before yesterday or today, you would have seen it when you went look-ing through the property records in 1958, right?"

"Yes."

I thought over our progress so far. "Maybe if we run the photo you have of Betty, we'll hear from someone who has seen her since 1958."

"Maybe," he agreed. "If she's alive, I don't think she's anywhere near here, though."

"And maybe we should start trying to find out more about Griffin Baer's friends and associates."

"I'd bet anything Lefebvre is already at work on that, but sure."

"Lydia mentioned the heirs fighting over a property on the beach and the farm, but I don't recall anything about a mountain property, do you?"

"No. But it could have been sold to someone else since 1958." He noticed that it was about eleven-thirty. "We'd better work through the rest of this another time. You'll be late for your date."

"Not a date," I said.

He began packing up the box. He even let me help him.

"I think you should ask Wrigley to move Lydia over to news side," I said. "We could use her help."

"Lefebvre was right," he said sourly. "You're a menace."

"Nuisance."

"Both," he said, but there was no heat in it.

33

I STOPPED BY MY DESK AND PICKED UP MY SHOULDER BAG, WHICH WEIGHED a ton, because it had the big hardcover library book in it. My intercom buzzed. Geoff, the security guard, told me that a gentleman by the name of Max Ducane was waiting for me.

That made something clear. Admonishing myself to call him Max and not Kyle, I made my way downstairs.

Max Ducane didn't look as happy as I would have expected a new multimillionaire to be. If anything, he seemed troubled. We made small talk as we walked out of the building. His car was around the corner—a new BMW. "Your first purchase?" I asked.

He nodded. "I had my reasons—or thought I did—but are you embarrassed to ride in it? Is it too ostentatious?"

"For someone with your bucks?"

"Maybe I'll sell it," he said, glum again.

Once we were settled inside it, he said, "I made reservations at the Cliffside. Is that all right? If you'd prefer, we can just go to a restaurant near here."

The suggestion gave me pause, but I thought about the fact that I was now living rent-free, had paid off my bills from the Bakersfield move, and had just put a paycheck in the bank.

"I've never eaten at the Cliffside," I said, not adding that I had never thought of myself as someone who could afford to eat there, "but I've always heard that it's a great place. And it's a smarter choice for us than anywhere nearby, I think, unless you want half the staff of the *Express* trying to eavesdrop on us."

"The Cliffside it is, then."

We were seated in a private room at the restaurant, which is part of a luxury hotel with stunning ocean views. Our waiter had a manner that suggested he was on loan from a palace somewhere. He seated me, placed a fine linen napkin on my lap with a flourish, and handed me an open menu with a smile. Before I even looked at what was sure to be the cause of a painful chapter in my financial history, I made myself say, "Will there be any difficulty giving us separate checks?"

He said, "Not at all, miss, but—" just as Max tried to protest that this was his treat.

"It can't be, Max. I'm supposed to be working, remember?"

He glanced nervously at the waiter, who was feigning just the right amount of indifference, and said, "All right. But another time, then."

"Another time."

I had decided that I would do my best not to appear shocked at the prices on the menu, but the real shock turned out to be that my menu didn't have any prices on it at all.

"Excuse me," I said to the waiter, holding the menu out for him to see. "I think I have a misprinted one."

Max said, "The Cliffside is a bit old-fashioned, I'm afraid. Why don't we switch menus?"

At that point, I finally figured out what was going on. "I can't believe it," I said. "Only men get menus with prices on them?"

He smiled. "Neanderthal, I agree. I promise not to drag you by the hair into a cave after dessert."

The indignation I felt over the "ladies" menu allowed me not to faint when I finally did get a look at the prices. The waiter was placing bread on the table and filling our water glasses while reciting the specials with a level of enthusiasm that suggested the chef had chosen these items in our honor. I thought about ordering nothing but a side salad, then told myself that it would be worth it to pack a lunch every day next week in order to not look like a pauper just now. I thought Max—a recent college student—would understand a low-budget order perfectly, but I didn't want to appear to be a nobody to the waiter.

So I ordered duck in blackberry sauce, which came with grilled vegetables and little pancakes stuffed with wild rice. Max ordered a porterhouse steak. We considered and rejected the idea of having some wine, both of us having a lot of work before us that afternoon.

Max asked me how long I had worked for the *Express*. I told him that I was new there, but had worked at the *Californian*. He tried asking about that, but seemed to quickly pick up on the fact that I didn't want to reminisce about Bakersfield.

When the waiter brought the salads, he nearly tripped on my shoulder bag, which I had set on the floor. He acted as if people tried to trip him all the time, that keeping his balance while treading a path of hidden obstacles was part of the service a member of the staff of the Cliffside was happy to render to its customers. I apologized as Max picked up the bag and set it on an empty seat. "What the hell do you have in this thing," Max asked, "a brick?"

"A library book. Mind if we stop by the downtown library on the way back to my office?"

When I told him I was reading *Interview with the Vampire*, he said he had already read it, and talked about it enthusiastically, but he was good about not spoiling the ending for me.

"You okay these days?" I asked, thinking that by now he had relaxed enough to tell me what was on his mind.

"Sure. Well—no. Actually, I don't know how to answer that." He sighed and set down his silverware. "I don't know what to do." He smiled a little crookedly. "Can we talk off the record for a while?"

I agreed that would be all right. He had tensed up again, and I knew that as it was, he was feeling so uptight, I wouldn't get much out of him otherwise.

He took a minute to figure out how to begin, then said, "When the story came out—about them finding the real Max Ducane—I felt horrible. I mean, I already feel like a fake, you know?"

"Why? Because of a name? Lots of us have names that others have had before us. Think of all those John Smiths."

"But they weren't believed to *be* someone else. Each John Smith is who he is, and his grandmother and his uncle know which one he is. Few people got their names the way I did."

"Right. You could have been in my situation, named after an old song, and have everyone sing the damn thing to you whenever you leave a party."

He laughed.

I liked his laugh; it was one that made you want to laugh with him.

The strangest thing happened, though. Maybe because I had been looking at pictures of Katy and Todd Ducane all morning, I could see why Warren Ducane had mistaken him for his brother's child. I decided to keep that to myself.

"Max, if you think about it, all of us have made-up names. So you got this one in a courtroom. You're hardly the first person to legally change his name. Unless you don't like the name?"

"No, it's fine. In fact . . . do you know who I was named after? When I was Kyle, I mean?"

"No," I admitted.

"It was my uncle's middle name. Adam Kyle Yeager. A man who died in prison. Now, *there's* a hero. It wasn't even anything glorious like civil rights or civil disobedience. He was a felon. A thief, among other things. From all I've heard, he was a local gangster."

"He must have meant something to somebody, for you to be named after him."

"Oh, my father thought the world of him." He caught himself and said, "Mitch, I mean." He looked away for a moment, then said, "For the most part, not knowing who my birth parents were hasn't bothered me. After Mom— Estelle—died, I really wanted to know who they were, and every now and then I wondered about them. But on the upside, by the time I was ten or so, if I saw Mitch Yeager acting like a jerk, I knew he wasn't my father. I was always free of him—I hadn't inherited anything from him."

"I can see both sides of it, I suppose. I think curiosity would have gotten the best of me by now."

"That's really all it is for me at this point—curiosity. I've met people who can trace their ancestry back to the *Mayflower,* or farther back than that, but whose own lives haven't been worth much of anything at all. So I told myself that what mattered was what I did with my life. Who I am, what I made of myself."

"I agree."

"And I've had incredible advantages. I don't deny that. Estelle Yeager loved me. I didn't grow up in poverty, or being discriminated against for the color of my skin. I've never had health problems. Hell, just being born in this country is something to be thankful for. There are plenty of horror stories about what can happen to orphans, so for a bastard, I'd say I've done really well. Mitch Yeager might not love me, and maybe he's always planned to use me for his own purposes, but he has spent a lot of money on me."

"I know what you mean about the advantages," I said, "and maybe you were better off than some other orphans, but didn't you feel kind of bad about being shipped off to boarding school?"

"If I hadn't gone to boarding school, I would have been raised by Mitch, and I don't think that would have been so great. As it is, the headmaster of my school sort of took me under his wing, became a better adoptive father than Mitch was. So I was lucky there, too."

"Back up a second. You said Mitch wanted to use you. How?"

He toyed with his steak, then said, "Sonya, his new wife? She's nice. But not too bright. The kids he's had with her take after their mother, according to Mitch. I hardly know them, so I couldn't say. Anyway, he wanted me to be a kind of caretaker of his businesses, along with my cousins—Eric and Ian. We'd see to it that his kids died wealthier than he did."

"And would you have been compensated for that? Or were you supposed to just be grateful to have a chance to repay him for adopting you?"

"No, I would have been compensated. And generously."

I studied him for a moment. "But you turned him down by accepting Warren's offer."

"Oh yes. Mitch is furious with me. I don't blame him. I even offered to pay back what he spent on my upbringing and education. I'd be embarrassed to repeat what he said to me, but he ended by telling me he didn't want the money because I was his responsibility, and he had never backed down on one yet."

"Ouch. I grew up Catholic, so I recognize that weapon. Guilt."

"Yes. But to be honest, I don't feel guilty about Mitch. Maybe I should, but I don't. I hated the way he treated Mom. I've even wondered if . . . well, never mind that. I haven't ever been close to him, but that's not the problem. It's just that he . . . how can I describe it? He *ensnares* people."

"So Warren Ducane and Auburn Sheffield gave you a way out of his trap."

"Exactly."

"You know, I can't help but think there was more to it than that. Auburn said you had turned them down."

"Believe it or not, Lillian convinced me."

"How?"

He was silent. I waited. I concentrated on my lunch for a while. He hadn't been eating much, and still didn't. That made me feel a little self-conscious, so I stopped and looked up at him.

"That night," he said, "at the dinner party? After you left?"

I turned crimson, but said, "Don't tell me . . . you threw something, too?"

He smiled and shook his head. "No. I meant, after everyone else left, Lillian and I talked. I can't explain it, really, but I feel comfortable around her."

"I know what you mean, or at least—I went over there with a chip on my shoulder, totally expecting her to look down her nose at me, but ended up liking her in spite of myself."

"Same here. I thought she might want me to be some kind of replacement grandson or something."

"That would have been pretty creepy."

"Creepy. Yes. This whole thing has lots of creepy aspects to it."

"But she didn't pressure you?"

"Not openly," he said, amused, "but subtly? Maybe she did. She got me to talk about school and my plans to work for Mitch. Like I said, it was easy to talk to her. She also said that whether I called myself Kyle or Max, she'd like to get to know me, because she had known my mom, and liked her."

"She meant Estelle?"

"Yes. Then she asked Hastings—her butler—to bring out some photos. They were of Mom when she was young, maybe nineteen or so. I guess Mom had been dating a friend of Lillian's then, because the man she was with in the photos wasn't Mitch. She looked . . . so beautiful, so happy. I don't remember her that way. I guess she was sadder, more fearful, when I was a kid. She drank a lot, and it made her look older than she was. Even her posture had changed from that of the girl in the photos. Maybe because she was always cowering around Mitch."

"With reason?"

He hesitated, then said, "Yes. Anyway, Lillian said that she didn't think she could ever forgive Mitch for what he did to my mother. She said that if I wouldn't take Auburn's offer, she'd like to know how she could help me to become free of Mitch, because she would never believe that Estelle would have wanted me to live my life always doing just what he wanted me to do."

"So you decided to take Warren's offer?"

"Yes. As for Mitch and all his schemes—I haven't ever seen them do anyone any good. Not even Mitch, really."

"So what do you want to do?"

"Invent things," he said, then blushed. "I mean, I have some ideas, and know some people I'd like to work with, guys from school."

"Like the GPS thing you were talking about the other night?"

"Yes. I want to be part of what's happening with that." He paused, then said, "At least, that was my plan until yesterday."

"Do you lose the money now that they know the real—well, I mean, the original Max Ducane is dead?"

"No, it's mine," he said, without much enthusiasm.

"Okay, you have an idea, some people to work with, and the funds to try it. So what's the problem?"

"Max Ducane," he said quietly.

"But you just said—"

"I'm using his money. I'm using his inheritance. He's a murder victim."

I thought about that for a moment, then said, "He was a murder victim twenty years ago, Max. You didn't cause that to happen by agreeing to Warren's plan."

"No, but it wouldn't be right to just—let me put it this way. Maybe some-one else could say, 'Too bad, that's just the past.' But I can't. For one thing, well—not many people know this, but I'm living at Lillian's house."

I must have raised a brow or something, because he quickly added, "Just for a few weeks. Then—well, never mind."

"What?"

"There was a plan that I would move into the house where her daughter lived. I was going to rent it, maybe buy it from her if I liked it. But I don't know—it seems morbid."

"She still owns that house?"

"Yes. I think—I think she still had some hope that Kathleen or Max would come home again."

"Twenty years of that. Wow. Did she rent it out to someone else in the meantime?"

"No."

"Weird."

"People hold on to hope," he said. "They have to, don't you think?"

"I suppose so. So . . . living with her, though. Why did she want you to live with her?"

"She wanted to get to know me. I've been spending a lot of time around her and Helen Swan and Auburn Sheffield, and I even spent time around Warren Ducane just before he left. I like all of them, but I especially like Helen and Lillian." He paused, then said, "I was there yesterday, when the police told Lillian what you'd found."

"Oh no . . ."

"It was so hard on her, even after all this time. Thank God your friend Helen came over to be with her, because I felt strange as hell, to say the least. And that's my point—I can't have this name and be befriended by these peo-ple and then pretend I don't know who that other Max Ducane was. When you looked in that trunk—that was her daughter, her grandson. Warren loved his brother—he set me up to get all of that money because I reminded him of Todd. Don't you see? I couldn't live with myself if I didn't do something to . . . to bring about justice, if at all possible. I have to use the money to try to find out who killed them."

"All of it?" I asked, startled.

"No, I couldn't do that even if I wanted to. Auburn and Mr. Brennan will still manage the trust until I'm thirty. Let's just say that I have been given enough right now to offer a big reward without becoming a beggar myself."

At this point, I started giving him the pitch. I asked to write his story, including the part about the reward, and started working through a list of things he had told me that could be published without hurting anyone. Some of it—mostly negative personal comments about Mitch and Estelle—he still wanted to withhold. He said I could tell O'Connor or Lefebvre anything that would be of help with investigating the murders, provided it was off the record, too. He didn't want to see anything he had said about Mitch and Estelle's marriage in the paper. I suppose I let what was beginning to be a friendship get in the way and didn't push him about that.

I told him about Mitch showing up at the coroner's office.

"I'm not surprised," he said. "Mitch thinks he has special privileges. I guess he does."

"Your cousin was the one who did the actual talking, I think."

"My cousin? Eric or Ian?"

"Ian—at least, Lefebvre said it was Ian."

"Silver streak in his hair?"

"Yes."

He made a face and gave an exaggerated shudder.

"That bad?"

"Ian and Eric are evil."

I laughed.

"I'm not joking," he said.

I was startled by his tone, his seriousness.

The awkwardness that produced was relieved a moment later, when the waiter came back and asked if we wanted dessert or coffee. We both declined, and soon he was back again, presenting the checks, taking our credit cards with thanks and an appearance of sincerity in his pleasure in serving us.

I could see Max fretting as the waiter walked off. "Don't worry," I said, "my card won't be declined."

He smiled. "I hope someday I'll be able to make this up to you. You know, that we'll be able to do something together and it won't be work for you." He turned red after he said it.

"Do you have a girlfriend at Dartmouth?" I asked.

"No. Not many girls go to Dartmouth—they just started admitting women six years ago. So there weren't many in my graduating class. Not many at all in computer science."

"Oh."

I was scared to death that he was going to say, "Why do you ask?" But he asked a worse question.

"Did you have a boyfriend in Bakersfield?"

"No," I said, breaking eye contact. "No . . . just friends. That's all."

"I must have missed that news story," he said.

I looked back at him. "What?"

"The one about all the guys in Bakersfield suffering from blindness."

"It's my charm that allowed them to resist, I'm afraid."

He shook his head.

"I didn't go to Bakersfield in what you'd call a receptive mood," I said.

"Somehow, I sense there's more to this."

"There is, but I need to get back to the paper."

He laughed. "You didn't come back to Las Piernas in a receptive mood, either, I see. Okay, I won't pressure you to talk about it."

The restaurant had become more crowded by the time we left, and the parking lot was full when we stepped outside. Most of the cars were Jags, Mercedes, or BMWs. There was a gaggle of black BMWs parked near the place where we had left Max's. "Are you going to be able to figure out which one is yours?"

"I'll have to look at the plates," he admitted. "Mine will be the one without any yet. But before we do that, let's go over to the fence—have you ever seen the view from this parking lot? It's one of the best in Las Piernas."

He was right. The fence was about waist-high. We could see Catalina Island in the distance, and nearer, sailboats passing the oil islands—man-made islands with oil well drilling rigs on them, the rigs covered and disguised as condos. And beyond, dappled with bright sunlight, a vast expanse of blue-gray sea. The wind brought sea spray and the scent of the ocean up the cliff, and below us breakers roared and hissed.

Max moved a little closer to me, not quite touching me. That inch or so of distance might as well have been the edge of the cliff—tempting and dizzying, but a wise woman would watch her step. I was trying to decide if I would be wise when a deep voice behind us said, "Who have we here?"

He startled the hell out of both of us, and we turned to see a big man who looked enough like the man I had seen at the coroner's office to allow me to guess who he was. Eric Yeager had no white streak in his hair, and wider shoulders than his younger brother.

"Kyle—no, Max," he said, stepping closer to Max, even as I stepped away from both of them. "Oh no, wait—we can't call you that, because Max Ducane is dead." He grabbed Max's shirtfront and said, "I know, I'll just call you cocksucker, since that's what you are." He leaned forward, so that Max was bent backward over the rail. I saw Max's feet leave the ground.

"Let go of me, Eric."

" 'Let go of me, Eric,' " he mimicked. "If I do that, cocksucker, you'll fall and die. Not a bad idea."

"That would be a stupid fucking thing to do in front of a newspaper reporter," I said.

He turned to look at me and narrowed his brows, as if he had just noticed that I was there.

"You've got a filthy mouth, bitch," he said.

"Like you're Emily Post come to teach me manners."

"Irene—" Max said. "Don't."

Eric continued to stare at me. Almost absently, he pulled Max back onto his feet. He let go of him and took a step toward me. "Maybe I will teach you some manners."

I took a step back without thinking, then stood my ground. I let the shoulder bag slip off, but kept hold of the straps in my hand. I moved it a little, trying to get a feel for the best use of its weight.

He saw the step back and laughed. "Talk big, but you're scared, aren't you?"

"Of your breath," I said. "You have a different kind of filthy mouth."

He lunged. I swung the bag up toward his balls as hard as I could.

The bag hit Eric full in the face instead of his family jewels, making a satisfying cracking sound on his nose. I didn't miss the more vulnerable target because I had aimed badly, but because Eric had already been on his way down to the asphalt. He hit it much harder than I had hit him.

I never saw exactly what it was Max had done to him, but he had moved like lightning.

Eric, in contrast, didn't move at all.

"I'm almost sorry we aren't on a date," I said shakily. "Dragon slayers are so damned rare these days."

"Come on," Max said, putting an arm around my shoulders and hurrying me away. "We'd better get out of here."

"Where did you learn to do that karate or whatever it was?"

"Military boarding schools, remember?"

I glanced back at Eric and saw that he was getting to his feet. I started running toward the car. Max ran, too.

We backed out just as Eric came at us from between parked cars. His face was bleeding down the front of his shirt. For a moment, I thought he was going to step in front of the Beemer, but Max hit the accelerator and Eric had at least enough sense left in him to stay back. We burned rubber out of the parking lot and drove lickety-split down a series of side streets, squealing around turns, braking hard, and narrowly missing objects mobile and immobile.

I don't know if seconds or minutes passed that way. I do remember thinking that my father might outlive me after all, and worrying about who would take care of him. The things you think of when you are full of adrenaline.

Almost as suddenly as our wild ride began, it ended. Max pulled over to the curb of a suburban street and parked in the shade of a big oak tree. We sat there, listening to the little clicks and small noises of a cooling engine. He rolled the windows down. Birds chirped up in the tree, a soft breeze blew, and I could hear the stutter of a pulsating lawn sprinkler two houses away.

We were both shaking.

"I've probably made you late to work," he said, "so I'll take the book back to the library for you."

Don't ask me why, but this struck me as one of the funniest things anyone had said in the twentieth century. I started laughing, and so did he.

When we paused for breath, he added, "You'll have to tell me how to get out of here. I'm lost."

That set off another round of laughter.

I looked at him, and what I wanted to do, in all honesty, was kiss the hell out of him. I would swear that he was looking at me in exactly the same way. But neither of us leaned closer, and the moment passed, and we both looked out the front windshield as if the scenery before us would change somehow, must have changed with whatever else had just changed.

"If you go straight ahead to that intersection," I said, "I can read the street sign and probably guide us from there."

"Okay," he said, and started the car.

I figured out where we were and gave him directions until we reached streets he knew. He talked about how someday his GPS devices would be in cars and guide people to their destinations, even if they were in totally unfamiliar places.

It sounded a little far-fetched to me, but that wasn't what really bothered me about it. "Getting lost isn't always so bad, is it?" I asked. "I mean, if you only go where you intend to go, and travel only on the recommended roads, you only see what everybody else sees all the time. You miss the out-of-the-way places."

He smiled and said, "Those who want to be adventurous can simply turn the GPS off."

"Or disobey it."

He laughed and said, "You don't need a dragon slayer, you'll take care of them on your own." He glanced over at me, then back at the road. "Hurry and finish that story, Irene Kelly."

34

I WAS SURPRISED TO LEARN THAT O'CONNOR HADN'T COME BACK IN YET, and wondered what he might be up to. I had plenty to work on, though. I started writing the story of how Max Ducane was reacting to the news that he could not possibly be the lost heir, and telling, for the first time anywhere, why he had accepted Warren Ducane's offer. O'Connor hadn't been able to get that story out of Max.

With some reluctance, I called Lillian Linworth. I wanted to reach her before Max came home. She was understandably still upset about yesterday's discoveries, but said that she was not about to ask Max to stop using her grandson's name. "Max is a good man, and his support and presence here have been a great comfort. You saw him today, didn't you?"

"Yes. I interviewed him at lunch."

"Oh." She sounded a little disappointed.

"He tells me that you want him to live in your daughter's house."

"If he wants to, yes."

"Any chance I could look through it before the change in ownership?"

There was a long silence, then she said, "If Max goes with you, I don't see a problem."

"Do you know about the reward?"

"Reward?"

"He's offering a twenty-thousand-dollar reward for information leading to the arrest and conviction of the murderers of . . . well, Max Ducane. And Kathleen and Todd."

"Is he?" she said, clearly surprised. "What a wonderful idea. Please print that I will match that amount."

*　*　*

I called Lefebvre to get his reaction. "Isn't that great?" I asked him. "That's more money than most people make in a year."

"It may help," he said.

"You sound tired."

"Didn't get much sleep. You know, the first twenty-four years in a homicide investigation are the ones that matter most."

"Years? I thought it was hours."

"I have never," he said sadly, "been good at making jokes."

"No, I'm just not up to your speed."

I guess I had made a joke, because that made him laugh.

"So, Phil, will it help?"

"It might. It might also keep us busy chasing false leads. But on a case this old, it will probably be a good thing."

"Any hope of getting fingerprints from the car?"

"Certainly. You and that construction crew put your paws all over it."

"You know what I mean."

"Tough call. I think we'll have better luck with hair and fibers."

"Bloodstains?"

"Yes."

"You are intentionally being irritating."

"Picked up on that, did you?"

"Yes."

"Well, Irene, I am irritated by this case. But perhaps offering this big reward will bring us an honest eyewitness, and not just a lot of greedy so-and-sos. What do you think my chances are?"

"Get some sleep. I'll let you know if I find anything at the Ducane mansion."

"What?"

I hung up.

My phone rang less than ten seconds later.

"That was rude," he said.

"Are you apologizing?"

"I meant," he said, laughing, "that you were rude."

I owned up to it. "I thought we were going to have a spirit of openness here, that's all."

"I can't tell you everything. You know that."

"Likewise. But I will tell you that it's apparently sort of a Miss Haversham scene over at the former Ducane household."

"What a relief."

"That Lillian preserved it the way it was on the fatal night?"

"No, that *Great Expectations* is still being taught in school."

"I didn't like it much, to be honest."

"No surprise. So, is there a cobwebbed wedding cake up in a dark and dusty chamber here in Las Piernas?"

"I'll let you know when I get back. If Max will let me tour it with him."

"Perhaps you wouldn't mind a third person to make it a crowd?"

"Because you've been doing me so many favors lately?"

"Are you waiting for me to say 'please'?"

"No, I wouldn't want you to die from the strain. Besides, you'll get a search warrant and probably tape it off and prevent me from seeing it at all. This way, you don't have to bother a judge or waste your yellow tape, and I get a homicide detective's comments. So I'll call you when I hear from Max. And you'll call me—?"

"If I can. I promise."

"Lefebvre?"

"Yes?"

"Were they in the car when they were killed?"

There was a long silence, then he said, "Perhaps."

"Let me put it this way. Did anyone other than the Ducanes die in that car?"

"I couldn't say."

I sighed. "Do you think the Ducanes were made to ride in the front seat or the backseat?"

"If I tell you, will you feel the urge to write about it for tomorrow's paper?"

"I can hold on to it, if you're willing to let me know the minute you're about to make it public."

"All right. We have seen signs that they were in the backseat."

"Thanks, Phil. I won't break my promise."

"If I thought you would, I wouldn't have told you a thing."

I wrote quickly. I decided I'd get it all down for now and make it pretty later. I kept my promise to Lefebvre.

When O'Connor showed up, he had changed shoes. "What happened to the ones you were wearing earlier?" I asked.

He looked down, as if surprised to see what he was wearing on his feet. "I got something on them at lunch."

"That's too bad." I also realized that his hair was a little damp, and he smelled like soap. He had taken a shower after lunch? The obvious meaning of this struck me—O'Connor had a girlfriend and had grabbed a quickie while I was at the Cliffside. And he had the nerve to tease me about Max? I tried not to smirk.

"No big deal," he was saying. "What's going on?"

I figured if I told him about Eric Yeager threatening us, I'd start to hear something about why this was no job for a woman. So I told him about my lunch with Max—leaving out the dragon-slaying—and about my plans to tour the Ducane mansion.

"I can't believe Lillian moved that kid under her roof," he said.

"He's not so bad."

He narrowed his gaze at me. "You're smitten, I suppose?"

"For God's sake, all I did was have lunch with him—unlike what some people might be doing on their lunch hours. And I paid for my own lunch. So there."

"You gave him your number at Lillian's that night, but he didn't call you until the story broke, did he?"

If there had been another bowl of strawberries at hand, he would have needed another shower. My fists clenched, but I kept my mouth shut. I turned and went back to my desk, back to writing the story about Max.

A minute later, O'Connor leaned over my typewriter. "Wrigley said no to adding your friend to the news staff," he said.

It smarted, coming as it did on the heels of his previous insult, but I tried to keep that reaction out of my voice as I said, "His loss."

"I told him it would make it easier for you if there was another woman working news side."

"Well, no wonder he said no—that would be a lame-ass reason for him to bring her over here. Besides, it isn't true. I'm fine. But thanks for fucking things up for Lydia."

"Why do you talk like that? Like a sailor?"

"Why should men have sole ownership of swear words? Why should you be the only ones who get to express your anger?"

"It's un—"

"Don't you dare say 'unladylike.'"

"All right. It's unbecoming. And unprofessional."

I stood up and stepped onto the seat of my wooden chair and shouted, "Any man in this room who has never said the word 'fuck,' please raise your hand."

Dead silence, broken only by the sound of the Teletypes. No hands went up. I saw Wrigley move to his office door. He was looking at O'Connor and grinning.

"Thank you," I said. "O'Connor believes you are all unprofessional. Take it the fuck up with him."

There was laughter and applause, a lot of hooting and hollering at O'Connor, who left the room as I got down off my chair.

I went back to writing, and the newsroom settled down—as much as it ever did.

Max called. I arranged to meet him at the Ducane place that evening. He didn't have a problem with Lefebvre joining us. "Bring O'Connor, too, if you'd like."

"I'll see," I evaded. "He's out at the moment." I asked if the power was still on at the house, and when he said yes, I arranged to meet him there at eight o'clock. "I've got a story to get in, and I won't be able to stay long—I've got to get home to my dad."

"To your dad?"

"Yes. He's ill. I'll explain it all later." Which in a way was a lie, because I couldn't fully explain it to myself.

I called Lefebvre, who thanked me and told me he'd try to return the favor. The weird thing was, even though I acted cheerful when I called him, I had the distinct feeling that he had read my true mood, anyway. Over the phone. Scary.

I used Lydia's notes to figure out who was the most talkative of the heirs of Griffin Baer. I called him and got the names of a few of Baer's friends. I even learned the name of a bar Baer used to hang out in.

Who else do old men talk to? I wondered.

I asked if he golfed, but the answer was no. I asked if he used to get his hair cut by a barber. This time, the answer was yes—in fact, the barber had come to his funeral. With a little searching through the Yellow Pages while I waited, the grandson was able to come up with the name of the barbershop. I thanked him and ended the call.

It occurred to me that it would help to have some of the photos from O'Connor's collection with me. I was wondering if I should try to find him, or just leave him alone and ask about it tomorrow, when I got a call from Aunt Mary.

"How's your friend?" she asked.

"My friend?" Did everyone in Las Piernas know I had gone to lunch with Max Ducane?

"The one you sent by to check on Patrick at lunchtime today."

I felt a cold sense of dread roll through me from my shoulders to my knees. First question. "Is Dad okay?"

"He's sleeping. Doing fine. He enjoyed the visit. In fact, he answered the door."

"Dad did?"

"Yes. Patrick was up for a little while, you know—walking around the house a bit like he's supposed to—and he answered the door."

"Oh."

"When he told me that you had arranged it just to give me a little break, I have to admit I was surprised, since you never mentioned a word to me. Well, I don't mean to criticize. That was very thoughtful of you, Irene, but not necessary. It did allow me to get a little grocery shopping done—"

"You're sure Dad's okay?"

"Why, yes."

"Uh . . . a couple of people have offered to help out. What did this friend look like?"

"A big man, dark hair with gray in it."

"A streak of gray?"

"No, more salt-and-pepper."

"He was from the newspaper, then?"

"No, he wasn't wearing a suit. Dressed more casually than that. But that was probably because of the lawn."

"The lawn?" I said, totally baffled now.

"Yes. He mowed and edged the front and back lawns. Made me realize how much I've neglected Patrick's garden."

Maybe it was O'Malley, I thought. Dad would have let him in. But why tell Mary he was a friend of mine, and not just call him an old high school buddy?

"You haven't neglected Patrick," I said. "That's the main thing." And I spent some time telling her how much I loved and appreciated her, which is the kind of thing you start doing when someone close to you has rung death's doorbell and run away.

"You sound worried," she said, cutting past all that. "Patrick is fine, and I am, too. Honestly, Irene. Patrick enjoyed the visit. You should be telling your friend how much you appreciate him."

"I would if I knew who it was."

"Drives a Nash. Does that help?"

"A Nash? A Nash? A Nash Rambler?"

"Didn't I just say so?"

"Thanks, Mary. I know who it is now." I told her about my schedule for the day. As usual, she was fine with it. She wanted, she told me, all the time she could get with Dad.

I hung up and sat there thinking that I wanted to quit my job. I wanted to go home and read to Patrick Kelly, and laugh with him, and mow his lawn.

But first, I decided, I needed to find O'Connor.

Mary thought I should thank him.

I had a different idea. I wanted to kill him.

35

I TRIED THE PRESS CLUB FIRST. HE WASN'T THERE. SOME OF THE NEWSROOM boys were already knocking 'em back, and it took me a little while to turn down offers of drinks without causing offense. Wildman, of all people, came to my rescue, telling the rest of them to back off and escorting me to the door. "You might try O'Grady's," Wildman said. "And you be sure to tell Conn I was a perfect gentleman." This last came out as "gennelmum," but I assured him I'd convey the message.

O'Connor wasn't at O'Grady's, either. The place was almost empty. I asked the bartender if he'd seen him, and he said O'Connor hadn't been in all week. I took my roll of dimes and went to the pay phone, which was in the hall outside the gents, and called Helen.

The problem was, by the time I reached her, I was out of steam. So when she asked me if anything was wrong, I told her, "Not with him. I, on the other hand, have lost my mind." I gave her a brief rundown of the afternoon. "So I was going to tell him off for sneaking behind my back to visit my dad, but—somewhere along the way, I guess I started to hear what Mary was trying to tell me."

"That your father enjoyed the visit. That it was a relief to her."

"Yes."

"You'll have to share him, won't you?"

"Yes." I took a deep breath and tried to change the subject. "How are you?"

"Rough day. But I'll be all right."

"Anything I can do?"

"No, and you have enough to contend with—but listen, if you're looking for Conn when he's upset, try Holy Family Cemetery."

"What?"

"Jack's grave. He goes out there to have a word with him once in a while."

"I wouldn't want to intrude," I said. "I'll catch up with him later."

*   *   *

I wasn't far from Griffin Baer's favorite barbershop, so I drove over to it. It was a clean little shop, with the traditional pole mounted outside the door, revolving in a pattern that must have inspired early psychedelic art. I walked into a room of white linoleum, maroon leather chairs, chrome, and mirrors. A thin, gray-haired man was sitting in one of the chairs, reading the sports section of today's *Express*, but he quickly stood when I came in. He looked at my shoulder-length hair and said, "Good afternoon! Two dollars to trim off those split ends and even it up a bit. The length is good on you, so we won't take off much."

Normally, I have to work up some courage to let anyone with a pair of scissors in his or her hand come near me, having had a couple of bad experiences with hairdressers who couldn't control their impulses—but this old guy didn't strike me as the type who felt the need to experiment on humans. "A deal," I said, taking a seat in a comfy chair. "But I want to be honest with you—I didn't come in here for a haircut."

"Sales?"

"A reporter for the *Las Piernas News Express*."

"I already subscribe," he said, indicating the copy he had set down. I saw that he had been circling horses' names on the handicapper's page.

"No," I said, "I'm not selling the paper. I'm a reporter."

"A reporter! How about that . . ."

He draped a cape over me and fastened it at my neck, then began combing my hair. No one had done this for me for a long time. I suddenly seemed to be able to feel every hair on my scalp. It almost tickled, but not quite. The sensation was both relaxing and gently stimulating. While it wasn't sexual, there was all the same a kind of intimacy in this personal attention. No wonder people confessed everything to barbers and beauticians.

"A natural brunette," he said. "Don't ever color it. It's gorgeous."

"Thanks, but how can you tell it's my natural color?"

"Do you know how to type?"

"Better than some congressional employees."

He laughed. "Well, you also know news. And I know hair."

"I wanted to ask you about Griffin Baer."

He stopped combing, then began again. "Old Griff, huh? Why ask about him now? Man has been dead for some time now."

I nodded toward the paper. "You read the story about the bodies in the car?"

"A little of it—don't be insulted, I just haven't had time to get to it yet. I was just catching up on sports when you walked in. I like to start the day with a smile, so I read the funny pages, then the sports, then 'Dear Abby,' and by then I'm ready for the news. But I do read the whole paper. I have to, in my business. Never know what a customer will want to talk about."

"Griffin Baer owned the farm where the bodies were found."

"Well, I'll be damned. I used to think that old man was just telling me tales, trying to make me think he'd had a wild youth. And after I went to his funeral and everyone was so nice and normal, I thought he'd made it all up!"

"He told you he had buried a car on his farm?"

"Oh no—hell no. Never said anything about that. But tell me—the people in the car, were they bootleggers?"

"What?"

"Bootleggers. Rumrunners. That's how Griff got that house by the ocean."

"You mean he smuggled booze into Las Piernas during Prohibition?"

"Yes, exactly. Told me they'd bring it into his house down there by the water, and then he did the work of getting it over to the old farm. Had a whole operation for distributing it from there."

"His heirs believe he got the house on the beach by selling mineral rights to the farm."

"Griff used to say—and lordy, I thought he was just being dramatic—that he was approached about letting them use the farm first. I guess it was a big place—a lot of acreage—and private. Set back from its neighbors. So then they arranged for him to get the house for a song, provided they could use it to land their hooch. He had a legitimate reason, see, for going from the house to the farm, and all that."

"Why not just buy the farm from him?"

"I don't know. Maybe they didn't want their names on too many records." He frowned. "That mineral rights story—you know who bought them?"

"No, but I'm going to find out."

He shook his head. "I get a few odd ducks in here, and I figured old Griff was just reading too many spy novels. He always acted a little paranoid. Would come in on a weekday afternoon, just like you have now. Wouldn't say a word if there was another person in the shop. He told me the government men never suspected that farmhouse, but I guess he had a false floor in the barn and a secret cellar. You can see why I didn't believe him."

I thought about all of that while he started to trim my hair. Maybe it really was nothing more than a paranoid old man's stories.

"What year did Prohibition end?" I asked.

He paused in his trimming and said, "Oh, let me see. Sometime during the

Depression. Around the time we had the big earthquake here—1933." The scissors went back to snipping. From what I could see in the mirror, he was doing a good job.

"The car was buried in 1958," I said. "So I don't know how it can have anything to do with bootlegging. And the people who were murdered were a young family. A man and woman in their early twenties, and their baby."

He shook his head sadly. "Honey, I don't like to think ill of Griff, who was always kind to me, and generous, even if he was a little odd. But the fact of the matter is, that kind of bootlegging would connect him up to some folks who weren't very nice."

The absurdity of talking about killers and gangsters as "not very nice" might have made me laugh if I hadn't become caught up in wondering about the Ducanes possibly having mob connections.

He finished his work with the scissors and put them and the comb into a jar of blue liquid to sanitize them. He was using a big soft brush to dust the clippings off my shoulders when I asked, "Did Mr. Baer ever mention a place up in the mountains? Near Lake Arrowhead?"

"No. And I don't think he ever went up there. He stayed in town. He didn't like the cold, but then, that just might be something that was part of old age. When he was younger, he could have been a ski champ, for all I know."

I thanked him both for the haircut and the information and promised I'd be back. I tipped him very generously.

First the Cliffside and then a big tip. I was walking around town as if I was in high cotton, as the Louisiana branch of the Kellys might have said. Ludicrous behavior for someone making an entry-level reporter's salary.

But then again, what had all the money in the world bought the Ducanes?

36

"YOU'RE LUCKY SHE DIDN'T BREAK YOUR NOSE," IAN SAID, HANDING his brother an ice pack. "I can't believe you let a chick do that to you."

"Wasn't her," Eric said. He would have said more, told him to fuck off, that the one who had really hurt him was their former cousin, but speaking through his scraped and swollen lips was too painful. Eric didn't think that wienie Kyle had landed all that many blows—he wasn't even sure he had made contact more than once before that bitch hit him in the face with the handbag from hell—but there were places along his neck, shoulders, back, and legs that ached from whatever the fuck he had done. Eric never saw it, never even saw it coming. Hit him from behind, then let a girl finish his fight—like the wienie he was.

When the purse hit his face, his teeth had cut into his lips and the inside of his cheek. The corner of whatever the hell it was she had in that bag had struck his eye, and it was now nearly swollen shut. Planting his face in the asphalt hadn't helped. His nose had stopped bleeding now, but it was tender and swollen, as was most of the left side of his face. His head throbbed.

"Man, your face is completely fucked up. You sure you aren't going to lose any teeth?"

If Ian didn't shut up soon, Eric was going to risk another set of injuries to make it as difficult for his brother to talk as it was for him.

As usual, though, Ian read his mood. He could always do that more quickly than anyone else. "Sorry, that was a shitty thing to say. If that asshole Kyle—wait, Uncle Mitch is right. He shouldn't have ever had even one part of our dad's name. I don't know what to call him. He's dead as far as I'm concerned."

Eric managed something close to a smile. "Deadman."

"Good one. Because he should have been dead a long time ago."

Eric nodded slightly. Even that much movement of his neck caused excruciating pain.

"We are getting way too old for this physical shit, you know?" Ian said.

"No kidding," Eric said. Guys in their early forties shouldn't have to do this kind of thing. They both kept in shape, worked out, and spent time out at the firing range, but they hadn't done this kind of job for Uncle Mitch in many years.

Uncle Mitch's businesses had changed. For the last twenty years, there hadn't been much rough stuff. Oh, every once in a while, Eric or Ian had to do a little collections work, but they seldom had to get physical. And Uncle Mitch hated to hear any report of that kind of action.

Uncle Mitch had wanted to be respectable now. He had a big thing about it. The Ducanes, the Linworths, the Vanderveers—that whole crowd had looked down their noses at Uncle Mitch. So Uncle Mitch was always on the climb, wanting to look right back down at them. Eric admired that about him. When he was a kid, Uncle Mitch owed that crowd money. Now he had more money than any of them.

For the past ten years, Eric and Ian had drawn a fat salary and had the titles of vice president in Yeager Enterprises, as Uncle Mitch's biggest company was known. That meant they went around to his various businesses and kept people honest, voted the way he told them to at board meetings, ran little errands. Nothing too challenging.

Except for one other task, the one they were told was their primary job— to keep an eye on Warren Ducane. Make sure he didn't go near any reporters. Come back and tell Uncle Mitch if he did anything out of the ordinary.

Ian and Eric used to wonder why Uncle Mitch didn't just kill the miserable son of a bitch. Over time, Eric began to understand certain things. One was that Warren Ducane and Uncle Mitch were in some kind of standoff, and that if either one of them made a move, the other could do serious harm.

He knew better than to put Warren Ducane out of his misery, because Uncle Mitch enjoyed seeing that misery. Warren wasn't the only one. There were these people in Las Piernas whom Uncle Mitch had never forgiven. Eric wasn't even sure what they had done to Uncle Mitch, but he knew that Uncle Mitch was paying them back for something. Uncle Mitch wasn't in a rush— he wanted them to suffer.

Uncle Mitch felt superior to all of them, but no one as much as Warren.

Eric had observed Warren for many more hours than his uncle had, and didn't share his uncle's complacency. He once told Uncle Mitch that he might have underestimated Warren Ducane. Eric would never forget the ranting and raging that had followed that—Uncle Mitch had a fire poker in his hand, and had threatened Eric with it. Ian had stepped in to protect him, and Uncle

Mitch had hit him. That's why Ian's hair had a white streak in it—it grew that way out of the place where he had been hit.

For a time, Uncle Mitch had seemed to be right about Warren Ducane. Over the years, except for a little change in his manner after he visited Auburn Sheffield, Warren Ducane seemed to be a beaten man.

They all knew better now, didn't they? And did Uncle Mitch remember Eric's warnings? No. He berated Ian and Eric, blamed them for becoming bored out of their minds with watching a dull little wimp like Warren Ducane go through his dull little life.

Uncle Mitch always made it clear that he didn't think they were smart. Maybe they weren't as smart as his adopted traitor—but they weren't stupid. They weren't as interested in some of the business stuff as Uncle Mitch wanted them to be, but that didn't mean they were dumb.

Uncle Mitch didn't respect them, but he took care of them. It had been that way from the beginning of their lives. He wasn't always an easy man to please, but he was there when you needed him. He was good at protecting them, and they did their best to return the favor. But he had younger guys on his payroll, and Eric wished one of them had been over at the Cliffside this afternoon instead of him.

"He can't let anyone else handle this," Ian said, again following his thoughts. "And you know why."

Eric nodded and instantly regretted the motion.

"I guess I'd better try to find the Deadman," Ian said. "Why'd you get in his face, Eric? Now they'll be watching for us."

Eric flipped him the bird.

Ian didn't say anything for a minute. When he spoke, he took up another sore subject. "I can't believe he bought a Beemer. A black one, like ours?"

"Yes," Eric said, deciding that it was easier to talk than to nod.

"He's trying to show us up, isn't he?"

Eric thought the Beemer was the Deadman's way of telling Ian and Eric that he didn't need Uncle Mitch in order to have a car. He could buy his own.

For a few moments, Eric found himself wondering what it would be like not to have to go to Uncle Mitch for everything.

He thought about the little treasure box he kept hidden—his insurance, as he thought of it. A few things to help him out if Uncle Mitch's will turned out not to be so generous to his nephews after all. Eric had been collecting small but valuable items in it from the day Uncle Mitch took an orphan into his home. Still, nothing in the treasure box would allow Eric to live as he did now.

"Do you think our little cousin is getting it on with that chick from the newspaper?" Ian asked, breaking in on these thoughts.

Eric managed to mumble, "Don't know. But he's after her."

Ian suddenly sat up straight. "Do you think he's trying to get Warren's side of things into the paper, now that Warren thinks he's safe?"

Eric's one good eye widened. He hadn't thought his cousin was on anything more than a mission to get laid. But Ian was right. "Shit," he said.

The biggest problem was, Warren did seem to be safe. They had learned not to mention him around Uncle Mitch. Warren and that little wiener and now a reporter from the *Express*—not a good mix.

Ian frowned, growing more worried. "No wonder Uncle Mitch wants us to keep an eye on them. Fucking weirdo, Warren! Why couldn't he just leave things alone?"

Eric was in complete sympathy with these feelings.

"A reporter," Ian repeated. "A reporter! Damn!"

"That's not all," Eric said. "She's O'Connor's friend."

"What! O'Connor!"

"I shit you not."

"The Deadman couldn't have given them anything from Warren yet," Ian reasoned, "or it would already be in the paper. So what's the deal? We've gotta find a way to stop him. Maybe we should just kill the Deadman—and this reporter."

"No."

"Why not?"

"Warren could still tell O'Connor. Or someone else. Warren is the problem."

"So what do we do?"

"Set a trap for Warren."

"How?"

"The Deadman—make him the bait."

Ian liked the idea. "I'll tell Uncle Mitch."

"No," Eric said quickly.

Ian looked so stunned, Eric found it almost comical.

"No?" Ian said, his hand going to the silver streak.

"He's mad at us for letting Warren get away from town, right?"

"That wasn't our fault!"

"Of course it wasn't. But you know how he is."

"So if we say this will work, and it doesn't . . ." Ian said.

"Exactly. We're screwed. He'll just say we fucked up again. When we have Warren in our hands, we tell Uncle Mitch."

"But if Warren doesn't show himself . . ."

"He will."

Ian looked doubtful.

"He will," Eric said again, with the confidence of a hunter who had studied his prey for twenty years.

37

I LEFT THE BARBERSHOP AND DROVE BY THE ADDRESS I HAD FOR GRIFFIN Baer's beach property. I couldn't blame Baer for trading a farm in for a place in this neighborhood. Baer's was one of the homes that formed a single row along the wide four-lane avenue—known in that stretch as Shoreline Avenue. On the other side of the avenue, a narrow, grassy park lay along the top of bluffs. At the foot of the bluffs was the sandy, south-facing shore, and beyond that, the Pacific Ocean.

Along that section of Shoreline the homes were huge, with mammoth picture windows, large balconies, and steeply sloping lawns. Many of the mansions were built in the 1920s and 1930s, although here and there one had been torn down and replaced with a contemporary structure. The newer homes seemed to be made of steel and tinted glass.

There was no parking available anywhere near the Baer place on this warm, sunny day, at least not on Shoreline, but I slowed as I neared it. A white Spanish-style home, with arched windows and a red-tiled roof, it didn't look as if it had changed much from when it was first built. The paint looked fresh and the yard was well maintained. A low white stucco fence surrounded the front yard. There was a For Sale sign in the yard. I wrote down the real estate agent's name and number. Someone honked behind me.

I drove to the end of the block and turned right, and right again at the alley behind the homes. I found the Baer house and parked blocking the door of the detached, flat-roofed garage in the back. I glanced at the latch on the garage door. It was padlocked shut, so I didn't think there was a danger that anyone would throw it open and bash my car.

I got out of the car and tried the back gate. It proved to be padlocked as well. I peered over the fence, wondering how this place could have been used for smuggling. Maybe there weren't as many houses along here then. Shoreline had been a much narrower road in the 1920s, and the park wasn't in existence yet, but the bluffs had been there. A few miles from this point, they rose into steep, rocky cliffs, but here they were lower and made mostly of clay and sandstone, and in places were covered with ice plant. Although they weren't as high as the two leg-shaped cliffs that gave Las Piernas its name, a fall from the bluffs would have caused serious if not fatal injuries. Would a bootlegger scale them?

Maybe there had been stairs along this spot in those days. Perhaps the goods were landed somewhere else along the beach and brought by car to this place. But that didn't seem to make much sense. Why stop here? Why not just go on to the farm?

The house was quiet and from where I stood, it seemed to be empty. After a moment, I got back into the Karmann Ghia. The alley didn't go through to the next street, but it was fairly wide, and I was able to maneuver the Karmann Ghia around rather than having to back up the whole way.

When I got back to the paper, the late-afternoon siege was on, the troops battering away at deadline. I looked over what I had written so far. I couldn't add what I had heard about Griffin Baer; that was all unsubstantiated.

I called the real estate agent and told her I was with the *Las Piernas News Express* and asked for a tour of the house, but she apparently didn't understand why I mentioned the paper, because she tried to "qualify" me. I bit back a laugh—mortgage interest rates were at a double-digit historic high; I had only held my current job a few months, and would have been a first-time buyer. Another big obstacle was the known fact that no lender wanted to make a home loan to a single woman. But the biggest one of all was that a reporter's salary wouldn't have allowed me to buy a single square foot of that neighborhood. So I told her I wasn't a potential buyer, I was working on a story for the *Express*. She hung up on me.

I went to work on my story about Max.

I glanced up and saw O'Connor enter the newsroom. He saw me, checked for a moment, then came toward my desk with determined strides. He opened his mouth to say something to me, but I spoke first.

"I'm to tell you that Wildman was a perfect gentleman," I said.

"Wildman? He's drunk as a brewer's fart. I just saw a couple of the boys loading him into a taxi outside the Press Club. He was passed out cold or they never could have managed it."

"All right, so—a couple of hours before he passed out, Wildman was a perfect gentleman. I should explain that I asked for his help in finding you this afternoon."

We went through what was now becoming a ritual exchange of apologies. I thanked him for visiting my dad and mowing the lawn.

"I told your aunt not to tell you about that," he said testily.

"She's my great-aunt, and she probably thought you were too young to give her orders. Did you tell her your name?"

"Of course I did!"

"She's also a troublemaker," I muttered.

"Kelly, no wonder you are as you are. All this uppity-woman stuff is inherited, I see. You haven't a chance." He shrugged. "Or perhaps it's the rest of us who haven't a chance."

"True. Aunt Mary says you can tell a Kelly woman anything but where to sit and when to shut up."

"What have you been up to this afternoon, my fine young renegade?"

"I went to the barbershop." I told him what I had heard about Griffin Baer.

"Good work," he said.

"Thanks, but I don't know if what he told me is true." I told him about the house. "It doesn't seem well situated for bootlegging."

"It's not as unlikely as you may think. Those old houses have tunnels that lead from their basements to the bluffs. Most of them are sealed off now, but in the twenties they would have been functioning."

"But wouldn't just having one of those tunnels make the prohibition agents suspicious of you?"

He smiled and said, "I was only five when Prohibition was repealed, you know."

"I know you didn't fight in the Civil War, either. But did Jack or Helen or anyone else ever talk to you about it?"

"From what I've been told, almost all of the homes along the bluff had them, and the owners always claimed that they were just a convenient way to get to the beach or take small sailboats out on the water. The government never put enough money into hiring federal prohibition agents, and locally, there were certain cops and judges who were getting protection money to shield the bootleggers."

"So the town had speakeasies and all of that?"

"Of course. And there was the gambling ship."

"Gambling ship?"

"A big ship that was anchored offshore, with a sign on its side telling people where they could get speedboats to come out to her. There were a number of ships that were moored between the coast and Catalina in those years, run by gangsters. They sold booze out there, too. The one off Las Piernas caught fire and burned."

"I didn't realize Las Piernas had such a wild history."

"No better or worse than most cities its size."

"So I should walk along the beach and try to find a tunnel exit?"

"You could, I suppose."

I told him about the meeting I had arranged with Max Ducane and Lefebvre. "Do you want to join us? I think it would be good to have you there, since you saw the house the night of the murders."

He hesitated, then said, "Sure."

We talked about what we'd do for the next set of stories. He showed me what he was working on—an interview he had done with Auburn Sheffield this afternoon about the trust and why he had taken on Warren's unusual request. O'Connor had asked Auburn how he felt about it now that the coroner had identified the true Max Ducane's remains.

"While I feel the deepest sympathy for Lillian Vanderveer," Auburn had said, "and for Warren Ducane—assuming he may learn of these recent discoveries—I have absolutely no regrets regarding the trust. It is being given to a young man in whom Warren took a sincere interest, a young man who will, I am certain, bring honor to the memory of the Ducanes."

"This fits really well with what I've been working on," I said. I waited as he read what I had written about Max. He gave me some useful feedback about it—he was right, I needed to pull back a bit.

"I have too much sympathy for him, I guess," I said, and told him some of the things Max had said to me off the record.

"Even if it hadn't been off the record, you were smart to leave all that out, especially since we've no quotes from Mr. Yeager. Not that I doubt for a moment that he abused his first wife." He paused, then added, "It's not bad to feel sympathy. Reporters who pretend they are objective, above-it-all recorders of the truth are lying to both their readers and themselves, and that lie can be found everywhere in their stories. They often develop a kind of cynical disdain for everyone and everything they write about. Cynicism is just another way to lose objectivity."

"But you can't just be a sap, either," I said glumly.

"No. It's what degree of that sympathy ends up in the story that you need to watch, especially if you haven't balanced it with the other side of the tale. If I hadn't caught that, H.G. or John would have, but in time you'll be able to catch it yourself, long before it ends up on the page."

My phone rang. It was Lefebvre.

"Do you know where Bijoux is?"

"The jewelry store on Third Street?" I asked.

"Yes. Can you meet me there in twenty minutes?"

"Hang on." I covered the phone and told O'Connor about the request.

"I take it he's not buying you a ring?"

"Yes, for me to put through your nose, if they've got one that big."

"Go," he said, laughing. "Take advantage of Lefebvre's cooperative mood while it lasts."

"But deadline—"

"I'll polish the story a bit, add what I have from Auburn, and turn it in—if that's all right with you."

I told Lefebvre I'd be right there. I thanked O'Connor, grabbed my camera, and took off.

I was closer to the store than Lefebvre was—the police department used to be headquartered nearer to the newspaper, but they had moved to a newer and bigger facility in the 1960s, generally regarded as one of the ugliest buildings in Las Piernas, and not just by those brought to it in the back of a squad car.

Lefebvre greeted me, then looked up at the store and said, "I'm told Mr. Belen is a diamond expert, and the most reliable jeweler in town."

"I don't know about that, but Bijoux has been around forever."

"As if you would have any sense of forever," he said. "Bijoux, eh?"

"It's hard for most of the locals to say it," I said. "I've actually heard it pronounced 'buy jocks.' You, however, make it sound exotic."

"I was just thinking that it is a bit plain," he said. "In French, the word means 'jewelry.'"

"So are we here to get the Vanderveer diamonds cleaned?"

He smiled. "And I had thought to surprise you."

"I couldn't think of any other reason you would invite me to come to a jewelry store."

"Why, to get a ring for O'Connor's nose," he said, holding the door open for me.

"Next time, I'm using the hold button," I said, and entered the store.

"Speaking of putting things on hold," he said, following me, "I need you to hang on to the information you hear today. Not run it in a story until I let you know that we can release it. Can you promise me that?"

I tested his resolve on this a bit and found that he wouldn't budge, so I agreed, with conditions. "If you'll promise me in return that you won't wait just for the fun of it," I said. "Oh—and if I can get this information any other way—"

"You can't," he said. "But yes, I agree to your conditions."

Mr. Belen was an elderly man with a charming accent of his own—one I couldn't quite place. He had some photographs in hand.

"Mr. Belen is Mrs. Linworth's jeweler," Lefebvre said. "Before she gave the necklace to her daughter, she asked Mr. Belen to clean the diamonds and repair any loose settings. Today he told me that he photographed his finished work."

"Yes, I did," Belen answered. He sighed. "I'm so sorry that the next time it was seen was under such terrible circumstances. I knew Miss Kathleen. A lovely girl."

He showed us the photographs—two lovely double-strands of round diamonds. He laid out a black velvet cloth, and Lefebvre gently placed two small sections of the necklace that were still united and twenty-six loose diamonds onto it. At my look of puzzlement, Lefebvre said, "We found most of them under the bodies and in the crevices of the trunk."

They were in a range of sizes, and Mr. Belen spoke to us as he quickly sorted them. "There should be one hundred and twenty of them," he said.

"We collected forty-one."

Mr. Belen raised a brow.

Lefebvre said, "I won't tell you that our evidence control is always perfect, but with something this valuable, and in a case like this, we are extremely careful. These diamonds were collected under the highest security possible."

"Could some of the diamonds still be in the car?"

"Every inch of that car, and everything in it, has been searched and sifted through. We've gathered much more minute evidence than diamonds." He turned to me. "That is not for publication."

"No, why should I tell anyone you're doing your job?"

Mr. Belen went back to sorting diamonds. Before long, it was clear that most of the missing stones were from a middle section, the part that would hang lowest—and which had the biggest diamonds in it.

"Maybe whoever killed her grabbed the necklace and yanked down," I said, "and kept whatever he still had in his hands. Stuffed a few more in his pockets."

"In a hurry," Lefebvre agreed.

"And took them after he killed her," I said.

"How could you know that?" Belen asked.

"If she had been alive, I think he simply would have made her take them off and hand them over. The loose stones wouldn't be in the trunk."

"They won't be hard to identify if the killer still has them, just as he took them," Belen said, "but I suspect he has had them recut. This style of diamond cutting is passé. The newer ways of cutting disperse light in the stone in a way that makes them brighter."

Lefebvre and I both took photos when Belen had the diamonds laid out in the order they belonged. Belen gave Lefebvre copies of the photos he had taken in December 1957, and looked at me apologetically.

"I'm sure Detective Lefebvre won't mind making copies for me," I reassured him.

Detective Lefebvre ignored me as he studied the pictures. "I have some photos of her wearing the diamonds at the party," he said, "but none of just the necklace itself. Thanks—this will help."

We left not much later. I mentioned to Lefebvre the Chesterfields and the lighter Jack had given to Katy. He took notes. I thanked him for bringing me along to the jewelry store and told him I'd see him later that night. I had just enough time to have dinner with Dad and Aunt Mary.

As I drove home, I thought I saw someone following me in a dark car. I made a few unnecessary turns to get to streets that were emptier, where it would be harder for a tail to hide from me. Nothing.

I told myself not to let myself get spooked so easily and kept driving.

38

As O'Connor stepped into the foyer, the last of the four to enter the Ducane home, he felt himself surrounded by ghosts. The house was much as he remembered it. He thought of the four murder victims—of Katy, Todd, and the baby, but most especially of the nursemaid, whose blood he had seen on that rainy evening more than twenty years ago. He thought of all that had happened that evening in so short a space of time, and much of it centering around this household.

He recalled the urgency with which Jack had insisted he look for Katy that night—how Jack hadn't cared about his own injuries (or sending O'Connor out into the rain) half as much as he cared about Katy. He remembered now that Jack said something had been troubling her. He remembered the note to Jack, asking if Mitch was her father, and wondered if that was what had disturbed her that evening. He felt sad for her, thinking of her now from nearly the same age Jack had been, while she had been about the age Max Ducane was now.

When Max turned on the lights, the cleanliness of the house only emphasized its emptiness, made it into a well-kept museum, and added to O'Connor's feelings of disquiet.

He watched Irene and Lefebvre. As Lefebvre looked around, nothing in his facial expression gave away his thoughts or feelings. He had a large brown envelope in his hands—crime scene photographs, he had told them. Irene, he thought, should never let anyone talk her into getting into a poker game. She was bothered, he could see—by the thought of what had gone on here twenty years ago, or perhaps because the house seemed frozen in another decade. She had a small camera with her, the one she had brought to the groundbreaking ceremony, hanging by a strap around her neck. She wasn't using it.

"I thought you said this place has been empty for twenty years," she said to Max. "There's no dust."

"Lillian has paid someone to keep it clean," Max said. "Weird, huh?"

"Seriously weird." She glanced uneasily at O'Connor. "I mean . . . Lillian seems to have moved on with her life, but then there's this house, sitting here."

He thought of his protectiveness of Maureen's room, how hard it had been when his eldest sister had moved into that room. "The families of the missing can't live in the same way other people do. If you know what happened to someone—that the person moved away, or died, or chose to be with someone else—your mind can let go, even if your heart takes a little longer to do the same. When a person you love is missing, inexplicably gone, perhaps you want to cling to anything associated with them, anything solid and normal, any reminder that they were here. If you keep a place for them, they might return. You worry that if you stop remembering them—and memories do fade—then the missing person will disappear in a more final way. That seems as if it would be a horrible betrayal, and so you fight it. And besides, the physical gives you something to focus on, other than the endless questions."

He became suddenly self-conscious, and especially aware of a change in Lefebvre's scrutiny.

Irene said, "Max, you've lived away from Las Piernas, so you probably don't realize that O'Connor is kind of famous around here for all he does to help families of missing persons, and to help find the identities of John and Jane Does."

"You were going to show us the house, Max?" O'Connor said quickly.

"I suppose we should start upstairs," Max said, and led them up the large, curving staircase.

"Check out the phone," he said to Irene, pointing to one that sat on a small marble-topped hall table.

The phone would have been an old one when Katy lived here; it was made of black Bakelite, and had no dial on it.

"An extension only," O'Connor said.

"So is this place exactly the way it was the last time you were here?" Irene asked.

"No," Max answered, before O'Connor could reply. "Lillian hired someone to repair the door off the kitchen, and she's had the place painted. I think . . . well, a new floor was put in the nursery. Let's go there first."

As he led them into it, he said, "At least I can stop wondering if this used to be my room."

"Did you wonder?" Irene asked.

"Not really," he said. At the doubting looks of the others, he moved over to the empty bassinet and ran his fingers lightly along its rim. "I mean, everyone who is adopted has that fantasy at some point in his childhood—you were always the kidnapped prince, of course, and never the abandoned pauper. Warren seemed so certain that I had once been this little prince, I asked myself if it could be possible. But if you mean, did I ever have some mystical experience in here, some faint memory from infancy? No."

O'Connor thought of the way the room looked that night—really looked. Not this sanitized shrine.

The bloodstains.

He heard paper rustling and saw Lefebvre opening his envelope. Photographs. Lefebvre set a small stack of them on the changing table. Almost against his will, O'Connor drew nearer to look, standing next to Irene.

In stark black-and-white, the top photo showed him what the room had looked like when Dan Norton had arrived, when Rose Hannon's body still lay on the floor. He saw what Dan had seen that long-ago night—the bloodstains and the position of the body indicated that she had been crawling on the floor toward the bassinet. The poor woman had bled to death trying to reach the baby.

Max glanced over their shoulders, shuddered, and moved away.

"There was another member of the house staff. A maid, right?" Irene asked, picking up the photo and looking through the next three. They were far more gruesome shots of the body.

"Yes. She wasn't implicated," Lefebvre said.

She handed the photos back to Lefebvre. "I'm just thinking that Gus Ronden must have known a lot about this household. He knew that the Ducanes wouldn't be at home, and that the baby wouldn't be with his mother. He knew that Rose Hannon would be here alone with the child."

"He might have come here ready to kill two women," Lefebvre said.

"Maybe," Irene said. "But that would be much more chancy, wouldn't it?"

"Yes," O'Connor said. "But Dan and I both checked up on the other maid. Doesn't seem likely at all that she knew Gus Ronden."

"Is she still living?" Irene asked.

"Yes," Lefebvre said. "Why on earth does that make you smile?"

"Because you wouldn't know she was alive unless you had already contacted her. What did you find out?"

"That I should watch what I say around you."

"You've both lost me, I'm afraid," said Max.

"You have to think of everything that was going on in Las Piernas that night," Irene said. "Too much was going on at once for it to be explained as just a random, terribly unlucky night." She frowned in concentration. "I think it was supposed to look as if the Ducanes happened to drown on the night of a kidnapping. In the end, that's the way most of Las Piernas looked at it, right? A horrible coincidence, and the kidnapping of the child was sad, but the Ducanes' tragedy at sea was a combination of foolishness and unpredictable weather."

"Don't forget Jack's beating," O'Connor said.

"I haven't," she answered. "I'm as sure as you are that the beating was planned, but I doubt he was supposed to see the burial of the car."

"I agree," Lefebvre said. "No one was ever supposed to find that buried car. They didn't dump Jack Corrigan in a grove and hope he'd wake up in time to watch—I think that was a mistake. If they had wanted him to see it, they would have given him a front-row seat and a ride back to town. Instead, they tried to kill him."

"They came damned close to succeeding," O'Connor said.

"Okay," Irene said, "but back up. We've found the car. So we know there wasn't simple coincidence at work. Think about it—there had to be a ringmaster of this circus. That person knew about the Ducanes' yacht, and that they planned to take it out that night."

"And planned to take Kathleen and Todd with them," Max said.

"Right. And like I said, he or she knew that Rose Hannon would be here alone with the baby."

"And the trio that went to work on Jack either followed him or knew he'd be at the party," O'Connor said.

"Did they have invitations?" Irene asked.

"Yes," O'Connor said. "But no one was ever able to verify where they got them from. Lillian gave a stack of invitations to the Ducanes, and she has always believed that the Thelma and Barrett Ducane must have given one of their invitations to someone who knew Bo Jergenson—but the Ducanes weren't around to tell us who that might have been."

"So think of it as a circus from hell. Three rings—Jack in one ring, Thelma and Barrett Ducane in another, and Katy, Todd, and their baby in the third."

"So who's the ringmaster?" Max asked.

O'Connor thought of mentioning Yeager, recalled this young man's defense of him at Lillian's dinner party, and decided to keep his theories to himself. It occurred to him that Irene might be doing the same.

"The ringmaster? Someone who had a connection to the people in all three rings," Lefebvre said.

"Who benefited the most?" Irene asked.

"Warren Ducane, more than anyone," Lefebvre said. "With every other Ducane out of the way, he inherited a bundle."

"He disappeared just before that shopping center broke ground," Irene added.

"Not in a million years," O'Connor said.

All three stared at him in surprise.

"First of all, Jack and Warren knew each other. Warren was a party boy in those days. I can't think of a reason in the world he'd do something like that to Jack. They always got along fine."

"But the money . . ." Max said.

"I've never known a man who loved his brother more than Warren loved Todd. Looked up to him—not that Todd was any great role model, but Warren didn't see that."

"Maybe his hero failed him in some way," Irene said. "It has been known to happen."

O'Connor eyed her narrowly, then glanced at Lefebvre, who was suddenly busying himself with putting the photos back in the envelope. "That isn't the only reason," O'Connor said. "I was there when he got the news. Warren was shocked to hear that Todd was dead."

"But not shocked that his parents were dead?" Lefebvre asked.

O'Connor shrugged. "Neither Dan nor I were ever sure about that. We both thought he was hiding something. But he had a solid alibi and if someone got a payoff from him, Dan never saw it—and he looked hard for something like that. Warren let him look at his bank accounts and all of that without throwing any obstacles in his way."

Irene turned toward Lefebvre, who shook his head and said, "Oh no, I'm not talking to you about the man's finances. But what O'Connor said is true."

"Well, Warren didn't mastermind it, anyway," she said.

"What makes you so sure?" Max asked.

She turned to Lefebvre. "The department watched him closely after his parents disappeared?"

"I never said so."

"Come on, Lefebvre. The heir and everyone else in the family missing, he cashes in big time, and your department didn't think you guys ought to watch him?"

"I know I seem very old to you, but I wasn't with the department then. But let's assume Dan Norton checked into his alibi and kept an eye on him."

"Good," she said. "Because I think the police would have noticed if he had gone up into the mountains and shot someone and stuffed the body in the trunk of a car."

"True," Lefebvre said. "But maybe he killed the man earlier in the proceedings."

"When? Gus Ronden was up in the mountains before O'Connor and Norton found Warren over at Auburn Sheffield's place. Ronden must have left not long after he killed Bo and dumped Jack in the marsh."

"I used to wonder why they would have bothered moving Jack," O'Connor said, "and knew it had something to do with the Buick, but—I was missing too many pieces of the puzzle. Everyone who knew Jergenson said he wasn't too bright, so I suspect he wasn't supposed to take Jack to the farm."

"They thought they had drowned Jack, right?" she asked.

"They probably thought they had finished him off," he agreed.

He watched her brows draw together.

"We know Gus Ronden was connected to both the kidnapping and the attack on Corrigan," Lefebvre said. "Our crime lab found bloodstains on clothing at his house, and it wasn't his blood—he was type A. The blood on the clothing in the hamper matched Rose Hannon's blood type—she was AB, which is found in only about four percent of the population. Jack Corrigan was type O—we found type O bloodstains in the trunk of Ronden's car, but we also found fibers from Jack's clothing and his keys inside the trunk. The gun in Ronden's car fired the bullet that killed Jergenson, so we know he was at the marsh that night."

"And you found the weapon that killed Rose Hannon," Irene said.

"Yes. It was a knife among Gus Ronden's possessions." He sighed. "He had previously assaulted a woman. Today, we could have run many more tests for proteins on the bloodstains than we could in 1958, and narrowed down the possible contributors of that type O blood. And Gus Ronden would have shown up in the NCIC."

"The FBI computer project?" O'Connor asked.

"Yes. National Crime Information Center. Back in 'fifty-eight, it wasn't all that hard for criminals to relocate. No easy way to track them between jurisdictions. This system changes all that. Soon we're supposed to be getting hooked up to an automated fingerprint system from the FBI. So—"

"Back up," Irene said. "The bloodstains—what was the baby's blood type?"

"Type O. Katy and Todd were both type O."

She looked toward Max. "I've given blood, so I know I'm type A. Do you know your blood type?"

"Yes," he said, "I'm type O, but it doesn't matter now—the real Max Ducane has been found. Besides, it's the most common blood type."

"Was all of the blood inside the Buick type O?"

"We aren't sure we'll be able to work with any of those bloodstains. They are quite old and most have been contaminated by dirt or degraded by bacteria."

"Most? Does that mean you may have some you can work with?"

"I'm not going to discuss that now."

She muttered, "Spirit of openness." Lefebvre ignored her.

"The police checked out Warren's alibi, right?" Max asked.

"Yes," Lefebvre said. "Warren Ducane could have paid others to do his work for him, of course."

"I don't think it's Warren," Irene said. "If his motive was the inheritance, and he already knew the baby was dead, it wouldn't make a lot of sense for him to set up a trust fund for his lost nephew and then actually give that trust—worth much more now than it was then—to Max. Even if setting up the fund was just some way of throwing you off his trail, it made no sense for him to keep it going so long—if he had arranged to have the baby killed, why not take the money back after ten years? He could have told everyone, 'I tried my best to find him, but I've given up hope now.' No one would have blamed him. Instead, he went out of his way to find Max and talked him into taking the money."

"That's true," Max said, and O'Connor heard the relief in his voice.

"Let's look through the rest of the house," Lefebvre suggested.

As they made the long trek toward the master bedroom, Irene said, "Katy slept so far away from her baby," voicing the same thought that had crossed O'Connor's mind twenty years before.

"No," Max said. "There's a bassinet in her room, too."

"Oh, good," she said, then added in a quieter voice, "I don't know why I mentioned it. I guess it doesn't matter now."

"But it mattered while he lived," O'Connor said.

"While he lived . . ." she repeated softly. "Wait! Why wasn't the baby killed here?"

All three men stopped walking and turned toward her.

"I mean," she said, looking self-conscious, "if you were going to kill an infant and bury him in a car trunk, why not just kill him here? It would have been easier to kill him than the maid, right? And if he was dead, you wouldn't need to worry that he'd cry or scream or . . . cause you any trouble."

Lefebvre got a thoughtful look on his face.

"The police must have considered that question before now," Max said. "What's the answer?"

"Until yesterday," Lefebvre reminded him, "we thought the Ducanes had probably been the victims of a boating accident—although there were questions, there was no proof that it had been anything else. We thought the child had been kidnapped, to be held for ransom. And perhaps killed when the possibility of ransom disappeared. And we really weren't sure how Jack Corrigan's beating figured into anything, other than some kind of connection between the man who assaulted him and the one who murdered Rose Hannon. So, sorry, but no. No ready answers to that question."

They went into Katy's room first. O'Connor watched Irene, curious about her reaction to the other woman's room. "It was her sanctuary, wasn't it?" she said. "Everything a young 1950s society girl could want . . ." She strolled around, touching objects as she named them. "Music in high fidelity, *color* television, books, a comfy bed with baby close by, and . . . a dog bed? Oh, how sad. What happened to the dog?"

Max and Lefebvre looked to O'Connor.

"The pug? No one knew. I thought it might have run away after the nurse-maid was murdered."

"No . . ." Lefebvre said slowly. "No, wait . . ." He started looking through his envelope of photos again. He pulled out an eight-by-ten black-and-white glossy—a photograph taken at a party. A half-dozen elegantly dressed people stood near a big birthday cake. *Happy Birthday, Kathleen!* was inscribed in flowing script on the cake. O'Connor immediately recognized the six people—Lillian and Harold Linworth, Thelma and Barrett Ducane, Katy and Todd Ducane. Katy was holding a dog. Her pug.

"The dog was with her!" Irene said. "The Ducanes never came back here that night, right?"

"Right," Lefebvre said. "Her roadster was at Thelma and Barrett's home. There were no signs of violence there. We don't think anyone entered the house. The trouble must have started at the marina or on the boat."

"So when she got to her in-laws' home, she either left the dog in the yard there—no, you would have found it. She must have taken it with her."

"By God," O'Connor said angrily, as understanding dawned on him. "Woolsey! That dumb bastard can't tell a dog's bones from a child's?"

"You're saying those could be a dog's bones in the trunk of the car?" Max asked. "A dead dog, not a baby?" He sat down on the bed, looking pale.

"Hold on, hold on," Lefebvre said. "We don't know what happened. And just because we don't know what happened to a dog doesn't mean those bones weren't those of the baby. The dog could have been lost off the *Sea Dreamer* or thrown overboard. The dog could have run away that night and ended up living on a neighboring farm."

"Or Mitch Yeager could have pressured or paid off the coroner," O'Connor said.

"It could also be an honest mistake," Lefebvre said. "Have you ever seen the bones of an infant that age? I have." He paused and looked away for a moment. "The bones of a two-month-old baby are so small, so fragile. Found in fragments, as most of these were . . . a dog breed with a rounded skull . . . you can't assume that a preliminary finding couldn't be honestly mistaken."

"That's kind of you, that is!" O'Connor said. "And I understand that you need to keep working with the man."

"O'Connor . . ." Irene said, looking between him and Lefebvre.

But it was Max who spoke next. "Perhaps you should tell the coroner that he might want to take another look at those bones and make sure he's right, because Mitch Yeager is not the only person in Las Piernas who is . . . concerned. I am concerned. I'm sure my friend Lillian Linworth will also want to know the true facts. As will Auburn Sheffield. If the coroner's not willing to take a closer, honest look, then tomorrow morning I'm calling . . ." He looked to Irene.

"The State Attorney General's office," she said.

"Yes, the State Attorney General's office, and asking for an independent investigation."

"Sounds like a newspaper story to me," Irene said.

"Oh, it is," O'Connor said. "And if anyone on the County Board of Supervisors reads the Sunday morning edition of the *Express,* then they just might finally decide it's time to replace Old Sheep Dip."

"Have you thought about the possibility," Lefebvre said, "that he could be right, that those bones are the baby's?"

"I consider that slim, knowing who was visiting him," O'Connor said.

"And what reason would Mitch Yeager have to influence him?"

"I can tell you that," Irene said. "He hoped to ruin Max's chances of living independently of him. Mr. Yeager didn't know the terms of the trust and figured Max would have to give up all his money and become dependent on him again. He's had big plans for Max."

"Does that possibility seem likely to you, Max?" Lefebvre asked.

"Absolutely. He wanted me to manage his businesses. Now I don't have to. He's furious with me."

"This will take tact," Lefebvre said.

"You're screwed then, aren't you?" Irene said, and he laughed.

"I don't mean to get you in trouble," Max said, "but—"

"Mr. Ducane," Lefebvre said, putting the photos back into the envelope, "a homicide detective who is at war with the coroner might as well stay home. Give me a day to try to find a way past Dr. Woolsey's defenses. If I can't manage it, then I'll let you know."

"The crime scene photos," Irene said.

"What about them?"

"I saw your photographer at work. He took photos of everything—every step of the way. If we're on to something here, then he probably has a photo of some bone that will give it away. A pug must have . . . oh, a jawbone, for example, or a nose cavity or some other bones or teeth that are very different in shape from a baby's, right?"

"Yes, but . . ."

She held up her camera. "Tell him that before the police had a chance to secure the scene, that nosy broad from the *Express* took a bunch of photos of the contents of the trunk of that car, and that today I started asking you questions about dog bones."

"Irene . . ." O'Connor warned.

"I'm not making news here, O'Connor. That's the truth. I took a lot of photos. I asked questions about dog bones. I wondered about a killer who would keep a baby alive, just to kill him later in a car trunk. That's all."

"Do you know what, O'Connor?" Lefebvre said, touching his chest. "I think I feel a little something here. What is it?" He feigned a look of concentration.

"In a human, it would be a heart. In a jackass, indigestion. But what do you feel?"

"Oh yes, now I know. Sympathy for you."

39

WHEN WE LEFT THE DUCANE HOUSE, O'CONNOR FOLLOWED ME HOME again. It wasn't that late, about nine o'clock. The lights were on, so I figured Mary and my dad were still up. I invited O'Connor in. He declined. I felt noble for offering.

Once inside, though, I was glad he had declined, not because my dad was in bad shape, but because he and Mary were laughing. Recently, Dad hadn't laughed all that often.

"Glad to see you're having a good time here," I said.

"I was remembering the camping trip."

We had gone camping together a lot, but "the camping trip" always referred to one adventure in Joshua Tree National Park. On that trip, I was about ten, Barbara fourteen. Barbara and I had caught a bad case of contagious giggles, and infected my parents with them. After three warnings from the ranger, the whole family got kicked out of the campground for laughing too loudly after curfew. Just as we were getting in the car, the ranger asked in a pleading voice, "What was so darn funny?"

It broke us up again. In fact, for some time after that, all you had to do was say "Joshua Tree," and we'd lose it.

The truth is, I don't have the slightest idea what the original joke was, or even if there was one. If there was and I heard it again, I suspect I wouldn't be more than mildly amused. The laughter itself wasn't really what mattered. What mattered was that all our lives, from that moment on, there was that time in our memories of our family so closely drawn together, a one-of-a-kind something that happened over nothing.

My father looked at me now and took my hand. "Call Barbara," he said.

"Now?"

"No, tomorrow. Arrange to have lunch with her. Something. Just the two of you. Don't mention me. Don't ask her to come here."

If he hadn't mentioned Joshua Tree just before he asked, I probably would have made excuses. But I knew what he was remembering, what he wanted of me, and so I agreed that I would.

So I left a message for Barbara. I specified that I wouldn't be asking her to talk about or take care of Dad. Sister time.

I walked Mary out to her car and thanked her again. After she left, I had an odd sensation of being watched. I looked around, but couldn't see anyone.

I went back inside and called Barbara again.

I didn't hear from her.

It didn't bother me much, because the next few days were wild ones.

40

WHEN SHE FIRST SAW THE PHOTOGRAPHS ON THE FRONT PAGE OF THIS morning's *Express*, the woman who had once been known as Betty Bradford became so alarmed, she threw the paper in the kitchen trash. Her husband came downstairs as she did and teased her as he retrieved it, telling her she was becoming absent-minded. "Just because it's Saturday doesn't mean I don't want to keep up with the world," he said.

She laughed it off, told him she didn't know what she had been thinking. She was a convincing actress. All the world had been her stage for fifteen years.

She had become the woman in the part she played. A respectable woman. How she loved that word, respectable.

She hadn't been able to eat breakfast at all. From the moment he took the newspaper in hand until the moment he left to take the boys to Little League, she worried that he would see her photograph and ask questions. Twenty years, a few pounds, and a change in hair color—was that enough to keep a man from recognizing a photo of his wife?

Now, several hours later, while he took the boys to their swimming lessons, she stood stock still at the kitchen sink, staring out through her greenhouse window, her hands in yellow rubber dishwashing gloves. The warmth of the sudsy water came through the gloves, and she enjoyed the plain, everyday feel of that.

She looked out at the front lawn, looked out at her neighborhood. A good neighborhood. One where they thought the problem kid was the long-haired boy who played in a band. He wasn't a problem. He smoked a little dope with his friends once in a while and played his guitar too loud, but he was a sweet kid at heart. He wasn't going to do anyone any real harm. They should all keep an eye on the quiet, sullen boy who lived three doors down.

She knew how to spot a troublemaker.

She had been one.

She didn't like to think of it, but there it was, right in the paper. She glanced over at the place where it lay on the counter, stained by coffee grounds that had been in the trash, and quickly looked away from it, looked back to the sunny day just beyond the window. She thought about a little box that held something she had stolen from a powerful man, something she had nearly thrown away a half a dozen times. Maybe, she thought, she should throw it away now.

She told herself that even if he learned the truth, her husband would love her, would stand by her.

She didn't really believe it, though.

She had known only one man who had stood by her, accepted her as she was. A tough man who was, all the same, gentle with women, gentle with her. Who had helped her to find her way from being a wild and restless thing into being a woman. Not some silly mimicry of womanhood, but something real. Just by respecting her.

But that man had died in Mexico. His name was Luis—she had stopped calling him Lew, the anglicized version of his name, not long after they had become lovers.

"Luis," she whispered now, "what am I going to do?"

41

On Saturday, the coroner made a special announcement. He was placed in the embarrassing position of admitting that further examination of the bones had shown them to be those of a small dog believed to be Katy Ducane's pet. Lefebvre later told me that he had talked his partner, Matt Arden, into being the bearer of bad news. I had a feeling Arden was often the ambassador for Lefebvre.

Woolsey blamed an assistant for the error. The *Express* and the rest of the fourth estate did not go easy on Woolsey, but it would have been worse if he had tried a cover-up.

Max stayed in touch over the weekend, calling me a couple of times each day, usually just to ask if I had learned anything new. I gave him my home number, and he called me there a few times, too, always careful not to call too late. More than once, I got the feeling that it was more difficult for him to be "possibly-the-kidnapped-one" than "not-the-kidnapped-one."

The reward was published. Lots of calls came in, both to the paper and to the police. I didn't see a lot of promise in those made to the *Express*.

One call, from a woman, might have been an exception. Within a moment after she asked if I was Irene Kelly, something made me believe she knew something. Exactly why I was so sure she wasn't another crank, I can't say. Maybe it was her nervousness, when other callers had been cocky, more eager to know about the conditions attached to the reward than to tell me anything. She said she didn't want the reward money. She just wanted to talk to me. Just me, not the police. She sounded upset. I found myself praying I could keep her on the line long enough to get her to tell me her phone number. But she hung up before I could respond with more than, "I'd love to hear whatever it is you have to say . . ."

I stayed off my phone for two hours, hoping she'd call back. I pissed off everyone near me because I used their phones instead. That was all I got out of that.

On Monday, I learned that the Baer house was sold—apparently over the weekend—but the real estate agent would not reveal the name of the buyer to me. Telling her I would eventually see it on county property records did not make the least impression on her.

I talked O'Connor into going over more of his notes from 1958 with me. We talked about the property records for the area near the cabin where Gus Ronden's body had been found. He mentioned that Katy Ducane, Lillian and Harold Linworth, and Thelma and Barrett Ducane owned cabins not far from Baer's. Katy's was then bequeathed to Jack Corrigan. Helen owned it now.

I gave her a call and asked her if she remembered a guy named Griffin Baer living near her mountain cabin. She said no. I asked about the enclave of folks from Las Piernas; she said the Vanderveers had owned two or three cabins and a lodge up there for as long as anyone could remember, and the Ducanes were merely trying to keep up with them. A few members of Lillian's social circle had bought cabins after visiting hers. "And naturally, there were friends of friends, too."

"Why did Katy give her cabin to Jack?"

There was a long pause before she answered. "To be honest, I was surprised about that. Jack and Katy were very close. She called him 'Uncle Jack,' but the truth is, Jack was more of a father to her than Harold. Harold Linworth wasn't home more than two days out of seven, and he never paid much attention to Katy. Jack spent a lot of time with her. She probably realized that he'd never have enough money of his own to afford a second home. She was a generous girl. Jack loved to go up there, although at first, I think it was hard on him—he missed her."

"O'Connor said she made the will just a day or two before she died. Do you know why?"

She seemed to weigh her words carefully. "No one knows what was on her mind with any certainty, of course. I believe Mitch Yeager said something to upset her."

"What do you mean?"

"She tried to talk to Jack about it at the party. Gave him a note. Didn't O'Connor tell you about it?"

"No," I said, looking over to his desk, where he was typing a story.

"I'm sure it just slipped his mind."

"Helen, I can handle it if he lies to me, but not if you do, too."

There was a brief silence. "I'm sorry," she said.

"So tell me about this note."

"Katy worried that Mitch might be her father."

"What?"

"Irene, it was a lie. I will never forgive Mitch for upsetting her. She should have had a happier birthday. She should have . . ." She broke off.

She was crying. I felt terrible. "I don't mean to upset you, Helen—"

"I know, I know. I'll be all right. I thought I had accepted the fact of her death years ago. I guess I didn't."

"It hasn't been so long since you lost Jack," I said. "That can't make this any easier."

"No, it doesn't," she said. I heard her take a steadying breath. "You were asking about Mitch and Katy."

"Mitch said that to her at her birthday party?"

"No. Mitch wasn't at the party. You should call Lillian. She may be able to tell you more about it."

"I will," I said.

She seemed to be doing better by the end of the call, but I felt so bad, I almost forgot to be angry with O'Connor for not telling me important facts.

Almost.

I asked him to go to lunch with me. We told Geoff where we could be found and went to a little café that was about half a block from the paper. We talked over the weird and basically useless calls we had received from people trying to collect the reward. We ate our sandwiches. I waited until we were done with all of that before I confronted him.

He wasn't bothered in the least. "Mitch lied to her. Why am I obliged to repeat his lies?"

"Gee, because maybe it's important information all the same?"

He shrugged. "How could it be?"

"For God's sake, O'Connor—"

"I talked to Wrigley again. He said if your friend really wants to lose an editorial position to work news side, it's up to her. But he wants thirty days to find a new food editor. And he wants to be the one to tell her."

I stared at him a moment. "You are trying to change the subject."

"I am trying to make amends."

Before he could say more, a man walked up to us and said, "I've been looking all over for you." The remark was directed to O'Connor.

This guy was a little older than me, tanned, muscular—and handsome, I suppose, but there was something about him that I disliked immediately. He was wearing a tight-fitting T-shirt, blue jeans, and work boots. He knew exactly how good he looked in them. Maybe he overestimated on that score. Spoiled brat, I thought.

"Irene," O'Connor was saying, "this is my son, Kenny."

"Pleased to meet you," I said, holding out a hand he glanced at, but didn't shake.

He returned his attention to his dad. "Look, about that car loan—"

"Let's not discuss that here," O'Connor said, folding his arms across his chest.

Kenny opened his mouth to protest, then seemed distracted. He was looking toward the entrance of the café. I was seated facing the other way, but at the radical change in his expression, I turned around—just in time to see disaster approaching.

Kenny was staring in adoration at a tall, good-looking redhead with big green eyes. I was looking at my sister, thinking that she always did have shitty timing.

I introduced her to everyone. Kenny suddenly found his manners and shook her hand—holding on to it a little longer than civility required. As for Barbara, I strongly suspect she hadn't planned to be as polite to me as she was. O'Connor and I exchanged a glance.

"Barbara," I said, "we have to get back to the paper, but I'd like to talk to you. Want to walk with us?"

"I haven't had lunch yet," she said, in a voice you might hear from a starving kitten, if starving kittens could talk.

Kenny had the charm turned on full blast by then. "Hey—I need to talk to my dad, you need to talk to your sister. Let me buy you lunch, then I'll walk with you over to the paper and we can talk to them there."

"How sweet of you!"

O'Connor and I exchanged another glance, silently agreeing to pay up and leave before it got any worse.

As we gained the sidewalk, O'Connor said, "I don't mean to be disloyal to Kenny, but if you care about your sister, you'll do anything you can to keep them apart. Let's just say he doesn't have a great track record."

"If I thought for one minute that anything I said to that mule-headed sister of mine would make an impression on her, I wouldn't have left them alone together." I sighed. "Her own track record isn't so great, but then, neither is mine. I guess the only consolation is that if her history keeps repeating itself, it will all be over soon."

"Whatever happens to them, let's promise each other we won't let this get in the way of our own working relationship."

"Oh hell," I said, "I was hoping one of us believed they'd just have lunch."

But it was good to know he thought we had a working relationship.

During those days, I tried hard to manage the balancing act required with Lefebvre—to do my best to get information, but not to become such a pest that he shut down on me forever.

On Monday afternoon, he gave me a little more information about what had been found in the lab's search of the car. He let me know that he wasn't giving me the complete list, that this was just what I could mention in the paper if I wanted to. These items included a gun believed to be the murder weapon; a large metal flashlight that had apparently been used as a club, because there were bloodstains and hair matted on it; other hairs and fibers; cigarettes and cigarette butts. Some of the hair on the flashlight seemed to be dog fur.

"You said you found cigarettes. What brand?"

"Chesterfields and filtered Pall Malls. From what you told me, the Chesterfields might be Katy's—none were smoked in the car, though. We found stubbed-out Pall Malls in the ashtray of the car, and on the floor of the backseat, so those might be the killer's. No lighter."

He also told me—not for publication—that among the bloodstains in the car were ones the lab had been able to type, from blood that had soaked into the foam of the seats before it dried. A section of the backseat cushions had type O embedded in them, and spatter patterns on the headliner were consistent with someone striking several blows with a blunt instrument, most likely the flashlight. Stains in the area of the driver's seat were type O. There were also stains of type B in the backseat.

"Type B? So another person was wounded or perhaps killed there?"

"It's a possibility, although there is much less of the type B. We can't say that all the stains are of the same age."

"But no third body? Human body, I should say?"

"You think Woolsey might claim the dog was type B?"

"I wasn't trying to be funny," I said. "Where's that other person?"

"He could be living next door to you, for all I know."

"Lefebvre, there's something else you should know about that farm." I told him about the bootlegging story.

He was silent.

"Sorry, I should have mentioned that earlier."

"Mmm-hmm."

I waited. Eventually he said, "I may have to tell your friend the construction supervisor that more excavations are needed because you mentioned this bootlegging theory."

"Bullshit," I said. "You were already planning to dig when you realized missing diamonds and other evidence might still be buried out there."

He laughed and told me it served me right for not continuing our spirit of openness, but I could tell it was okay between us.

"Am I invited to be there when you dig?" I asked.

"I'll let you know. It will be sometime tomorrow, I think."

I told him I was going to think about things and would call him back. He told me he was always interested in my theories. I tried hard to detect any possible amusement in his voice when he said that, but either he was serious or I was fooled.

"Are you dating Max Ducane?" he asked.

I was surprised by the question. "No, I'm not."

That was met with silence.

"I don't have anything against Max," I said. "It's just that I'm still hung up on someone I was interested in back in Bakersfield. Which is so stupid, because we never really dated, just spent time around each other on the job. And besides, someone called me a few weeks ago to tell me he's seeing someone else."

"He's a cop."

"How on earth—did you check up on my life in Bakersfield, for God's sake?"

"Not at all. The other day at Woolsey's office, the things you knew, the way you spoke and reacted—I don't know, gut feeling, I suppose. I found myself thinking that you had dated a cop."

"Well, I hadn't. Dated, I mean. And it doesn't matter, anyway."

"No. And it's not my business."

"No, it's not!" I said with indignation.

He didn't hide his amusement at that.

42

H.G. GAVE ME PERMISSION TO BORROW A CONFERENCE ROOM FOR A couple of hours. I gathered some colored scrap paper, scissors, and tape together, then left a note for O'Connor and went to work. By the time O'Connor walked into the conference room, I was separating a string of paper dolls.

"Good God," he said, halting in the doorway.

"Come in," I said, "I'm trying to figure something out."

"What grade are you in?"

"Very funny. Have a seat. I need to make a dog, a boat, and some cars."

He started looking over the layout on the table. I'll admit it looked like a poor imitation of a Playskool village that had met up with a steamroller.

"It's the first Friday in January 1958," I said.

I pointed out the locations first. White sheets of paper I had labeled *cabin, marina, farm, Linworth mansion, in-laws' mansion, Katy's house, Warren's location,* and *unknown.*

Next, I showed him my blue, golden rod, and lavender paper dolls. The blues ones were labeled *Rose, Jack, Katy, Todd, Thelma,* and *Barrett.* A smaller one was labeled *Baby*—I hadn't been able to make myself write "Max" on it. I finished the paper dog and put him with Katy.

"Victims in blue?" O'Connor asked.

"Yes—innocent ones, anyway. There are some dead people in these other groups, too." The goldenrod ones were labeled *Gus, Bo, Lew,* and *Betty.* I put question marks on all but one of the lavender dolls. That one was labeled *Boss.*

"God, do those colors look horrid together," O'Connor said with a wince.

"You want to be an art critic, we'll put you in charge of the funny pages."

"Some days, I think they make more sense than the front page. Are you going to tell what you're doing?"

"Wait—I'm almost done." I cut out eight green rectangles. I labeled six of them *Buick, Imperial, Ducanes' car, Katy's car, Bel Air,* and *Sea Dreamer.* I put question marks on the seventh and eighth.

I surveyed my handiwork and said, "I've been hearing about what went on that weekend, but I haven't been able to work out the logistics or get an overall picture."

He frowned, then moved all of the people except the baby, Gus, Boss, Rose, and the question marks to the Linworth mansion. Good. He was going to play.

"Don't forget their cars," I said. He moved the Bel Air and both Ducane cars over to the Linworths' as well.

I put Rose, the baby, and Gus in the Ducane house and parked the Imperial nearby.

"Let's start with Jack," I said. "I think his being taken from the party was one of the first things to happen." I put Jack, Betty, Lew, and Bo in the Bel Air. "We don't know where they took him for round one of the beating, or how long that went on, but eventually they drove out of town and left him on the farm."

I drove it along the tabletop, past the marsh and out to the farm, resisting the temptation to make car sounds. "What time did you say he was taken from the party?" I asked.

"No one noted the exact time. Between eleven and midnight."

"Just before Katy and Todd left the party with Todd's parents, right?"

"Right."

"Okay—so probably before Jack is dumped out of the car at the farm, the Ducane party is on its way to the boat."

"Yes, that sounds right," O'Connor said. "Except they stopped off at Thelma and Barrett's mansion first."

"Yes. Katy and her in-laws were in separate cars," I said, putting Katy, Todd, and the dog in the paper roadster. "We know they stopped by her in-laws' mansion, because Katy's car was found there and Thelma and Barrett's car was found at the marina."

I moved Katy's roadster to the paper marked *in-laws' mansion*, and brought Thelma and Barrett's car there, too.

"Did Katy and Todd ever get any farther than the mansion, though?" O'Connor asked.

"I don't know. Someone was waiting for them, either at the in-laws' place or at the marina. The marina is more likely."

"Why?"

O'Connor agreed that a stranger's car would look less out of place there, and less likely to draw attention than in the Ducanes' neighborhood. It would be darker at the marina, even darker in 1958 than it was now.

"So let's say they all get into the in-laws' car, and Thelma or Barrett drives." I left Katy's roadster at the in-laws' mansion. I moved all four people, the dog, and the elder Ducanes' car to the marina. I put a couple of the question-mark figures there, along with the Buick and the *Sea Dreamer*. I frowned.

"What's wrong?"

"Just trying to picture the seating arrangement in the Buick. I talked to Lefebvre." I told him what Lefebvre had said about where the bloodstains were.

He got a distant look in his eyes, as if he was trying to picture the car and occupants. "You don't really need the bloodstains to see it. A man working alone wouldn't leave Todd and Katy together in the backseat. They might attack, or try to escape. The killer forced Katy or Todd to drive, and rode in the backseat with the other hostage."

"And the other man took Thelma and Barrett out to sea?"

"Yes."

"How did he get back ashore?" I asked. I picked up a piece of paper and started shaping it with the scissors.

"You're making a second boat?"

"There had to be one, and someone else to operate it while the killer was aboard the *Sea Dreamer*. They left the *Sea Dreamer* adrift and returned to shore in the smaller boat."

"No—too many people. They wouldn't involve so many."

"Are you kidding? They used three people to beat up Jack."

"They had to get him away from a party—the middle of a crowd. They had to make sure he wasn't going to interfere with their plans for Katy. And he had a reputation for being able to defend himself."

"I hear you used to finish his fights for him."

"Not true, especially not when he was younger. He finished plenty on his own. And for that matter, they might have assumed I'd be with him that night."

"True. Lucky you weren't."

"I happen to disagree. If I had been there . . . but there's no use wishing it."

We talked it over, and decided that Lefebvre's theory made sense—that the original plan had been to keep Jack alive, a plan which had only been altered when Bo Jergenson had left him in the wrong place. There was no other explanation we could think of for moving Jack from the farm to the swamp.

"Back to the *Sea Dreamer*," I said. "If you're right, how does the killer get back to shore?"

"He didn't need to abandon it far from shore. The storm probably took the *Sea Dreamer* farther out than he left it. He could have been closer and used a scuba suit."

"Okay, I like the scuba idea. Less manpower and fewer boats involved."

We talked about the possibility that all four of the Ducanes and the dog went aboard, and weren't taken hostage until they were out at sea, away from any witnesses, but decided their captors would see that as full of risks. The killers would have been forced to try to follow the *Sea Dreamer* in the dark, and without attracting attention. The Ducanes might have been able to fight back or use the radio or manage to escape, especially—on a boat that large— if they weren't all grouped together.

"Pirate movies make boarding another vessel look easier than it is," I added. "And you told me that the fisherman who found the yacht didn't see any signs of a struggle or that anyone had used life jackets. The killer was aboard from the start and abandoned the yacht after Thelma and Barrett Ducane were dead. My guess is, they were drugged or knocked unconscious and drowned."

"Why not just shoot them, too?"

"Because that would show up if and when the bodies washed ashore. If you want people to stop looking for Katy and Todd, you have to make it seem as if everyone might have been lost overboard that night." I looked at my notes. "The coroner found salt water in Thelma's and Barrett's lungs, so they were alive at some point when they were in the water. In cold water, in evening clothes, they would have had difficulty swimming even if they regained consciousness. I think someone took them so far offshore, they didn't have a chance of getting back in alive. And if they were taken out into the fog, the Ducanes might not have even known which direction to swim in to reach shore."

He nodded. "The killer then brings the *Sea Dreamer* closer to shore, abandons it, and swims to the beach. He made a couple of mistakes, though. He left it too pristine, didn't turn the radio on, and took the key. Probably force of habit. Maybe he expected the yacht to break up in the storm that was on its way. But the boat survived."

"Yes—do you know what became of it?"

"Warren sold it to Lillian. She has it maintained, but I don't think she uses it much, if at all."

"Another museum?"

He shrugged.

I was beginning to get a picture of how tightly Lillian held on to the past.

O'Connor pointed to the sailor question-mark doll and said, "What became of this one after he finished with the Ducanes?"

"For now, let's put him in the unknown headquarters of the Boss, the unknown mastermind of all these activities." I also put the question-mark car there, for the Boss to escape in.

"Unknown?" O'Connor said. "I think I know his name: Mitch Yeager. I think I've known that for years."

I studied him. He had mentioned Yeager before. Time to ask some hard questions. "Did you believe that before you knew Kyle Yeager might be Max?"

He paced, and rubbed a hand through his hair, making a mess of it. "I suppose so. I never had an ounce of proof, mind you, and never came close to finding any. He wasn't even in Las Piernas that weekend, from all I could discover. But there was that note Katy left, and—frankly, I couldn't think of anyone else who would have the power to do it, or who hated Jack more than he did."

"Hated Jack? Why?"

"Jack wrote stories that ultimately helped to put Mitch's brother in prison, and almost sent Mitch there himself. Cost him a fortune in legal fees. Mitch nearly got Jack fired from the paper—Old Man Wrigley had enough spine to say no to that, but he wouldn't let Jack write about Yeager."

"Spine? I'll bet Jack's stories sold papers. And Jack could have had his pick of the L.A. papers."

"That's true," O'Connor said.

"What about the others? Did Mitch hate the Ducanes?"

O'Connor shrugged. "I don't know. They socialized and seemed to have been friends. The Ducanes helped him out when he was in trouble, bought his companies so that he'd have the cash he needed. There weren't many people in a position to do that during the Depression. He bought the companies back, eventually."

We were silent for a long time, looking at all the paper figures on the tabletop.

"Let's leave the question of the mastermind open for now," I said. "Let's just try to figure out what happened, okay?"

He seemed ready to object, then nodded. "We know the couples were separated, and that only Thelma and Barrett stayed at the marina. While all of that was going on, Katy and Todd and the dog were killed and put in the trunk of the Buick."

"Which ends up on the farm. Griffin Baer might have been there that night, operating the tractor." I looked at my notes again. "Jack told you he saw an old man operating it, right?"

"Yes."

"Griffin Baer was sixty-two in 1958."

"Jack had a skinful of martinis and a concussion."

"Was he wrong about anything else?"

"No," O'Connor admitted. He started pacing again.

None of this was going to get any easier on him, so I watched him for a minute or two before I said, "I think the killing must have taken place after the Buick was driven to the farm. And I think Katy or Todd fought them."

He halted and stared at me. "What makes you say so?"

"The windshield. The fact that the car was wrecked. Maybe one of them was already dead when the other struggled—I don't know. But Jack said the car's grill was smashed in before it was buried."

I told him about the dog fur being found on the flashlight, the signs that someone in the backseat bled—perhaps after being struck with the flashlight, too. "That had to be Katy, I think. When Woolsey finally releases the autopsies on Katy and Todd, we'll know more. Todd was probably driving. Maybe Katy started fighting the man who took them."

"More likely her than Todd," he said quietly.

I tried to picture it. "Something happens to make the car go out of control, maybe the struggle in the backseat distracts Todd, or he's shot—I don't know. Blood ends up on the windshield. The dog is probably killed by a blow from the flashlight. Katy is hit with the flashlight, several times. She's also shot, so maybe he shoots her after she's unconscious."

I heard him make a sound, as if he had been struck himself, and waited a moment before going on. He sat down.

"The killer puts Katy and Todd and the dog in the trunk, probably with Griffin Baer's help. He takes off in a car that's already waiting for him at the farm." I moved the second unknown car to the farm.

O'Connor didn't say anything. He looked toward the paper version of Katy's house.

"Gus Ronden kills the nursemaid, Rose Hannon," I said. "He doesn't mind that part of it—he's cruel. He might have someone with him, but I think it's more likely he's alone."

"I agree."

I put Gus and the baby in the Imperial, but before I moved it, I said, "Now, this is really important—blood matching Rose Hannon's was found on clothing at his house, but nothing indicating the baby was there, right?"

"Right. Dan Norton searched the place for any sign of the child. Nothing was found. And the neighbor didn't hear or see a child."

"So he either killed the baby before he got home, or handed it off to someone else. No type O blood on the clothing Gus left in the hamper?"

"No," he said slowly, "but an infant that young could be smothered or killed in any number of other ways that wouldn't cause bleeding."

"Yes, but this goes back to what I was saying when we were over at the Ducanes'—if the baby was supposed to be killed, Gus Ronden would have killed it there. And if the baby was just supposed to be held for ransom, why not take the nurse along as a hostage, too?"

"Adults are harder to manage."

"Okay. But the fact is, no ransom note was ever delivered."

"Maybe Gus bungled the kidnapping and the child died," O'Connor said. "In truth, we just don't know what happened to that little boy."

"No, but Warren Ducane thought young Kyle Yeager—now Max—was that child, so that's still a possibility. And if that's true, we keep coming back to the same name again and again, and it's the man you've suspected. Mitch Yeager could be the person who orchestrated all of this."

O'Connor sighed. "Doubtless this has occurred to Lefebvre as well. But so far, there isn't a thing anyone can do to prove that."

"My guess is that the Baer farm was kind of a hideout for this gang, and had been for years."

"Prohibition was long over by 1958," O'Connor said.

"Yes, but that doesn't mean smuggling was over. Or that criminals didn't have a use for an out-of-the-way place."

"Maybe."

"Think about it—Gus has come back from killing Rose Hannon and handing the child off to someone. Bo Jergenson arrives and says he's left a reporter at a hideout, where a double homicide was about to be covered up. Gus must have been rattled; he leaves a knife and his bloody clothes at his house. Of course, he thought he'd be able to go back to get them. He had a busy, busy night. He killed Bo, and maybe one or both of the other two, and then took off for the mountains. Or . . . maybe the other two are buried near the cabin, too."

"Betty Bradford and Lew Hacker haven't been seen or heard from in twenty years," O'Connor said. "It's not likely they're alive. We would have heard from them after Lily and the new Max Ducane offered that reward."

"I'm not so sure they're dead."

"Why, because of that phone call you got the other day?"

I shrugged. "A hunch. Maybe not a good one. I don't know. Anyway, that night, or soon thereafter, Gus is dead. The only people left on the mastermind's team are the murderer from the *Sea Dreamer* and the one who killed Katy and Todd in the Buick."

"I can think of two people who are loyal to Mitch and wouldn't have minded doing a night's work like this," O'Connor said.

"Eric and Ian? How old were they?"

"In their twenties."

I thought about Eric holding Kyle over the railing. "I wonder if Ian and Eric know how to scuba dive."

Barbara and Kenny never came by the paper.

I had Tuesday off and spent most of it taking my dad in for chemo and catching up on household chores and errands.

O'Connor called me at nine o'clock that evening to tell me that when he came home, my sister and Kenny were sitting close to each other on his living room couch. O'Connor wasn't happy about finding them together, and neither was I, but we agreed there wasn't a thing we could do about it.

When I told my father about it, he asked me if I had so few worries, I needed to borrow some from Barbara.

No. I had plenty of worries of my own.

I worried that my time with him was too short to waste with anything other than staying at his side. Nothing worried me more.

I worried that Mary would feel that I had trespassed on her kindness too often.

I worried that I'd never figure out what really happened that weekend in 1958, and more people would be harmed.

I worried that if I didn't find something solid to back up all my great theories, I'd be covering a PTA fund-raiser by the middle of next week.

I worried that O'Connor and the other men in the newsroom were just humoring me.

I worried that someone really was following me all those times I felt watched, and I worried that no one was following me and I was losing my mind.

I worried that I liked Frank Harriman, the cop in Bakersfield, more than was healthy, because at the end of each day, no matter what else had occupied my mind, I found I had an urge to make a long-distance call to him, to ask if he was seeing anyone, to ask who was meeting him for coffee at the end of the shift these days, and—just to talk, to see if talking to him and listening to him still made me feel comfortable, at ease, in a way no one else seemed to make me feel at ease.

I didn't make the call.

43

My mystery woman called early on Wednesday morning.

"The boss had a cabin up near Arrowhead," she said, and gave an address. "Maybe they took the baby up there. I don't know."

"Who was the boss?"

She ignored the question. "The cabin was in Gus's name. Gus Ronden."

I took a chance. "Betty, where's Lew?"

There was a long pause, then she whispered, "Luis died in Mexico."

She hung up.

She had spoken those last few words with grief in her voice—and pronounced his name in a way that suggested she might speak Spanish.

Lew Hacker had meant something to her. Luis. I wondered if "Hacker" was also an anglicized version of a Hispanic name. It wasn't surprising that Luis might have found it easier to be Lew in the 1950s. Mexico. Had the two of them made an escape there?

I looked through everything that had been published about Gus Ronden. Nothing mentioned the exact address of the cabin, or even the road it was on. O'Connor had the address in his notes, from when he had gone to look up property records all those years ago. But it had never been in the paper. Whatever doubts I had that the mystery woman was Betty Bradford vanished.

I was making calls to find out if Ian Yeager was scuba-certified, when O'Connor told me Lefebvre was on the other line, asking for me. I took the call.

"I'm in your friend O'Malley's office on the construction site. You might want to come out to the farm," Lefebvre told me. "Bring O'Connor if you'd like."

I told him we'd be there right away.

Before we could leave, Max called. O'Connor rolled his eyes when I motioned for privacy, but he stepped away.

"Want to explore the inside of Griffin Baer's former home?" Max asked.

"You know I do. But it was sold this past weekend."

"I know. I bought it."

"You—what?"

"I wanted to tell you earlier, but thought I had better wait until it was official."

"Wow . . . I thought . . . did you decide against living in Katy's house?"

"You said it—Katy's house. I don't think Lily would be happy if I changed anything in it, and I don't think I'd be happy if I kept it as a museum."

"I can understand that. I drove by the Baer place the other day and saw it from the outside."

"Come by and see more of it. Bring a flashlight—the power won't be on until Friday."

"Can you give me a couple of hours? I was just heading out."

"No problem. I'll go on over and open some windows to air the place out. It's a beautiful house. And the view—well, wait until you see it."

I hung up and stood there in a daze. O'Connor came back over and said, "Much as I hate to disturb your daydreams about your rich Romeo, we are keeping Lefebvre waiting."

"I doubt he'll wait for us. Listen, I'm going to drive separately. I'm meeting Max later."

I saw a look come into his eyes, and his lips tighten across the front of his teeth. His hand clenched, then opened. But he didn't say a word.

"Thanks," I said.

"For what?"

"Biting your tongue."

He laughed and said, "I'll meet you there."

Lefebvre and Matt Arden had caused most of the work on the mall to come to a complete halt. O'Malley wasn't happy about the huge costs involved, but his employers didn't blame him, so he didn't blame me. He admitted to me that he had enjoyed helping Lefebvre with the investigation. Currently, that included lending the use of the backhoe and operator to the proceedings, which were taking place about two hundred yards away from the place where the car had been.

Lefebvre had found some building plans filed on the farm in the late 1940s, plans that showed where various structures had stood. By the time we arrived there, Lefebvre, those who were helping him from the department crime lab, and O'Malley's crew had worked together to uncover a strange metal contraption. They had set it aside and continued digging. O'Connor identified the object to me as a still.

"So he was making booze as well as shipping it?" I asked.

"It may have been the way he got connected with the bootleggers in the first place," O'Connor said.

They were working slowly and cautiously now, and we weren't allowed to get too close. I learned from O'Malley that a few minutes before Lefebvre called us, they came across a hidden room similar to the one described to me by Griffin Baer's barber.

While we waited, I told O'Connor about the call from Betty Bradford. "So at least she's alive."

He was interested in this, but before much more time had passed, he gave in to an urge to lecture me on reporting rather than creating news, especially where Max was concerned. If I didn't believe, somewhere deep down, that I needed to watch my step, I suppose it would have bothered me more.

When other media arrived, O'Connor broke off a story about Corrigan to swear. I considered this further progress in our working relationship.

Lefebvre reached us before the other reporters did. He said there didn't seem to be anything in the room other than signs that some booze had been stored there during Prohibition.

"Irene has some theories about the night of the murders, you know," O'Connor said.

"Tell them to me later today?" Lefebvre asked.

"Sure." I glanced at my watch. "I have an appointment right now, though."

"I'll stay here," O'Connor said, "and get what I can before deadline. See you in . . ." He broke off again, this time as we heard brakes squeal. A black Datsun 280Z pulled up, double-parking next to my Ghia, blocking me in.

"Hey!" I said in protest.

A bearded man with long dark hair tied in a ponytail emerged from the car. Although we had never been formally introduced, I recognized him immediately as one of the staff of the *Express*. He was dressed in blue Adidas, torn jeans, a white T-shirt, and an Army jacket, and within moments was carrying two cameras and a backpack full of film and accessories.

"Stephen Gerard," O'Connor said to Lefebvre. "Word must have come into the *Express*, too—Wrigley has sent one of our best photographers."

"One of our best head cases," I said. "He makes Wildman look tame."

"You shouldn't believe every rumor you hear, Kelly."

I shook my head. "Lydia was trying to interview the author of a vegetarian cookbook. Gerard came in to shoot photos—eating a hot dog."

O'Connor and Lefebvre started laughing.

"He did it on purpose!" I said.

"I have no doubt of that."

"Is he some sort of pet of yours?"

"He's paid his dues," O'Connor said. "And most of them in Vietnam—he's a veteran, you know."

"So is Lefebvre."

O'Connor looked at me in amazement. It was clear to me that he had no trouble believing Lefebvre was a vet, but was miffed that I knew about it and he didn't.

"Air Force," I added, just to rub it in.

Lefebvre smiled, but said nothing. Gerard reached us, and O'Connor introduced him all around. Gerard held on to his cameras as if using them as a protection against having to shake hands with anyone.

"Nice to meet you, but you're blocking my car," I said.

"I know. I recognized it. That's why I parked there."

"How could you be sure it was my car?"

He shrugged. "Observation, mostly. I've seen you drive into the lot at the paper in a red ragtop Karmann Ghia. A similar car is now parked where you are supposed to be covering a story. When I got closer, I saw that it has a white license plate frame with black lettering that says 'Las Piernas Auto Haus.'" He paused for about half a second before reciting my plate number, then added, "There's a place near the right rear taillight where you didn't get all the Turtle Wax off the last time you washed the car."

I was seriously creeped out by this, but all I could manage to say was, "I don't use Turtle Wax."

He shrugged again. "All right. Whatever it was, you didn't get all of it off."

O'Connor grinned, and Lefebvre suddenly took an interest in the toe of one of his shoes.

"I've got to go," I said.

"I didn't mean to offend you," he said.

"You didn't. Look, I'm in a hurry." I said good-bye to O'Connor and Lefebvre, and walked off. Gerard followed me.

We didn't talk on the way to the cars. A couple of other photographers called out to him as we passed them, and he waved but didn't stop to talk to them.

Before he got into his car, he stopped to take some quick photos. I glanced in the direction he had aimed the camera, but didn't see anything unusual.

"Do you mind?" I said impatiently. "You can take photos of traffic after I leave."

"The car I wanted to photograph won't be here then."

"My Ghia? You are starting to freak me out, Gerard."

"I freak you out? And the guy who's been following you doesn't?"

I felt the color drain from my face. "What guy?"

"I don't know. Drives a black Beemer. I've seen it near the paper, but only when you're there. And he was just here. I don't know anyone on staff who can afford a BMW."

A black BMW. Max? I wondered. "What does the driver look like?"

"I haven't had a chance to get a look at him. For that matter, I'm not even sure it's a him and not a her."

"You know where I missed a spot of car wax," I said, bending to clean the offending dried paste off the taillight, "but you never saw the driver?"

"You didn't even see the car, so don't give me grief about not seeing the driver."

I had to admit the justice of this. "New black BMW without plates?"

He closed his eyes. "No, there were plates. Don't know how new it is. Shiny, well-cared-for car." He opened his eyes again. "I'll see if I can get a plate from the photos I've just taken."

"Thanks," I said. "And sorry for snapping at you."

In a gesture I was starting to anticipate from him, he shrugged that off. He got into his car without saying anything more.

He took my great parking spot when I drove away.

I nearly wrecked the Karmann Ghia twice after that, a result of looking in the rearview mirror too often. No black BMWs. I was feeling a little shaky. I told myself it was the near misses, then called myself a liar. I tried to figure out why anyone would want to follow me around, and couldn't come up with any clear answers.

I didn't know if Max had his plates yet. After a moment, I realized that it didn't matter.

If Max wasn't the one following me, I was upset.

If Max was sneaking around, shadowing me, I was upset. Maybe not quite as much, but still, it was weird.

I'd have to confront him. Then I thought about how awful it would be if he wasn't the one following me. How could I even hint at such a thing to him without sounding really paranoid—or as if I thought he was some kind of creepy freak? I started rehearsing how I'd talk to him about it.

Closer to the beach, an afternoon wind was coming up, causing the roof of the convertible to flap noisily. It added to my sense of unease.

At a traffic light, I felt that sensation of being watched again. No black cars behind me. I glanced to the side to see a woman quickly face forward after staring at me in an amused way. I then realized that I had been rehearsing aloud.

Maybe I'd just wait until Stephen Gerard's photos were developed.

I was almost to the house when I remembered that it had been a while since I had used my flashlight. I pulled into a convenience market parking lot, took the flashlight from the glove compartment, and tested it—sure enough, it gave only a dim glow. I bought batteries, and after checking to see if any black cars were following me, I was on my way again.

I turned down the alley that ran behind the Griffin Baer mansion, wondering if I would be able to park in front of the garage door again, or if Max's BMW would be in that space. The BMW was not in sight, so I pulled as close to the doors as possible to allow any traffic in the alley to get past me. It occurred to me that I could check the plates on Max's car, to see if they matched whatever plates might show up in Gerard's photos. The garage was unlocked now, but I was so close to it, I ran the chance of scratching the Ghia if I opened the doors. I thought of moving my car, but decided I'd wait until I was leaving and take a look then.

The gate to the backyard was latched but no longer locked, so I went in that way and walked toward the house, carrying my flashlight. Several windows were open, and I smiled thinking of Max running around opening the place up, trying to get the mustiness out of the house. The wind would help—if it didn't cover everything inside with a fine layer of sand.

A note on the back door said, "Bell broken. Come in."

A man of few words.

I turned, entered the house, and found myself in a huge kitchen. There was enough light coming in through the windows to allow me to save my new batteries. The appliances, to my disappointment, were not what they had been in the 1920s and 1930s. Even a big white oven and a curvy refrigerator from the 1940s would have been okay with me, but they were boxy and blah and appeared to have been installed in the late 1960s. An avocado green electric stove. A harvest gold refrigerator. A glass-topped wrought-iron table. Lots of white tile interspersed with a line or two in the avocado color.

"Max?" I called. I heard my voice resonate in that not-quite-an-echo way sound travels through the emptiness of a big house.

I heard the wind whistle through the little gaps and crevices only the wind can find in a house. No other reply.

I walked over to one of the kitchen doors and opened it. An empty pantry. A second one opened on to a laundry room. Harvest gold washer and dryer. I was glad Max had enough money to replace appliances.

I crossed the kitchen and pushed on a swinging door that led to a dining area. Sun-faded orange carpet here, with dents showing that a heavy table had taken up most of the room. Max had his work cut out for him.

"Max?" I called again, a little louder.

I walked out of the dining room into a large open space and fell in love.

Wooden floors, alcoves and arches, built-in cabinetry and bookcases, a huge stone fireplace, an old chandelier. The room was spacious and bright, with high ceilings and large double-paned windows that looked out toward the park along the bluffs and the Pacific beyond.

The room was beautiful, the view was spectacular, but after that first admiring moment, I began to feel uneasy. Perhaps it was because the room was quiet. No sound of the traffic on Shoreline penetrated the windows. No sound of the sea, either. The open windows were all at the back of the house, it seemed. That didn't make any sense—the coolest air would come from the ocean. Why didn't Max open some of the windows on this side of the house?

Why hadn't Max come downstairs, for that matter? With the windows at the back of the house open, he must have heard the Karmann Ghia coming down the alley—my father always complained that it sounded like the arrival of a Panzer division.

As if, I chided myself, you are so special, Max is listening for the sound of your car.

There was a short hallway leading to other rooms on the ground floor, but my eyes were drawn to a staircase with an ornate banister that appeared to be made of mahogany inlaid with a geometric design of brass and mother-of-pearl. I stood at the foot of the stairs and called up. "Max? Are you here?"

I heard a soft creak above me.

Upstairs, then.

At the top of the stairs was the short end of a wide L-shaped hallway. As I turned the corner and stepped into the longer section, I was nearly in darkness. A small amount of light came from one partially opened door at the end of the corridor. That was it. Nine or ten other doors, each of dark wood, flanked the rest of the hallway.

I turned the flashlight on.

I heard another creaking sound; it seemed to be coming from the open room at the far end.

"Max!"

I yelled his name at the top of my lungs that time. It felt good to shout, because the rest of my body seemed unwilling to move. Stephen Gerard's confirmation that I was being followed by someone was getting to me. Even as I told myself it was just an empty house, my imagination led me to believe someone or something lurked behind each closed door.

I had just decided to leave when I heard a soft moan.

I stood frozen for a brief moment, then hurried down the hallway. What if Max had been hurt?

I stayed in the middle of the hall and glanced nervously at the closed doors as I passed them, expecting at any moment that someone would jump out from behind them to grab me. I reached the open doorway and looked in.

I heard myself give a little scream.

Max lay curled on his side on the floor, bound and gagged. His face and shirt were covered in blood. I quickly knelt beside him. "Max!"

His eyes fluttered open briefly, then closed again as he moaned—the same moaning sound I had heard moments before. I don't think he really registered my presence. There was a cut above his brow, but some other wound had caused blood to flow down his neck and back.

I wasn't sure what to do first. I glanced around. The room was an empty bedroom. The whole house was vacant—no medical supplies would be in the bathrooms or elsewhere.

I tried to remember my first-aid lessons.

Air. Everyone needed air. Worried that the duct tape gag might make it hard for him to breathe, I decided I should remove it. I turned the flashlight off and set it down, not needing it with the light coming in through the windows. Using both hands, one to hold his skin, the other to grasp an end of the tape—and wincing on his behalf—I slowly pulled it away from his skin and off his mouth. That made him moan again, but his eyes didn't open.

Bleeding. I should try to stop the bleeding.

I carefully moved his head onto my lap, grabbed a pack of tissues from my purse, and held one of them to the cut on his brow. I gently searched through his hair for the wound on his head—I found a gash at the back and pressed the rest of the tissues to it. They quickly became soaked, as did my hands, my pants suit, and my blouse. I took off my jacket and tried using it to apply pressure.

I attempted to free his hands, which were taped behind him at his wrists, but that nearly caused me to drop his head on the floor, so I gave that up.

Maybe I should just go to a neighbor's house to get help, I thought. I looked down at my blouse. Would anyone in this snooty neighborhood open the door if they looked through a peephole and saw a blood-covered stranger standing on the front porch? I doubted it, but maybe I could shout to them to call an ambulance.

As I worried over this decision, the closet door behind me flung open and a man in a ski mask rushed toward me. Before I could do anything other than look up at him in a dumbfounded way, he had covered my mouth and nose with a cloth soaked in something with a sweet medicinal scent. His other hand grabbed the back of my head and pressed me forward into the cloth. I tried clawing at his hands, which were gloved, but the pressure only increased. I quickly grew dizzy and felt slightly ill. The room was spinning wildly—spinning away my ability to think clearly. I felt an odd sensation of floating, even as I struggled in discomfort. Fear stayed with me—a cold, raw terror that wasn't softened by my confusion. Within seconds, I felt myself hovering on the brink of passing out, tried to use the fear to fight against that. Now I was going to be sick after all, I thought. I became dimly aware of a second pair of gloved hands pulling mine away from the hand that pressed the cloth.

I did not float into darkness. I plummeted.

44

O'CONNOR CAUGHT HIMSELF MUTTERING UNDER HIS BREATH AND STOPPED. Was he turning into such an old man that he couldn't understand what young people were like when they were in the throes of love? Or lust, at any rate.

Kelly hadn't come back to the paper this afternoon after her meeting with Max Ducane. He didn't mind Max—for all the grief O'Connor gave her about him, he liked the young man. But he had hoped she would take her responsibilities at the paper seriously enough to return in time to contribute something before deadline.

He had covered for her with H.G. and the others, told them she was pursuing leads and he wasn't sure if she'd make it back. He said—and this much was true—that she had given him plenty of material for today's story already. H.G. seemed to buy it, but O'Connor wasn't confident of being able to keep up the charade more than this once.

It was a shame. She'd have to be taken off the story. He found he was deeply disappointed. He enjoyed working with her. She sparked something in him, made him work harder.

He was working hard tonight. He sighed and went back to writing the story of the rooms found today on the farm. It wasn't much of a story in and of itself, but it made O'Connor feel surer about Mitch Yeager's involvement. The Yeagers were the biggest bootleggers in Las Piernas, whether they had been convicted of it or not. And if Griffin Baer was involved with bootlegging, chances were good he was involved with Mitch Yeager.

Lefebvre also told O'Connor—on the condition that he held the information from publication—that they had found some shell casings in the trunk of the Buick, and other evidence (which he wouldn't talk about at all) that might help them find the killer. He wouldn't name the caliber, which made O'Connor suspect the caliber itself would give him a lot of information about the gun. Lefebvre had taken an interest in Irene's theories about that night in 1958. Lefebvre had been impressed, which made O'Connor feel a certain pride in her.

It had lasted until she failed to return to the newsroom.

O'Connor finally filed the story. He was putting his coat on when Stephen Gerard stopped by his desk.

"I thought you would have gone home long ago," O'Connor said.

Gerard held out a stack of photos. "Give those to Kelly, would you?"

"What are they?" O'Connor said, taking them.

"The plates on that car that has been following her."

O'Connor looked up sharply. "What?"

"The black Beemer. You've seen it, haven't you?"

"Yes," O'Connor said slowly. "Yes, I have."

"Maybe one of your friends at the DMV can run those for you."

"Who said I have friends at the DMV?"

Gerard shrugged and started to walk off.

"Wait!" O'Connor called.

Gerard turned back to him.

"When did you take these?" O'Connor asked.

"Today. Out at the construction site."

O'Connor let him go, but he sat staring at the photos for a moment, an uneasy feeling coming over him. The phone on his desk rang, startling him. "O'Connor," he answered.

"Mr. O'Connor? This is Mary Kelly, Irene's aunt. We met the other day."

"Yes, of course," he said, his worries taking a new direction. "Is Patrick— is Patrick all right?"

"Patrick? Oh, he's fine—sleeping at the moment, which is why I thought I'd call now. Forgive me for disturbing you, but I wondered—you see, it's so unlike Irene not to warn me if she'll be late, and—"

"She's not home?"

"No—that's why I'm calling you. What time did she leave the paper?"

"She went out with Mr. Ducane this afternoon," O'Connor said. "I haven't seen her back here since."

There was a long silence, then she called him a series of names he was surprised she knew. "I thought you were keeping an eye on her!" she ended.

"I defy anyone to keep an eye on your grandniece," he said. "But I'm worried, too. I'll look for her, and I'll keep you posted."

She thanked him, apologized for losing her temper, and hung up.

O'Connor quickly looked through his notes and found the address for the house that had once belonged to Griffin Baer. He started to leave, hesitated, then went back to his desk and called Lefebvre.

45

MITCH YEAGER STOOD UP FROM THE DINNER TABLE.

Ian and Eric exchanged a glance, then realized that Uncle Mitch had seen the exchange, and was smiling. It was not a good kind of smile.

"Eric, Ian, in my study," Mitch said. To the rest of his family, he said, "You'll excuse us. We have a little business to discuss."

"But, Daddy!" his daughter protested. "You promised you would help me with my homework."

Eric felt hope rise.

Mitch smiled at her. "And I will, sugar, I will. This won't take long."

His brief moment of optimism crushed, Eric followed his uncle into the study, as Ian lagged behind.

When they had taken seats across from him, Mitch asked, "Tell me all of it, and tell it to me right now."

"All of what?" Eric asked.

Mitch threw a glass paperweight at him. Eric ducked just in time. The paperweight shattered behind him.

Mitch looked at Ian.

Within minutes, Ian divulged everything. He started out nervously, then warmed with the enthusiasm he felt for the project. Ian discussed what he believed to be the more brilliant aspects of the plan, including the place where they had hidden their hostages. "So you see, Uncle Mitch, Warren will have to come back."

For a full fifteen seconds, Uncle Mitch said nothing, but Eric knew he was unhappy. His jaw clenched, his eyes narrowed, and he turned red.

"You fucking imbeciles!" he exploded. "I work all these years to clean up the family name, and you do this? I give up lucrative opportunities, donate to charities I could give a crap about, and spend time with people I like even less. I pay off half a dozen hoods to shut their yaps, and permanently shut the yaps of the ones who aren't smart enough to be satisfied. I send my kids to good schools. I make sure your own little youthful escapades never lead to an arrest or bad publicity—that wasn't easy. I take care of you, and what kind of thanks do I get? One fuckup after another, that's what!"

He ranted at them, telling them that he would be lucky to be able to save their miserable hides this time, then going on to a familiar speech about their lack of intelligence. All the while, Eric thought of the bag he had packed and concealed in the trunk of his car, of the one-way plane tickets, cash, and other treasures, of the private residence he had bought under another name. He was so pissed off at Ian, he wasn't sure he'd give him the other ticket.

He wondered at his own ability to foresee this moment. Maybe he had always been expecting something like this to happen, maybe he had always known in his heart of hearts that Ian wouldn't be able to stand up to Uncle Mitch. At least Uncle Mitch thought he was too dumb to have a Plan B, which was actually an essential part of said Plan B.

He suddenly realized that Uncle Mitch had asked him a question.

"Well?" Mitch said impatiently.

"No, they didn't see our faces. We had masks on," Ian answered for him.

Okay, Eric decided, Ian could come with him.

"Did you say anything in front of them?"

"No, we were absolutely silent," Eric said.

"Thank God for that!" Mitch said. "You go back there and make it possible for them to escape, you understand? You will do this immediately, then come back here. Go. Now!"

When they were outside, Eric insisted on driving. Ian was apologizing profusely, paying no attention to where they were going, until Eric pulled into Ian's driveway.

"This is my house," Ian said. "What are you doing?"

"Thought I'd give you a chance to pack. You want to buy your underwear in Belize, that's fine with me."

"Belize? What are you talking about?"

"You can stay here and let Uncle Mitch ride your ass for another twenty years, or you can come with me to the Caribbean. I've had it. I'm getting out of here. What you do is up to you, but I've got phony passports, and all the other arrangements made if you want to come along with me. Plan B."

Ian swallowed hard. He was silent for so long, Eric began to feel certain that he was going to stay behind. He wondered if he'd really have the nerve to go alone.

"I'll go with you," Ian said.

Eric smiled. "You will not regret this. I promise. Now grab a change of clothes and let's go—don't fuck around in there, we've got to get out of here before Uncle Mitch figures out what's going on."

"What are we doing for money?"

"I've been putting some in an account down there." He thought about telling him about the bag in the trunk, but decided that could wait. "Hurry. I'll tell you the rest on the way to the airport."

Eric kept the engine running. Ian was inside for no more than a few moments. When he returned, he had a canvas bag with him. "I brought underwear, a pair of jeans, and three thousand bucks," he said. "That's all the money I had in the house."

"That's great, Ian," he said, and pulled away from the curb.

They were on the freeway when Ian said, "What about Kyle and the girl?"

"Not our problem," Eric said, and moved into the fast lane.

46

LEFEBVRE ARRIVED AT THE DARKENED MANSION ON SHORELINE ALMOST at the same moment O'Connor did.

"Doesn't look as if anyone is here," Lefebvre said.

"You have someone looking for the BMW?"

"Yes."

"Who's it registered to?"

Lefebvre didn't answer. O'Connor hadn't really expected him to, but he had learned long ago that unasked questions never get answered, so he had taken the chance.

Lefebvre took a portable police radio and a large flashlight from his car. O'Connor already had his own flashlight in hand. It was windy here, and he pulled his jacket closer about him.

They tried the front door and found it locked. Shining their lights in through the big windows, they saw no sign of Irene or of Max.

"Maybe they've been and gone," Lefebvre said.

"Let's look around back."

The side gate was unlocked. They went through it into the backyard.

"Windows are open," Lefebvre said, and called out, "Irene! Max! Anyone there?"

No answer.

While Lefebvre tried knocking at the back door, O'Connor walked toward the alley.

"Lefebvre!" he called a moment later.

The detective turned toward him.

"Her car's still here."

Lefebvre joined him, shining his flashlight into the car while O'Connor squeezed his large frame between the little import and the garage door. There was no lock on the door and so he unlatched it, trying to peer inside. The wind caught the door, banging it against the Ghia.

"She's gonna have your hide for that one," Lefebvre said.

"Another item on a long list, I'm afraid." He pointed his flashlight into the garage and drew a sharp breath. "A black BMW." He bent to shine the light on the license plate, and sighed. "Not the one we were looking for."

Lefebvre's radio crackled and O'Connor saw him turn away to speak into it. O'Connor didn't try to listen in—he hurried back toward the house. If she wasn't still in the house, it was the last place she had been. He had no doubt that she was in trouble. If he knew anything about her at all, it was that she was devoted to her father, and would not have left him.

He thought of his own sister's disappearance and momentarily lost himself in remembered helplessness—how like that night this seemed to him. The thought filled him with dread, and he took himself to task—think of Irene, he told himself. Concentrate on the here and now.

He ran to the back door. He rang the bell, knocked, tried the knob. The door was locked.

He stepped back, then slammed against it. He felt it start to give. He slammed against it again just as Lefebvre came into the yard and asked him what the hell he was doing. The door gave way. He pushed what remained of it aside and went into the house.

He quickly went from room to room on the ground floor, calling to her. Moonlight came in through the windows, enough to see by in most of the rooms. Where it wasn't enough, he used his flashlight. Lefebvre had followed him in and was doing the same. They met up at the stairway. "Let's take a look around up there," Lefebvre said, shining his light on the stairs, "then maybe I'll arrest you for—"

Lefebvre grabbed his sleeve just as O'Connor was about to step on the first tread, and pulled him back. "Hold it," he said, bending closer to the stair.

O'Connor saw what he was focusing on. Blood. A large splotch of it on the left side of the tread, another on the banister just above it.

"Oh God . . ." O'Connor said. "Oh God."

Lefebvre seemed unperturbed. He used the radio again and called for backup and a crime scene unit and said to stand by, they might need an ambulance. He mentioned that the power was off, adding that they might want to bring a portable generator.

O'Connor, impatient, tried to break away from him, to rush up the stairs, but Lefebvre held tight.

"Listen to me!" the detective said, commanding, yet calm. "We're going up there, but don't touch the rails, and step to the right edge of the treads. I'm going first—try to step where I step. Watch that you don't put your big feet in any evidence." In a lower voice, he added, "Hold your flashlight away from your body, just in case we're not the only uninvited visitors, all right?"

Lefebvre's calm steadied him, forced O'Connor to struggle to regain his own.

Lefebvre watched him, then added, "Nothing is for the newspaper unless I say it is, or I handcuff you now and we wait here for a squad car."

"Do you think for a moment that the damned front page is more important to me than she is?" O'Connor asked, outraged.

"Maybe you bleed ink, O'Connor, like some of your friends at the paper."

"No more than you bleed blue."

Lefebvre smiled and said, "All right. Just so long as we understand each other." He took his gun out and started to climb. O'Connor concentrated on stepping where Lefebvre stepped, seeing the reddish brown spots they avoided, all the while telling himself that it wasn't really so much blood, perhaps no more than a small cut would produce.

Then Lefebvre's flashlight caught a smear of blood on the wall of the hallway. Much more blood than they had seen before. It was up high, at about the height of a man's waist. "Someone was carried, I think," Lefebvre said softly. "Not very carefully."

They turned a corner; this hallway was much darker than the rest of the house. Moonlight came through an open doorway at the end of the hall. Lefebvre stood for a long moment, listening. Gradually, cautiously, opening doors one by one, they worked their way down the hallway. Below, they heard patrol cars pulling up, doors opening.

Lefebvre called to them once, telling them that O'Connor was with him, and to be careful not to step on bloodstains on the stairs, but otherwise continued his methodical clearing of each room.

Two of the officers caught up with them. They carried powerful portable lights and brightened the hallway with these. With the additional light and more men to check the rooms, they made progress more quickly. Lefebvre noticed some faint bloody shoeprints and again warned the others to avoid stepping near them or the drops of blood along the floor.

The rooms were empty and only briefly held their interest, save the last one—the open one.

It, too, was unoccupied, but the bright lights illuminated several large bloodstains and bloody shoeprints on the hardwood floor. A closet door stood open. There were several objects scattered on the floor. O'Connor immediately recognized one of these and felt woozy, as if he had taken a hard, unexpected punch.

"Her jacket," O'Connor said brokenly, starting forward, then heeding the pressure of Lefebvre's hand on his shoulder, did not move into the room.

"Yes. I recognize it, too. The one she had on today," Lefebvre said. "And that's her purse, isn't it?"

"Yes, I think so."

They could also see a wallet, some bloodied tissues, a rag, and a small bottle.

Lefebvre moved cautiously into the room, avoiding the bloodstains and spatter. O'Connor saw him briefly glance at the shoeprints—which seemed to have started when someone stepped in blood in this room, and became fainter as he had walked down the hall, toward the stairs. Lefebvre spent a little more time studying a handprint on the floor, and then looking at the bottle, although without picking it up.

"Chloroform," he said.

O'Connor leaned against the door frame. "Jesus . . ."

Lefebvre looked up at him. "She probably left here alive. They wouldn't have bothered moving the body if all they wanted to do was kill her."

O'Connor said nothing, but Lefebvre perhaps read his next thought, because he added, "No use thinking the worst just yet."

He put on a pair of gloves and carefully opened Irene's handbag. He held up a reporter's notebook, then a wristwatch.

"Hers. If he's done something to her . . ." O'Connor said angrily.

Lefebvre ignored him and reached back into the bag. He found another wristwatch, a man's watch—and a wallet.

O'Connor felt briefly puzzled. Two wallets? Two watches? Were they both attacked?

Lefebvre verified that the wallet from the handbag was Irene's. "There's some cash and a credit card here, so apparently she wasn't robbed." He gingerly opened the man's wallet. Something wrapped in a piece of paper fell to the floor. Lefebvre ignored it for the moment and looked through the wallet's contents. "Max's temporary California driver's license. And it doesn't appear that he was robbed, either. I'd say they're both in trouble, though."

Lefebvre reached for the fallen paper and opened it. "A New Hampshire driver's license. Kyle Yeager—Max's old license." He read the note that had been wrapped around it—the paper had been torn from a spiral notebook.

"What does it say?" O'Connor asked anxiously.

"It says, 'Warren Ducane knows where we are.'"

47

I OPENED MY EYES IN UTTER DARKNESS. FOR A PANICKED MOMENT I WAS convinced I had been blinded. My cheek lay against a cold surface—hard and smooth. Concrete or marble, I thought. I could smell dried blood on my clothing. I remembered Max then. I tried to move and found that my wrists were taped together, as were my feet.

"Who's there?" a voice called from nearby.

"Max? It's Irene."

"Irene? Oh God . . ."

"How's your head? You were bleeding . . ."

"Never mind me—did they hurt you?"

"Not really. They used some kind of drug on me—chloroform or ether— I don't remember anything after that."

"Are you all right?"

"A little woozy, that's all. Max, it's you I'm worried about. Your head was bleeding so much. And you sound—I don't know, you just don't sound like yourself. Worse off than I am, anyway. Are you still tied up?"

"Yes. I'm—I'm okay. I don't think I'm still bleeding, but I'm tied up. You are, too, I take it?"

"Yes. Your head must be killing you."

"They hit me pretty hard, I guess."

"Your cousins?"

"I can't be certain, but I think so. Whoever it was hit me from behind."

I had no idea how long I had been knocked out, and began to wonder how late it was. My father—I had to get out of here. He would worry . . .

No use thinking of that right now, I told myself. I felt groggy, but the chill air was helping to clear my head.

"Any idea where we are?"

"No."

"Somewhere in the house?"

"It has a big basement," he said. "Maybe that's where we are. No—wait. The basement floor has linoleum on it."

We decided to try calling for help. We shouted a few times. It made my head ache worse than before.

"We could be anywhere," Max said. His voice sounded odd, with a drowsy quality to it.

"I'm going to try to scoot over to you."

I moved slowly and not in a very controlled way. I was now sure the surface below me was concrete; too rough to be marble. It felt like a cold, damp sidewalk.

I lost track of Max's location in the dark. "Talk again," I said.

"What?"

"Are you falling asleep?"

"I guess I kind of drifted off."

It was enough to help me find him. Sort of. I found his shoes with my face. It startled him as much as it did me.

"Okay, I'm going to work my way up to your hands. You're lying on your right side?"

It seemed to stump him for a moment, then he answered, "Yes."

I remembered that his hands had been bound behind him with duct tape, as mine were now. It took me a while, but eventually I positioned myself so that we were lying back to back. He must have passed out again or fallen asleep by the time I reached his hands. A horrible third alternative occurred to me, and I called his name.

"What? Huh? Oh . . . Irene?"

"Try to stay awake, Max. I think you have a concussion. Talk to me while I try to get the tape off your hands."

So he talked while I fumbled with his hands and tried to find an edge or end of the tape. His wrists had been bound much tighter than mine. I noticed his wristwatch was missing, and only then realized that my own was gone, too. While I worked at freeing him, he told me about Estelle, his adoptive mother. He told me about the military school, and about befriending the son of one of the instructors, a boy who was also a student at the school, of that boy's family virtually adopting him into their own. His voice kept that sleepy quality. As I gradually started to work the tape off—a process that was not as easy as it looks on television—I urged him to keep talking. Every now and then I'd hear him start to drift off, and I'd yank a little harder, and he'd keep going. I began to wonder if he would pass out just as I got his hands free and be unable to help me.

But when that moment came, he was awake and fairly focused. I heard him let out a breath in the darkness. "Thank you," he said. It took a little while for the circulation to return to his fingers. Both that and his head injury must have been painful, but he didn't complain. He rolled toward me and, as soon as the numbness left his hands, tried to free mine.

It took him less time to return the favor, but undoubtedly longer than it would have if he hadn't been injured. I spent a moment savoring the easing of the tension in my shoulders and back, then went to work on the tape around my ankles and helped Max to do the same.

We moved to our knees on the hard floor, staying close to each other, at first holding on to each other's shoulders just to steady ourselves. Without speaking, we embraced in the darkness, held fast to each other in sheer relief. He felt strong and warm and good, and I could not help but think of how much worse it would have been if I had been there alone.

"Are you okay?" he asked.

I nodded against his shoulder. "Yes, and you?"

"I'm doing okay."

"Dizzy?"

"A little. Weird in the dark."

"I don't think they took us far. I can still smell the ocean."

"Yes, I can, too. Maybe we're in the basement, just some part of it I haven't explored yet. There was a laundry room and another storage area that I didn't look into."

"I guess we'd better try to find a way out of here before they come back to finish what they started." I thought for a moment. "Maybe we should crawl along on all fours, shoulder to shoulder. Trying to walk might cause us to trip over objects we can't see, or run into things, or fall into a pit or something."

He agreed with this plan. It wasn't the fastest or most comfortable way to move, and was especially hard on the palms and knees, but it seemed the safest.

Before long, we realized that the space we were in was long and relatively narrow, and its walls as well as its floor seemed to be made of concrete. The utter darkness made it hard to be sure of much, though. We decided to stay along one of the walls, thinking we'd eventually come to some kind of opening or stairway. I took the position along the wall, since Max seemed to be having difficulty keeping his balance.

We came to a turning and moved to our right.

A glimmer of light came from some distant source, and we could hear the sea. The dampness increased, but the air was fresher. I felt wisps of my hair brushing against my face with a breeze. I could hear sounds of surf and wind.

This cheered me immeasurably. It also relieved some of the disorientation I had been feeling in the pitch darkness of before. And where light could get in, maybe we could get out.

It suddenly occurred to me where we were. "The bootlegger's tunnel."

"What?"

I told him what O'Connor had told me about the passageways.

"Then this leads to the house or the beach, right?" he asked.

"My guess is, we're nearer the beach right now. Let's try to stand."

We traded places so that he could lean his right hand against the wall. We took careful, shuffling steps forward. Eventually, I felt a change in the surface under my shoes. We were still walking on concrete, but there was something gritty on it—sand. The air continued to grow cooler and fresher.

We reached the end of the passageway. The light turned out to be moonlight, coming in through chinks in an opening sealed with a thick, iron-plated double-door. On our side, a wide iron bar secured with heavy padlocks held the doors shut. The other side of the doors seemed to be covered with a thick lacing of bougainvillea vines. The wind caused the bougainvillea's sharp, needle-like thorns to scrape against the metal doors as if it wanted to come in out of the weather. We tried dislodging the bar, to no avail. We pushed against each of the doors. They didn't budge. We called out again, but I could tell that no one was nearby.

Max sat down, leaning his back against one of the walls.

"Let me rest a little," he said. "Then I'll try to think of something."

I felt around the hinges, which were on our side of the doors, but they seemed rusted in place. Next I looked at the bottom edge.

To my delight, the concrete floor came to an end five inches or so before it met the doors. I began to claw at the sand with my hands.

"What are you doing?" Max asked, coming closer to see. "We can't fit between the doors and the concrete."

"No, but I think I could get an arm out, and maybe wave something to attract attention. Plus, it might give us more light and air."

"Or a better chance to be heard," he said. "Let me help."

He lasted five minutes before he passed out cold again.

48

ORTY MINUTES AFTER THEY HAD DISCOVERED THE ROOM WITH THE bloodstains, Lefebvre and the rest of the LPPD were making every effort to find Max and Irene. O'Connor tried—and failed—to comfort himself with that thought.

The "be on the lookout" order for what Lefebvre had since admitted to him was Eric Yeager's black BMW had been expanded to all local jurisdictions—an all-points bulletin saying that Eric and Ian Yeager were wanted for questioning in connection with an assault and kidnapping.

The crime lab team was at work on the shoe print, bloodstains, latent prints, and other forms of evidence from the scene.

Matt Arden was on his way, with another detective, to talk to Mitch Yeager. When O'Connor asked Lefebvre if Arden would have the balls to pressure Yeager, Lefebvre laughed. "Matt? He's wanted to have a go at Yeager for a long time now."

"Why?"

"You think you're the only one who believes Mr. Yeager isn't as respectable as he'd like everyone to believe? Besides, Eric and Ian have been thumbing their noses at the department for years. Skating just so close, just managing to keep clear of an arrest."

"Paid-off witnesses and the like. No need to tell me."

"You can trust Matt. He's good at interrogation, you know."

"I hear you're better."

"I learned from him, that's all." One of the uniformed officers came up to him just then and said that Haycroft from the lab wanted to show them something in the basement. "Do you know Paul Haycroft?" Lefebvre asked O'Connor. "He does excellent work with blood spatter patterns."

Haycroft theorized that one of the victims had received a blow from behind in the room upstairs and had fallen forward and injured his face. "A guess based on the cast-off blood on the walls and on the ceiling by the door, and from some of the staining on the floor. At least one of your attackers will have flecks of the victim's blood on his clothing. I'll want to study it more carefully, but I can't immediately see signs of more than one person being attacked in that way."

"Probably Max," O'Connor said. "He was here before Irene arrived."

"Yes," Haycroft said. "It's possible she found him after he was injured and used the jacket to stop the bleeding—the pattern of staining on the jacket indicates it was bunched up and held to a wound. The stains are on the outside, not on the lining. If she was wearing it and had been, say, stabbed or shot, the wound would bleed from the lining to the outside. And the staining is not consistent with, say, a wound to the head bleeding down onto the collar and back."

Seeing O'Connor's relief, he added, "I'll know more when we do more tests, but Ms. Kelly's father told us that her blood type is A, and all we have found so far is type O. According to Lillian Linworth, that's Mr. Ducane's blood type. The bleeding had nearly stopped by the time the victim was carried down the hallway and stairs. But what I want to show you, Detective, are small spots on the stairs leading to the basement."

In the basement, the spots of blood ended at the bottom of the stairs. O'Connor began to explore, looking carefully at the walls, which were covered with cheap paneling.

"What are you looking for?" Lefebvre asked.

"This is the bootlegger's house, remember? Somewhere along here, we might find an entrance to a passageway."

"Why would it be hidden? I thought the locals claimed to have legitimate uses for those tunnels to the sea."

"Most of the owners sealed them off years ago—in the early 1960s, a gang of thieves figured out that the passageways allowed easy access to and from some of the wealthiest households in Las Piernas. That and the possibility of homeless people camping in them put an end to most of the tunnels."

"But if the entrance was used this evening, we should see signs of it, don't you think?"

"Maybe. Or maybe they took the time to seal it up again."

Together they knocked on the walls, listening for some sign of a hollow space behind them.

A uniformed officer came down the basement stairs and drew Lefebvre aside. Lefebvre spoke briefly with him, then the officer hurried back upstairs.

"What was that all about?" O'Connor asked.

"They've taken the Yeager brothers into custody."

"Have they said anything about Max and Irene?"

"So far, no. They were apprehended at LAX. They're being brought back here, with their car. Let's keep looking."

They looked beyond the finished area of the basement. O'Connor searched through the storage room, but the walls in it and the laundry room were unfinished. Lefebvre had just followed O'Connor to the laundry room—which held an old washer and dryer, a large water heater cabinet, and a fold-down ironing board—when something occurred to him.

"Wait a minute," he said. "Why would one old man need two laundry rooms?"

Lefebvre frowned. "Yes—you're right—there's a newer washer and dryer upstairs." He walked over to the water heater cabinet. "And why would he need two water heaters?"

He opened the cabinet. It was empty. The back wall of the cabinet was a narrow metal door, sealed by a thick steel bar, which was held in place by three heavy padlocks. New padlocks.

Lefebvre banged the end of his flashlight on the door. "Irene! Max!" They listened, but heard no response. Lefebvre called to one of the uniformed officers and instructed him to keep tapping at the door.

"Let's try to find the other end of it," he said to O'Connor.

They met Haycroft on the way out. Two uniformed officers would wait for him to look for fingerprints, then work with bolt cutters to remove the locks. "I'll have my radio with me—call me the moment you're through that door. Oh—see if we can get someone from the beach patrol to meet us down at the bluffs."

On the way out, he asked another uniformed officer to cross the street and walk to the railing at the top of the bluffs. "Stand directly across from the house. Use your flashlight to signal me toward your location when we're on the beach."

The beach patrol received the message and met them with a Jeep at the bottom of the public stairway that led from a nearby parking lot down to the beach. They drove until they saw the signal made by the officer at the top of the bluffs.

"Now what, sir?" the driver asked Lefebvre.

"Let us out. Keep your headlights on the section of the bluffs just below where that officer stands."

O'Connor and Lefebvre hurried toward the vine-covered section of the bluffs.

"All this bougainvillea," O'Connor said. "We'll never see an opening through it."

"Irene!" Lefebvre called. "Max!"

They listened. The tide was coming in, but over the pounding of the surf, O'Connor swore he heard a voice.

Lefebvre had heard it, too. "Keep calling to us!"

It was a faint sound, nearly lost in the wind. Try as he might, he could not find its source.

Suddenly, O'Connor saw a flash of white. "There!" he cried, pointing a few yards away. "Near the ground. She's signaling us."

"What in God's name is that?" Lefebvre asked.

"If I'm not mistaken," O'Connor said, "it's her blouse."

49

I FELT MIXED EMOTIONS AS I WATCHED THE AMBULANCE LEAVE. I WAS relieved to know Max would be getting medical attention, but I felt as if I were abandoning him, even though it was I who stayed behind.

Lefebvre and O'Connor had waited patiently on the beach, talking with me and relaying information I gave them about Max's condition to the paramedics, while our rescuers worked to break in through the other end of the tunnel. They brought lights, water, and a stretcher for Max. I had my blouse back on, but I was still cold, so I was grateful for the blanket they gave me to wrap around my shoulders. Eventually someone found a way to bring me a cup of hot coffee.

I felt really bad about not being able to give much of a description of my assailants, but Lefebvre assured me that they would be caught whether I had seen them or not. I was starting to feel shaken, now that the main emergency was over and someone else was in charge, but Lefebvre's steadiness reached me, kept me from giving in to an urge to fall apart.

Lefebvre was watching me and said, "O'Connor put a big dent in your car."

"What?" Outrage snapped me out of fear into anger.

"For the Lord's sake," O'Connor said, "you're as full as you can hold, Lefebvre. Making it sound as if I hit it with a sledgehammer."

"I told you she'd be mad," Lefebvre said, but by then I had seen that glint of amusement in his eye, and caught on to his game.

"I'll be all right," I said.

"Do you have any guesses who might have attacked you?" Lefebvre asked.

"Eric Yeager," I said without hesitation. "I suppose his brother might have been the other one."

He exchanged a look with O'Connor and asked me why. I told him about our encounter with Eric at the Cliffside.

O'Connor was outraged that I hadn't told him about that. I had the pleasure of hearing Lefebvre tell him to lay off.

Lefebvre said some objects had been found near the basement entrance of the tunnel. "Including a long-handled flashlight that looks as if it was used to hit Max."

"Like the flashlight that might have been used to hit Katy Ducane?" I asked.

Lefebvre said, "The thought has occurred to me that it might be a familiar method for Max's attacker."

"But they wore gloves today, right?" O'Connor said. "Probably no fingerprints on it."

"Probably not," I said, then remembered my own flashlight. "Wait—the batteries! They might have worn gloves today, but I'll bet they touched the batteries in their flashlight with bare fingers!"

"That would be the natural thing to do," Lefebvre conceded. He called to one of the men from the lab and asked him to check for fingerprints on the batteries in the flashlight used to strike Max.

"And on the one left in the buried car," I said.

The lab man looked from me to Lefebvre.

"It's worth a try," Lefebvre said.

Eventually, I was told I could go home. O'Connor walked me to the Karmann Ghia.

"I'll pay for any damage I did to your car," he said.

"Don't be an idiot. There is no damage, and besides, I owe you big time."

"I'll follow you home," he said.

I didn't object. In fact, I thanked him.

50

Eric and Ian had been caught trying to flee the country with large amounts of cash and false passports in their possession. That gave the police enough reason to take them into custody, and later, it helped to ensure that bail was set astronomically high. Mitch Yeager paid it, but it took him a couple of days to do it.

Lefebvre's case against them for their assault and kidnapping of Max and me began with fingerprints found on the batteries, but was supported by other evidence. They literally had a trunkful of it. The end of a roll of duct tape found in the trunk of the car was compared microscopically with the ends of the pieces of tape used to bind and gag us—they matched. There was blood matching Max's blood type on gloves found in the trunk and on clothing stashed there as well. My flashlight, with my fingerprints on my new batteries, was also in the trunk of the BMW. And sensitive chemical tests showed traces of chloroform on one of Eric's gloves.

The note about the doorbell being broken was found wadded up in their trunk. The questioned documents expert in the Las Piernas lab was also able to match the perforated edge of the note about Warren Ducane with the edges left behind in a spiral-bound notebook in the car, as well as handwriting characteristics in the printing, and the ink type in a fancy pen carried by Ian.

There was trace evidence as well—hair and fibers found in the room where we were attacked matched samples taken from Eric and Ian, and strands of our hair and fibers from our clothes were found on theirs. The photos Stephen Gerard took, and his testimony about the places and times he had seen the BMW, convinced the jury that Eric had planned my kidnapping for some time.

Together with testimony from Max and me, they were convicted.

Eric and Ian Yeager were each sentenced to twenty-five years in prison.

Max, O'Connor, and I went drinking with the boys from the newsroom. The events in the Baer mansion seemed to have moved my status on the staff from that of outsider to team member—they closed ranks when they heard that one of their own had been attacked. That didn't stop several of them from asking me, from time to time, to take my blouse off and demonstrate how I had signaled for help, but their regard for me seemed to outlast the joke.

The *Express* had covered the story from one angle or another for almost a year by the time the Yeager brothers were sentenced, and nearly everyone on the news staff had worked on some related story. Time to celebrate.

The victory was bittersweet, though, because that was the Yeager brothers' second trial.

The first one, for the murders of the Ducanes, ended in a mistrial, with a hung jury. Although Lefebvre was clearly a genius at interrogation, the confessions obtained were ruled as inadmissible in pretrial—the Yeager brothers' lawyers claimed their clients were not properly Mirandized when taken into custody in Los Angeles. If there had been no other evidence, I suppose I would have understood the holdout juror's reluctance, but there was plenty of other proof of their guilt.

Among the treasures found in Eric's trunk, sewn into the lining of his suitcase, were seventy-nine diamonds. Diamonds that matched exactly the cut and style and size of those missing from the Vanderveer necklace. Also in the trunk was the lighter Jack had given Katy, monogrammed with her initial. Eric claimed that he and Ian had found these items while scuba diving. The fact that the lighter worked and showed no sign of having been exposed to sea water was something he could not explain.

Ian swore that he knew nothing about any of these items. Lefebvre didn't immediately challenge this. Instead he asked, "You like reading James Bond books?"

"Yes," Ian said warily, apparently puzzled by the abrupt change of subject.

"I wondered. Maybe you liked the writer's name. You know—Ian Fleming, Ian Yeager."

"No, that's not it. I just like them."

"I thought you might. Is that why you've hung on to that old Walther PPK of yours? What caliber is that? A 7.65 millimeter, isn't it? James Bond's gun. Your gun."

"You found . . ." But Ian's voice trailed off.

"You look surprised," Lefebvre said. "But you know, we look in all kinds of places when we have a search warrant, so it's a little hard to hide things from us. That business of taping the gun to the toilet tank lid—that's an old one."

Silence.

"You probably won't be surprised," Lefebvre said, "if I tell you that the bullets that killed Katy and Todd Ducane were 7.65 millimeter. I'll bet the rifling patterns and all those other little things we check when we match a weapon to a bullet just might tell an interesting story."

But Ian was surprised. "That fuckwad Eric killed them with my gun!" he said, and immediately provided an alibi for himself: he couldn't have been in the Buick—he had been invited to join Thelma and Barrett on the *Sea Dreamer,* and helplessly watched as they were swept overboard by a rogue wave.

"While you, on the other hand, could use your scuba tanks to breathe."

"Yes! No!"

It was only a matter of time before Ian admitted that he and Eric had been involved in the murders of all four Ducanes. Asked whose plan it was, he claimed that Eric had been the mastermind.

"Why would Eric want to kill the Ducanes?"

"They always looked down on us, that's why."

"Why spare Warren, then?"

Ian's voice took on a quality of recital as he answered. "If you kill your enemy, he's dead. He's not feeling another thing. But if you kill the people he loves and hide the bodies—you kidnap them and never let them be found— then you make him wonder if they're alive or dead, if he'll ever see them again. He starts to think about what might be happening to them. That way, your enemy suffers all his life. Nothing you could do to him is worse than that. Nothing."

Like Lefebvre, I was certain Ian's confession was a mixture of truth and lies, but those few minutes were the most disturbing. Ian had spoken with utter sincerity, as if this was his religious creed, rather than a declaration of his depravity.

Ian claimed complete ignorance about other events of that evening in 1958— the attack on Jack Corrigan, the kidnapping of the infant Max Ducane, the murder of Rose Hannon. His denials were convincing, and no further interrogation shook Ian from this position, or made the slightest change in his avowal that Eric had planned the murders of the Ducanes.

Eric denied everything—until he listened to a few minutes of Ian's confession. He then told of taking the younger Ducanes hostage, forcing Todd to drive while he sat in the back with Katy and the dog. As they went up the drive toward the farm, Eric had been bitten by Katy's dog on his gun arm, and he had clubbed the dog with his flashlight. That had so upset Katy, she had attacked him. During the ensuing struggle in the backseat, Todd lost control of the car and crashed the Buick into a tree. Eric had clubbed Katy as well then, and shot Todd as he sat dazed after hitting his head on the windshield. Griffin Baer had already prepared a burial place for the Buick, so Eric hadn't worried much about the crash.

Eric shot Katy just to make sure she was dead. He placed the bodies in the trunk. He wasn't supposed to take anything from them, but the diamond necklace was too big a temptation. He grabbed hold of it and it broke.

He could see Baer on his way over with a tractor, ready to tow the car to the pit. Eric rushed to pocket as many of the diamonds as he could before Baer reached him.

"Why not kill Baer to keep him quiet?"

"I knew Griff wouldn't talk. He was a friend of my father. Of my grandfather. You think I would kill an old family friend?"

Lefebvre was silent for a long moment, then said, "Thelma Ducane was a friend of your uncle Mitch, and so was her husband."

"This has nothing to do with my uncle Mitch."

"What is it he's promised you?" Lefebvre asked.

"Not a thing."

"I'm supposed to believe it's a coincidence that all of this took place on the same night that the Ducane heir was kidnapped?"

"I don't care if you believe it or not. That's the way it happened. I know nothing about any kidnapping."

"Why was Warren Ducane spared?"

"You ought to ask him. Have you found him yet? Besides, if you really want to hurt your enemy, you don't just kill him. That's quick. He doesn't suffer at all. You want to make your enemy suffer, you kill the people he loves and hide the bodies—you make him wonder if they're alive or dead. Nothing is worse than that."

O'Connor was convinced the Yeager catechism was a direct quote from their uncle Mitch. While I didn't doubt it, there was simply no way to prove it, or to prove that Eric and Ian had any connection to the disappearance of Max Ducane or Jack's beating or even the death of Gus Ronden.

Mitch Yeager had been present at the trials, publicly playing the role of the shocked and saddened uncle who couldn't believe that these "boys" would do such terrible things.

The D.A. at the time was not as skilled as his opponents. The prosecutor told Lefebvre and Arden that he was concerned about the age of the cases, lack of witnesses, and the little physical evidence that tied Eric and Ian to the murders. Under public pressure he decided to prosecute the cases, but he sought the death penalty—which had only been reinstated in California the previous year.

Lefebvre later told me that he didn't think the D.A. did a good job of screening the jury. Post-trial interviews revealed that the possibility of a death sentence had weighed strongly with the most reluctant juror. After five days of deliberation, the jury informed the judge that it was hopelessly deadlocked, and the judge declared a mistrial.

Ian and Eric weren't free—there was still the problem of the little housewarming party they had thrown for Max and me. Rather than pursue a second murder trial, the D.A. brought them up on the assault and kidnapping charges—not even attempted murder, which was arguable.

But the safe bet paid off, and the D.A. won that case. I was relieved to know the Yeager brothers wouldn't be free, but it didn't seem right that they were going to jail for hitting Max and locking us in a tunnel for a few hours rather than for taking four—or more—lives.

In the months before the trial, Max and I figured out that dating would ruin a perfectly good friendship. By then, the friendship meant too much to us to risk that. He recovered from his injuries and went back to New Hampshire to pursue his MBA at Tuck. He came back to Las Piernas often, though—he hired some friends from Dartmouth to help him start a company that would develop applications of GPS technology, and based the company in Las Piernas, where he planned to live after graduation.

The day the verdicts were handed down, he left our post-trial celebration early to catch a flight back East. Before he left, he gave me a hug and said, "Write to me. Call me collect. And keep slaying dragons."

Lefebvre stopped by the party for an hour or so, and was the first person to notice that I wasn't drinking. "Driving tonight?" he asked when he was sure he wouldn't be overheard.

I glanced at O'Connor, who was quietly downing one scotch after another. "I think that would be best."

"You two are getting along now, I see."

"We still have our occasional differences of opinion," I said, which made Lefebvre smile. "But I like it when we tackle a story together. It's hard to describe, but there's a kind of energy there that I don't always feel when I work on my own." I shrugged. "This is going to sound corny, but I like him because he tries so hard to do the right thing."

"Corny, huh? Maybe not. I've been reading some of the articles you've written together—it's a good partnership, I think. And speaking of partnerships—I hear that you'll soon be related by marriage."

I sighed. "For as long as it lasts. Yes, my sister Barbara and his son Kenny are getting married. The only upside to this is that Kenny has moved out of O'Connor's house and bought a place of his own."

"You don't place much hope in their future?"

"I shouldn't be so negative," I admitted. "They'll probably be together forever. Kenny needs constant care and attention. My sister loves providing it—to a healthy male like him, anyway."

He studied me after I said this, and I found myself hoping he didn't ask me what I meant by it. He probably knew about my father, but he changed the subject.

"I wanted more of these old questions to be resolved," he said, "but I have worked in law enforcement long enough to feel relieved that at least Ian and Eric now have felony convictions on their records. If they fail to win appeals, I'll be happy."

"I know what you mean. I just wish Betty Bradford had called me back."

"Maybe she will, one of these days."

"She's passed up a huge reward, and if the person who was her boss was convicted today, she should have stepped forward."

He shook his head, but didn't comment. We both knew the big fish got away. And neither of us thought there was a hope in hell he'd be caught.

When last call rolled around, O'Connor and I were the only ones still in the bar. O'Connor was under full sail. Still, he managed to walk fairly steadily to the Karmann Ghia, and didn't have too much difficulty getting in.

I drove him home. He was sobering up a little by then, and invited me in for coffee. I had been to his house many times by then, and he to mine, but this was something he had never done before. I accepted the invitation, but watching the clumsiness of his movements, seated him at the kitchen table while I made the coffee. Never let a drunk loose in a kitchen. Too many sharp implements, and the simplest tasks will take forever.

I made coffee that was the equivalent of forty-weight motor oil. He drank three cups of it. I could see him coming into focus, so I asked, "What is it, O'Connor?"

"What's what?"

"What's eating at you?"

He shrugged. "I was thinking of Ian and Eric's catechism, and wondering if I could have become Mitch's Yeager's enemy before I was eighteen."

"When you were a copyboy?"

"Maybe before that, even."

"What do you mean?"

He didn't answer. I poured him another cup of coffee.

"I was thinking of Maureen tonight, that's all," he said. "I think of her every day, but sometimes . . . like that night when you were in that tunnel . . . God, did that worry me."

"Who's Maureen?"

He seemed surprised I didn't know, then looked down at his coffee. "Was . . . who *was* Maureen."

After a long silence, he told me the story of his missing sister, and how he blamed himself because he had not walked her home that night. He talked of the misery his family had experienced, of the years of waiting for her to return. Of how even the discovery of her remains, while a relief of one kind, hadn't brought him the peace he had hoped for. He spoke with bitterness over the fact that her murderer had not been caught. He seemed to blame himself for that, too.

I thought of the many times, over the past few months, when we had talked of unidentified bodies and missing persons. Not once had he mentioned Maureen. I realized that not even the loss of Jack could compare with the painfulness of this wound.

"We had been so close," he said quietly. "I miss her to this day."

I couldn't think of a thing to say or do to comfort him. I wanted to hug him, and while in later years that would become a natural part of our friendship, it was not yet. Finally, I said, "When you told me about the way she felt about your work—she was proud of you. I think she still would be proud."

"Do you?" he asked. "I wonder."

"I'm sure of it."

He smiled softly then said, "It's late, Kelly. Will you call me to let me know you've got yourself home safely? Don't worry you'll wake me."

I called him when I got home, thinking of that night when he searched for me along the bluffs, and of his admission tonight that he had been afraid for me. I vowed that if he ever again wanted to see me safely to my door or wanted me to call him when I got home, or check in with him during the day, I would not fight it or refuse to do as he asked. These requests were not, I saw at last, overbearing protectiveness. His fears came out of a devastating loss, one that had haunted him all his life.

At work the next day, thinking of how drunk he had been, I wondered if he would remember telling me about his sister. He drew me aside and said, "I know you heard my sad tale with a kind heart, Irene, so I won't regret the telling of it. But I have no right to use my sister's memory in such a way. I would be grateful if we did not speak of it again."

We never did, directly. We often did, in a thousand other ways.

Neither of us ever forgot Maureen O'Connor.

PART III

LEX TALIONIS

"Did I appeal to the law—I? Does it quench the pauper's thirst if the king drink for him?"

—MARK TWAIN, *Life on the Mississippi*

February 2000

51

WHEN THE DOGS STARTED BARKING, FRANK WAS IN THE SHOWER AND I was in the bedroom, getting dressed. I had just pulled my pantyhose up around my knees when the doorbell rang. I glanced at the clock. Seven-thirty on a Wednesday morning. Who the hell was at my door at this hour?

I hastily pulled the pantyhose up the rest of the way, got a big run in them as I quickly put on some shoes, swore, and went to the door. I opened it to see—to my utter surprise—Kenny O'Connor.

Kenny was not the same man who had walked into that café all those years ago. He and Barbara had married and divorced, and were talking seriously about remarrying now.

Over those twenty years or so we had all changed to some degree, I suppose, but Kenny's growing up had been recent. He had received a savage beating at the business end of a baseball bat, a beating that had left doubt about whether he'd live, and, if he survived, whether he'd walk, be able to speak without slurring his words or stop seeing double. The latter two problems cleared up fairly quickly. After years of rehabilitation work, he was walking now, with the help of a cane, and although his features were perhaps not as handsome as they had once been, anyone who had seen him immediately after the beating was now a believer in the wonders of plastic surgery and dental prosthetics.

He still worked in construction, but had been forced to sell his own company to pay medical bills. Now he was employed by O'Malley's company, as a supervisor. Working for O'Malley had been good for him—better for him, in many ways, than working for himself. These days, Kenny never took his job—or much of anything else—for granted.

"Hi, Irene. Mind if I come in for a minute?"

"Sure, great to see you. I was just about to make breakfast. Have you eaten?"

"Yes—I've eaten. But don't let me hold you up."

I motioned him inside. "Come and talk to me while I get busy in the kitchen."

"Is your husband here?"

"Yes, he's in the shower. Let me tell him you're here."

"That's okay—I came here to talk to you, anyway. I just thought—well, I'll ask him later."

He followed me into the kitchen, sat at the counter, and accepted an offer of coffee. He watched while I put a couple of slices of bread in the toaster.

"So, what's up?" I asked.

"Barbara tell you we're moving?"

"Yes. A house not too far from here, right?"

"Right. Thought we'd make a fresh start this time around."

"You'll like the area," I said, not commenting on the fresh-start part. I kept trying to make myself forgive him for some of the horrible things he had said to Barbara when he was going through man-o-pause. For fooling around on her. I supposed I should get over it, since obviously she had.

There is a distance between "should forgive" and "have forgiven" that is sometimes hard to cross.

"Well . . ." he said, then stalled.

I waited. Eventually he started up again. "I have some old stuff of my dad's. I thought you might like to have it."

"Stuff of your dad's? Kenny, I saw what was left of his house when he was . . . when he died. Everything burned to the ground. You lost everything . . . right?"

"Yeah, *everything*." He fell silent again. The toast popped, and I set it on a plate. Maybe Frank would want it. My appetite was gone.

Deke, one of our big mutts, sidled up to him. "Well," Kenny said, reaching down to pet her, "you might not remember this, but after Barbara and I separated, I moved back in with my dad. He had filled my old room up with a lot of papers and stuff, and so when I came back home, he dumped it into boxes and carted it all over to this storage place." He opened his wallet and pulled out a business card and handed it to me.

"U-Keep-It Self-Storage," I read. I flipped it over. Scrawled on the back, in a hand I would have recognized anywhere, O'Connor had written "#18B."

"It might just be junk," Kenny said quickly.

"Haven't you looked through it?"

He paused, went back to petting Deke, then said in a low voice, "I can't."

After a moment, I said, "I understand."

He nodded, not looking up at me. Dunk, our other dog, saw what he was missing and crowded him on the other side of the chair.

"If they're getting obnoxious, I'll put them out," I said.

"No. No—I like dogs. Might have room for them at this new place."

"You've been paying the rent on this storage place all this time?"

He nodded again. He reached for his keys and pulled one off. "Almost forgot. You'll need this to open the padlock. The code to get into the gate is four-six-four-five."

I frowned. "Everyone who rents there knows that code?"

"No, Dad made that one up for himself. Each person has his or her own. And there are cameras all over the place. But you can change the code if you want to—just see the guy at the counter, and he'll put your new one in the computer. I guess he was a friend of Dad's."

"He made them wherever he went."

Kenny smiled. "True."

"You sure you want me to have whatever is in there? Maybe there will be things you'll want."

"If it's just papers and stuff like that, I don't really want them. Otherwise—you can let me know if there's something you think I'll want. I trust you."

That statement left me speechless.

Frank came out then, and Kenny visibly relaxed. "Hey, Frank—how's it going?" They shook hands and almost immediately began talking about weekend sports.

Frank glanced over at me, his gray-green eyes full of amusement, and reached for the cold toast.

"Let me heat it up for you," I said, a bit of domesticity that made him raise his brows even as he thanked me. I put the toast back in the toaster.

Kenny said, "Do you know much about this DNA stuff, Frank? I mean, being a homicide detective and all, of course you do, but . . . well, can I ask you about it?"

"Sure. What's on your mind?"

"My dad's only living brother is coming over from Ireland in a couple of months."

"Dermot?" I asked.

"Yes. What I was wondering is—I've heard you can tell about paternity from DNA, even if you don't have a sample from a living parent."

"Yes, that's true. You just need a relative descended from the same person."

"So I could find out if my dad was really my dad from a sample of Dermot's blood?"

"Yes. You'd each have to provide a blood sample, and you'd have to have it done by a private lab. It can be expensive—about fifteen hundred or more. Takes about four to five weeks."

"Oh. Well, that makes sense, I guess."

"Is that something you want to do?"

"I don't know. I'm just thinking about it, that's all." He sniffed the air and said, "I think your toast is burning."

Later that morning, I sat at O'Connor's desk in the newsroom. It was my desk now, at least as far as the newer staffers were concerned, and I called it mine, but that was for convenience' sake. I could never truly think of it as mine rather than his, and I know most of the staffers who had known him felt the same way—I was a tenant, not a proprietor. It's one of the last of the old-style desks in the newsroom, and I have resisted all attempts to get me to exchange it for a piece of plastic on metal tubes. The publisher has heard me threaten to quit if it's moved an inch from where it is.

Winston Wrigley III, the jerk who inherited his late father's job, knows that isn't an empty threat. I quit the paper in the late 1980s after he failed to fire someone for sexually assaulting another staff member. I was gone from the *Express* for a couple of years. I came back because it was the only way I was going to find out who had killed one of my closest friends—my mentor, Conn O'Connor.

The same people who had been responsible for Kenny's beating had been responsible for O'Connor's murder. O'Connor had died because he got too close to the truth while covering a story. I followed the leads he had worked so hard to discover, and his killers were brought to justice. It didn't ease the loss.

The homicide detective working on the case was a man I had known in Bakersfield, Frank Harriman. Though he moved to Las Piernas in 1985, we didn't manage to reconnect until O'Connor's death. To the shock of everyone who had written me off as a woman who would be single all her life, we had married.

I'm Irish enough to think O'Connor's spirit had a hand in that.

Maybe because I held the key to his storage unit in my hand, I could feel him looking over my shoulder in the newsroom that morning. I still missed him terribly and often wished I could hold another conversation with him, to tell him he was right, that newspaper work was in my blood, and that I had wanted to come back to the *Express* all along—but mostly to listen to his voice, his laughter, at least one more time.

I looked around me and wondered if he would want to work here these days. Not so much as a whiff of cigarette smoke, but that wouldn't have bothered him. A bigger problem would be that a Starbucks Double Latte was about the strongest drink anyone kept near his desk.

No, that wouldn't be the biggest problem. The biggest problem would be that someone had come by, vampirelike, and sucked the life's blood out of the place while we were all trying to make deadline.

Nearby, I heard other reporters murmuring into headsets and the soft snicking of computer keyboards. The hum of the fluorescent lights overhead provided the loudest noise in the room. Quiet as a damned insurance office, and looked like one, too.

A few faces would be familiar to him. John Walters, Mark Baker, Stuart Angert, and Lydia Ames—who was now the city editor. Most of the men who had been hired in the late 1950s and 1960s had taken advantage of retirement packages in recent months, unable to watch the paper change as it had under Winston Wrigley III's latest overhaul. We were losing a lot of people who had ten to twenty years in, too.

Circulation was down, and Wrigley was engaging in desperate measures these days. In the past few months, photographs had taken up more room than text on the front pages of every section. "What are we afraid of—readers?" one veteran reporter had said to me, just before he left. "Soon we'll be giving out crayons to new subscribers."

Another plan involved keeping stories to about two column inches each. All right, that's an exaggeration, but as one of my colleagues said, "We used to have sidebars longer than these stories."

The paper would have been even worse off if Wrigley's father had not foreseen that his son might not be up to the job. While he had spoiled his son to a large degree, by the end of his life he had become less willing to excuse his only child's weaknesses, and grew impatient with his lack of judgment. He couldn't bring himself to deny him the position held for two generations by men named Winston Wrigley, but he made sure that Wrigley III didn't inherit controlling stock, and established a Publisher's Board that his son had to answer to.

Wrigley had less-than-subtle pressure from the board to keep me around, and John Walters covered my back—a loyalty I tried hard to continue to deserve.

To keep costs down, Wrigley insisted that John replace veteran staffers who left the paper with young reporters fresh out of J-school. I didn't mind working with these newcomers, but I stopped expecting to get to know them very well, because most of them left us after a few months to work for bigger papers. We were becoming a "nursery paper"—a training program for people who would win the Pulitzers at some other paper. That was another sore point among the older staffers. They became unwilling to invest time and effort into teaching the ropes to people who would be gone in less than a year.

My tolerance—and my friendship with Lydia, who had reign over the general assignment reporters—had earned me the keep of two of these fledglings, Hailey Freed and Ethan Shire. They had been assigned desks near mine. As I logged on to my computer that morning, I felt tired just thinking about them.

They had graduated in the same year from the journalism department of Las Piernas University (formerly Las Piernas College—my own degree was issued before the upgrade, and I shuddered to think what they might make of that fact). They had a lot of confidence in themselves and were competitive as all get out, but otherwise, they were as different as they could be from each other.

I sometimes wished they had a little less confidence. Hailey was fairly sure that two years on the campus paper and a summer internship meant she already knew it all and ought to be left alone so that she could pry journalism from the clutches of crones like me, abandon our archaic methods, and improve the paper for the twenty-first century. She didn't mind letting me know she resented my old-school style of journalism. Clean writing, balanced coverage, fact checking—boring stuff. A little more of her beautiful, semi-poetic but inaccurate reporting and I was going to FedEx her to Tom Wolfe, to force him to live with the results of what seeds he had sown. I would have, until she told me that Wolfe was an old man and that was the old new journalism—she was going to be part of the new new journalism, a revolution on the World Wide Web. I couldn't wait. In the meantime, I tried to teach her that the lead—the most essential and dramatic information in a news story—was not an acorn to be buried beneath several other paragraphs.

Ethan, who had been a city editor on that same college paper, was damned sure he was destined for better things than the *Express*. The rest of us just hadn't realized that we had Jesus in our carpenter shop.

He was also our budding newsroom politician. He shamelessly brown-nosed Wrigley, who in turn made him a pet. He had talent, I thought, but he didn't seem to be able to concentrate on his work and often took the easy way out on a story. I didn't think he had quite found the style that was his own, either, because his writing approach was all over the map. When he focused on what he was doing, I recognized a style that needed a little time to mature, but held a lot of promise. Two days later, I would get stories from him that were so obviously a patchwork of other styles, they didn't read well. I would tell him that while he had done the basic job of collecting facts in these cases, he'd be better off not trying to imitate other writers.

Ethan thought he had charmed me into believing he paid attention to what I told him about his work. Perhaps he thought I couldn't read—the proof that he was ignoring me was writ large in nearly every story he filed. Lydia was tough on him—stories got kicked back to him or rewritten by surer hands. While Hailey was going to have problems because she hated anyone touching her lovely words, Ethan seemed almost unnaturally detached from his. He never minded a rewrite of his work—Ethan was on to the Next Big Thing by then—and was happy just as long as his name was on the story.

No problem. A byline was no longer an honor to be earned. Everyone got one. Most of the time, they got a mug shot pasted next to it, too. Lydia said it was just as well that the public knew who to blame.

Hailey peered at me over the top of her monitor now and asked, "What agency has jurisdiction over cemeteries?"

"No simple answer. California has a Cemetery and Funeral Bureau, which is part of the Department of Consumer Affairs. The federal government maintains veterans' cemeteries. Some cemeteries belong to religious groups, some to counties, some privately to families."

"What about the Las Piernas Municipal Cemetery?"

"The city owns that one, and believe it or not, that's under the care of the Parks and Recreation Department."

"Oh."

"What have you got in mind?"

We heard the sound of laughter, and turned to see Ethan talking with Lydia, apparently amusing her. Hailey frowned, probably envying the attention he was getting from the city editor. She had a hard task ahead of her if she was going to compete with Ethan's charm.

"You were saying something about the cemetery?" I said.

"Nothing much. Kind of a crazy thing—I have a friend who swears some-one has been disturbing his grandfather's grave."

"Modern-day grave robbers?"

"I don't think they've taken the body. Just messed with the grave. Al-though my friend thinks someone might have tried to break into the casket to steal this antique ring the old man was buried with. I thought I might try to find out if there's anything to it, that's all."

"You run it by Lydia?"

She shook her head. "I'm not sure I want to do anything about it. Besides, Lydia has given me a couple of other things to work on. And I don't know—the whole thing creeps me out."

"Maybe she'll cut you loose from some of the other things you're handling right now."

"Maybe."

I wasn't going to do any hand-holding. I went back to my own work.

Most of my time is spent covering local politics—being married to a homi-cide detective prevents me from covering stories about crime, but there's enough intrigue in city government to keep me busy. I read through some notes I had made about current issues before the harbor commission, but found my thoughts constantly drifting to O'Connor, and wondering what might be in the storage locker. I was curious, but also aware that Kenny had burdened me with what was undoubtedly going to be an emotionally draining task.

On the other hand, maybe it would just be a lot of crap that would be easy to toss out, and nothing more complicated than laziness had kept Kenny from doing it himself.

Except that in the time since he was injured, Kenny hadn't been lazy at all.

I left the paper and spent a couple of hours at city hall trying to get some answers to questions I had about a planning commission proposal. When I returned, Ethan was talking to Lydia again. He soon rushed out of the news-room. Well, I thought, he's finally catching on to the fact that you can't cover the news if you stay inside the building. That, or he was going to lunch.

I glanced at my watch and realized that it was almost noon.

I suddenly recalled an appointment of my own and hurried over to the city desk. "I'm having lunch with Helen Swan and my great-aunt today. You want to join us?"

"I'd love to," Lydia said, "but I can't get away. Give them my best."

"I may be back a little late." I told her about Kenny's visit and the storage locker key. "I'll have my cell phone with me if you need me."

Despite the fact that, as usual, she had three phones ringing, four people walking toward the desk from various parts of the newsroom, and more "highest priority" e-mail messages waiting for her than I wanted to think about, she said, "You need some company when you do that?"

I shook my head. "I'll be all right. If it starts to . . . to bother me, I'll lock it up and come back to it when I can handle it."

Would that I could have lunch with Helen and Great-Aunt Mary every day. Each time I do, I'm reminded of how strong and smart and wise and downright ornery they are, and how much I hope to be like them someday. If I have half as much energy when and if I make it to my eighties, I'll be happy.

It was the perfect way to prepare myself for going over to the storage unit. Helen had grown a little deaf over the years, and had voluntarily given up driving, but otherwise was doing well. Mary had become one of her closest friends. Mary was still driving her red Mustang, and seemed to enjoy taking Helen out and about. Mary was sharp and in good health and remained one of my anchors in times of trouble.

I told them about my fledglings, which amused Helen no end. She kindly didn't mention her own trials with me, when I was her student. I mentioned to Helen that some of O'Connor's papers had apparently been in a storage locker, and that Kenny had given me the key to it. "I'm on my way over there after lunch. If I find anything that might be of interest to you, I'm sure Kenny won't mind if I give it to you."

She seemed surprised, then distracted. Aunt Mary was going on and on about what a pack rat O'Connor was. She has drawings I gave her when I was in first grade, so I didn't pay much attention to her. I became worried that I had upset Helen. O'Connor had been so close to her and Jack.

After O'Connor died, Max Ducane told me that Helen had been severely depressed and talked of having lost almost everyone who was dearest to her. She was, as always, resilient, and eventually seemed more herself, but I was concerned.

"Helen?"

As if coming out of a trance, she said, "Yes, let me know what you find.

But you needn't give anything to me. If it were up to me to choose one person to have O'Connor's writing and notes and other treasures, I would choose you."

I was flattered, and as I made my way to the storage place, I couldn't help but remember the time I had told O'Connor that Helen's counsel had kept me working with him. He had admitted then that she had been working just as hard to keep him from giving up on me. I owed her thanks for one of the most important friendships of my life.

U-Keep-It Self-Storage was typical of those built in the mid-1970s. Cinder block and steel roll-up doors. I pulled up to it in the Jeep Wrangler we had just bought from a friend, Ben Sheridan. Ben is a forensic anthropologist. Thinking of him, I wondered if he might be able to help Hailey out with her story.

A sign warned that anyone entering the premises was subject to video surveillance. I entered the 4645 code, and a security gate opened to let me into the parking lot. I was parked and out of the car before it rolled shut again. O'Connor's unit was on the second floor. I thought that was probably good—a little more secure. I took the stairs. The wide hallway was windowless and dark, but apparently a motion detector sensed my presence, because a series of bare bulbs lit overhead.

I found the unit, shoved a small flatbed cart away from the door, and fit the key in the padlock. The lock was a little stiff, but it opened. I flipped the bolt aside and pulled the door up.

Before me were about forty boxes and plastic containers, and two metal trunks. Some boxes were labeled, some weren't. Some looked relatively new, but most appeared to be old and bore signs of long storage.

One was immediately familiar to me. Written in that misunderstood scrawl of his was a beloved friend's name: Jack.

I heard myself exhale, hard. Seeing the box made me think of the day I first saw it, of O'Connor walking across that dusty field, holding on to it as if he were a priest carrying the last tabernacle, asking me—a green reporter—if he could help me with my story. He had worked so relentlessly to discover what had really happened on that night in 1958. For all that had been learned, there was still a great deal that was unknown.

Eric and Ian Yeager were already out of prison, supposedly living on a Caribbean island, but every now and then someone said they had seen them in town. Mitch Yeager—that old buzzard—would probably survive World War III. The only punishment he had received came from his three kids, spoiled brats who had never done an honest day's work.

I shook off thoughts of that family from hell and stepped inside, found a light switch for the unit (a luxury item), and was surprised to find that the bulb wasn't dead. I rolled the door down a little more than halfway. I wanted some privacy, but claustrophobia is a problem for me—I counted being able to pull the door shut at all a major victory.

The old trunks intrigued me. One was brown, the other green. They were side by side. Neither was locked, although they were latched shut. I snapped the latches open on the brown one, which looked older to me.

It was full of fragile, yellowing papers covered in a childish scrawl. I carefully lifted a few from the trunk. Each had a title, written in small and large caps, headline style: "THE MAN WHO FIXES MOTOR CARS." "THE HOUSE WHERE MY MOTHER WORKS." "HOW MY DA GOT HURT." "HOW DERMOT HELPS A HORSE WIN A RACE." "LUCKY THINGS IN MY HOUSE." "WE MOVE TO A NEW HOUSE." Each of these stories was clearly marked, "by Conn O'Connor."

Lucky things in his house included a horseshoe that had come from a stakes winner, various religious medals and other artifacts, a piece of wood "from a true fairy tree" back in Ireland, a crow's feather that "Dermot says isn't lucky at all, but he's wrong," and a "dollar from my benefactress." This last word appeared to have been carefully copied from a dictionary.

I smiled. After he had known me for a few years, O'Connor told me of the day he had met Jack Corrigan, and that Lillian had tipped him a silver dollar. I looked around me, thinking that it might well be in one of these boxes.

Maybe not. He was such a superstitious old Irishman, he probably had it in his pocket the day he died.

For some stupid reason, I started crying.

I pulled myself together after a bit and looked in the trunk again. Not far from the top were nine diaries.

The oldest one was dated 1936. I opened it carefully and read the first entry.

52

"TODAY MAUREEN GAVE ME THIS DIARY. SHE IS THE BEST SISTER IN THE world." A little below that was written, "Jack would say that's hipurboily, but it's not."

"Best" and "not" were heavily underlined. The word "hipurboily" had been crossed out and carefully corrected to hyperbole. I sat on the other trunk and kept reading. As I read on, again and again I saw corrections. I found myself feeling amazed that a boy his age wrote so well, and had taken the time to correct his mistakes.

"Jack gave me another boxing lesson today."

"Da had a bad day today. I tried to be quiet."

"Jack liked the story about the horse but he is making me redo it anyway."

"Jack said to call it rewrite, not redo. Said my diary is for me, not to show it to him again. Said I could get mad as fire at him in my diary—say anything here."

"Miss Swan scared me again today. Asked if I am writing Jack's stories. Told her I am only a kid."

That one made me laugh aloud.

"Jack still likes Lily, I think. She is mad at him."

"A good day. Jack took me upstairs to the newsroom. Met Mr. Wrigley. He is very old. Jack told him I will be a reporter for the *Express* one day. Mr. Wrigley did not say no."

"Jack and Miss Swan had dinner tonight. Jack calls her Swanie. He is brave."

Hardly a day went by without a reference to Jack Corrigan. Helen had told me they were close, as had O'Connor, and O'Connor was always full of stories about him. But seeing this day-by-day record of O'Connor's boyish adoration of him gave me new awareness of just how close they were. Jack seemed to treat him like a much younger brother, at times almost as a son. He must have taken him under his wing from the start and had infinite patience.

Well, no, I thought—even at eight, O'Connor was obviously an amusing companion.

As I read on, I realized that while Helen clearly thought of him in that way, Lillian seemed to have been annoyed with him. She probably wasn't aware that her snide remarks were not only overheard but dutifully recorded by O'Connor. Gradually, through the observant if not fully comprehending eyes of an eight-year-old, I saw a picture of a young, willful rich girl who was enjoying a bit of rebellion by dating Corrigan. The picture that emerged of Thelma Ducane was even less flattering. Corrigan, for his part, seemed unfazed by Lillian's tantrums or threats, and not far into the entries, either Jack stopped seeing her or O'Connor became uninterested in reporting about Jack's love life.

I guess Jack sought company with his colleagues for a time, because then the stories were of other reporters, often Helen Swan. I had a feeling that Jack had been smitten with her long before he married her, something that was going right over O'Connor's young head. Maybe over Jack's as well.

I got a fascinated child's view of the staffs of the two papers.

In that same summer, O'Connor, the little rat, had spied on Jack one night—and saw that he was out with Lillian again. "It is wrong. She is married." The kid should have been a gossip columnist. I turned the page and repented of these thoughts.

This page was tearstained. It said, "Jack hurt in his car. Might die. Please, God, help him. I will be good."

The next entry thanked God "even though I was not so good." O'Connor had managed to sneak into the hospital to visit Jack, apparently by charming a kind janitor and a sympathetic old nun. This went on for a few days. The entries were worried ones—"Jack's ankle broke. The doctor can't fix it." "Jack is sad. I can't help him." Then, one day, "Miss Swan visited." A report of what she said to Jack made me realize she was as tough then as she is now. But the entry ended with, "Jack likes her. He will be better, I think."

He noted a date not much later, when she left the *News*. I hadn't known about that. O'Connor wrote, "Jack misses her, I think. Talks about her a lot."

The outside hallway light had turned off at some point, but it suddenly snapped on again. I waited, heard someone's footsteps at the other end of the hall, the sound of another unit's door being rolled open and down again.

For no real reason I could name, I felt uneasy.

I glanced at my watch and nearly swore. I had certainly whiled away the afternoon. Lydia probably thought I'd gone to work for another paper. She hadn't called, though. I pulled out my cell phone to see if I had missed a call. No signal.

No way to know if Lydia had tried to reach me or not.

I decided I'd look through the contents of the two trunks in the comfort of my own home. Still uneasy about the other visitor to this floor, I crept toward the roll-up door on O'Connor's unit, eased it higher, and looked up and down the hall before I pulled the flatbed cart inside. I loaded the two trunks on it, pushed it out, and started to close up the unit, then stopped and grabbed the box labeled "Jack" before locking up.

The elevator was at the other end of the hall. I pushed the cart past the unit that was occupied and paused briefly to listen, but the person visiting it wasn't making any noise. I hurried out.

I wasn't all that far from the house, and the parking lot of the Wrigley Building is far from secure, so I stopped off just long enough to place the trunks and box in our guest room, and close it off from our pets.

At work, I had about ten calls on my desk voice mail, but nothing that needed immediate attention. All around me, computer keyboards softly clicked away. Reporters furiously at work as they always were this late in the afternoon, trying their damnedest to make deadline.

Happily, I had earned the luxury of being able to work on long-term projects now, and knew that nothing in the day's "budget" was being held up by me—there wouldn't be a hole in the front page because I had become caught up in reading O'Connor's first diary.

I should have felt relatively relaxed. I didn't. Something was going on in the newsroom. But what?

More than twenty years of newspaper work had made me attuned to those times when someone on the staff was onto something hot. Any veteran could feel that. Some reporters could hide their excitement about a hot story from their fellow reporters, but I seldom met a first-year who could pull that off. You might as well play the *William Tell Overture* over loudspeakers in the newsroom whenever a green reporter was on the chase.

I looked around. Hailey looked bored. Mark Baker was over at the city desk, talking to Lydia and Ethan.

Ethan. That's who it was. Lydia had something up on her screen, and

Ethan was smiling as she talked to him about it, while Mark took notes. I left my desk and walked over to them.

"I'll see what I can find out," Mark was saying.

"Find out about what?"

"Oh, hi, Irene," Mark said. "I'm doing a sidebar for this A-one story of Ethan's."

"Ethan's got a story on tomorrow's front page? Hey, that's great."

"Thanks," Ethan said, but he wouldn't look me in the eye.

"What's it about?"

Lydia answered. "He's found disturbances of graves at Municipal Cemetery. Called someone from the Parks Department and the State Cemetery Bureau to see what they had to say about it, and he's spent the afternoon covering their mutual investigation. Turns out the city subcontracts with a private company that gets paid for administering the burials there. This company was moving caskets from unmarked graves, burying them two-deep in marked graves, and then reselling the plots they had 'vacated.' And looting the caskets they moved—and that's just what they learned today. It's going to take months to sort the burials out and figure out who belongs where. Great story. Congratulate him."

Instead, I said, "You little shit."

Lydia's eyes opened wide, and Ethan's chin came up.

Mark said, "What's wrong?"

"I'll tell you who's the looter here—he is. He stole a story."

"I did not!" he protested hotly.

"Hailey was asking me about this very subject this morning."

"Irene," Lydia said reasonably, "don't jump to conclusions. Ethan came to me with this idea—"

"Hailey!" I called.

The muted clickety-clack of keyboards all across the newsroom came to a halt. It was like disturbing crickets that you hadn't noticed until they stopped singing.

She sauntered over. "What's wrong?"

"Did you talk to Ethan about your story idea, the one about the cemetery?"

"No," she said hesitantly.

"Did you say anything about it within earshot of him? Leave notes about it out on your desk?"

She looked over at Ethan, who stared back at her defiantly. "No," Hailey said quietly.

I glanced at Mark, saw him studying the two of them.

"Irene," Lydia said. "It's just a coincidence."

"I'm sure Lydia's right," Hailey said. "You're the only one I've spoken to, and when I talked to you about it this morning, Ethan was talking to Lydia. I remember because—" She seemed to change her mind about what she was going to say. "I remember because he made her laugh."

"That's right!" Lydia said, with obvious relief. "Ethan was telling me about an old roommate, one who works for the *Bee* up in Sacramento."

"Satisfied?" Ethan said.

"Not by a long shot. Hailey, Ethan has just happened to discover cases of burials being moved and looted in Municipal Cemetery."

There was a moment, just a brief moment, when Hailey's sense of hurt and betrayal showed on her face. She hid it quickly and said, "Cool. I'll tell my friend who mentioned it to me. You might want to talk to him about it for follow-up."

"Thanks," Ethan said.

Hailey murmured, "No big," and hurried away from the city desk—and out of the newsroom.

"You see?" Lydia said to me.

"Oh yes, I see all right." I walked away before I gave in to a desire to throttle someone.

I logged off my computer, thought about how close Ethan's desk was to mine, then logged on again and changed my password.

I decided to try to talk to Hailey again. I called the security desk. Geoff said she hadn't left the building. That being the case, my guess was that she had gone into the women's bathroom.

I got up from my chair and walked through the *Express*'s warren of hallways. As I made the hike, I kept thinking that in the course of two decades, it should have occurred to someone to spend a little money to put a women's room closer to the newsroom, and a men's room closer to features, but Wrigley claimed that all the funds available for updating the building had gone into earthquake retrofitting.

As recently as two years ago, features would have been jumping at this time of day, but Wrigley had decided to pick up the vast majority of our features content from wire services—the result being massive layoffs in this department. The room was completely deserted—a journalistic ghost town.

As I stood near an abandoned desk, Hailey came out of the bathroom. She froze when she saw me.

"You and I need to have a little talk," I said, sitting down in a big rolling chair, and motioning her toward another.

For a moment, I wasn't sure if she was going to deny everything, run back into the bathroom, or try to make it past me. Then her shoulders slumped, and she sat down in a nearby chair. "I'm not going to try to take that story from him."

"The way he took it from you?"

"Past experience tells me I won't be able to prove that. He's very slick when it comes to computer stuff. Besides . . . you don't know Ethan."

"What's that supposed to mean?"

She bit her lower lip, looked toward the door, then said, "He's a trouble-maker."

"No shit."

"I mean—he makes trouble for people who cause him problems. In school? He had the chair of the J-department completely by the balls."

"How?"

"He starts by kissing up. But he does research—finds out things about people." She paused, then said, "It's so weird. He can do good work, really good work. But he's lazy. And I think he has problems with . . ."

I waited. When she didn't say more, I said, "Problems with what?"

"He likes to party, that's all. I don't know if it's that," she added quickly, "so I shouldn't be saying that about him. Besides, I don't think it's the biggest reason he acts like he does. I mean, he has all this talent, right?"

"Yes," I agreed. "When he focuses on something, that's apparent."

"But the problem is, he spends more time covering his butt and playing games than he does working."

"Maybe if you told Lydia—"

"Forget it. I told you. He kisses ass. He's already done it here. Mr. Wrigley thinks he has a new hotshot."

"So why would you cave in to him, the way you did today?"

"Just trying to stay on his good side, I guess. You don't want Ethan to think of you as anything but a friend."

I sat thinking for a moment, then said, "Have you filed your story for today?"

"Yes. Not that it's going to set the world on fire or anything."

I smiled, remembering saying something like that about the first stories I covered.

"What's so funny?"

"I won't bore you with tales of my life on the frontier."

She looked at me curiously. "Is it true that you were the first woman reporter here?"

"No. No, there were others before me. You want to meet one of the first women reporters?"

"Sure," she said.

I laughed. "I was going to suggest that you interview Helen Swan, but not if you're just being polite."

"No, I wasn't just being polite."

"You'd better be telling the truth," I said, "because Helen's one tough old lady. If you are just being polite, she'll make you cry for your mommy before the dust settles."

She swallowed hard.

"Go down to the morgue—I mean, the library—and ask for microfilm of the *Las Piernas News* from around 1936—"

"Microfilm! It's not on the computer?"

"Don't try my patience. Now, get this straight—you want the film for the *News* and not the *Express*. We were two papers back then, and Helen worked for the morning paper. Read a few issues before you talk to her. I have a feeling this assignment will help you. Helen has a way of inspiring people."

She left a few minutes later. I stayed in my ghost town, thinking up ways to trap a troublemaker.

53

"MOVING INTO THE GUEST ROOM?" FRANK ASKED. HE WAS SURROUNDED by two adoring dogs, who pressed up against his legs while our cat, Cody, yowled a greeting.

"No," I said, standing up and stretching over the menagerie to give him a hug. "Just going over some papers from O'Connor's childhood."

"His childhood?" He hugged back. Still had his gun on. His face had been chilled by the night air—and felt wonderful.

"Yes. Believe it or not, he was keeping a diary when he was eight. He started writing little stories for Corrigan around that same time. You should read a few of them—they're hilarious. He was such a bright kid. And Corrigan obviously had a gift for teaching—O'Connor was learning how to identify reporters' work by their style. He made a game out of it."

"That's wild. I hate to think what I would have been writing at that same age." He gave me a kiss.

"I saved some chicken for you," I said. He had phoned at five to say he had caught a new homicide case, and might be delayed. I glanced at the clock on the desk. "Only eight—you got out of there faster than I thought you would."

He grinned. "Case went to L.A. County Sheriff's. Turns out it all started in their jurisdiction."

He changed into jeans and a sweater and put the gun away. It isn't easy for me to watch that man get undressed and dressed again without making him keep his clothes off for a while in between, but he was hungry, so I didn't interrupt the process. Still, I noticed a certain knowing light in his eyes, one that told me he was completely aware of the direction my thoughts had taken.

We went into the kitchen and talked about the day while he had dinner.

We've had to work out rules with each other, given our occupations—he doesn't talk about my work at his workplace, I don't talk about his at mine. He won't tell the police what's going on at the newspaper, I won't tell the newspaper what's going on in his department. I don't ask him for information that would compromise an investigation, he doesn't ask me for information that would cause me to reveal sources.

This has driven our employers crazy at times, and every now and then the pressures we've each been under at work have put a strain on our marriage. But over the long run, it has helped us to stay together. In our workplaces, others may suspect us of being less than loyal to our employers, of something akin to consorting with the enemy, but at home, our trust in each other remains.

And every once in a while, we manage to help each other.

"I left a voice mail message for Mark Baker about something you might be interested in," he said, putting his dishes in the sink. "There's an old prisoner up in Folsom who claims he's got religion and wants to confess to a couple of murders he committed here in the 1940s."

"In the 1940s? Wow. How old is this guy?"

"They told me he's seventy-seven."

"You know which cases?"

"Yes. He named them—a couple of young girls who were buried in an orange grove. Carlson's handed the cases to me."

"You've been getting a lot of these lately."

"We can do more with these cases than we could before—even five years ago, the DNA testing wasn't where it is now. It's not just the DNA, either—we can do much more with fingerprints and other lab work than we could back when the murders took place."

"Who were the victims?"

"Young women. I don't have the information with me—haven't even had a chance to go into storage and pull what we have on them. But ask Mark to give me a call tomorrow morning and I'll fill him in on it."

"Great. Hoping for some local help?"

"You never know. Sometimes people come forward. But I don't expect it. Bennie Lee Harmon isn't going anywhere, even if they don't."

"Harmon—that name is familiar . . ."

"He was paroled in the late 1970s—model prisoner and all that. About two years after he was released, he attacked and killed a woman in Riverside. But at that point he had a sheet, we had better labs and computers, and he was caught."

"Wait, now I remember him. He had been serving on death row up in San Quentin. He got out when the court overturned all those death penalty convictions in the 1970s."

"Right."

"O'Connor wrote about him. He was upset that he was going free."

"Well, O'Connor was right. Harmon's confessing to seven murders, two of them here in Las Piernas."

The phone rang. I answered it.

"Irene? It's Max."

"Max! Are you in town for a while?" I saw Frank frown. It always takes him a moment to remind himself that Max is a friend and not a former boyfriend.

"Yes, I'm here for a few weeks. In fact—well, I called to let you know I'm engaged."

"Engaged!"

Frank's frown became a grin. I was grinning, too.

"Yes, well, you weren't available any longer, so I had to pick someone else."

"Oh, right. As if you aren't the most sought-after bachelor I know."

He laughed. "You'll like her, Irene. She's as good for me as Frank is for you."

"Then she must be perfect for you. And in that case, I'm sure I will like her. Does this perfect woman have a name?"

"Gisella. Gisella Ross." The way he said her name told me all I needed to know. Max Ducane, who had withstood more matchmaking attempts, more women chasing after him, more flat-out onslaughts on his single status than any man I know, had fallen for someone.

"Is she here with you in Las Piernas?"

"Not right now. She's going to join me here in a few days. Actually . . . I was wondering, do you think I could get together with you and Frank sometime before Friday?"

"You want Frank to do a background check on her?"

He laughed. "No. I've met her family. Very upper-crust New Englanders."

"I'll read up on my Emily Post before we meet. I don't want to embarrass you."

"You couldn't do that. Besides, she's not as stuffy as her parents are."

"Hang on," I said. I talked it over with Frank, then said, "Are you free tomorrow night? Why don't you come over?"

He agreed to it, and we arranged for him to come by at about seven. I hung up and looked over at Frank. "Wonder what's on his mind?"

"I don't know," he said, gently pulling me closer and nuzzling my ear. "How about if I tell you what's on mine?"

I have always liked the way Frank's mind works.

54

AT WORK THE NEXT MORNING, I FORGOT TO USE MY NEW PASSWORD, AND was immediately locked out of my computer. Computer services was tied up on another problem and couldn't help me right at the moment.

"I thought I was supposed to get three tries before it locked me out."

"You do," the technician said. "I'll check on that when I get a minute."

I was going to try persuading him to take that minute right now, but one of my outside lines was ringing, so I hung up. It was Frank, calling from LAX.

"Hi, sorry I didn't call you earlier, but everything has been rushed this morning. I'm flying up to Sacramento."

"Today? I mean, of course you're going today, but—"

"I need to talk to Harmon. Just a preliminary interview."

"Oh."

"Look, I haven't forgotten about our dinner plans—I might be able to make it back, since it's only an hour's flight, but I might not. So—you and Max go on ahead without me if you haven't heard from me by six, okay?"

"I can call Max, try to reschedule . . ."

"No, don't do that. He's excited about the engagement, and you're the one he really wants to talk to, anyway."

"Frank—"

"You'll make me feel bad if you cancel. I'll call you when I leave Folsom to let you know what's going on."

Over the next twenty minutes, I reached for the phone several times, thinking I should call Max and reschedule anyway, but ultimately I decided I'd take Frank at his word.

I began reading though a packet of materials that was part of the agenda for the city council meeting next week, circling points I needed to ask questions about, and making notes.

"Computer not working?" Mark Baker asked, seeing that I was doing all of this in longhand.

"No, it's not." I told him my password problem. "Someone is supposed to fix it with an override code or something, but there's some bigger problem with the software that runs the presses, so you know how high I am on the priority list."

"Just remember that it will never, ever be as bad as it was when we had those first computers."

"No kidding." We spent a few minutes recalling hardware and software disasters of the 1980s—whole pages that would have to be reentered, bizarre line justification that produced odd gaps in type, stories lost somewhere in the ether, and worse.

"And all the headaches for the designers—what a mess. I went to bed every night wondering if the paper would get out the next day."

"Same here," Mark said. "Say—if you have a few minutes, why don't you walk with me down to the morgue?"

This is one of the things I like about Mark. He's one of about a dozen people at the paper who still call the paper's archives "the morgue," rather than "the library."

"You talked to Frank before he left?" I asked as we made our way downstairs.

"Yes. His lieutenant released the story to other media, too, of course, but we've got the inside track, anyway—we covered these murders. I'm going to see if I can find the stories the *Express* ran on the cases. Interesting stuff—the cases go back to 1941 and 1943. The bodies weren't found until 1950."

I stopped walking.

He looked at me and said, "You know."

"O'Connor's sister. But she disappeared near the end of the war—1945, I think."

Mark shook his head. "That's the weird thing. Frank said Harmon didn't mention her. He said two victims here, and their names are . . ." He looked at his notes. "Anna Mezire and Lois Arlington. Anna disappeared on April 30, 1943. Lois on April 18, 1941."

"Wait—he's saying that God inspired him to admit to two murders but not a third? That doesn't make sense."

"None whatsoever. But it makes me wonder. If he had something to gain in this lifetime, I'd say he hasn't told us everything. But no one asked or coerced him to talk about these two—he doesn't get any better treatment or time off at this point. The only break it's going to give him is on the other side—when he meets his Maker. So why not make a completely clean breast of it?"

"You're looking up what we had on it then?"

"Yes. And any background I can find on Harmon."

"I've got some of O'Connor's old papers. I'll look through them and see if I can find his notes about his sister's disappearance. Knowing him, he must have had his own investigation going."

"Thanks. Listen—I appreciate your help with the story, but that's not why I wanted to talk to you."

"Oh?"

"This computer business makes me wonder about something. This morning, I got here early and caught Ethan snooping around your desk. He claimed he was just looking for a pair of scissors. I told him off, but I wanted you to know about it."

"Was he trying to log on to my computer?"

"I don't know. I didn't actually see that, but . . ."

"But I think I just figured out why I couldn't log on this morning. If you log on with the wrong password three times, it shuts the computer down until a system administrator can log you back on, right?"

"Right."

"Last night, I changed my password. This morning, out of habit, I entered the old password—but I only did that once before I was locked out of the system."

"So someone else had tried it twice and failed?"

"Yes. I don't think I need too many guesses about who it was. He failed twice and knew better than to enter it a third time. If I had entered the new one this morning, there never would have been a sign of anything wrong."

"How'd he get the old one?"

"Sits right across from me. He could have easily watched me log on dozens of times without my noticing it."

Mark took a deep breath and let it out slowly. We stood there in silence. After a while, Mark said, "He could be fired."

"Not any time soon. He's such an ass-kisser, if Wrigley turns a corner, that kid's nose will break."

"You've got that right. He's trying to suck up to me now, too. I think he realized yesterday that I didn't buy his version of events. And getting caught at your desk this morning scared him."

"Mark, you know I don't like newsroom gossip, but—let's just say I've heard some things that make me think we need to keep an eye on him."

"I wouldn't need to hear any gossip to know that."

"Why?"

"Call it intuition. I think he's a phony. He's got some kind of problem."

"What do you mean?"

"He's come to work hung over more than once. You haven't noticed?"

"This is a horrible thing to admit, but I guess I expect young men his age to do that once in a while."

Mark shook his head. "This isn't once in a while, Irene."

"I'll pay more attention."

He laughed. "Sorry, didn't mean to scold—or to make it sound as if you are supposed to be the kid's mama while he's here. You aren't even his editor."

I hesitated, then said, "I think the biggest problem is going to be Lydia."

He put a hand on my shoulder. "To be honest, I'm glad to hear you say that. I was worried I was going to have to be the one to mention it."

Back at my desk, I got a call from the computer services department and learned that I could log on again with a password the technician gave me. "But change it again to one of your own right away," he said.

I followed these instructions. Ethan was schmoozing with the executive news editor, John Walters, at that moment, so I wasn't worried that he'd be spying on me. He hadn't had as much success with John as he had had with Lydia and Wrigley. I was fairly sure that if Ethan did manage to ingratiate himself with John, it wouldn't last long.

Lydia was another story.

By choice, our careers had taken separate paths. I chose to stay with reporting and writing, she moved into editorial work.

Not all reporters get a reputation for being writers. You can be invaluable to the paper because you have the persistence to ferret out the facts, the ability to get people to confide in you, and other news-gathering skills. There are reporters who can do all of that, but are then unable to express what they've learned in clear terms.

Conversely, there are those who can't figure out what question to ask next, but can take the dullest, most completely jumbled story you've ever seen and rework it into something clear and exciting to read.

Lydia was both reporter and writer, but she excelled at writing. Before she had worked on the news side for very long, the paper put her to work in rewrite, then as a copy editor, and soon after that, an assistant city editor—the first woman to have that job on the *Express.*

She was now the city editor, and her skills in that job were unquestioned. All hell could break loose, she'd stay calm and divvy up the crises of the moment to those most capable of handling them. She was good at assigning stories, and although there would always be someone who thought he or she would have been the better reporter for this story or that, no one thought Lydia was arbitrary or showed favoritism. She not only knew which reporter would best handle a story, she knew how to get the best out of each reporter.

She was known for her loyalty to the reporters, for sticking up for them with the bosses—she might tell someone off (in her quiet way) in private, but she'd take on John Walters or Wrigley III in defense of that same reporter. She had won both the trust of the veterans and the respect of the newer reporters.

The problem was, when it came to seeing a guy like Ethan for what he was, I wasn't so sure of her abilities. If you're working on the street as a reporter, you usually spend time around a wider variety of people than editors do. You start to learn what most liars look like when they're lying to you—not all, by any means, but the garden variety becomes readily apparent, and eventually some of the most expert find it harder to get past you. You figure out who's uncomfortable with attention just because they're a little shy, and who is hoping you will not ask a dreaded question. You don't always find what's hidden, but you almost always sense when something important is being kept out of view.

I had no doubt that Lydia could tell if something in a story didn't ring true. But I wondered now if she had lost some of that ability to read people as well as she read stories.

Then I remembered Mark's comments about how often Ethan showed up hungover, and also that I had failed to notice that the little twerp had watched me enter my password. I decided I should worry about my own inability to keep my BS detector working.

Even if Ethan had managed to log on to my computer before now, I wasn't too worried about him looking at my notes. I was, you might say, a third-generation cryptographer.

O'Connor had been trained in newspaper work by Jack Corrigan, who had worked for the paper at a time when the morning *News* was the rival of the evening *Express*. Reporters spied on one another all the time. Corrigan wrote his notes in an oddball code—a mixture of a kind of shorthand, initials, and ways of referring to things that might not be readily apparent. RCC, for example, was not the Roman Catholic Church, but "the rubber chicken circuit," or political fund-raising banquets.

O'Connor learned it and added his own layer of code to it, and once he decided I was worth the trouble, taught it to me. Even though there was only one paper by then, the code helped. If you're in a room full of professionally nosy, often competitive people, sooner or later a slow news day will lead them to be curious about one another. It's frowned upon. It happens anyway.

So the code remained useful. Maybe one day I'd pass it along to a younger reporter—but Ethan was not going to be a candidate to inherit.

I had just thought this when Ethan came over to his desk, smiling. He logged off his computer and gathered his notebook and jacket. He looked over at me and his smile widened to a grin. "See you in a few days," he said.

"A few days?"

"I'm flying out this afternoon. Mr. Wrigley wants me to go up to Folsom and interview Bennie Lee Harmon."

55

"I DIDN'T KNOW THAT ABOUT O'CONNOR'S SISTER," MAX SAID. We were sitting together in the living room after dinner, during which we had heard about Max's fiancée, courtship, and future plans. They hadn't known each other long, about three months now, but he had apparently fallen for her almost on sight. Her family was wealthy, so she didn't seem to be after his money. He had shown us a photo of a lovely, almost ethereal-looking blonde. If she had given him the smile she wore in the photo—no mystery in why he had pursued her.

Frank had made it back in plenty of time. Harmon was ill, he said, and not able to talk for long. Frank told Max about Harmon's two-out-of-three confessions on the old cases.

"O'Connor rarely let anyone know about Maureen," I said.

"It explains so much, though," Max said. "I remember how he used to speak about the missing." He turned to Frank. "Will you be able to use DNA to tell if Harmon killed O'Connor's sister, too?"

"Possibly," Frank said. "I have to take a closer look at the evidence we gathered at the time, and how it has been stored. We had a good lab man back then. I'm told our coroner—this was before Woolsey—was a big believer in freezing tissue samples and the like, so if no one has dumped them out of the freezer at some point along the way, we may be in luck. But I'm not getting my hopes up just yet."

"Can Ben Sheridan help in a case like this?" I asked.

"He might. He's been called in on the investigation into Municipal Cemetery—they're digging up a lot of graves over there trying to straighten out who belongs where, so he's been really busy with that. But we're going to have him take a look at the photos, see if he thinks it's worth exhuming the girls' remains." He turned to Max. "Have you met Ben?"

"Not yet. He's your forensic anthropologist friend, right? The one who stayed here with his dog for a while?"

"Yes. A good friend, and good at his work, too. He's agreed to come by tomorrow and take a look at the photos."

"Any idea why Harmon is so adamant that he didn't kill her?"

Frank hesitated. "I can't back this up with proof yet, but I think he's so adamant because he didn't do it. I'm beginning to think he's telling the truth."

"What?"

"I'm not the first to see that there are differences in the way the bodies were left, or what had been done to them. Dan Norton, the detective who worked on the case in the 1950s, left a lot of notes on this one, and he had the same feeling I do—he thought it was possible that someone else had killed Maureen."

"But the timing—in April, every two years," I said. "And what you're saying would mean that the person who killed Maureen knew those other girls were buried there and never told anyone."

"Believe me, I see the problems."

"I don't know," Max said. "The best place to hide a body must be a grave. Think of that story in this morning's paper."

Frank laughed. "Don't mention that story to Irene."

I told Max about Ethan.

Max shrugged. "He still had to do a lot of work in order to write the story, though, didn't he?"

"Yes. But it isn't cool to do what he did to Hailey."

"I can see that," he said. He looked at Frank. "Actually, I have an interest in the contents of a grave, too. I hope you might be able to help me."

"One of these ones in Municipal Cemetery?"

"No, in All Souls. The Ducanes are buried there."

"What exactly do you have in mind?"

He shifted a little, then said, "Gisella's family has . . . expressed concern about my parentage."

"What? In this day and age?" I said, outraged. "Are they 'Granny came over on the *Mayflower*' types?"

"No, no, I'm sure that's not it," he said, not sounding all that sure to me. "What they said to me was, well, if we want to have children . . . it's a legitimate concern."

"A legitimacy concern, maybe?"

"Maybe," he admitted with a sigh. "They say they are worried that without knowing my parentage, there may be hereditary diseases I could pass on to our children."

"And?" I asked, sensing that wasn't all there was to it.

He spoke softly when he answered. "They also say that if our children are indeed the great-grandchildren of the Vanderveers and Linworths, they should know their heritage."

After a moment, I said, "And take Grandmother Lillian Linworth's inheritance?"

"I've told them there can be no need, given my own situation. I can already provide more than enough financial security for any children we may have."

"And they said, 'You can never be too rich or too thin.' "

He smiled. "Something like that. I pointed out that Lillian would not be obliged to leave a dime to me, even if we are related. She may decide to leave her money to her pet cat for all I know."

"But Gisella's parents don't think the cat would be a contender if you could be proved to be the missing heir."

"Look, it's just what her parents hold dear. They can trace both sides of each family back to—I don't know, Stonehenge, probably—and I don't know what my own birth name is, let alone my parents' names. Gisella tells me not to worry about it. But I don't really have a family, and I guess I don't want to start out by causing division within hers."

I finally caught on. "This isn't about the Ross family, is it? You can finally answer a question that you've had on your mind for the last twenty years."

For a moment he looked stricken. Then he let out a long sigh.

"Yes," he said. "That's it." He laughed. "I just needed to talk to a friend who would be brutally honest, who could make me own up to it."

"Was I brutal? I'm sorry."

"No. Not at all."

"How do you think I can help you?" Frank asked.

"As I understand it, there are DNA tests now that could be done on remains as old as Katy and Todd Ducane's."

"As old as Egyptian mummies—and older. Remains from the 1950s won't be a problem. But if you're thinking that we need to exhume Katy Ducane to find out if she was your mother, we don't. Lillian could give a private lab a small blood sample, and you could know the answer in a matter of weeks."

He shoved his hands in his pockets and sighed. "The problem is, Lillian won't do it."

"Won't do it! Why not?" I asked.

"She says that she loves me as I am, doesn't care who I once was or where I came from, and that all this talk of biological ties is insulting nonsense. She's furious with the Ross family for bringing the matter up. I won't repeat what she has to say about them. She became very upset. I have to admit that I was surprised at the vehemence of her reaction."

Frank and I exchanged a look.

"What?" Max asked.

"I don't know," I said. "Just a feeling, I suppose. Her reaction makes me wonder what she's afraid of. All these years, not knowing what became of her grandson . . ."

"If the DNA tests show that they aren't related," Frank said, "she may fear that Max will no longer care about her."

I looked at Max. He shrugged. "It's the only explanation I've been able to come up with myself. To be honest, if that's the case, it's kind of insulting. It's as if she's saying she stood by me and took me under her wing when she had no real proof that we were related—if anything, proof that we weren't. But I'm supposedly so shallow, I'll stop caring for her if she's not my biological grandmother."

"No other Linworth or Ducane relatives?" Frank asked.

"Warren Ducane," I said. "If you can find him."

"Warren may show up someday," Max said, "but he chose to make himself scarce more than twenty years ago."

"You haven't heard from him since then?" I asked.

He shifted uneasily in his chair, then said, "I haven't seen Warren since the day he disappeared from Las Piernas." He anticipated my next question and said, "Please don't put me in the awkward position of lying to you, Irene—I'd hate that. I'll just say that I don't know where he is right now, and even if I could locate him, odds aren't good that he'll come out of hiding while Mitch Yeager is alive."

So Warren was alive, and he had contacted Max at some point. A letter or an e-mail, or a call, perhaps. I was curious, but respected Max's request.

"Does Lillian have any siblings?" Frank asked him.

"Lillian was the only child of two only children. I suppose I could look for distant cousins, but why do that, when the people whose DNA would tell the true story once and for all are buried not far from here?"

"Katy and Todd Ducane." Frank thought for a moment, then said, "I'm not saying it's a sure thing, but in the interest of investigating a kidnapping and murder case, I suppose we could exhume one or both of their bodies. I hope we can talk Lillian Linworth into cooperating before we reach that point. I'd also want to be sure there are no samples that might already tell the story—that way, there's less trauma for the families involved. And lower cost for the department, too."

"What do you mean?"

"If we can find enough DNA in a sample frozen in 1978, and it won't compromise the other cases involved to process them—in other words, we won't use up some tiny fragment that's all we have—then we may not need to go to the trouble of an exhumation."

"That's great!"

"I don't think there will be a problem, but I also don't want you to look at this as a sure thing yet. I'm going to have to talk this over with my lieutenant, and I'm sure it will go to the captain as well. If I get approval from the department, I'll have to look for the simplest way to get the tests done. That would mean talking to Lillian and trying to get her to change her mind."

"Maybe you'll have better luck than I did," Max said.

After Max left, I asked Frank if he had met Ethan up at Folsom.

"You think he's in the slammer?"

"Deserves to be, but no. He left today, telling me that he was on his way to Folsom to interview Harmon."

Frank shook his head. "I know there are reporters up there, hoping to talk to him, but not many are going to get a chance. Harmon had knee surgery last week, and he ended up with some sort of complication—an infection. The doctors tell me that in a few days, he'll be up to longer conversations, but right now, he tires quickly. I can vouch for that—I was able to talk to him for about two hours, but he drifted off and dozed every few minutes."

"I wonder why the *Express* is going to the expense of sending Ethan up there now?"

"I don't know. You ought to be glad he'll be gone."

"True."

"I mean, a trip to Folsom—is that really such a big prize?"

I laughed, but in truth it was something of a prize. I saw it the way the others in the newsroom would see it—that Ethan was being trusted with the kind of assignment few young reporters would be given. A fledging out of the nest.

Why Lydia—or whoever else had been involved in the decision—thought he was ready for something like that was more than I could say.

Maybe, I thought, Lydia's little Icarus would be tempted to fly too near the sun.

Though I scolded myself for actually wishing that one of my colleagues would fail, it didn't change the wish.

56

By Monday, I was ready to concede that my wish had not come true. Ethan somehow managed to get in to talk to Harmon, and when I saw his story, which would run in Tuesday's paper, I had to admit he had done a fine job with it. Word was, Wrigley went bananas over it, and decided to give it big play. Lydia assigned supporting pieces to several other staff members. She didn't make eye contact with me during that process.

I thought I ought to mend fences with her, so I invited her to go to lunch with me. She gave me a look that made me uneasy, but accepted. We didn't talk much on the way out of the building, or even as we made our way to a café that was currently known as Lucky Dragon Burger, but which changed names a lot. The food was consistently good, though. "Think dragons have been the secret ingredient all along?" I asked her.

It was a weak joke and it won a weak smile.

We ordered, and I said, "Congratulations on being able to see that Ethan could handle that story. I guess that's why you're such a great city editor. You know the staff and what they are capable of."

She studied me for a moment. While she did this, she crossed her arms—a signal of fury that few others would recognize for what it was, but which startled me. Lydia's maiden name is Pastorini. A good Italian Catholic girl. She needs her hands to talk. If she confined her hands, I knew she felt the need to exercise control over what she had to say. I was trying to figure out what I could have done to make her so angry, when she said, "You believe that I am the one who sent Ethan up to Folsom?"

"Didn't you?"

"No. I never would have sent him up there. That was Wrigley's decision."

"Oh." I suddenly recalled Ethan's words. He never mentioned Lydia. "I jumped to a conclusion, Lydia. I was wrong. I'm sorry."

She shook her head.

"Look, I can see why that makes you angry, but—"

"Can you?"

"Yes. I thought you were championing him, and now that I think back on it, you didn't actually do that."

"That's the symptom. Not the problem. I may not treat a first-year reporter the way you and the Old Boys Club do, but I can see his faults. I'm not completely stupid just because I'm not on the street, you know. I am not incapable of seeing when a twenty-two-year-old is full of himself."

This was so close to what I had thought of her, I turned red. Worse, she had known me so long, I knew she was reading that blush for the guilt signal it was. "Like I said, I'm sorry. Really sorry. I mean it."

Silence. The food arrived. Nobody made a move to touch it. As the minutes passed, I went from feeling contrite to feeling injured by her refusal to at least give some token acknowledgment of my apology. Did she want me to grovel?

"Lydia, please. Let's not let a little creep fuck up our friendship, okay?"

She looked me right in the eye and said, "He's not the one messing it up."

"You know what? You're right about that."

I stood up, threw a twenty on the table—much more than I owed, but I wasn't going to be accused of sticking her with the bill on top of everything else—and though I knew I was letting my Irish temper get the best of me, I left.

I needed to cool off, and sitting in the newsroom with Lydia would not accomplish that. I glanced at my watch. I thought of my options, used my cell phone to call John Walters and tell him where I'd be, and walked around the block to the newspaper's parking lot. I got into the Jeep and drove home.

Cody and the dogs were delighted. The friend and neighbor who usually spent time with them during the day was out of town, so I got an especially enthusiastic welcome. My mood of righteous indignation couldn't withstand that. I played with them for a while—tossing a catnip toy for Cody, stuffed squeaky toys for the dogs. That worked off some tension for everyone involved.

I went back to reading O'Connor's stories and diary. One of the best stories was from April 1936 and was called "What I Saw in the Court." He told about sneaking into a courtroom to watch Mitch Yeager's trial, and later telling Corrigan about what amounted to jury tampering.

Mitch Yeager had been on trial for something? O'Connor, boy reporter, hadn't provided details. I made a note to look it up.

Max might know about it. I called him and had the good fortune to catch him at home. "I'm leaving to go see Lillian in a little while," he said. "Do you have my cell phone number?" He gave it to me.

"Are you in a rush? I could call you back later."

"I can talk now for a few minutes. What can I do for you?"

"I hope you won't mind my asking, but do you know if Mitch Yeager was ever arrested?"

"Mitch? Not that I know of. He wouldn't have told me about it if he was, though—he was really hung up on being thought of as respectable. Which, come to think of it, argues for a shady past, doesn't it?"

"Maybe."

"Oh, wait—are you sure you heard something about *Mitch* and not *Adam* Yeager?"

"Adam Yeager . . . why is that name familiar?"

"He was Mitch's brother. Ian's and Eric's dad. In fact, my former name—Kyle—was his middle name."

"Did you know him?"

"No, he was dead long before I was born. My mom always said Eric and Ian were going to grow up to be just like their father—jailbirds."

He suddenly broke off, then started laughing.

"What's so funny?"

"I was just thinking that she was right."

"Yes, although she probably didn't predict the part about life on a tropical island."

"No. I wouldn't mind that, if they'd stay there."

"So you've heard the rumors, too."

"Oh, it isn't rumor. They come back to the States on a fairly regular basis."

"What? Are you sure?"

"Absolutely certain. I have them watched, Irene. If I thought for a moment that they were going to harm you, I'd . . . I'd make sure it didn't happen."

I was stunned.

"You're angry," he said.

"No—not angry. It's just weird. I mean, I wish you had told me sooner."

"I've thought about it, even came close to telling you a couple of times. But two things stopped me. One was that you've been through some horrible experiences in the time since they've been released, and it just happened that whenever I'd come back into town, certain that I was going to tell you, the timing was always wrong—I didn't want to upset you with talk of people who might not ever come near either one of us again."

"What was the other reason you didn't tell me? That they're too old?"

"No. Evil does not retire."

"No pension plan."

He laughed. "I guess that's it. Besides, they both keep in good shape, so I wouldn't feel safer from them because of age. No, the other reason I didn't tell you was Frank. If I told you, you might tell him, and . . . I didn't want Frank to feel obligated to mention my surveillance of them to his department."

"I understand," I said. "But it won't be a problem."

"Good."

"I know you're running out of time, but can you give me a little more information about Adam Yeager, the jailbird uncle?"

"Oh—not much, really. Mom was upset that she always had to say that he died in the war, because he died during the Depression, in prison. She said something about how he didn't live more than a year in prison. That's why Eric and Ian were raised by Mitch. I remember Mitch always kept a photo of him on his desk. I know that's not much information, but you might say that by the time I was old enough to ask about him, I had learned not to ask about him."

"What do you mean?"

He took so long to answer, I thought we might have lost the connection. But then he said, "Not long after Mom told me that Adam had died in prison, I asked Mitch to tell me the truth about him, since I had to go around with his name. A mistake I'll never forgive myself for. That's when I got packed off to military school. Mitch told me my mom wasn't feeling well, so she couldn't say good-bye."

"Oh, Max . . ."

"I never saw her alive again. She died two years later. She fell down some stairs." After another silence, in a much quieter voice, he added, "Or so I was told."

57

He ended the call just after that, but I was uneasy. A minute or two later I called his cell and told him that I just wanted to make sure he was all right. He said he'd be fine, thanked me for my concern, and promised to call me again later.

Adam Yeager's death would be worth looking into. I hooked up my laptop and tried to find him in the Social Security Death Index, but he wasn't in it. That index began in 1937. Since he wasn't in it, it was possible he was dead before 1937. Or at least not earning wages. I supposed prisoners might not have had Social Security numbers at that point.

I decided to do more research when I got back to the paper.

Thinking about Max made me think about the days when we first met. Here we were, two decades later, and he still didn't know if his parents were the people who had been found in the trunk of that car. That in turn made me think of all the other unanswered questions I had about the night Corrigan had been attacked and the Ducanes murdered. I decided I'd go through the notes O'Connor had made. Maybe after all this time, giving it a fresh look, I'd see something we had missed before.

Opening the box marked "Jack" brought a flood of memories. At first, it was difficult to concentrate on the task of studying the contents rather than to sit reminiscing about those early days of working with O'Connor.

I came across the photo of Betty Bradford, she of the pink underwear, owner of the buried Buick. Jack Corrigan had been set up by her, and nearly died as a result. "I wonder if you're still around," I said aloud. She looked to me now as she had the first time I had seen this photo—pretty woman, young but hard-edged—although now thought I perceived a little insecurity beneath the cool.

I kept searching. I came across a set of O'Connor's notebooks I hadn't seen before. They ranged over a number of years. I smiled to myself. If I had seen them in 1978, I probably wouldn't have known enough of his shorthand and code to figure them out. I glanced through the first few and saw that they were devoted to one story: the events connected to that night in January 1958.

They began not with Corrigan's beating, as I had thought they might, but with O'Connor meeting Dan Norton at the home of Katy and Todd Ducane. His notes brought to mind the day we had toured the house with Max, and I wondered if Lillian still kept it as a museum.

I glanced at my watch and decided I needed to get my ass back to the paper. I'd have to live with Ethan and his gloating over the Harmon story, with Lydia and her anger. I had work to do.

I fed the dogs and Cody and hurried out. Overhead, gray clouds thickened, and darkened the sky. I went back in and grabbed an umbrella.

As I drove, O'Connor's voice echoed in my thoughts. I missed that old man as much as I missed my own father. Perhaps because of Ethan's story, a memory came to me—of the night he told me about his missing sister.

I slowed the car a little, but kept driving.

By the time I reached the paper, rain was falling. I hurried inside.

My plans were twofold: to spend some time reading up on the Ducanes, and to look back at the articles O'Connor wrote about Harmon.

The presses were already running, sending their pulse through the building. As I climbed the stairs, I half-hoped Lydia would be gone for the day, then decided that was not only extremely unlikely, but showed a sad lack of courage on my part.

When I got up to the newsroom, she was arranging furniture, helping Ethan move his desk nearer to her own. She saw me right away. She ignored me after that.

I went down to the morgue, as much to get away from the newsroom again as to do some homework. Hailey was there, but she was focused so intently on whatever she was reading, I didn't disturb her. The rumble of the presses was a little louder here. I found it soothing.

I asked the librarian to get microfilm for specific dates in 1936, 1958, and 1978.

"The 1978 reels—I've got them right here. Haven't had a chance to file them again."

"Again?"

He sighed. "That asshole Ethan—you know him?"

"Yes."

"He's in here looking through back issues all the time. Pesters the hell out of me."

"He was probably doing background work on the Harmon story."

The librarian shrugged. "Maybe. Seems to be an old news epidemic. Hailey has the reels for 1936 over there," he said.

Hailey looked up at that, apparently only then noticing my presence. "I'm working on the story about Helen Swan," she said. "I've already called her to set up a time for an interview. I'm going over to her house on Monday night."

"Good. She was married to Jack Corrigan, you know. She used to teach journalism at the university."

She knew nothing of her, I realized, other than what she had just read—but at least she already had an admiration for Helen from the stories she found in the old issues of the *News*. I gave her a quick rundown of the *News Express* staff, at least what I knew of it. "I didn't get to know many of the people who worked here before I came to the paper in 1978," I said.

"What happened to Wildman?" she asked.

"Killed in a car accident," I said. "He was drunk. Family in the other car didn't make it, either."

"That really sucks."

"Yes."

She let me have the reels for April 1936, near the date of O'Connor's childhood story "What I Saw in the Court." I looked back a few weeks before the beginning of his first diary and came forward. It didn't take long to find it, big and bold across the front page. An A-1 headline, as befit a story written by Jack Corrigan, the star reporter of the *Express*. I imagined an eight-year-old Irish kid shouting the headline from a street corner:

YEAGER BROTHER TRIAL BEGINS TODAY

58

T HE STORY TOLD OF THE OPENING OF THE TRIAL OF MITCHELL YEAGER, the twenty-one-year-old brother of Adam Yeager, who had been convicted earlier that year of receiving stolen goods, the biggest charge local officials seemed to be able to bring against him. He was currently serving time, it said, in San Quentin. Mitch Yeager had been arrested on a bribery charge in connection with his brother's arrest. Apparently, he had made his offer to the wrong official. Corrigan also noted that the defense in Mitch Yeager's trial had asked for a continuance, due to the illness of the defendant's brother. The motion was denied.

Illness. I had imagined a prison fight or escape attempt.

I watched for mention of Adam's death as I scrolled on, and kept reading. I wasn't surprised to see that Mitch Yeager's first trial was declared a mistrial, given what I had read of O'Connor's account of what he had seen in the courtroom. Yeager, who had previously been granted bail, had his bail revoked and was taken into custody pending a trial on charges of jury tampering. A new trial on the bribery charges was also ordered by the judge.

I learned from Corrigan's accounts that the charges of jury tampering were later dismissed. No one could prove that Yeager had ordered a man everyone knew to be his lackey to intimidate the juror. Deep in the story, in a last paragraph more than a page in, Corrigan noted that Adam Yeager, the defendant's brother, had recently died of tuberculosis. I was surprised, and wondered if there had been other complications or if he had been denied treatment.

I used a terminal in the morgue and looked up the history of tuberculosis treatment on the Internet. Effective anti-TB drugs were not in use until after 1944. Adam Yeager became ill eight years too soon.

The second bribery trial resulted in a conviction, but the conviction was later overturned. Mitch Yeager was free.

The large and sympathetic—to Yeager—article on the overturning of the conviction was not written by Jack Corrigan. I didn't recognize the name of the reporter. The story seemed to go out of its way to quote Yeager on his own innocence. I noted the dates so that I could cross-check the story in the *News*.

I asked Hailey if she'd like to help me out with some stories about old crimes that might be solved thanks to DNA technologies, and she jumped at the chance.

"Here's the deal," I said. "First, I've got to clear it with John and Lydia. Second, you have to promise me you'll keep your files and notes secure— especially from Ethan." We talked for a while about how she could do that— codes, using paper instead of the computer when possible, frequently changing passwords, clearing her Web browser's history files, keeping her notes with her—I think the espionage aspects interested her more than the story itself.

I reviewed the stories from 1958, distracted by memories of looking at these same reels in 1978, and working with O'Connor.

At ten o'clock, the librarian wanted to lock up, and I decided to call it a day. Hailey had left some time before.

I thought I'd make another stab at patching things up with Lydia. She was gone, as was almost everyone else. The paper had obviously gone to bed. Only a handful of people were still around. John Walters was one of them. He had just come back from the press room, where he had been checking the "first-offs"—the first papers off the press. "Got a minute?" I asked him.

"To settle a catfight? Hell, no."

"Since no one asked you to do that, no need to let the very thought of women disagreeing cause you to pucker up."

"Okay, what's the problem, then?"

I looked over my shoulder at the four or five people still in the newsroom, all of them pretending too hard to be busy with things that kept them within earshot. "How about holding this discussion in your office?"

I could see that he was tired and not happy with the idea of a private chat, which he probably assumed would be about the "catfight" after all, but he studied me for a moment, made a grunting noise, and waved to me to follow him to his office.

He sat down at his desk with a sigh and said, "At my age, if I sit down at this time of night, I damned well might not be able to get to my feet again."

I suddenly forgot everything that was on my mind, because it was clear to me that something was weighing on him, that he had some big worry.

"What is it, Kelly?" he said impatiently.

"Is something wrong?"

"Yes, I'm here on a rainy night long past the time when I wanted to go home. You wanted to talk to me, remember?"

I let him in on everything I had been researching down in the morgue, and told him that I wanted Hailey to work with me.

"Kelly, you told me this wasn't about the catfight."

"Well, not directly."

"You want that little greenling cut loose to help you, though."

"Yes, as much as possible. And quietly."

Another grunting sound. "If you don't mind my asking, just what the hell is the *new* part of this news?"

After swearing him to confidentiality, which insulted him, I said, "Four or five weeks from now, a question will be decided once and for all—the question of whether or not the person known as Max Ducane is also the actual missing heir." I told him about the possible DNA tests, although I didn't mention a word about Warren Ducane. I had John's intense interest, so I added that if Max was the kidnapped baby, other questions would arise. "It means the child Mitch Yeager supposedly adopted in November 1957 was still living with his birth parents in January 1958. Mitch Yeager will have a hell of a lot to explain. The *Express* should be ready to talk about the events of 1958 and 1978 again if need be. Which reminds me—his offshore nephews could still be tried for murder."

"No double jeopardy, because it was a mistrial, right?"

"Right."

"And someone ought to be talking to Lillian Linworth now—try to find out what made her hesitate. You'd think she'd be the one asking for the test."

I smiled. I had him, and we both knew it.

He rubbed his face. "Damn, you are a pain in the ass."

"You say that whenever I get you to change your mind about something."

"Hmm. You better work all this out with Mark Baker, too. And Kelly, if any little bit of this comes near the police department, or even speaks of what it did in the past, you are not writing that part of the story."

"Absolutely not. Same rules apply."

After another moment of brooding, he said, "You don't like Ethan much, do you?"

"No."

"I hear rumors about password problems on your computer."

I narrowed my gaze.

"No one in the newsroom told me," he said, understanding that look perfectly. "I was contacted by computer services. Which, I might add, is a damnable thing, because I would think a certain reporter would know enough to come in here and talk to me about it."

"Would you? If I didn't have any proof?"

"No," he admitted grudgingly. After a long moment, he sighed and said, "Wrigley thinks we're all getting too old. At first I thought he just wanted young women to sexually harass, since that's a favorite pastime of his. But he thinks the world of Ethan—thinks of him as the bright new hope of the *Express*."

"That's because Ethan could be *his* own long-lost son. His moral twin, anyway."

John smiled. "Maybe. Maybe. Sometimes I look at what Wrigley wants the paper to become, and I'm not sure I want to be a part of that . . . vision, shall we say? But then I ask myself what the hell else an old newspaperman like me could do with himself."

"Nothing else anytime soon, I hope. You have the faith of the staff and the board, John. You know the board will oust him if need be. And if I'm wrong and they let him lead us to disaster and the whole paper is sold, then, well, we'll leave together. I guess we can take up jumping off bridges, or something else that will provide the same adrenaline rush."

He didn't say anything.

"Shit," I said, sitting down. "The board is seriously talking about selling it."

"Shut up, Kelly. It doesn't do either of us any good to talk about it, or the newsroom any good to worry about it. Although knowing this bunch, they'll know about it soon enough. It's impossible to keep a secret in the newsroom."

"They won't hear it from me."

"I know."

I looked out beyond his office, back into the newsroom. Most of the lights were out, large areas of the room lit only by the glow of one or two terminals not set to "sleep mode." At its busiest, the newsroom was never the noisy one I had first worked in, but this quiet, abandoned space was eerily still, even by current standards. I thought of all the men and women who had worked hard as hell for low pay and little thanks, worked to pull thousands of words together to describe the day in Las Piernas, who had done that day after day for more than a century. Who would tell the story of those days if the paper wasn't here?

I heard and felt the thrum-thrum-thrum of the presses.

Only sleeping, that's all. The paper had gone to bed, the newsroom was asleep. In a few hours, the early staffers would arrive, and it would start all over again.

"John," I said. "Let's make a pact."

I turned to see that he had been watching me all the while.

He said, "Why do I think I'd be safer making a deal with the devil?"

"I say, no surrender."

"We both know it may not be up to us."

"When it comes to that, fine. Not until then."

He reached out a big paw and we shook on it.

I went through the darkened newsroom to my desk. My voice mail light was blinking, so I checked my messages. I had one from Max, saying he was sorry he missed me. He sounded happy. While I listened to it, John waved to me as he left.

The next five were the usual messages from people who held local political offices, hoping I'd give them some ink.

The last caller didn't leave his name, and I didn't recognize his voice. He had called at seven-fifteen. The message was brief.

"I haven't forgotten you."

I slammed the receiver into the cradle and backed away from the desk, as if the phone itself were the menace. I was shaking. I told myself I had had dozens and dozens of similar ones over the years. Maybe Wrigley was right, and I was getting too old for this work. I wasn't as sure as I used to be that no harm would come to me. Harm had come to me over the years, and although I had survived it, I didn't feel the need to welcome another visit.

The phone rang. I took a deep breath and lifted the receiver.

"Irene?"

"Frank! Oh—I'm just getting ready to leave."

"What's the matter?" he asked. "You sound upset."

I never can fool him. That didn't stop me from trying.

"Nothing, nothing. In fact, it's the stupid sort of thing that never used to bother me at all. A crank call on my voice mail, that's all."

"Threatening?"

"No threats." I told him what the caller had said.

"Did you save it?"

"No," I said. "Sorry, I know that irritates you."

"Just keep any others, okay?"

"How fun that will be. Where are you?"

"Just outside the front door of the *Express*. I've got the dogs with me in the car. We got tired of sitting around the house."

"Oh?"

"Okay, I worry about you being downtown alone this late at night, and you know it. It's a nasty night out, too."

"To be honest, I'm really relieved you're here. I'll come out to where you are and you can take me around to my car."

"Great," he said.

I thought of the presses, then said, "Do you think the dogs would be okay in the car by themselves for a few minutes?"

"Sure, I'll crack the windows for them and hope the seats don't get soaked."

"Come inside, then. I'll meet you at the security desk."

As I came down the stairs, I saw Frank talking to the night security guard. Frank is about six foot four, lean and muscular. He was dressed in jeans and a sweater. His hair was damp from the rain. He looked damn fine. Best of all, although I am sure that after my long day I looked completely bedraggled, he looked up at me in a way that made me wish the security guard would have to go put out a fire somewhere or something.

The guard, Leonard, is one of Frank's biggest fans, and it was all I could do to free my husband from the clutches of that applicant to the police academy.

"Frank," I asked, "have you ever watched the presses run?"

He shook his head. I took his hand and led him into the basement.

Danny Coburn, a pressman who used to work days, had recently moved to the night shift. He saw us and brought over earmuffs that were hearing protectors. I shouted an introduction, and Frank and I donned the heavily padded headsets.

They were running full bore at that point. I watched Frank's fascination with the overhead wires and rollers, the presses themselves, the movement of paper as it unspooled from giant rolls and was printed and cut and divided and folded.

We walked through a maze of small offices to look above us and see finished sections flying toward machines that would bundle them for distribution to the delivery trucks.

I realized after a moment that Frank had guided me out of the sight of the security cameras. He cornered me against a wall, an absolutely wicked grin on his face. The vibration from the presses was so strong here, I felt it all the way through my body.

He pulled one earmuff a little away and said, "I never thought I'd meet a girl who looked sexy in earmuffs."

"Frank, I don't think—"

He kissed me, earmuffs and all.

After a few minutes of that, I lifted his earmuff and said, "I am so tempted to give the crew down here something to tease me about forever, and to try to forget the dogs, and Cody, and all of the world."

He laughed. "Come on, I'll take you home. I guess I'll just have to take you into the garage and turn the washing machine on to the spin cycle."

"Deal. I think I even have a pair of earmuffs somewhere."

59

On Tuesday morning, I was surprised to get a call from Helen Swan.

"Irene, I need your help."

"Whatever I can do, Helen."

"I need someone to take me over to Lillian's as soon as possible."

"All right, I think I can manage that." I told her I'd be right over.

The morning was chilly and overcast, the kind of dull weather that saves itself for the weekend, when it can really make you miserable. Helen was bundled into a coat that probably fit her once, but she seemed lost in it now. She complained that the Kelly women's cars were either too high or too low as I helped her into the Jeep.

She seemed extremely agitated, but after an attempt to get her to tell me what was on her mind was met with a polite but firm rebuff, I stayed quiet.

She noticed and said, "Tell me about your search through the storage unit. Anything interesting?"

"A great deal." I told her about going through O'Connor's early diaries, but given her mood, decided not to tell her of his first impressions of her. Instead I generally described some of the things I had found so far. I wasn't entirely sure she was listening to me. We spent the last few minutes of the ride in silence.

When we reached Lillian's house and pulled into the big circular drive, she said, "This won't take long." Then she paused and said, "I've been rude, and you've been so kind. I'm sorry."

"Don't worry about it. I'm fine."

"That's my girl!" she said.

"Need help getting out?"

"No," she said, and jumped down, scaring the hell out of me.

I saw her walk up to the house—apparently uninjured—and knock on the door. I waited.

She rang the bell. I waited.

She knocked again. I got out of the car.

"Was Lillian expecting you?" I asked.

"Of course she was." She turned toward the house and shouted, "That's why she's not answering the damned door!"

"Did you call her?"

"She has that obnoxious thingamajig that allows a person to screen calls."

"An answering machine?"

"No! I've got an answering machine. She's got—oh, what do they call it?"

"Caller ID?"

"Yes! That's it! Incredibly rude."

"Are you telling me she got a call from you and refused to answer when she saw your number?"

"Yes."

"And you came over here, anyway."

"If you have somewhere else to be, you needn't wait for me. I'll stay here until she"—turning toward the house again—"opens the damned door!"

I took my cell phone out of my purse. "What's Lillian's phone number?"

Her eyes lit up in appreciation. She gave me the number.

Lillian answered on the second ring.

"Hello, Irene."

"Lillian, I'm on your front porch. Helen's here, too. Please don't make her stand out here. I'm afraid she'll get a chill, and even if that doesn't kill her, the guilt will kill me."

"That stubborn old woman!"

"Please, Lillian."

"All right, all right. Might as well get this over and done with."

A pale, thin housekeeper, who must have been just on the other side of the door—the damned door, Helen would have said—opened it and asked us to come in.

"I miss Hastings," Helen murmured, not as softly as she probably thought she did.

"Now, Swanie, why on earth have you dragged Irene into this?" Lillian asked as she came forward to meet us.

"Because she and Lydia are the closest thing I have to daughters these days," Helen said sharply. "Granddaughters, I suppose I should say. The point is, I'm old as hell and I want to make sure that if I croak in my sleep, someone else will know full well what you are up to."

Lillian looked as if she had been slapped.

"Yes," Helen said. "Unlike some people I know—"

"That's enough!" Lillian snapped.

They stood glaring at each other.

I glanced toward the housekeeper, whose wide blue eyes indicated she was a fascinated audience.

I ventured onto the battlefield with, "Maybe we could move into a room where we could discuss this calmly and privately."

They both fixed their glares on me, seemed to recognize that I was not the enemy—yet, anyway—and thawed a bit. Lillian glanced at the housekeeper. "Yes. Let's go into the library."

"Do you need me to bring anything, ma'am?" the housekeeper asked hopefully. She had an Eastern European accent that I couldn't quite place.

"No, thank you, Bella," Lillian replied.

"I'll just clear the—"

"Let that wait, please," Lillian said. "Thank you. That's all for now."

In the library, a fire was already burning in the hearth, a coffee urn had been brought in, and several china cups—three of which had been used—rested on saucers on a side table.

"Oh, Lillian, how could you?" Helen said in despair. "You've already done it, haven't you?"

"Yes," Lillian said.

"Done what?" I asked.

"Agreed to give a blood sample for a DNA test," she said offhandedly. "Please be seated, Helen. You, too, Irene. The coffee's still fresh and hot. Would you care for some?"

We both agreed to it. I studied Lillian while she played hostess. She was impeccably dressed, as always. A lovely silk suit. Simple but striking jewelry. She was still a woman with presence, and appeared younger than her years. But in ways that weren't easy to name, she hadn't aged as well as my aunt Mary or Helen. Although she had apparently had face-lifts, no one seemed to have done the same for her spirits. Unhappiness had made its mark over the decades. Although she enjoyed far more luxuries and comforts in life than either Mary or Helen, I found myself feeling sorry for her.

We all sat. We all drank coffee. No one said a word. Hell if I was going to be the one to light the fuse. I was starting to worry about Helen, who looked twice as upset as she had been before we arrived. I couldn't figure it out. I knew Max must be happy. Why was Helen angry?

Eventually, Lillian said, "How have you been, Irene? I haven't seen you in a long time."

"Fine," I said. "And you?"

Instead of answering, she asked me about Frank. Easy for me to talk about Frank.

After about five minutes of this, Helen suddenly said, "You really don't care about him, do you? Not really."

"Frank?" Lillian asked.

"You know I don't mean Frank! You don't care about Max!"

"Of course I care about him. That's why I did what I did."

"Oh, really? What do you suppose is going to happen when the Yeagers learn that you've submitted blood for a DNA test?"

"Mitch is not stupid, Helen—"

"I never inspected him as closely as some others did."

"—however little you may think of him," Lillian went on. "He has known for several years now that this would be possible. News stories about the power of DNA tests have abounded recently, and I'm sure he has imagined that Max would want to know his origins. Mitch has been thinking that at any time, I could participate in the testing, and Mitch would have awkward questions to answer if Max proved to be the missing child."

She turned to me. "Perhaps it's for the best that you are here today. Perhaps a story could run in tomorrow's paper, saying I've already submitted a blood sample? If you think it would be newsworthy, that is."

"She doesn't lay out the front page, you know," Helen said. "Why can't you ever learn what it is a reporter does and does not do?"

"I can provide you with the name of the doctor who drew the blood," Lillian said, ignoring her. "And give you the name and address of the lab that has the sample—or will have it in a few hours, anyway. Max is flying it up to Seattle. He's chosen a lab up there."

"Thank God he's out of the area, anyway," Helen said.

"He'll be back Monday."

"My God," Helen said. "What can be done?"

"Nothing," Lillian said. "Will you please use that brain of yours? The key has been to get the test in progress before Mitch could do anything about it. If I waited, he might kidnap Max again, just to keep him from being tested. I felt as you did, until Max told me he was willing to take some extreme measures. Exhumations are not done quite so speedily as blood tests, Helen. If it were to become known that Kathleen would be exhumed—a thought I find unbearable to begin with—Mitch would have the time he needs to make sure something horrible happens to Max."

"What do you think has stopped him before now?" I asked.

"My very well-known refusal. Knowing that I refused the tests, and that I would fight an exhumation, has been enough."

"You egotistical fool," Helen said.

I said, "But Max might have gone to the other side of the family for help. If Warren Ducane—"

Lillian interrupted. "Mitch probably doubts that a man in hiding for over two decades will come forward just to make the parents of Max's fiancée happy."

"Exactly why is he in hiding?" I asked.

"I have no idea," Lillian answered.

"Because," Helen said, "he has known that no one—*no one* has a longer memory than Mitch Yeager when it comes to avenging slights or injuries. If he needs twenty years to carry out his revenge, he'll happily take that long to do it. As Lillian is fully aware."

"Yes, and Warren would be a target of that revenge," Lillian said. "He took Max away from Mitch and caused questions to be raised about Mitch and his nephews. Mitch had worked hard to make everyone forget his beginnings."

"She means," Helen said, "that his father was a good-for-nothing who abandoned his family, his mother was a drunk, and his brother was a thief and a bootlegger. Mitch's own business practices have never been entirely above-board, either."

"He tried to change," Lillian said, "but there were always those who were ready to snub him or remind him of his past. Perhaps he was right. Perhaps if the *Express* had left him alone, he would have been just another successful businessman."

"I don't believe it!" Helen said furiously. "A woman your age cannot be so hopelessly naïve! After that speech, I could swear you're still carrying a torch for Mitch Yeager. Good God, Lillian! Have you forgotten what he's done?"

"No," Lillian said quietly. "How can you possibly ask such a thing?"

"I can ask it when you do things on impulse, things that will only hurt Max. You haven't solved a problem, Lily—you've only created new ones, as well you know. Or is this your own—" She stopped herself, with a visible effort, from finishing that sentence. "You really don't care about what this will do to Max or anyone else, do you, Lily?"

"He's all I care about in this, Helen."

"Helen," I said, "what aren't you telling me?"

That silenced them both.

"I know you both adore Max," I said. "And you know I would never want any harm to come to him, either. I'm trying to figure out what's really going on here. There are only two possible outcomes for these tests. One is that Max is Lillian's grandson."

"I feel sure he is Katy's son, don't you, Helen? He is so much like her."

"Don't play games with me, Lillian! You've put him in danger!"

"I can't help but think she's right, Lillian," I said, "although if we alert the police, they may be able to help us. Because if he is your grandson, Mitch Yeager's ties to the events of that night in 1958 will be difficult for him to refute."

"You go right ahead and tell Frank."

"But, Lillian, you have to face the fact that there is a possibility that the tests will prove he is not your grandson, which—"

"Which will again leave him with no idea who he is," Helen said. "And no real possibility of ever finding out the truth. Don't you remember what he went through when all this began? How confused and unsure he was? He'll feel he came by all his wealth and advantages dishonestly, that he has robbed the estate of some poor murdered infant who will never be found. Oh, Lily, why didn't you tell Gisella Ross's parents to stow the Mayflower Compact where the sun don't shine, right alongside the blue book and all the other trappings of their stupid snobbery?"

"You might as well ask me why I didn't assassinate Watson and Crick when I saw what their DNA discoveries might lead to," Lillian said. "Don't you see, Helen? You're the one who's being naïve. Max has never felt sure of his identity. Never. From the moment I learned that DNA was being used to determine paternity, I knew that sooner or later he would want to have DNA tests done. He has, in fact, asked many times before. He cares for my wishes, and without this added pressure from Gisella's family, perhaps I would have been able to go to my grave without having to face what I'm facing now. But the Rosses' request is only an excuse that he was all too happy to grab hold of." She sighed dramatically. "I understand they can test hair from a hairbrush. I feared it was only a matter of time before I'd discover Max combing through my brushes."

Both women fell silent again. Helen stood and said, "Irene, please take me home."

"So you see it my way now?" Lillian asked.

"Oh no, Lillian."

Lillian suddenly went white. "You wouldn't say anything about— Helen, I've made the right choice. You'll see I'm right."

"I don't want to hurt you, Lily, but I can hardly believe you've considered all the implications. I think you're wrong about why Mitch hasn't harmed Max."

"What do you mean? What do you mean by that?"

"You tell me Mitch is intelligent. And you tell me you think you're the reason Mitch hasn't harmed Max." Her hands clenched and unclenched. "I've never told you this, Lillian, but there was a reason Katy asked Jack to come to her birthday party that night, and it wasn't just to spite you."

"Helen, there's no need to go into this now, is there?"

"She was upset about something and she tried to talk to him, but Jack said you and Todd made sure she was never alone with him for more than a minute. So she used one of those minutes to slip him a note. Conn found it in the pocket of Jack's overcoat. It probably should have ended up with the police, but both Jack and Conn knew what it might do to your reputation."

Lillian glanced at me and said, "Perhaps we should discuss this—"

"Irene has all of Conn's old papers now, so I'm sure she'll come across it, if she hasn't already. Jack kept the note for years, because it was the last thing Katy had given to him, even if it only hurt him to see it. I finally told him to give it to Conn, that Conn could keep it in the collection of things the two of them gathered while they were trying to investigate all that happened on that night."

"You don't know that Conn kept it!" Lillian said. "Please—"

"Oh, he kept it. He mentioned it to me when Eric and Ian were facing charges in 'seventy-eight. If he had it then, he kept it."

Helen turned to me. "The note said, 'Is it true Mitch Yeager is my father? You're the only one who will tell me the truth.'" She stared hard at Lillian as she said this last sentence.

"Katy thought Mitch Yeager was her father?" I asked, stunned.

"Damn it, Helen! What have you done to me!"

"All about you, isn't it, Lily? Well, I'm tired of it."

"But . . . Helen," I asked, "are you saying that Mitch Yeager thinks Max is his grandson?"

"Yes. At least, there's a real possibility that he does."

"Is it true?" I asked Lillian. "Was Mitch Yeager Katy's father?"

"No. I've told him that again and again."

"But he has reason to believe he could be?"

"I don't think I should answer that."

"Cut the crap. You tell her or I will," Helen said.

"You horrid old bitch!" Lillian said.

I thought back to O'Connor's diaries. "Katy was twenty-one in January of 1958, so she was born in January of 1937, and would have been conceived in April or early May of 1936. Possibly a little later, but prematurely born infants weren't as likely to survive then, so it's more likely she was conceived in April or May. Mitch Yeager was on trial around then, but out on bail for most of April."

"Go on," Helen said, which drew another plea from Lillian. Helen shrugged and said, "Tell her yourself, then."

"I . . . I was a stupid young girl," Lillian said bitterly. "Mitch and I had been having an off-and-on affair for some time. I had been rather sheltered, and I rebelled. I found there was something exciting about him."

"You dated Jack Corrigan in April of that year, too," I said. "I've seen that in O'Connor's diaries."

"Diaries! He was a child!"

Helen smiled. "Jack told him to keep them, Lillian. Conn also wrote little stories about everything he had seen and heard."

"Everything?" Lillian said weakly.

"Jack showed a few of them to me when he first started giving him 'assignments'—they were uncanny. Jack used to say that Conn was born holding a pen, and I believe it's true."

Lillian frowned, then admitted, "Yes, I dated Jack. Mostly to make Mitch and Harold jealous, I suppose."

I remembered O'Connor's observations and wondered if that was true. But I didn't say that—couldn't say that in front of Helen. I was already wondering if I should have kept my big mouth shut about Jack's previous affairs.

I glanced at her and found that far from looking injured over Lillian's talk of dating Jack, she looked knowing—almost smug. Maybe she didn't care about Jack's past, since she was the only one he married. Of course, Jack and Helen had been friends long before they married, so she must have known that "Handsome Jack" hadn't lived a celibate life.

Lillian said, "You may not be aware of it, but Winston Wrigley—the first one, I mean—was my godfather. He was furious when he found out that I was dating Jack. One of his own reporters! Then later, Mitch told him that if the paper printed so much as one more negative story about him, he'd tell the world a few stories about me."

"What kind of stories?"

"The kind that might have caused problems for my marriage."

I waited.

"You have to understand that Harold was my parents' choice," Lillian said, "and though I liked him, he didn't seem as romantic as the other fellows did to me. Then he did something very romantic—he asked me to elope with him, and I did, in late April."

Helen stood and walked toward the big windows, looking out on the gardens below them.

"Was Mitch upset?" I asked.

"Upset! I should say so. Mitch had this insane notion—he was sure I had married Harold as quickly as I did because I was pregnant with his—Mitch's, I mean—child. According to this cockamamie theory of his, since Mitch was in jail and would likely go to prison, there was nothing else I could do, and so in desperation I made a fool out of Harold."

"You mean he believed Harold was raising his daughter?"

"Exactly."

"But then, why would he harm Katy?"

"I've never been as sure as others are that Mitch himself was behind all of that," Lillian said primly.

Helen made a noise of derision. "Lillian, tell the truth."

"All right, I will. Katy hated him and made no secret of it. She never failed to be rude to him, and he resented it—she publicly insulted him, and Mitch won't tolerate that from anyone. Jack and Helen had something to do with her attitude toward him, I'm sure."

"If that's so," Helen said, "I'm glad of it."

"Are you?" Lillian said. "What if it cost Katy her life?"

Helen didn't answer right away. After a moment, she said, "I was always proud of Katy. If Mitch Yeager had anything to do with her murder, and I can prove it, I don't care what she did to him. Don't make it sound as if she deserved what happened to her. I didn't cause her to be murdered, either, Lillian. And you know it."

"Yes, of course," Lillian said. "I didn't mean that. I—oh, Helen, you know I loved her and was proud of her! It was just that you made me so damned angry! Forgive me?"

Helen didn't answer.

"Helen," I said, "it seems to me that what's done is done—the tests are going to be in progress soon. Lillian is right about one thing—Max seems determined to find out whether or not he's Katy's missing child. You won't be able to stop him from doing that."

She sighed and turned toward me. "Yes, I suppose you're right. Let's go, Irene. I'm suddenly very tired."

She fussed a little when I offered to help her climb into the Jeep, complained about how much she hated seat belts when I refused to close the passenger door until she had hers on. Warned me not to slam the door when she gave in and exaggerated a startled jump when I shut it.

I stood outside the passenger side of the Jeep for a moment, a sensation of being watched suddenly coming over me, causing goose bumps to prickle along my skin. I spun around, as if I might catch some watcher unawares, but saw nothing. I looked around me. The street was quiet. No faces stared back from windows in the few houses I could see from here. There were trees and shrubs planted for privacy all along the borders of Lillian's property. I scanned them, looking for a glimpse of a face, a sign of movement.

Behind me, the passenger door to the Jeep opened. I didn't need to fake being startled.

"What's wrong?" she asked.

"I thought I heard someone call my name," I said. "I was mistaken."

"Liar," she said, and shut the door. It didn't close all the way. She reopened it, on an impressive list of expletives, and slammed it shut again.

The ride to her home was silent. She let me help her out of the Jeep. She gave me a big hug and said, "You've endured a morning with two stupid, querulous old women. I'm sorry, Irene."

"Oh, one of those women is dumb as a fox, getting me to tag along," I said. "What aren't you telling me?"

She touched a dry, thin hand to my cheek and said, "I'd tell you everything if I could. I meant what I said to Lillian—you and Lydia make me very proud. But I've made promises, Irene. I intend to keep them, at least for now. But you keep digging, and don't be discouraged or afraid of what you may find, and my little promises won't matter at all."

"All right, I will."

I walked her to her door. "Helen, I just remembered something I wanted to ask you about."

"Yes?"

"In 1936, you left the paper for a while."

A look came into her eyes, one I had seen a few times before. In college, if I turned in something she especially liked, she got that same look. "Yes. Come in for a moment, won't you? I won't keep you, but it's too brisk out here for this talk."

We went inside and shed our coats. We sat together on her sofa.

"I did leave the paper," she said. "For about a year. How do you know about that?"

"O'Connor's diary mentioned it. Why did you leave?"

"Several reasons. I'll give you a few of them. First, I wasn't being paid the same wage my male counterparts were making, even though I was supporting myself."

"Wrigley the first was still in charge?"

"Yes. An old man by then. I went in to ask for a raise, he told me he couldn't give me one—didn't I know there was a Depression on, and there were men who wanted my job, and so forth. Take it or leave it, he said."

"So you left it."

"Yes. That's why everyone thought I had left. But you see, I knew what his reaction would be, so it served as a way for me to disguise my other reasons for leaving."

"Which were?"

"First and foremost, I was madly in love with a man who felt a great deal of affection for me, but whom I could plainly see was not ready to settle down."

"Jack."

"Jack. Gorgeous as all get out, and a devil to boot. He was younger than I, and still sowing his wild oats." She smiled. "You can't change them, you know. They have to outgrow it."

"You knew about Lillian?"

"Oh yes. Lily was as beautiful as he was. They made a striking couple. And of course, her old man was loaded, so she thought that would keep Jack chasing after her. What he liked about her was her spirit, not her father's money."

"Is Lillian why you left?"

"No, being jealous or angry of Jack's women would have been exhausting and useless as well. He also had a way of—oh, at the time I was convinced it was some rogue's trick of his, but he made me believe I was something special, that he might flirt here or there, but that I truly mattered to him. Besides,

I liked Lillian. I admired that spirit in her, too. She was barely out of high school, but she could put a woman twice her age in her place. A bit spoiled, but she's smart and if you get her interested in something other than herself, she can surprise you with her generosity and drive."

"She was married by the time you left the paper, right?"

"Yes, although Harold was never much of a husband. They weren't married a month before he moved to Europe without her. He traveled all over the world. He was involved in the sale of supplies to military groups, including ammunition—just barely kept his nose clean as far as the government was concerned, but many American companies profited from wars in other countries during those years. Barrett Ducane was one of his business partners. I think he even did some business with Mitch."

"Lillian was pregnant when Harold left for Europe?"

"Yes. She had lost both parents not long after her wedding—a car accident. She wanted to get away for a while after that happened. It was summer and terribly hot, so she decided to go up to a huge cabin owned by her family—a lodge, really—in the mountains. She later told me that she felt alone and abandoned and began to think about women who were less fortunate than she, and that's when she got the idea that she'd start a place for unwed mothers."

"I didn't know about that."

"It's still in existence. She purchased another, smaller cabin nearby. If the Vanderveers had known of the scandalous use she had made of the lodge, they would have come back to haunt her. But she made the right choice. I think it kept her occupied, kept her from dwelling on her problems. And away from Thelma Ducane, who was a terrible influence on her. Those unwed mothers were better women than Thelma, who had the morals of a jackal."

"How did you get involved?"

"She heard that I had left the paper and was looking for a job. She was Wrigley's godchild, and he was fond of her." She smiled. "Dear Lillian. She gave the old man a great deal of misery over letting me go, and told him that she was going to hire me just to spite him. So she invited me to come up there to help her run her home for unwed mothers. And fiercely refused to let me consider coming back to the newspaper. We got along famously."

"Wasn't that frowned on back then, a single woman working around unwed mothers?"

She laughed. "Irene, what do you think they thought of women who worked for newspapers?"

"Oh. The cabin—the smaller one? That's the place where Katy was born?"

"Yes."

"No wonder you were so close to her."

"Yes, I was a part of her life from the very beginning."

"And later, Lillian gave the cabin to Katy, and Katy willed it to Jack?"

"Yes."

"I've always wondered about that will. Do you know why she wrote it?"

Helen hesitated, then said, "I can answer that, but—I can answer it more fully if you will first call Lillian and tell her that you want her to give me permission to tell you all about the day Katy made the will."

I looked at her as if she were nuts.

"Courage failing you? She is younger than I am, but I still think you'd beat her in a fair fight."

I pulled out my cell phone and pressed redial.

Lillian answered, and when I told her what I wanted, she said, "Put her on the phone."

I handed it to Helen.

After a moment, Helen said, "Yes, of course I forgive you. And you forgive me, I hope?"

There was another long pause, during which Helen rolled her eyes. "Yes, it was a terrible thing to say to you."

Another pause. "Yes, I will . . . this will be for the best. You understand that? . . . I'm glad. . . . Thank you. . . . Yes, I'll see you then. Good-bye."

She looked at the phone, handed it to me, and said, "You'll have to hang up. I can't stand those things. And the buttons are so small. Who designs such things?"

I disconnected the call and put the phone away. I turned to her and said, "Wow."

"Wow?"

"You two had a hellacious fight, one I was afraid would end in blows, and that's all it took to patch things up?"

"We've had lots of practice over the past sixty or so years. Eventually you figure out that you'll never have enough time to enjoy the company of your closest friends, so it's best to learn how to mend damage quickly." She paused, then said, "Lydia called me yesterday."

I felt my spine stiffen.

"Do you know," Helen said, "I think she's in the wrong."

"Not entirely," I admitted. "Really, my attitude started it."

"Perhaps, but the thing is, she knows that for the most part, it's she who is in the wrong now."

"She knows?"

"Yes. Which is why you'll have to be the one to make another effort, Irene—so that she can admit it."

I frowned.

"Is the worst thing she said to you worth more to you than the best thing she's ever done for you?"

"Not even close."

"Then let go of it. Call her. Invite her somewhere. Not to talk things out, just to see each other, and when the time comes you can tell each other how stupid all of this fighting is. All right?"

"If she snubs me again, I am siccing you on her."

"I doubt it will be necessary."

"Tell me about the will."

She sighed. "All right. I want you to understand two things. The first is that I didn't know the answer to this until very recently. I threatened to sell the cabin, and I suppose that was enough to make Lillian cave in and tell me what had happened. The other is that this is absolutely confidential. If you feel you might have to tell someone at some point in time, it will have to be after Lillian has given you permission, or because she's dead. If you can't promise that, I can't tell you."

"All right."

"Here's what Lillian told me. A few days before Katy's birthday, Mitch came across Katy and Lillian when they were together, doing some shopping downtown. Their hands were full, holding the handles of their shopping bags—you know the type of bag—big fancy paper bags with twine handles. The chauffeur had already gone ahead with an armload of boxes, and was going to bring the car around. Mitch offered to help carry the bags until the car arrived, and Katy snubbed him. He asked her why she was always so rude to him. She said something like, 'Uncle Jack has told me all about you.'"

"I remember O'Connor mentioning that she called him that."

"She had always called Jack that, from the time she was little. Jack was much more of a father to her than Harold was—Harold spent less than a half-dozen nights a month at home. But whatever she called Jack, she probably shouldn't have mentioned him to Mitch. Jack's name was always enough to make him lose his temper."

"Because of the stories he wrote about Mitch?"

"I think so. Although God knows Mitch's mind works differently than a reasonable person's—he can't forgive any injury, he's quick to perceive a slight, and he sees the smallest criticism as a major insult. Which is why what happened next was—was the worst thing that could have happened.

"According to Lillian, Mitch took her by the chin and said, 'Uncle Jack, is it? He's not your *uncle*, any more than Harold's your father. Didn't your mother ever tell you how close we were, all those years ago?' Katy spit in his face."

"Not that I blame Katy," I said, "but given what happened later, why didn't Lillian tell the police about this?"

"Irene, you must remember that for twenty years, we thought Katy had drowned in a boating accident. Lillian told me she thought of going to the police about it in 1978, when you found out what had really happened to Katy and Todd, but when she saw that even Ian and Eric wouldn't be convicted, she realized that it would be her word against Mitch's and Mitch would claim it never happened."

"No one else saw it?"

"Someone might have seen it, but to be able to recall a relatively minor incident twenty years later? She doubted anyone heard him. At the time it happened, she was hardly in a state to take down names from witnesses—she was *hoping* no one had seen it. She apologized to Mitch and fortunately her driver pulled up just then, which is probably all that kept Mitch from striking Katy."

"What happened after that?"

"Lillian dragged Katy into the car and, once they were home, scolded her. She tells me that Katy retaliated by asking certain uncomfortable questions about Lillian's past, and why there had never been any other children in the family, and so on. Lillian refused to answer them, and told her she should be less worried about Lillian's youthful foolishness and much more worried about her own—that insulting a man like Mitch Yeager could be extremely dangerous. When she asked if Mitch was her father, Lillian said that if she didn't want someone to spit in *her* face, she'd better stop asking such things."

"And the will?"

"Ah, yes. The will. Katy said Jack should have been her father, and that she loved him more than anyone she was related to by blood. Lillian said, 'This is your family, and it will be Max's family, and you ought to be grateful that you weren't raised by a drunkard without two nickels to rub together.'"

"Ouch."

"Lillian said that Katy managed a parting shot as she left the house. She told Lillian to roll up all her nickels and shove them up her ass—yes, I know, not very ladylike—and that drunk or sober, Jack could do a better job of raising a child in a shack than Lillian or any of the Ducanes could in a mansion."

"So she went from there to a lawyer?"

"Oh, that wasn't the mystery it seemed at first. Apparently she already had an appointment to see him. Dan Norton—the homicide detective who first investigated their disappearances?—did look into the business of the will back in 1958. The lawyer told Norton that she had come to consult him about getting a divorce from Todd, something she had told others she intended to do. She arrived early—probably a result of storming out of Lillian's house before she planned to leave. While she waited to see the lawyer, she talked to another client who was there to have a will and other papers drawn up—a young widow who said she wanted to make sure that if anything happened to her, her children would be left in the care of an aunt, and not her mother."

"Which made Katy think of her own child. And she made sure Jack had a shack to raise him in."

"Yes."

I thought about all she had told me. "I'm not sure this brings me any further along," I said.

"Perhaps not. Keep reading those diaries of Conn's," she said. "And come to me again if I can be of any help."

I thanked her for confiding in me. Just before I left, I asked, "Helen, are you hoping the tests prove Max is the missing child, or that he isn't?"

"I'm hoping for Max's happiness and safety. That above all and more than anything."

"Nothing more?"

"Oh, are you asking me if it would be a relief to know that Katy's child lived? Yes, because given what you and Conn figured out about that night, if Max isn't that child, I fear that child was murdered. I also hope that perhaps, one fine day, there will be justice. Justice would be sweet. It's one of the things that happens as you age, you know. The taste buds go like everything else, but the last ones to leave you are the ones that can taste sweetness. If the good Lord is willing, I'd like to taste a little sweet justice for Katy."

60

FOUR WEEKS LATER, THINGS SEEMED TO BE LOOKING UP. HAILEY'S STORY on Helen was nothing short of beautiful. We got letters from readers young and old after it ran. I had taken Helen's advice and called Lydia and pretended we weren't fighting, which happened to work, and eventually we had a long heart-to-heart about it that resulted in newsroom harmony, greater mutual respect, and increased local sales of Kleenex.

One unexpected result of this was that she became less defensive about Ethan, which ultimately made her more watchful. I decided not to tell her that Frank hated the Harmon story, mostly because he had only said, "This is bullshit, he never had this much access to Harmon," when he saw it.

One evening, I stopped by her desk before leaving for the day. I had found some quizzes among O'Connor's papers, and I told Lydia about them. "Middle sections of articles—no headlines, leads, or bylines—had been clipped out and pasted onto cheap paper—I suspect Jack took the paper from the newsroom. O'Connor had written names next to them. It took me a while to figure out what was going on. Jack used to have O'Connor read stories without knowing who had written them, to teach O'Connor to recognize the style of the different members of the staff." I shook my head. "He was ten or eleven years old, and he was getting most of them right. I don't think I could do that now."

"Sure you could," she said.

From her computer, she printed out a few things that would be in the next day's paper.

I was surprised. There was a little guesswork involved, but I got about eight out of ten. I missed twice—both were written by Ethan. Neither of us commented on that fact.

"Let's see how you do," I said.

Her test was a little harder to devise, because she had already read almost everything filed, so I waited at her computer until a few new stories were filed, and then added two sections from older stories of Ethan's. I picked harder passages than she did—odd snippets, paragraphs that wouldn't be recognized because of special content.

She also got eight of ten—she missed both of Ethan's, too.

"What the heck does that mean?" she said, frowning.

"Maybe his style is imitative," I said, hoping I wasn't about to start another fight.

"No," she said slowly. She asked the computer to give her everything written by him for the past month.

It pulled up a lot of material, but she quickly culled out two minor local stories. "You see?" she said. "These two—I would have known either one as his style. I like it, actually. Clear and direct. Doesn't overdo it."

I admitted they were well written. "Pull up the Harmon story," I said.

She opened it, and I read it over her shoulder. I kept my mouth shut, but I wasn't the only one who noticed a difference in what we were reading now and what we had read before. The style was also clear and direct, but there was something finer involved—a surer hand, more detailed observations, and words that evoked more powerful images. It stumbled here and there, but then the next sentence would redeem it.

I could see her posture change.

"I recognize that style—in places, anyway," I said. "It's not just one person, is it? But the strongest parts—I've read that writer before."

She folded her arms and leaned back in her chair, staring at the monitor.

Oh hell, I thought, here we go again.

Then she put her hands back on the keyboard and called up her connection to the wire services. She searched for stories on Bennie Lee Harmon.

Nothing matched the best parts of Ethan's story. Then she searched for a few exact matches of phrases in the story. Again, no matches. "At least that's a relief," she said. "For a moment, I envisioned telling Wrigley we'd need to make a public apology and who knows what kind of compensation to another paper for ripping off a story."

"I don't think there has been much access to Harmon," I said. "He's been ill."

"So where did this come from?"

I looked around the room, trying to picture who sat at each desk, and how they wrote. When I came to my own desk, I said, "Oh God."

"What?"

"O'Connor. He's ripped off O'Connor. And Lord knows who else."

A conversation came back to me. I checked my watch. "Lydia, call down to the morgue, ask the librarian to pull these dates." From Ethan's story, I read out dates that were key to events in Harmon's life.

Instead, when she called, she told the librarian, "I'll be down there in five minutes. I'll need everything Ethan Shire checked out on the day before he left for Sacramento. You'll have his signature on the sheet? Great." She gave the librarian the date.

She got an assistant to cover the desk, printed out two copies of Ethan's interview, and we went down to the morgue together. It didn't take us long to find what we were looking for.

"O'Connor interviewed Harmon," I said. "I had forgotten that."

"I'm going to kill him."

O'Connor was already dead, and I knew she didn't mean Harmon.

She told me later that it took some effort to convince Wrigley, but that she and John eventually persuaded him that yes, it was a serious matter when a person lifted a fellow reporter's words wholesale and made them appear to be his own, or quoted twenty-year-old interviews and tried to lead the public to believe they had just taken place. She thought Wrigley would have shrugged it off as youthful high jinks if John hadn't pointed out that Wrigley had probably reimbursed Ethan's expenses for a party trip to visit a college friend.

Lydia had the zeal of a convert, and began ferreting out other stories that seemed to her to be, as she said, "Assembled, not written." She found several. O'Connor was a favorite to quote, apparently because he was dead rather than retired, and therefore unlikely to call the paper to complain.

"A lot of research. You'd think it would have been easier for Ethan to just write the stories himself," I said.

"Don't ask me to explain the psychology of plagiarism," she said.

The *Express* ran an apology to its readers that ended up making the paper itself a news story for a day or so. No one doubted the need for it, but the shame the staff felt did nothing for morale, already low due to rumors of the paper being put up on the block.

We thought Ethan would be fired. He was put into an alcohol rehab program and told he could return on probation.

Hailey thought this was another scam on his part. I thought about friends of mine who had been alcoholics, and what it had taken them to try to turn their lives around. "He may be totally insincere about it, but this isn't the easy way out," I said. "Let's hope this has been a wake-up call."

"Yeah, right," Hailey said. "For some reason my heart refuses to break."

Ethan would be gone for at least thirty days. My teamwork with Hailey was intensifying.

We eventually took over a small conference room near the morgue, so that we would cause less interference with the functioning of the library. We camped at microfilm readers for hours at a time. The results of the DNA tests would be back within the week, and we had drafted background material on the Ducanes, the Vanderveers, and the Linworths, and recaps of stories about the crimes and victims of that night in 1958, and the discoveries of 1978.

We had stories written about Max, and thanks to Stephen Gerard, we had photos of Max, Lillian, and the two of them together to choose from. Helen had been at the house during the shoot, and Stephen—who apparently became a fan of Helen's when he was one of her students, years ago—had even talked her into sitting for a few group photos.

I loved those the best, although there was no reason to run a photo of Helen with this article. They looked happy to be together, though, and looking at the photo made me feel some hope that biology wouldn't call all the shots—Max would remain connected to these two women no matter what. I made Stephen promise to give me prints of the trio.

We had other artwork ready, including some about how DNA testing worked. Hailey wrote an article to go with that.

We eventually reached the point of having everything but the actual story, for which we'd have to wait. It was a little like trying to fall asleep in a starting gate.

Wrigley led small tours of potential buyers through the newsroom every few days. Rumors abounded. Anyone unknown who ventured upstairs was the subject of speculation and, from certain staff members, a kind of fawning attention the rest of us found sickening. The previous week, a guy with a briefcase was offered a comfy seat and a fresh cup of coffee and took advantage of both as he was entertained by the brown-nosers and asked his opinion of the paper—this went on for about fifteen minutes before he asked if it was okay if he fixed the copier now, because he had other appointments.

One night, as I worked late, the phone on my desk rang. I picked up the receiver and said, "Kelly." A long silence and a click were all I heard.

This began to happen frequently. I started letting my voice mail pick up all calls at night.

I kept going through O'Connor's diaries. After reading O'Connor's story about Harmon, I skipped ahead to the diaries for 1945.

Wedged in the pages for the first week in April was a photograph. It showed a young woman and a young man—I recognized him immediately, even though the photo had been taken before he had broken his nose in some barroom brawl: O'Connor. There was something else about him that seemed different. Perhaps it was the hat. They were both dressed up and stood arm in arm, looking comfortable with each other. On the back, a feminine hand had written "Conn and Maureen—Easter 1945." His mother's writing, I thought. Each of the diaries had been a Christmas present from Maureen, inscribed to him with some whimsical note, often asking him to please think fondly of his nobody of a sister when he became a famous newspaper reporter. I knew her hand by now.

Features that made her brother handsome did not quite do the same for her, but she was by no means plain. She had a face that was full of kindness, or perhaps I saw that there because I had read her brother's accounts of her. Her dress was simple in style, as was the hat she wore. No jewelry other than a simple necklace—a silver shamrock. Her hair was dark, her eyes were large and blue and full of mischief. She was smiling, looking as if she were just about to go from a smile to a laugh.

I looked back at O'Connor's image, and saw that he, too, was nearly laughing. That was it, then, the difference in him—I had seen him laugh, I had seen him smile, but I had never seen him as happy as he was in the photo.

There was only one entry after April 5, which had been devoted to plans for a date with Ethel Gibbs. On April 6, he wrote, "Maureen, please be safe. I am so sorry." There were no other entries that year.

There were no diaries between 1945 and 1950.

The Wednesday night of the week the DNA results were due, Frank and I managed to be home at the same time, and fairly early. We live near the beach, where the nights are often chilly, so he lit a fire in the fireplace. We snuggled close and talked about our days.

When I told him about having the stories ready to run, he told me that the police were watching Mitch and his family closely these days.

"Max said Eric and Ian are back in town."

"Yes. We're keeping an especially close watch on them."

"But they've served out their parole, so . . ."

"So, yes, all we can do is watch them." He held me a little closer. "Scared?"

"A little. I keep telling myself that Mitch Yeager is an old man, then I remember that an old man can own a new gun. Anyway, let's not talk about that. Tell me what you're working on."

"Looks as if we might have made a little bit of headway in the case of O'Connor's sister."

"Maureen? I just found a photo of her."

"I'd like to see it. Ben Sheridan and the coroner and our new lab director studied photographs of the bodies and the old coroner's reports—this was the coroner just before Woolsey. Turns out Harmon may be telling the truth, and we may be able to prove that he is without an exhumation."

"How?"

"Back in 1950, they collected hair evidence, and scrapings from under her nails. She fought her attacker. Guess where the nail scrapings have been kept?"

"A freezer?"

"Yes. The hair might have been enough anyway, but the nail scrapings look better. Some skin and some blood."

"So you could prove who killed her?"

"Well—let's say we can prove whether or not Harmon is lying. His DNA is on file, but if there's no match, then we'll try running it through CODIS— you know about that?"

"The FBI's Combined DNA Index System. The big computerized database of convicts' DNA profiles."

"Basically, yes. It has a long way to go—it's going to take a while to get all the samples processed, for one thing. Don't get your hopes up—if it isn't Harmon, I don't think we're likely to see a match."

"I understand. It's just so weird. If it doesn't match Harmon, someone had to know that Harmon was burying women in that orange grove, and then had to be a killer himself."

"Harmon was a loner, but we're not giving up on the possibility that he found a soul mate along the way."

"I'll see what I can find in O'Connor's notes. Maybe he learned something the police didn't—people Maureen came into contact with, or something like that."

"Worth taking a look, but I think Dan Norton was pretty thorough."

I intended to do that the next morning, but the doorbell rang just as Frank and I sat down to breakfast. Max Ducane stood on my doorstep. Before he gave me his news, I could tell by the look on his face what the DNA test results had revealed.

"Sorry to bother you so early, but I didn't know where else to go. I can't face Lillian or Helen right now."

"Max—come in."

He smiled ruefully. "Maybe you can help me come up with yet another name for myself," he said. "Because if there's one thing I know for sure, it's that I'm not Max Ducane."

61

PUBLICLY, HE HANDLED ALL THE RUDE COMMENTS, MEDDLESOME QUESTIONS, double takes, and stares that were to come his way over the next few weeks with a kind of fortitude and dignity that made all of us who loved him proud to know him. Privately, if you didn't know him well, he might have fooled you into thinking he was getting on with his life.

The *Express* broke the story about the DNA tests, and what that brought to Max made me wish something I rarely wished—that I didn't work for a newspaper.

Because we're friends, I didn't write any of the stories that directly involved Max, but Hailey did a good job on them. If it had all stopped there, he still would have faced a lot of public reaction. There wasn't a chance on earth it was going to stop there.

The story got picked up by the wires. He was a natural for national media attention. He was rich, good-looking, and quotable. His origins were mysterious. He had advantages that came to him through sheer luck and those he had obviously earned through his own abilities, but some of the media chose to insinuate that he was a charlatan who had slyly conned two tragic, wealthy families into handing over a fortune to him.

After a week or so, the story probably would have dropped off the public radar had it not been for an announcement from the Ross family. As the whole country soon learned, Max was an eligible bachelor again. Gisella had called him to break off their engagement just minutes before her father gave a press conference.

For a brief time, I fantasized retribution on Gisella Ross and her parents. As it turned out, my fellow media members did the work for me unbidden— after painting her as incredibly shallow, they found some dirt on her family that made Max's heritage seem noble by comparison.

"I'm so sorry this has happened to her," he told me, more upset by those reports than by anything that had been said about him.

He told us this over dinner at our house. Tuna casserole—lifestyles of the rich and famous.

He was spending a lot of time with us these days. Frank didn't seem to mind. They had formed their own friendship, and even though Max was now without a fiancée, I guess Frank had figured out what Max and I had figured out a long time ago.

"I wish I could be sorry for her," I said, "because it would fool everyone into thinking I am a much better person than I am. She didn't deserve you."

He shook his head. "She wasn't ready for what happened—all the publicity. She's a private person."

I decided not to respond to that.

He must have seen something of my thoughts, though, because he smiled and said to Frank, "God help anyone who harms someone Irene cares about."

"True," Frank said. He's smarter than I am, though, because he immediately changed the subject by asking questions that led to an animated discussion about the ways GPS could help with law enforcement. Max forgot his troubles for a while. He talked about how cargo containers could now carry signaling devices that could help locate stolen goods.

"Lots happening in the area of tracking the movements of parolees," Max said. "They could be tagged with lightweight devices and you would always know where they were. And even have the devices programmed to send a call to local law enforcement if, say, a sex offender goes into an area near a school or playground." Which was fine as far as it went, I thought, but I stayed quiet and didn't spoil their mood by asking if anyone had read any George Orwell lately.

At the end of the evening, just as he was leaving, Max said, "I have to try to find out what became of that child. The two of you understand that, don't you?"

"Yes," I said. "I've been trying to figure out what we could do."

"So have I," he said. "Frank, I know it didn't help much last time, but I want to offer the reward again. Maybe after all these years, someone will finally come forward. I'll up it to two hundred and fifty thousand. I'll add a grant to the department to help staff phones, if that's what it takes. I don't know what's allowed and what isn't, but—can you help me with this?"

"Sure," Frank said. "Let me run it by my lieutenant. I'll call you tomorrow."

The reward made our phones ring again. Sometimes the callers hadn't even been born at the time of the kidnapping. We got one "repressed memory" case of a woman who believed her father had buried the child in the family backyard, but real estate records showed the family hadn't moved to Las Piernas until 1961 or purchased the home in question until 1964.

I kept hoping Betty Bradford would call.

In the meantime, DNA tests on the scrapings from beneath Maureen O'Connor's nails excluded Bennie Lee Harmon—at least as the person who had been scratched when she fought off her attacker. Harmon was doing better now, but had become less talkative.

"The business of the graves bothers me," Frank said. "Harmon was mostly a drifter, didn't stay any one place for long. When he was here, though, he must have confided in someone. Or he was followed. I started to wonder if he had married or had a girlfriend, or had a crush on someone from work." Frank had looked up Harmon's Social Security records. "He was 4-F, so he wasn't in the military. No army buddy. I thought he might have worked for the aircraft plant, and maybe found someone nearly as odd as he was there. Or maybe he had been followed from there out to the grove."

"By someone who also knew Maureen. It makes sense," I said.

"Except he didn't work at the aircraft plant. He worked as a driver for a company that sold agricultural supplies," he said. "Probably how he chose the orange grove in the first place. He basically doesn't play well with others, so his job choices were usually ones where he could be alone much of the day."

"And he might have used the company truck to haul young women off to an orange grove?"

"Yes, I think so."

"Did he ever tell you why he chose April as his big month?"

"No, but that was something he told one of the other investigators this past week—I guess it has to do with Easter, not April. His mother died on Easter in 1939. His killings all took place within seven days after Easter."

"Then the person who knew about the graves in the orange grove didn't just follow him out there. The person who killed her knew about the Easter thing, too. Maureen was killed within a week of Easter."

"Damn. Once I knew it wasn't him, I didn't check the date against the Easter calendar. You're sure?"

"Yes. The last photo O'Connor had of his sister was taken on Easter Sunday, just a few days before she died."

*   *   *

Ethan came back to work. He looked as if he had lost about fifteen pounds. He didn't have fifteen pounds to spare. He also looked as if he hadn't been getting much sleep. His desk had been moved back near mine, placed just on the opposite side of it.

I said, "Welcome back, Ethan."

He nodded without looking up or saying anything. It occurred to me that he probably thought I was being sarcastic.

Lydia gave him every shit assignment that came into the city desk. She handed the plums to Hailey and other reporters. Ethan did his work without complaint. And without making eye contact with anyone in the newsroom.

He was careful to keep his eyes averted from the surfaces of other people's desks, too, and looked at no computer monitor other than his own, staring down at his shoes whenever he got up to get a phone book or moved for any other reason. Sometimes I wondered how he made it across the newsroom without bumping into anything. Every now and then, I saw another reporter go out of his way to jostle him. Ethan would apologize and move on.

More than once, he had to call the computer folks to supply a new password. It seems any new one he came up with was soon discovered and then used to change it to another password without his knowledge. I thought he might have complained to management about it, because after about a week of that, at a staff meeting, John said, "The next person who fucks around with another reporter's computer will be fired on the spot. I will set up security cameras in the newsroom if I have to. The fun's over, boys and girls." Ethan turned beet red and shook his head slightly.

I said, "John, who reported the problem to you?"

"Those propeller heads in the computer department," he said without hesitation. "I can't make sense out of half of what they say to me, so none of you are to make them talk to me again, understand?"

The next morning, I watched as Ethan navigated his way to his desk. He sat down and pulled a drawer open. All its contents fell out onto the floor with a tremendous clatter. Across the newsroom, there was laughter.

He said nothing, staring at the mess for a moment, then knelt on the floor and began picking up the scattered contents.

I stood up, went around to his desk, knelt next to him, and started helping.

"Please don't," he whispered.

"It's an old trick," I said, pretending I didn't hear him. "Don't open any of the others, they'll be upside down, too. Someone takes a thin piece of cardboard, uses it to hold the contents in while the drawer is flipped over and reinserted. Very hard to detect first thing in the morning."

At some point during this explanation, he stopped moving. Mark Baker and Stuart Angert came over and fixed the other drawers while I continued to hunt down paper clips, pens, loose change, and Post-it notes. The newsroom had fallen silent.

John's hearing is never so attuned to anything as a lack of noise in the newsroom. He came to his door, glanced over at us, then turned to the rest of the room and shouted, "What the hell are you being paid to do?"

It broke whatever spell had frozen the others, and work resumed.

Ethan said, "Thanks," as Stuart and Mark went back to their desks. Otherwise, he still hadn't moved or spoken.

"Let's get out of here for a few minutes," I said.

"I can't."

"Sure you can. Meet you downstairs in five. Don't forget your umbrella."

"I don't have one."

"We'll share mine, then."

I stood up, grabbed my purse, jacket, and umbrella, and left.

He met me in the lobby just when I thought I might have to go back up into the newsroom and haul him out by his ear.

I started walking, and to stay dry, he had to keep up. "Where are we going?"

"Lucky Dragon Burgers. Serves a great breakfast."

"I'm not hungry, really."

"I am," I said.

He didn't say anything more until we were seated in a booth. I asked him if he was a vegetarian. "No."

I ordered two Lucky Dragon omelets and a pot of coffee.

He was staring down at the table.

"I was trying to remember an acronym a friend taught me," I said. "Maybe you can help. It was the word H.A.L.T.—the H stood for hungry, the A for angry. The T was for tired. The L?"

"Lonely," he said. He looked up. "Your friend was in AA?"

"Yes."

"How's he doing?"

"She. That one is doing fine. Not always the story. But she remembers to do little things like taking care not to let herself get too hungry, angry, lonely, or tired. Like a lot of things in AA, that's not a bad idea for anyone, really."

"Are you—?"

"In AA? No. But try not to hold that against me."

"Actually, I'm glad to have a chance to talk to you. I need to apologize to you."

"Working your steps?"

"No—I mean, I am, but it isn't that. I'm not at that step yet. I'm—this is on my own. I just need to do this."

The long apology that followed wasn't something I needed, but I was fairly certain he had to get it off his chest. He spoke slowly and haltingly, in a manner far removed from that of the glib young manipulator who had put himself forward so often in recent months. The omelets arrived just as he was getting to the part about how he knew he had caused embarrassment to everyone on the whole newspaper.

"We'll get over it. Don't let that food get cold. Oh—thanks, and you're forgiven, and don't let any of this keep you from moving on from here."

"That's it?"

"No. Can I have your sour cream?"

He laughed a little nervously and dished it onto my plate. "It's not good for you."

"Oh yes it is. Hair shirts, on the other hand, are really bad for you."

"Hair shirts?" he asked, puzzled.

I sighed. "I should make you look it up, but—people used to wear them as penance."

"Oh. Okay."

We ate in silence for a few minutes. He was, I noticed, starting to tuck into his breakfast with earnest.

My cell phone rang. I apologized to him—I usually turn it off in restaurants.

His mouth was full, but he motioned me to go ahead and answer it.

The call was from Frank. "Lydia didn't know where to find you, so I worried a little," he said.

"I'm having breakfast at the Lucky Dragon. What's up?"

"I've been thinking about what you said about Maureen O'Connor. Harmon worked for Eden Supply of Las Piernas. Ring any bells?"

"Eden Supply? No, and there's nothing about it in O'Connor's notes that I can recall. Was it owned by some other company?"

"Haven't had a chance to look it up. It's not around now, though."

"I'll see if I can find anything about it in the newspapers from the 1940s. Maybe they advertised with the *Express*."

"Okay, but don't run anything in the paper yet—I'd rather Yeager didn't know we were looking in this direction."

When I hung up, Ethan said, "That was about O'Connor?"

I felt a little rise of anger.

"I didn't mean to eavesdrop," he said quickly.

"You could hardly help it. That's not what's bothering me. It's that—"

"That you were close to O'Connor and I stole from him."

"Yes."

"That was wrong, I know. You probably won't believe this, but—the reason was—I mean, I should never have done it, but—but I love the way he wrote."

"I do believe that."

"It makes it all worse, really."

"Ethan, if we could go back in time and pull all of O'Connor's writing out of your articles, believe me, I'd jump into the time machine right now. We can't. You have to live with that. But I knew O'Connor really well, and I know what he'd tell you."

" 'Why'd you steal from me, you stupid son of a bitch?' "

I laughed, which surprised him. "No. He'd tell you to keep your head up."

He looked down at the table, caught himself, and met my gaze. "Why are you being nice to me? You hated me."

"When I first came to work for the paper, I hid in the men's room of the *Express* one day, and eavesdropped on O'Connor insulting the hell out of me." I told him about some of my early troubles with O'Connor.

"What I've done," he said, "is pretty different from that."

"Yes, it is. But you aren't the first reporter to get off to a rough start at the *Express*, Ethan. You have talent. You've just got to show people what you've got, that's all. Never mind trying to impress them any other way—just use your own skill. Let it speak for itself."

"What if that's not enough?"

"If that isn't enough, nothing else ever will be. You'll need to find another line of work."

"No—this is all I want."

I smiled. "You'll be all right."

"I don't know. They'll never forget about this."

"You think you're so important that they'll remember your mistakes more than anyone else's?"

He smiled back a little. "When you put it like that, no." He drank some coffee, then said, "Thanks." After another few sips, he said, "It's going to be hard, because . . . I really fucked up. I'm not too proud of myself. And it's also going to be hard because . . . well, because until lately, it's been so easy. I know that doesn't seem to make sense, but what I mean is, no one ever stopped me before. I know how to get away with things, but now . . . I can't do it that way. Even if I know I won't get caught."

"You have to catch yourself."

"Right. So . . . I kind of have to reinvent myself. You know what I mean?"

"Yes, I think so." I stared out the window of the Lucky Dragon, watching a steady stream of downtown workers, panhandlers, shoppers, and others walk by. Each one a little bundle of troubles on legs, determined to make it through the day. I looked back at Ethan. "I've got a project for you. Something to do with O'Connor, so maybe it will be a way of paying him back."

"What?"

"A little background work for a story—nothing we can run with yet, but maybe it will go somewhere if you find a connection. Go down to the morgue . . ." I stopped, seeing his face go pale. "You can't avoid going in there forever, Ethan."

"No."

"All right, use the public library, then, but be careful not to mention to anyone else exactly what it is you're looking for. Find out if a company named Eden Supply, which was operating around here in the 1940s, was owned by anyone else—a larger company, for example. The city might have a record of it, although only with luck would that still be available. Try the ads for it first."

"Okay. If you don't mind my asking, what does this have to do with O'Connor?"

"It's the company Harmon worked for." I told him about the possible connections to Maureen's murder. "While you're at it, read up on her disappearance." I gave him some dates.

We talked about O'Connor for a while. I told him about the papers in the storage locker, and that O'Connor's brother Dermot would be visiting the States soon. It became clear to me, as he mentioned O'Connor's work, that he had read a great deal of it, and his enthusiasm for it made conversation easy between us.

I paid for our breakfasts, over his protests. The rain had let up, and it looked as if the skies were clearing. We walked back to the paper in a companionable silence. He seemed lost in thought, but at least he was lost with better posture. He was keeping his head up.

I thought he'd follow me into the newsroom, but he went downstairs to the morgue instead.

Until that moment, I wasn't really sure—for all my speeches over breakfast—that much could be made of Ethan Shire.

62

FOR A WHILE, I THOUGHT THAT GIVING ETHAN A CHANCE WAS GOING TO cause a bigger fight between Lydia and me than the one we had over him before. Somewhere along the line we both saw that, pulled back a bit, and she (a little gleefully, I thought) told me she thought it would be a good thing if I took him under my wing. "He's all yours," she said.

Not exactly what I had in mind, but I couldn't really back down.

Mark Baker, who was too tied up with writing stories about current criminal activities to be very active in the historical ones, told me that he wouldn't mind working with Ethan if I didn't want to be his scoutmaster.

"If it doesn't work out," I said, "you're my backup."

"He's not going to be your problem," Mark said. "Hailey is going to pitch a fit."

He was right. When I told Hailey that we were going to share our research with him, she told me I was crazy, that he was using me, and went on and on about it. "Ethan is going to be working with us," I said, interrupting her. "If you don't want to work with him, you can find something else to do."

She stood up. She didn't quite go so far as moving to the door, but I wouldn't have laid money on her staying. The success of the interview with Helen had produced a foreseeable side effect—Hailey, not exactly humble to begin with, now thought fairly highly of herself. I found myself half-wishing she'd walk away.

"Why should I be forced to put up with him?" she asked.

"You've never needed a second chance, I suppose? Or maybe you're looking for an excuse to go home earlier in the day."

She sat down, but said, "I love what we're doing, but—I don't trust Ethan!"

"I can't make you trust him. Not going to try. But if you want to keep working on stories with me, you're going to work on stories with Ethan."

* * *

He met us late that afternoon in a conference room just off the morgue. I learned that he had kept up with our stories about the old cases of 1958 and 1978, which had been running in the *Express* as a series in the weeks before Max's DNA test results were known. Hailey recapped what we had been looking into now—stories about the business connections between the Ducanes, the Linworths, and the Yeagers, as well as whatever personal backgrounds we could come up with.

"We think the Linworths and Ducanes screwed Mitch Yeager out of some money while he was under arrest in 1936," Hailey said. "His bail was set high, and he needed cash. He needed money to pay his attorneys, too."

"Wasn't his family wealthy?" Ethan asked.

"His family had been involved in rum-running," I said, "but Prohibition had recently ended, so bootlegging wasn't profitable."

"Barrett Ducane offered to help Yeager raise cash by buying some of his assets, assets that were worth much more than Ducane paid for them," Hailey said. "Linworth bought a few things as well, and those deals were in his favor, but not as lopsided as Ducane's. Ducane and Linworth both knew that money was going to be made from the coming war in Europe and elsewhere—so they chose companies that could be easily retooled to make aircraft parts and munitions and things like that."

"What did you find out today?" I asked Ethan.

"It's probably not worth anything," he said.

Hailey smirked.

He took a deep breath and explained to her why he had been researching Eden Supply. "It was owned by Granville Enterprises. Granville owned a lot of smaller, agriculturally related companies. Granville was a family name—Mitch Yeager's grandfather."

"Who was dead long before 1945," Hailey said, "so the company was Mitch's in those years."

"Which doesn't prove he knew that one driver in one subsidiary was taking a truck out to that particular orange grove after hours," Ethan said. "Or that he knew Harmon was killing and burying women all around a four-county area. If Yeager did know, it will be hard to show it."

"This is always the problem with him," I said. "He's there, but just out of reach."

"What do you mean?" Ethan asked. "I thought it was his nephews and minions who did all the killing."

"Which is *why* he's out of reach," Hailey said impatiently.

I tried giving her a look that told her to back off. Hailey doesn't really get the whole "back off" thing, which helps her as a reporter but makes working with her a pain.

"Tell me more about this," he said, looking at me.

"You've read the original confessions Eric and Ian made, the ones they recanted?"

"Yes."

"O'Connor said something to me about the statements they made—their theories about how to best punish someone. He called it the Yeager catechism." I flipped to a page in my notes and read, " 'You want to make your enemy suffer, you kill the people he loves and hide the bodies—you make him wonder if they're alive or dead. Nothing is worse than that.' "

"That was Eric," Hailey said, pulling out her own notes. "Ian was almost word for word the same—'If you kill the people he loves and hide the bodies, you kidnap them and never let them be found—you make him wonder if they're alive or dead, if he'll ever see them again, and he starts to think about what might be happening to them. Then your enemy suffers all his life. Nothing you could do to him is worse than that. Nothing.' "

"O'Connor once told me that when he heard those statements, he wondered if he could have become Mitch Yeager's enemy before he was eighteen," I said.

"He was seventeen when his sister disappeared," Ethan said. "I spent some time reading about that today. But what could he have done to harm Mitch Yeager?"

"He was a reporter," Hailey said. "He could have written something to harm Yeager's businesses."

"None of his early stories were about Yeager," Ethan said. "He seldom had any stories published with a byline until late 1945."

"You're the expert on O'Connor, all right," Hailey said.

Ethan looked mortified.

"Grow up or go upstairs," I snapped at Hailey.

She cast a dark look at Ethan, as though he were to blame for my loss of temper.

"Ethan's right," I said. "O'Connor didn't cause problems for Mitch Yeager as a reporter. He caused them for him when he was a child. A paperboy. He stood on a street corner after school each day and hawked newspapers. He managed to sneak into a courtroom gallery in 1936 and observe some jury tampering. He didn't know it by that name, of course. He just saw one of

Yeager's louts obviously threatening someone who looked like the brother of a juror. He told his hero about it."

"Jack Corrigan," Ethan said.

"Yes," I said, surprised.

"I—I saw one of the columns . . ."

I thought his courage was going to desert him, but he seemed to take hold of it again. He lifted his chin a bit and said, "I saw the tribute to Corrigan he wrote just after Corrigan died, so I know Corrigan was his mentor. You say O'Connor was Corrigan's source for the jury-tampering story—did Yeager know that?"

"Yes. As a kid, O'Connor wrote little news stories that he gave to Jack. I've got those papers now. One tells of a 'copper' keeping an eye on him and protecting him from Yeager's men. And of Yeager coming by one day and scowling at him. So somehow, Yeager must have heard of O'Connor. Maybe the man who was intimidating the juror figured out O'Connor was both in the gallery that day and connected with the *Express*. Or Thelma Ducane might have let word slip."

"Okay . . . Mitch Yeager might blame O'Connor for the jury-tampering charge," Hailey said. "Would he be involved in the death of O'Connor's sister over that?"

"No, not just that. From the articles I've been looking into down here, and what I've read from O'Connor's papers, here's what I know—Mitch's brother, Adam, was in prison while he was on trial. Granville, who had taken Mitch and Adam in when they were orphaned as kids, had died just a few months before—some said that Adam's arrest had been too much for the old man to take. Adam and Mitch were, by all accounts, very close. So Mitch probably lays the arrest of his brother and the death of his grandfather at the door of Jack Corrigan—whose articles probably did have a lot to do with the investigations that led to the Yeagers' arrests."

"It's not like Corrigan committed the crimes," Hailey said.

"Yeager wouldn't be the first to blame other people for what were really the consequences of his own actions. So while he's on trial, Jack is in the courtroom every day, gloating, no doubt. You would have to know Jack Corrigan to know how well he could do that. The woman Mitch had been seeing, perhaps hoped to marry—to bring himself up in social standing if nothing else—was sitting at Jack Corrigan's side and flirting with Jack during the trial."

"Who?" Hailey asked.

"Lillian Vanderveer. Now Lillian Linworth."

"Shut up!" she said in disbelief. "He wanted *her*?"

"She was a society beauty. You'll be lucky to age as well as she has."

"I'm beginning to see what you mean," Ethan said. "It wasn't just time and money lost to a legal hassle."

"I think the worst of it for Mitch was that Adam became seriously ill with tuberculosis while he was in prison. Mitch wasn't allowed to visit him, because the tampering charges caused his bail to be revoked."

"So his brother is dying, his bail's revoked, and though he owns a lot of assets, he doesn't have much cash," Ethan said.

"Right. And all the legal work for the family grows expensive. He's had to sell assets already, and now he has to raise more money. He eventually goes free, but in the meantime his brother has died, his reputation is shot, and the best of his assets have gone to people who snub him. He's left with the care of his brother's widow and children, estate taxes, and an inheritance he's been unable to properly manage while he's dealt with his legal problems."

"And it takes him a few years to get back on his feet," Hailey said.

"Yes, and to reestablish himself in Las Piernas society. Did you find out the date of his marriage to Estelle?"

"He married her in June 1945. He eventually took over her father's businesses, which increased his wealth enormously. His own businesses were doing much better then, so he didn't come to her poor. He didn't make the kind of money Linworth and Ducane made in the late 1930s—but he was better at manipulating. From what I could learn, he maneuvered them into positions where they had to come to him for supplies. Eventually, they were all doing a lot of business with one another."

"When was the engagement announced?" I asked.

She looked through her notes. "March. There was a notice in the Society pages on March 23, 1945."

"Two weeks before O'Connor's sister was murdered," I said. "I wonder if getting engaged to Estelle made him think about losing his chance with Lillian. And around that time the *Express* carried a story about how effective the new treatments for TB were."

"Maybe it wasn't as complicated as that," Ethan said. "Maybe he was just biding his time, making sure that no one would see it as retaliation. If he had killed O'Connor's sister right after the jury-tampering conviction was overturned, he would have been caught."

"Do you really think Yeager is the one who killed her?" Hailey asked me.

"You mean, killed her himself rather than arranging it? I don't know. Eric and Ian wouldn't have been very old—not even out of grade school—so they didn't help him. There's this whole question of Harmon, though—or so I thought until the DNA came back."

"No DNA samples on file for Mitch Yeager?" Ethan asked.

"No."

"Too bad."

"Why bother anyway?" Hailey said. "He's so old, people won't want him to go to jail. There are people who don't want old *Nazis* to be punished. We don't stand a chance. He's going to throw a big old pity party for himself and people will buy into it. 'I'm an old, old man who has served the community and the paper has always hated me.' People will feel sorry for him. They won't care about the dead."

"It's our job to make them care," Ethan said. "To show them why they should. It shouldn't be hard to do that, especially if he arranged the murder of a child. People want to see wrongdoing punished."

"Well," she said, staring right at him, "some people are found guilty of wrongdoing, and the world just seems to let them off with a slap on the wrist."

That arrow found its mark, not surprisingly. He gathered his papers. He said to me, his voice not quite steady, "Forgive me—I'm not giving up, but I think we'll have to talk more another time."

He left.

Hailey shrugged, to all appearances unconcerned. I wasn't exactly fooled by those appearances, but I was too furious at her to trust myself to speak.

"Do you want to know what I found out about the Ducanes?" she asked. "The business stuff is pretty boring, but I interviewed some people who knew the parents and they didn't have much good to say."

"Funny how some people are like that. I don't think we should continue."

"When do you want to meet again, then?"

"When is the big frost expected in hell?"

"Look, I know you're mad at me because Ethan has you under his spell or whatever, but—"

"Oh no—Ethan wasn't the witch in this meeting."

"Don't you think you should have *asked* me if I *wanted* to work with him, instead of just insisting on it?"

"No. Run upstairs and ask John or Lydia to explain to you why you are not in a democracy here. I obviously cannot get a single thing through to you."

"Okay, okay, I'm sorry about what I said about Ethan, all right? All right? So can we please just get back to business?"

"You're apologizing to the wrong person. Apologize to the right one, and maybe by tomorrow I'll change my mind about not continuing to work with you on this."

I left her sitting there and went back to the newsroom. Ethan was nowhere to be seen.

I had no sooner reached my desk than the phone rang.

"Kelly," I answered.

Nothing.

I hung up. It rang again almost immediately.

I picked it up and didn't say a word.

A woman's voice said, "Hello? Hello? Is anyone there?"

"Yes, this is Irene Kelly."

"Irene Kelly? I don't know if you'll remember me . . . you talked to me twenty years ago, but I didn't tell you my name."

"Betty Bradford," I said. "I'm so glad you called."

"I'm in Zeke Brennan's office. He's agreed you can be present when I talk to the police."

63

TWO HOURS LATER, I WAS PART OF THE GATHERING IN ZEKE BRENNAN'S office. I hoped Betty Bradford felt as comfortable as I did with him. Over the years, the attorney had saved me from more than one legal tangle. Only people who've never been in that kind of jam make lawyer jokes. Zeke is one of my heroes.

Zeke held the meeting in his mid-size conference room, which had just the right number of chairs for the small crowd that was there. Betty, Zeke, and I were joined by one of Zeke's assistants, the local D.A. and one of his assistants, Frank, a lieutenant and a captain from homicide, and Hailey, who was the last to join us.

Hailey had been paged by Lydia because next to me, she had the most background on the 1958 events, and since Zeke was my lawyer, the paper wanted to keep everything on the level and have another reporter there. Hailey looked more nervous than I thought she'd be—I supposed she was rattled because she was late. Zeke had already started talking when she walked in. She shot me a distressed look, then seemed to settle into the business at hand.

Betty looked nervous, too, but who could blame her? Although knowing she was the woman in the photos allowed me to see the resemblance, she seemed to have little in common with the blond floozy of the 1950s. She was in her sixties now. Her hair was carefully dyed to a natural-looking brown, her makeup was subtle and spare. She dressed conservatively.

The D.A. and Zeke had already come to a very clear-cut agreement about her protection from prosecution in exchange for information and later testimony—a negotiating process had been under way all day.

She had done a bit of negotiating with me, too. I could come to this meeting and bring one other reporter, but under no circumstances was she to be photographed. In exchange for an exclusive, the paper agreed.

She had contacted Zeke Brennan after reading about Max Ducane's reward in the paper. She didn't want the reward, and part of the agreement with the D.A. was that she would not receive it, and that in any announcements he made about the reward, it would be noted that it was her idea to refuse it.

"I came forward because Mr. Ducane seems like a good person, and he shouldn't have to spend money for someone he isn't even related to after all. I don't want to make money from what happened to that missing child and from my part in his being kidnapped—I am deeply ashamed of having any part in that."

She had wanted to come forward in 1978, but was afraid. "I have a new family, and a new life. My husband was living then, and my kids were all at home. My husband passed away two years ago, and my children are all married and moved away from here. This has been on my mind a lot, but I've been scared. So I sold my house, and I'm moving away from here just as soon as this is all settled and you don't need me to testify or anything else. I knew I needed a good lawyer, and Mr. Brennan's name was in the article about Mr. Ducane, so I contacted him."

She proceeded to tell us of her relationship with Gus Ronden, and her certainty that he had murdered Rose Hannon and probably the child as well, although she was less sure about the murder of the baby. "I read in the paper that blood tests have already proved that Gus did that, so that part you might think I got from the paper. But I know more than that."

She talked about that night, about being told by Gus that their boss had a big plan for them, of the role she'd played in setting up Jack for a beating—she shot an anguished look at me as she told about that. She told of going back to the house, escaping to Mexico with Lew Hacker, and marrying him there. She said she came back to the U.S. after he died, got a fake ID, and married her second husband. "I'm not telling you my new name or my husband's name or any of that, because Lex will go after my kids. I know he's older than dirt, but if he's drawing breath, he'll do harm where he thinks he has a right to do it."

She got a little flustered at that point, and Brennan said, "Ms. Bradford was for many years under a misapprehension regarding the name of the leader of this group. He used some intermediaries who deliberately misled those in the lower ranks about his name . . ."

"We never saw him," she said. "Only person I ever saw giving Gus orders was Griffin Baer. For a long time I thought he was this Lex, and that was another reason I didn't think it would do any good to come forward—Griff was dead. But then, back in 1978, these Yeager guys were caught by the police, and I realized Griff was connected to them. They were always meeting over at the farm Griff owned."

"Why didn't you come forward in 1978?" the D.A. asked.

"We agreed," Brennan said, "that she would be allowed to tell her story first, and then you would be allowed to ask questions, correct?"

"Sorry," he said.

"I didn't come forward," she said, "because the guy who had the D.A.'s job before you messed up and let those guys get away with murder. They're out now, aren't they? Have been for years."

Frank and all the other representatives of the police were suddenly putting their hands over their mouths, hiding smiles.

"Plus," she said, "I thought the boss's name might really be Lex Talionis."

"*Lex talionis!*" the D.A. said.

"For those of you who may not know," Brennan said, "that means 'the law of retaliation.'"

Betty said, "You should tell them that part, Mr. Brennan."

He nodded. "I believe by adopting the name Lex Talionis, the person who chose it was announcing that he thought of himself as the embodiment of retribution—the old 'an eye for an eye' rule of reciprocal revenge. He abused it, really, because *lex talionis*—first codified in ancient Mesopotamia—ensured that only the state, and not the individual or feuding family, would be allowed to seek that revenge."

"Whatever he thought he was," Betty said, "his name was Mitch Yeager."

But when more questions were asked, it was clear that she had only guessed this relatively recently. She had seen Griffin Baer and Yeager together, but did not know that Yeager was more than a friend of Baer's at the time, and had no solid proof that Lex Talionis was Yeager. "Although I might have," she said, a little defiantly.

"If you please," Brennan said, "allow Ms. Bradford to continue. I think what she has to say will be useful to you." He turned to her. "Tell them about Mr. Harmon."

"Bennie Lee used to work for Griff, too. Or—that's what I thought. He ran errands for Griff in that Eden truck. Not all of them had to do with farms. Someone got out of line, Bennie Lee paid 'em a visit. I once asked Gus what was in that truck of Bennie's and Gus said, 'Cold meat. Don't ask so many questions or Bennie will give you a ride in back,' and he laughed. I knew he wasn't talking about steaks."

The questions began, but once more, Brennan called for quiet. "Go on, Betty."

"Well, there's one other thing. Griff had an office. I never saw him use it, so maybe it wasn't his after all—maybe it was Mitch Yeager's. I was kind of snooping around in there on the night before all this stuff happened. I had gone out to the farm with Gus, and Griff wanted to show him something outside. He said he was going to borrow my car and drive him out somewhere in the field to show him something. I was supposed to just sit there, waiting for him, while this was going on."

She paused, and took a drink of water.

"Now, looking back on it, I suppose they were trying to figure out how big of a hole he'd need for my car. I didn't know that then. I just knew he was going to get my car dirty, and I was mad. So I went into the office and decided to have a look through the desk. I'm not proud of this, or much of anything from those days, but I thought there might be some money stashed away there, and so I took a look. There was this drawer with a false back to it. You know the kind I mean?"

Everyone nodded.

"I saw this pink envelope." She smiled wistfully. "In those days, I was crazy about pink. I knew Griff was married, so I figured, 'Well, here's a little insurance, in case I need it one day,' because a girl in my . . . in the situation I was in back then . . . never feels too certain of the future. Anyway, I heard the car— Gus and Griff coming back to the house—so I stuffed the envelope into my purse, and put the drawer back like it was, and got myself out of there before they could see what I was up to." She looked to Brennan.

"Ms. Bradford kept the envelope over the years," he said. "Although she opened it, and looked at the contents, they are intact." He handed a large manila envelope to the D.A., who opened and tilted it. A small pink envelope slid out onto the table, making a sound that seemed to indicate there was something metal in it. It sat untouched for a moment. The D.A. looked to Frank. Ever-prepared homicide detective that he is, my husband had a pair of latex gloves with him. He handed them to the D.A., who put them on, then gently lifted the flap of the envelope. He tipped it over the desk and out spilled a silver locket. It was shaped like a shamrock. The chain was broken and had dark stains on it that might be rust. Or blood. I stared at it in shocked recognition.

"Have you and Mr. Brennan handled this without gloves?" the D.A. asked her.

"Just me," she said. "He only looked at it."

"It's Maureen's," I said, finding my voice.

I had everyone's attention.

"It's Maureen O'Connor's." I felt a rush of emotion as I said it. All those years. All those years . . .

"O'Connor?" the D.A. asked.

"The reporter's sister," Frank said. "She was murdered in 1945. Irene, are you sure . . . ?"

"I've got a photo of her wearing it. I didn't realize it was a locket, but it looks just like this one."

The D.A. asked for a copy of the photo. I nodded, not trusting myself to speak, still trying to get the combination of rage and relief and sadness I felt under control. In spite of the company and the situation, Frank reached over and squeezed my hand.

"You okay?"

I nodded again, took a deep breath. "What's inside?"

The D.A. gently opened it. The locket had a thin middle section, so that it held four small photos in its hinged compartments. The first ones were two handsome young men, the youngest no more than a teenager. The second, a man and a woman. I recognized the faces. "Conn O'Connor, his brother Dermot, and their parents. Her family—part of it. The ones to whom she was closest."

The questions began again. Frank asked Betty about Gus's associates, and in a way that seemed to spark some memories. I was glad for this interlude—it helped me to focus again.

Frank seemed to get some kind of high sign from his lieutenant. While they conferred, Brennan said, "Ms. Kelly, do you have questions?"

"Yes. How did Gus know that Jack Corrigan would be at Katy Ducane's birthday party?"

"He said that she'd invite him because he was her uncle, and he thought that was funny, too, so I figured he was one of her mother's lovers or something. And Gus had a couple of people watching a bar or two that he might show up in— if Corrigan did, they were supposed to call somebody else, and they would come and get us and we'd try the same thing at the bar. But Gus was pretty sure of the party, so he got an invite from someone, and Bo carried that in."

"Did Gus know Rose Hannon, the nursemaid?" Frank asked.

"Not her," she said. "I think he had dated that other one—the one that had the night off. I don't like saying that, because it makes her sound bad, like she lied. But I don't blame her for not figuring it out. Gus knew that sooner or later, the boss wanted him inside the Ducane place, so months before all this happened, Gus was trying to chat up that housekeeper. He took her out once. But she decided she didn't like him, and he didn't get her keys off her, like he wanted—I remember that made him mad. But he learned where the baby slept and where the nurse's rooms were, and all of that."

She halted for a moment, briefly losing her composure. Brennan asked her if she wanted to stop, but she shook her head, brushed away tears, and said, "I never—not in a million years—thought he was doing anything but getting set to rob the place. I swear that's true. But I should have known, I guess. Somehow I should have known."

Frank and the D.A. asked a few more questions, and it was agreed that Mr. Brennan would come with her to police headquarters the next day so that she could look through some mug shots to help identify other people who might have connections with Yeager.

"I hope I helped," she said. "Did I?"

We all assured her that she did.

I wanted to talk to Frank, but that wasn't going to work out with the lieutenant and the captain there, so we just said a quick, "See you at home," and parted company. I could see that Hailey was anxious to talk to me, so as soon we were away from the others I said, "You'd better run if you're going to get this in before drop-dead deadline. And before you get any big ideas, we need to make sure we don't use Yeager's name in a way that will get us sued. We may need to bring the company lawyers in on this one."

"Irene—I'm really worried."

"About the paper being sued? We're threatened with it all the time."

"No—"

"You'll make deadline. I have faith."

"No! Not the paper. I'm worried about Ethan."

"Me, too. But now's not—"

"Then you know?"

"Know what?"

"He was going to go over to Mitch Yeager's house."

64

"TELL ME," I ORDERED HER, WISHING FRANK HADN'T JUST LEFT WITH HIS bosses.

"I felt a little bad about what I had said. I saw him leave the building tonight, and I followed him out to this bar—"

"Oh hell."

"He didn't go in. He kind of hung around outside it, then he walked down the street to this coffee place some of us hang out at sometimes—you know, people who were in J-school together. Anyway, I could see he was upset. He was calling someone on his cell phone, so I didn't come too near him at first. I wanted to give him some privacy."

"What happened?"

"He saw me and waved me over, said he had just been talking to his sponsor." She blushed. "I thought he meant he had some kind of deal, you know, like an athlete with a shoe company. Then he told me it was a friend from AA. Anyway, I tried talking to him, because I could see he was still really bugged by what I had said to him. Things were going okay, he was cool—but then I don't know, we got into it again. My fault, I guess. He was mad at me for saying we couldn't do any good. He said, you know, 'Then why show up for work at a newspaper, why tell anybody anything if nobody really cares . . .'"

"How did this lead to Mitch Yeager's house?"

"He said that the only thing anyone needed to do was get DNA from Mitch Yeager."

"And you told him that was a job for the police, right?"

She looked away, then said, "God, this is all my fault."

"You can enjoy your guilt trip later, Hailey. What the hell happened?"

"I was, like, 'Oh sure, just call him up and ask him for his toothbrush.' He asked if I had Yeager's phone number. I did. I had looked it up a few weeks ago, to try to get a comment from him for a story."

"You're telling me Yeager answered the phone and told him to come on over?"

"Ethan was awesome. He called and whoever answered said Mr. Yeager was with guests—some kind of party he's having tonight. Ethan says, 'Yes, I know, I'm supposed to be there now. Please ask Mr. Yeager to come to the phone. Tell him it's Mr. Harmon from Eden Supply.'"

"Jesus, Mary, and Joseph . . ."

"Yeager comes on and Ethan apologizes for getting him to the phone in that way, and quickly gives Yeager this story about how he—Ethan, I mean—was your worst enemy, and everyone on the *Express* hated Ethan because of what he had done, and how it made him feel sympathy for Yeager, because the *Express* was so unfair to both of them. If he could stay on staff, he'd try to tell some of these stories about Las Piernas's past from a perspective Irene Kelly might not like, but he needed a really good interview to do that, and he was hoping Mr. Yeager would grant him that favor."

"Yeager fell for that?"

"No. But then he kept him on the phone somehow, hinting around about a bunch of stuff, and ended up saying, well, okay, he probably wasn't going to be able to continue to be a reporter, so he'd have to look for some other way to support himself. Which was too bad, because he was good at interviews and learned things that other people might not know. And oh—that reminded him that Bennie Lee Harmon said Eden Supply was a good company, and that Bennie Lee would give Ethan a reference if Ethan ever contacted his boss. Yeager told him that maybe something could be arranged, but he was entertaining some people this evening."

"And that was that?" I said, hoping against hope.

"No, Ethan said matters were a little rushed, so Yeager said to come over at eleven, they could talk then."

"Oh, shit . . ." I looked at my watch. It was eight-thirty. Still plenty of time to talk Ethan out of this.

"At first I thought he had faked the whole phone call," she said. "I didn't believe him—told him Yeager's butler probably hung up on him two seconds into the call, and I was just hearing more bullshit from him. Ethan got really mad. He said fine, he'd tape-record the whole interview, and he'd get DNA from Yeager if he had to reach across the desk and stab him with his pen to do it."

I resisted my own impulse to do the same to her. "Where is he now?"

"I'm not sure, but I think he's at his place."

"Do you know Ethan's home phone number?"

"Not by heart, but it's listed. I've got his cell number."

"Okay, I'll call information, you call the cell phone. If you reach him, hand the phone over. If you don't, leave my cell number on his voice mail and tell him it's urgent—that he must talk to me before he sees Yeager. Tell him it's seriously a matter of life and death."

She called. As I was reaching information, she got voice mail. She left a message. I could hear in her voice that she thought the life-and-death bit was overly dramatic.

I got Ethan's number and asked if there was an address listed as well. "Oh yes," the operator said, and gave it to me.

Oh hell, I thought, as I wrote it down.

I called. He answered. That in and of itself nearly made me speechless with relief. Nearly. "Ethan? Irene. Do you want to keep working at the *Express*?"

"Hailey is such a little—"

"Never mind that, and it really doesn't matter who told me. You and I must talk face-to-face this evening. Immediately. No choice—you understand?"

"Yes."

"Do you have a deadbolt lock?" I asked.

"Yes."

"Bolt the door. Turn on your cell phone, because you may need it. Do not let anyone but me in the door. If your own mother comes to the door—"

"She's dead, so I'll assume it's just a zombie pretending to be my mother. But I won't let anyone else in. I won't go out in the corridor, even if someone sets the building on fire." His tone was flat—he sounded resigned, a little too resigned.

"Thank you. I'll be there as soon as I can."

"Don't you need directions?"

"Still living on Chestnut?"

"Yes—oh, you got it from the phone book. Apartment eight." He paused. "You think someone else could get my address the same way."

"Exactly. If someone tries to get in, call the police. Don't hesitate."

I hung up, then asked Hailey, "Did Yeager know you were there when he talked to Ethan?"

She shook her head. She was looking a little pale. I think she was starting to get the bigger picture.

"I want you to promise me that you will never, ever attempt something so stupid as going one-on-one with Mitch Yeager."

She promised. She promised to be careful driving back to the paper.

"Ask security to walk you out to your car when you leave," I said.

I tried to call Frank. His cell phone wasn't on, and he wasn't back at his office yet. I left a message on both voice mails, telling him I needed to talk something over with Ethan and would be home late, but he could reach me on my cell phone if needed. I also gave him Ethan's home number. "It's a long story, but—it might be a good idea for him to stay with us for a few days," I said. "Would that be okay? Let me know."

Ethan lived in an old apartment building in a tough part of town. I found a street lamp and parked beneath it. As I locked the Jeep up and set the alarm, I prayed I wouldn't have to call LoJack to find out where it was later that night.

The building was long and two stories tall, a flat-roofed Spanish-style structure, probably built in the 1930s. The mailboxes at the entrance indicated there were sixteen units in the building.

Although it was moving toward nine o'clock on a weeknight, I could hear voices and music and laughter coming from the building. A party palace. The noises coming from it were the kinds of noises you might hear in the hallway of a college dorm on a Friday night—a confined space occupied by individuals watching a dozen different television shows at high volume, listening to just as many different kinds of music, each trying to hear their own above others—apparently, not one of the tenants believed in headphones. The glass front door was framed by dark wood and could have easily been smashed open by anyone who really wanted to get in, but I took the easy route and pushed the buzzer above Ethan's mailbox. I pulled his name tag off it, which made it one of five blank ones. There was no sound from the intercom, but the door started humming and rattling, so I pushed it open.

My senses were assailed by both a louder edition of the noise I had heard outside, and a strong odor of urine and dried vomit in the foyer. I rushed back outside, remembering just in time not to let the door latch behind me. I took a deep breath, went back in, and held the breath all the way up the stairs, not exhaling until I reached the second level. The stairs ended at a short hallway at the front of the building. I glanced out a window there and saw that the Jeep was still where I had left it.

Apartment eight was to the right and at the rear of the building. The air quality was better in this dimly lit hall, but not by much. As I passed doors, the particular music of that apartment dweller intensified and became a little clearer. Two steps later, it was jumbled into the mix.

No wonder Ethan wasn't getting much sleep.

I knocked on his door, saw the peephole in it darken, and heard the lock click back. The door opened.

"Hi," he said, and gestured me inside.

He was still wearing his work clothes, a suit that hung loosely on him. His dark blond hair was slightly shaggy, but it actually looked better that way than it had in the shorter style he had worn before he went away to rehab.

The room we were in was neat and furnished in a spare way, with a table and chairs and sofa that looked as if they were not with their first owner. Or second or third, for that matter. I glanced around. It might as well have been a hotel room—nothing personal.

He had watched this perusal as he leaned against the back of the door, arms crossed. "No, it's not much," he said.

"Not home, either, is it?"

"I've only noticed that recently," he said, and moved toward the kitchen. "Can I offer you something to drink?" He smiled at my raised brow and added, "Coffee, water, tea?"

"Coffee would be great—but before you do that, call Mitch Yeager and tell him that you are sorry to have bothered him and won't be coming over, that you were trying to impress a girl who dared you to get an interview with him. That you never actually interviewed Harmon and will not be troubling him in any way. That will be the first call. I may have you make a second one to the homicide division of the Las Piernas Police Department, to tell my husband what you've done, so that he can tell you whether or not you have just completely fucked up a major investigation."

"I was trying to help it. I'm not so sure that I shouldn't still try to help it."

"Ethan, this is all very noble, but you cannot walk into the police department with Mitch Yeager's blood on your pen—yes, Hailey told me about that—and tell them that they now have what they need to arrest him for murder. For one thing, that's not your job. For another, I sincerely doubt it will stand up in court as a legal way for them to obtain evidence. And it is hardly ethical for you to have tried to blackmail Yeager into an interview by lying your ass off, is it?"

"No, but . . . no, it's not." He put his hands up to his face, ran them up through his hair. "I let Hailey get to me. She was—no, never mind, I'm not going to blame her." He opened his cell phone, used it to look up Yeager's number, then called from his land line. He hung up. "The line's busy."

"We'll try again in a few minutes. In the meantime—Ethan, I'm so worried about you."

"Afraid I'll start drinking again?"

"No—I mean, maybe you will, maybe you won't. Right now I'm seriously hoping you will live long enough to struggle with your alcoholism. You've undoubtedly pissed off a man who arranged for the deaths of more than half a dozen people because he wanted to seek revenge in the cruelest way possible. He was willing to scheme and wait for years to carry out vengeance the first time, but at his current age, I doubt he'll bother with long-range planning again. I'm hoping he didn't realize other people heard you talking to him."

He sat in silence. Then he said, "Maybe if he comes after me, he'd be doing the world a favor."

"Ethan, if you will just pull your head out of your ass, you'll see that you've got a bright future."

He laughed. "Okay. I'll call a halt to the pity party. Thanks."

"Good. Try Yeager again."

He called. This time, someone answered. I heard Ethan ask for Yeager, then say, "Oh . . . Well, listen—will you please tell him that Ethan Shire will not be coming by this evening after all? . . . That's right, I called earlier. . . . No, I'm not coming by . . . and please tell him that—that I'm very sorry to have bothered him, that I was just making stuff up, and it was all a stupid dare to impress a girl, and I'm sorry. And he can call me later and I'll explain and apologize for disturbing him. Did you get all that? . . . Yes, that's it. . . . Thank you. And sorry about earlier, when I made you bother him. . . . Thanks . . . Bye."

He hung up and said, "He couldn't come to the phone. Do you think that will be enough?"

"To be honest, I'm still worried."

My cell phone rang. It was Frank. "Collecting strays again?" he asked.

"Yes."

"I suppose you want to tell me that this one is a real doozy, but he's right there."

"Yes."

"That's okay, they're all doozies. Bring him over. Especially if that gets you home faster."

"Thanks. You know, I think your grandmother was the last person to use that word."

"Doozy? No, I picked that one up from you."

"Touché," I said, laughing. "See you soon."

"Where are you, by the way?"

"Over on Chestnut near Polson."

"Jesus—"

"We're leaving just as soon as he can pack an overnight bag. I'll be home soon. And, Frank—"

"You love me and you want me to hide the booze. I remember what you told me about him. No problem. We won't make it harder on him than it already is."

"Thanks."

He said he'd wait up for us, and we said good-bye.

"Are you allergic to cats or dogs?" I asked Ethan as I put the phone away.

"No, why?"

"I've got two big dogs and a cat." I explained to him that I thought it might be best if we put him up for a while.

"I couldn't . . ."

"Sure you could. You'll be safer, our animals will appreciate the added attention, and I won't be up all night wondering if Yeager has figured out that you're listed in the phone book. Stay at least until they have enough on Yeager to arrest him," I said. "Or until you can find another place to live."

"I've imposed enough on you."

"The imposition will be if I have to spend another hour or two demonstrating that I am really much more stubborn than you. Go and pack what you'll need for tonight and tomorrow, and then Frank can come back with you over the weekend."

He hesitated.

"Are you so attached to this place you can't bear to leave?"

He looked around the empty room and sighed. "No."

He stepped into the hallway, which led to a bathroom and bedroom, and opened the hall closet. He pulled a garment bag from it. "You know, I don't think what I said about Eden Supply bothered Mitch Yeager much."

"Let's not bet on it. He had no idea that anyone knew the name of the company or connected it to him until you blurted that out to him. That information wasn't public yet."

This had obviously not occurred to him, because his eyes widened in dismay. "Shit!"

"Too late to worry about it now, Ethan. What were you trying to say about Yeager being bothered?"

"Just that it seemed to me that he was more upset by something I lied about completely, you know, trying to get him to think I knew more than I did."

"Like what?"

"Well, I told him that I had helped you go through some things of O'Connor's before I got in trouble, and that while you were going through O'Connor's stuff, I was going through the things that belonged to his murdered sister. I said maybe O'Connor had been too heartbroken to ever look at them, or just didn't know what he was seeing, but that I had found a few items that belonged to Maureen that might be worth something to somebody. I said I was sure he knew why I thought he'd be interested in them. That was when he agreed to see me."

"What items?"

"I was bluffing, so I didn't get specific."

"The sooner we get out of here, the better. And I hope to God they don't break into the storage unit."

While he packed up a few items from the bedroom and bathroom, I told him about our meeting with Betty Bradford.

He glanced around the apartment again, then said, "I think that's everything." He patted the front of his suit coat and said, "Oh, I forgot—"

But before I could learn what it was he forgot, the door to the apartment came flying open.

Eric Yeager stood pointing a gun at us, and Ian came in not much behind him, also armed. Eric moved forward, and Ian closed the door.

"Must be my lucky day," Eric said.

65

THEY DIDN'T LOOK ALL THAT DIFFERENT FROM WHEN I'D LAST SEEN THEM, during their trial. Their clothing was dark and more casual this time, and they were wearing gloves. They had gained some weight, gone a little soft around the middle, but they were tall and big-shouldered. Nothing about them said they lacked strength. Their faces were a little more wrinkled. They had better tans. Their hair might have been dyed. I noted these things in nothing more than a glimpse, because I couldn't seem to make myself take my eyes off the business ends of their guns.

"Hands folded on top of your head," Eric said.

Ethan said, "No need to hold guns on us—"

"We'll decide that," Ian said. "Now hands up and shut up." He looked over at me. "What's she doing here?"

"I thought you two were enemies," Eric said to Ethan. "Wasn't that the story you gave my uncle? What's with the luggage?"

"I'm afraid our secret's out now," Ethan said to me, with a look that did an excellent job of mixing embarrassment with adoration.

"Ethan, for God's sake . . ." I said in exasperation.

"You two have ruined everything," Ethan said to them. "We could have been gone before her husband discovered us."

We are going to be killed, I thought, seeing Eric's anger. Right now. I'm going to die on the carpet of this crappy apartment.

"Eric!" Ian said sharply.

"You'll be gone all right," Eric said to Ethan. "Now shut your mouth."

They bound our wrists behind us with duct tape and took my purse and keys. They forced us to walk out to the Jeep. I kept hoping that one of the party animals in Ethan's building would open his door and see that two people were being led out at gunpoint. No luck. Eric and Ian probably could have capped us right there in the hallway without anyone knowing about it for hours.

Eric disarmed the alarm, and they put us in the backseat of the Jeep. I found myself thinking wildly that at least he couldn't stuff us in a trunk. Eric and Ian got in the front seats—after arguing briefly over who would drive, Eric took the driver's seat. He locked all our doors. He put on his seat belt and adjusted the mirrors. These little actions of protecting his safety as he stole my car with me in it had the effect of making me angry, which took a little of the edge off my fear. I calmed downed enough to find a slim hope. The LoJack.

Someone had to report the car missing, though, before police would try to track the LoJack's signal. How long before Frank would think he needed to call me, let alone come looking for my car?

I looked over at Ethan to see how he was faring. He seemed to have been waiting for my attention. He leaned toward me and whispered, almost too low for me to hear, "Trust me."

Right. I tried not to let him see just how stupid I thought that idea was. I saw Ian glance up in the rearview mirror.

At that moment, in a voice a little louder than a whisper, Ethan said, "Not the secret place. Tell them it's at the storage unit."

Ian, who had not put on his seat belt, whipped around and pointed his gun at us. "I told you to shut up, you sneaky little bastard."

Eric drove a convoluted route, and then, not more than three blocks from where we had started, the car turned down a ramp that led into a parking structure. Eric pulled out a key card and pushed it into a slot. This raised a heavy steel gate. He drove under it, and the gate lowered. I felt my hopes lower with it. It sealed us in.

He drove through the deserted structure, following the curve of the ramp to a level that could not be seen by anyone who might approach the other side of the gate at street level.

He came to a stop near a long limousine. He got out of the Jeep. The back window of the limousine rolled down. After a brief discussion, he came back and told Ian, "He wants them out."

We were taken from the Jeep.

Ian walked over to me, and without saying a word, punched me in the face. I lost my balance and fell hard to the concrete. My head was swimming. Ian stood over me, smiling down. "That's just the beginning of what I owe you," he said, and kicked me in the ribs. My feet were still free, so I kicked him back hard, on the ankle.

"God damn it!" he shouted, and aimed his gun at my head.

Ethan shouted, "No, don't . . . please . . ."

"Ian!"

Ian turned toward the man who had called his name.

Mitch Yeager was not frail. He stood straight and tall, his large, dark eyes boring into Ian's. His skin looked a bit translucent and his hair was on the thin and weedy side, but he was not, despite my hopes, someone who looked ready to pop off at any moment. He had been handsome in his day, but there was little sign of that now. His mouth had a bitter set to it that seemed to pull all his features into following its lead.

He was a big man, but a little shorter than his nephews. That he still stood in command of Eric and Ian was clear. Ian lowered his eyes and moved back from me, unable to meet his uncle's stare. Mitch glanced at Eric, who ducked his head as well. I looked for some sign of the rebelliousness Eric had shown in the past and didn't see it.

Mitch turned the stare on Ethan, who wasn't hiding his feelings so well now, and I knew that any second, the old man would notice the fear and remorse I was seeing on Ethan's face. I slowly maneuvered myself to my feet again and tried to convey to Ethan, with nothing more than a look, that I was okay, that he should calm down.

He got the message. He pulled himself back into his ace bullshitter mode.

He smiled at Mitch. "I'm glad you can see there's no need to hurt anyone. This is all just a simple misunderstanding."

"Is it?" Mitch Yeager asked.

"Of course it is. I can see that you might misunderstand our intentions, but we just needed a little traveling money, that's all. We both want to get as far away from Frank Harriman's reach as possible, and you know, that's not going to be cheap. We have to relocate outside the U.S., right, honey?"

I smiled weakly. It hurt my mouth.

"A little old for you, isn't she?" Mitch asked.

"No," Ethan said simply. I was relieved he didn't try to oversell that. I was feeling embarrassed enough as it was.

It seemed to work, because after Yeager looked between us, he said, "We haven't got time for your romance, Mr. Shire. Now. You have something of mine."

"It's in a storage unit not far from here."

Mitch looked at Ian. Ian hauled off and punched Ethan.

He lost his balance and fell onto the concrete.

Ian kicked him, making him cry out in pain. He curled his legs up to his chest, trying to protect himself from another blow.

"Stop it!" I shouted. My voice echoed throughout the structure, a voice lost in a concrete canyon. That earned me a gloved hand clapped over my mouth. I bit it. That won a slap hard enough to make me dizzy.

"Get him on his feet," Mitch said. He turned to me. "You shut your mouth, or I'll have him tape it shut, you understand?"

I nodded.

"Now," Mitch said to Ethan. "Where is it?"

Ethan's eyes were starting to tear up. He said, "I told you."

Mitch nodded. Ian hit him again.

Ethan hit the ground and groaned as he lay there. His mouth and nose were bleeding now.

"Hit him again," Mitch said.

"No, wait," I said. "Wait!" Eric reached into the pocket that held the duct tape.

Mitch turned toward me and motioned Eric to wait.

"It was never necessary for matters to reach this point," Mitch said. "You've forced all of us to do things we'd prefer not to do. But since you've brought all this trouble about, I should warn you that I don't mind the idea of killing you both. And it really wouldn't bother me at all to see you suffer before you die. I may only have a few minutes to do that, but I know ways to make your last few minutes seem like hours. Do you understand? Now, what were you about to say?"

I tried not to let him see how scared I was. He was an expert in suffering, all right—I thought of what he had done to O'Connor and his family by killing Maureen and hiding her body—and with that thought, I had my answer, as clearly as if O'Connor was standing right at my side to prompt it.

"The cemetery."

"What?" Mitch said. "What the hell did you say?"

"Municipal Cemetery."

Ethan's eyes had widened. He clearly thought I was crazy.

Yeager looked at him and perhaps misread his reaction—believed Ethan was upset that a secret had been told. He studied Ethan, then said, "Now, why should you pick a place like that?"

I tried mental telepathy, prayers, you name it, hoping he could see some reasons—the cemetery was not near here, so getting over there would give us some time. Openness, darkness, headstones, and statuary to hide behind. Better for our chances of survival than the narrow enclosed storage unit.

"I wrote a story about it," Ethan said. "I go there a lot."

"Why?"

"It's closed now, because of the investigations they did after the story broke. But who knows what they might find there? So I know which graves they're working on, and which ones they've finished with."

"An investigation, and they just let you have the run of the place?"

Ethan smiled up at him, his battered face not affecting his ability to look cocky. "They wouldn't have an investigation at all if it weren't for me, would they? And they're used to seeing me around, supposedly doing follow-up, so they don't pay much attention to me or anything I'm doing."

"Get him off the floor."

He groaned again as Ian pulled him up by an arm. He didn't look too steady on his feet this time.

"Keep talking," Mitch said. "Make it fast."

"There are a lot of empty crypts and graves. There are others that have too many bodies in them. Some vaults that don't have coffins in them—a nice place to store something if you need to. No one is going to be buried in Municipal Cemetery any time soon—the state is taking forever, having a forensic anthropologist work on it, all of that. Ben Sheridan. He's taken over part of one of the buildings just to sort bones."

I realized that some of what he was saying must be true—he must have gone by the cemetery fairly recently, or he wouldn't know about Ben.

"Never mind that," Mitch said.

"I'm just saying, I'm one of the few people allowed in there."

"At this time of night?"

"No, but I know a way in."

"No night watchman?"

"That's the beauty of it. The people who were robbing the graves and moving bodies around were with the company that operated the cemetery. The night watchman was in on it. He was fired."

"And not replaced yet?"

"No. There are police patrols. At first they came by a lot, but it's been over a month now, so they've cut back. The cops have already seen me there, too, supposedly hoping for a follow-up story, trying to get the mood of the place at night right. They think I'm kind of pitiful, really. If we're careful, they won't be a problem."

"Seems like too much trouble for a hiding place. Maybe I should have your apartment searched, just in case you're full of shit."

"Go ahead. You won't find what you're looking for. You ought to know why I chose the cemetery."

Mitch's eyes narrowed. "Me?"

"I got the idea from you," Ethan said. "From the orange grove. Let some-one else do all the digging, right? What's a better place to bury something than a grave?"

Mitch smiled. "Or bury someone."

He walked back to his limousine. If he left us in the garage with his nephews, we were as good as dead. Or, considering the Yeagers' ideas about suffering, maybe not that good.

He halted, then called Eric over to him. I felt a cold sweat break out on my forehead. I thought of running now, taking cover wherever I could, hoping Frank would be looking for the Jeep, hoping the LoJack signal would work two levels down in an underground garage. This plan seemed unlikely to do anything other than get both of us killed.

I glanced over at Ethan. His face was still bleeding, but he held his head up. When he saw that I was looking at him, he managed a small smile—not a cocky one this time. It seemed to say, *So far, so good. Hang in there.*

It reached me in a way no threat from Yeager could have. I stood straighter. He noticed and gave a little nod.

Eric came back. "We're all going in the Jeep."

"All of us?" Ian said.

"Yes. You drive, I'll get in back with these two. Smart boy here is going to show that he's not stupid enough to try to bullshit the Yeagers."

66

MITCH DISMISSED HIS LIMO AND DRIVER AND GOT INTO THE FRONT passenger seat of my Jeep, where he began barking orders. Although Ian had lived in Las Piernas for several decades, either he had no sense of direction or he had never learned where Municipal Cemetery was.

We drove into the hills above the city. At one point, I disagreed with Mitch on how to get there, trying to prolong the drive.

"Shut your pie hole," Eric said, leveling his gun at me. "And keep it shut. Far as I can tell, you've already been all the use you're going to be to us, anyway."

I sat back as far as my taped wrists would allow.

We came within sight of the cemetery. We drove past its front gates, which were locked. A tall, solid plywood fence stood behind the gates, the kind you sometimes see around construction sites, in this case, apparently to block a view into the cemetery. Just over the top of the temporary fence, faint moonlight reflected off the top portions of a yellow backhoe and a dump truck parked near it. A large sign read MUNICIPAL CEMETERY TEMPORARILY CLOSED and gave a number for families and others to call.

"All right," Mitch said, "where's this secret entrance of yours, kid?"

Ethan directed Ian down a small side road. The road ran along the eastern edge of the cemetery for a short distance before dead-ending at a field. "Park here," he said. To our left was an auto body shop and next to it, a screen door repair shop. Both businesses were dark and locked up for the night.

We sat there for a few minutes with the engine running while Eric got out and looked around, checking for traps. Eventually, he motioned that all was okay, and came back to help Ian take us out of the car.

Almost from the first breath, it was there—not overwhelming, but distinct. A mustiness, mixed with the slightly sweet scent that sometimes mingles with that of decay.

Ian sniffed at the air and made a face.

"I know," Eric said. "What is that?"

"Open graves," Ethan said.

The brothers exchanged a look. "You're shitting me," Eric said.

"He's telling the truth," I said.

There were other scents and sounds as well. Las Piernas Municipal Cemetery is a little over a century old and was at one time surrounded by oil derricks. Most of the derricks are gone, but the pumping units remain, and we heard the rhythmic growling sound of the rotating gears of several oil well pumps in the field beyond the cemetery.

I watched with irritation as Ian locked up the Jeep and set the alarm on it. He had kidnapped us, used my own car to drive us around, and he was already acting as if it were his to protect? From what, a criminal?

Eric's cell phone rang. He listened for a moment, then said, "Have the chopper ready. We'll call again."

"The chopper?" I asked.

"Nothing for you to worry about," Mitch said.

The look Ethan gave me then made my stomach drop. I supposed we were thinking the same thing. If the Yeagers left in a helicopter, they might be able to get to a plane and perhaps out of the country before anyone knew what had happened to us. And if the people on the helicopter were armed or used a spotlight, we would have difficulty hiding among the tombstones until we were free.

I watched Ethan. For the next few minutes at least, my life was going to be in his hands. Everything would be decided by his ability to stall them without being obvious about it and to convince them that he had hidden something here.

"Do you have flashlights?" he asked.

Eric looked at him suspiciously, perhaps suspecting a joke at his expense, given their previous problems with fingerprints on flashlights.

"There's only a little moonlight," Ethan said. "The cemetery is torn up. We'll need flashlights."

"You have any in your car?" Mitch asked me with exasperation.

I considered a lie, decided against it, and told him where to find the flashlights in the Jeep—one in the glove compartment, the other in the back storage compartment. Ian got back in the Jeep, found them, and reset the alarm.

"Okay," Ethan said, "untie our hands."

"Giving a lot of orders, aren't you?" Mitch said. "Not going to happen."

Ethan shrugged. "That's going to cause problems, but suit yourself."

The first problem became evident as soon as the flashlights were distributed. Eric and Ian had to hold both a flashlight and a gun or risk not having a light to use to reveal their target. I could see Mitch didn't like it, but he was too proud to back down.

Ian stayed with Ethan. Eric stayed with me. Mitch walked between us.

We followed Ethan as he walked slowly along a brick fence that had occasional panels of wrought iron. The view into the cemetery was again blocked by plywood panels temporarily in place over the wrought iron. There was already some graffiti on them.

I was glad for the slow pace, not only because we needed to stall but because I was feeling the effects of their earlier blows and the fall I had taken in the garage. Ian, impatient, told Ethan to move faster.

"If you hadn't kicked the shit out of me, I could," Ethan said, one hand on his ribs.

He led us toward the back of the cemetery. I wondered whether this was mere stalling on his part. If so, I hoped he walked us all around the perimeter.

As we moved from the street into the knee-high grasses of the field, the scenery changed a bit. The field was owned by the city, but was undeveloped. We were nearer some of the pumping units now, and could see their horse-heads bobbing up and down eerily in moonlight, their beams seesawing as the counterweights rolled.

The barrier along the back of the cemetery was a rusting chain-link fence—about seven feet high. It was not in good repair. Before the cemetery was closed for the investigations, visitors were spared a view of this ratty fence by the trees and the tall, thick oleanders that now blocked our view of the cemetery. I wondered if Ethan planned to have us crawl through one of the gaps near the foot of it, but he kept walking.

Eventually, we came to an asphalt driveway that led from the road on the western side of the cemetery to a pair of rolling chain-link gates near some large metal sheds. A heavy chain and thick padlock held them shut. As we came to a halt by the gates, Eric pocketed his gun and took hold of my elbow, apparently afraid I'd run off and leave Ethan behind.

"Why the hell didn't we come in this way?" Mitch asked angrily. "We could have parked on that other street and saved time."

"And have everyone in the world see a car parked here? That street isn't a busy one, but it gets traffic."

"Maybe I'll tape your smart mouth shut next," Mitch said.

Ethan stood silent.

Mitch smiled. "Hell, scream if you want to. Nobody inside that boneyard is going to come to your rescue. And you were stupid enough to bring us all the way out here. So now what?"

"We go in. As I said before, you'll need to untie our hands."

"Why?"

"I won't be able to squeeze through the gate if they're tied behind my back."

"I don't trust you."

"Okay, let Ian squeeze through. Once he's in, I'll tell him where to find the gate key."

Mitch took Ian's gun and told him to go in.

Ian, looking dubious, stepped up to the gates and pulled them apart. He got a leg through, then said, "I can't fit, Uncle Mitch. It'll take my balls off, trying to get through."

Mitch glanced at Ian's older brother and obviously realized there was no hope there, either.

"Get your lard ass back here, then. You two have turned into a couple of butterballs, lying on your big bellies on the beach all day. I still have to take care of things myself if I want them done right, don't I? Never know how much you two will fuck things up on your own." He eyed me briefly, then asked Eric what the fuck was wrong with him, standing there with nothing but his flashlight in his hand? Eric turned red, then switched off the light and exchanged it for his gun.

"Now grab on to her," Mitch ordered, "and put that gun right up against her head. . . . Good." He turned to Ethan. "Okay, smart boy, I'm going to promise you that once you are through that gate, you had better return in five minutes, or she's dead."

"That's not long enough!"

"That's how long you have. So Ian will cut you loose and give you a flashlight, and I had better be able to see where you are with that light every one of those five minutes—"

"Then we've come out here for nothing," Ethan said. "The spare key isn't hidden within sight of the gate, for God's sake. It's around the corner, on the other side of that maintenance shed. You won't see me the whole time and I can't do it in five minutes."

Held by a beefy arm around my throat, feeling the painful press of cold metal on my temple, I couldn't think very clearly, but I still managed to wonder if it was smart for him to be challenging Mitch in this way.

Then I saw Ian's face, and the hint of amusement on it. Maybe Ethan was trying to undermine Mitch's authority as much as he could.

"And why shouldn't I just save myself a whole lot of time and kill you both? I'm trying to remember . . ."

"You think we did this not knowing who we were up against?" I said. "We made sure that if we were to vanish or to be found dead, the truth would come out."

"Miss Kelly, I think you've watched too much television."

"I haven't had time for TV. I've been busy studying you for twenty years, you selfish old man. People have a habit of disappearing around you. Ian and Eric are too young to remember Gus Ronden or Betty Bradford, but—"

"I remember them," Eric said. "What happened to them, Uncle Mitch?"

"We're wasting time!" Mitch said. "Cut the smart aleck loose and let him get in there. And Eric, damn it, if she doesn't keep her yap shut, shut it for her."

Ian cut Ethan loose, and I watched Ethan wince as the circulation returned to his hands. Another moment passed before he had enough feeling in them to be able to hold the flashlight. Ethan walked to the gate, then held the flashlight out and said, "I'm going to tuck this inside my jacket. I won't fit through the gates myself if I put it in my hip pocket. I just don't want any misunderstandings." He slowly tucked it in the pocket, making sure his hands stayed visible as he did it.

He pulled the gates apart and began to squeeze between them. I heard his breath catch on a small sound of pain as his bruised ribs were pressed against the metal supports of the gates.

A moment later, he was through, and the flashlight was out again. Ian took Eric's flashlight and tried to position himself to fire on Ethan should he reappear with a weapon or some other surprise.

"Where are you?" Mitch called.

"On the other side of the shed," Ethan called back.

"I don't like this," Mitch said. "I don't like this at all."

We all listened, ears straining for sound. Nothing could be heard over the rumbling and creaking of the oil well pumps.

As what seemed like two or three eternities passed, I began to wonder if I had fooled myself into thinking Ethan cared about what happened to me. What if he just hared off, jumping over a fence on the other side of the cemetery and leaving me and the Yeagers standing in our little semicircle? Or hid in there the rest of the night, or at least until the police showed up? I could be long past being able to tell anyone my version of events.

I told myself that would not be the worst possible outcome. In all likelihood, that was the best we could hope for. Maybe Ethan was practical enough to see that.

But even with Eric's gun at my head and a cold feeling of certainty that I would not survive the night settling in on me, even knowing that Ethan had screwed up so many other times in his life and was a self-acknowledged liar and manipulator, I thought of how he toughed out those days at the paper and couldn't bring myself to believe he was abandoning me. I was not cheered by this thought. I didn't much want to die alone, but I wanted less for the two of us to die together.

In the next moment, he came back around the corner, his flashlight beam marking his progress as he returned to the gate. Fool, I thought, close to tears. You brave damned fool.

The Yeagers were relieved. I could feel Eric relax his grip slightly, and he eased the pressure of the gun away. A moment later, as Ethan fit the key into the padlock, Eric stepped back from me.

The chain fell free, and Ethan pulled the gates in. He looked toward me and said, "Welcome to my cemetery."

67

HIS CEMETERY LOOKED AS IF IT HAD BEEN TOSSED.

"Most of the grave robbing was done to the older ones," Ethan said. "They figured no one who cared about these people would still be around. But they also went for a few of the newer ones."

Mounds of dirt stood next to open graves, vaults were aboveground, and excavation equipment was parked here and there. The investigation had not yet extended into every corner of the cemetery, but where it was under way, it seemed doubtful the permanent occupants were resting in peace.

The odors were much stronger inside the cemetery. Rain had fallen during the weeks of investigation, and water collected in the bottom of the graves, intensifying the dankness and scents of decay. I could also smell traces of formalin and other chemical smells from embalming. Perhaps not in fact, but in my mind, the scent of human decay overrode all the others.

In a cemetery where no one had disturbed the burials, this rank smell would not have been present, but the practice of opening coffins and moving bodies from coffins into graves where more than one body was placed, or reburying bodies without coffins, had obviously made the soil here subject to saturation with it.

Ethan walked us past a few graves, then suddenly looked around, as if confused.

Not hiding his disgust, Mitch said, "You never found anything in Maureen's belongings, did you?"

"Not exactly," Ethan admitted.

"You son of—" Ian said angrily, but Ethan held a hand up.

"Irene got it from Betty. Betty stole it from your desk at the farmhouse. You know what I'm talking about?"

Mitch's eyes narrowed. "The locket. That bitch. I always wondered . . . but that doesn't prove shit, does it?"

"Oh, together with what we found among Maureen's papers, yes, I think it does. Which is why we had to find a safe place for it."

"Where is it?" Mitch asked. "Where'd you put it?"

"I have to find the right vault," Ethan said, looking around again. "I was afraid of this—they've done more digging. I need to find the tombstone of Alice Pelck." He spelled the last name.

"Who's Alice Pelck?"

"Hell if I know, I just used her tombstone as the marker. It's one of the big ones with an angel looking down from it." We looked across the cemetery and saw about fifty angels. He used his flashlight to make his way over to the nearest one. "No, that's not her."

"Don't go running off," Mitch said, ordering Eric to hand over his gun and stay close to Ethan and Ian. Mitch would stay with me. I didn't like that much—I had been hoping we could separate the brothers.

Ethan said to me, "They moved the excavator that was parked near here, and now I can't find her. Do you remember where she is?"

"I thought she was over there," I said, pointing to a nearby section, one that was crowded with equipment, old trees, and at least two dozen stone angels. They must have been all the rage at some point in Las Piernas's history.

Moving the flashlight in a sweeping motion, spotlighting grave markers here and there, Ethan walked toward the area where I had pointed, Eric close behind. Ian held both flashlight and gun and began to run the light over tombstones, joining the search for Alice Pelck. Eric, although far from helpless, now had no gun and no light. Glancing uneasily around him, he jumped when a breeze stirred the shadows of the tree branches over the tombs. He ordered Ian to give him the flashlight. Ian refused. "Uncle Mitch—" Eric called back to us in complaint.

"Damn it, Ian, give him the light," Mitch shouted. "Never mind looking at the graves, keep an eye on the smart boy there." Under his breath, he muttered, "Fucking morons." He waited to see that Ian obeyed him.

With Mitch staying near me, I gradually started drifting farther away from the others, supposedly to find dear Alice. "Try that one," I would say, and while he bent closer, I'd move to the next one.

I gradually lured him into a place with more treacherous footing, a muddy spot between two open graves. I could smell the stagnant water that lay along the bottom of each.

Despite his instructions, Ian got caught up in finding Alice Pelck's grave now, distracted by reading the tombstones Ethan illuminated, not paying close attention to Ethan himself. Eric was nervously darting his flashlight all around, peering into empty graves and pulling back with distaste.

"I think I see it!" I shouted, moving closer to one of the open graves, blocking Mitch's view of its monument.

Ian turned toward us. Mitch moved forward to try to read the tombstone, telling me to get out of the way. Eric turned his light toward us, but Mitch was now between me and Eric. Eric's beam of light fell on Mitch just as he bent over me, and just as I rose and shouldered into him with all my might.

I lost my footing on the slippery ground and fell face first into the mud, but Mitch was off-balance and fell backward into the stinking open grave. I heard him hit bottom with a splash as I hurriedly scooted myself behind the cover of the tombstone.

Ian fired at me, his bullet striking the wing of the stone angel above me. A shard of stone flew off and struck me on the cheek, but I ignored its sting and rolled to my feet. Eric came running toward me. Ian shouted at Eric to get the hell out of the way. I glanced back in time to see Ethan take his chance—while Ian and Eric started toward me, Ethan used his flashlight to deliver a cracking blow to Ian's head.

Even though I was some distance from them, I heard the sound of it. Ethan's flashlight broke. Ian pitched forward. Ethan disappeared behind some equipment.

I ran, dodging between trees and tombstones, watching for open graves. Glancing back, I saw Eric, unsure of which of several disasters to attend to first.

"Get your ass over here and get me out of this fucking grave!" Mitch screamed. "Now! And bring some damned light!"

I ran awkwardly from tombstone to tombstone, tree to tree, wishing my hands were free to allow me better balance and speed. I gradually headed toward the gates—until I saw Ian stumble to his feet and head in that same direction. He looked dazed, but not necessarily too out of it to fire a shot that might kill me. Not the gates, then. I altered my course and wound my way to the oleander, trying to see Ethan, thinking once or twice that I caught a glimpse of movement in the dark.

I reached the oleander and burrowed into it, then watched for Ethan while catching my breath.

I couldn't see much. There was only one flashlight now, and it was shining eerily up out of a grave, illuminating the face and wings of the angel above. Eric had taken off his jacket and was using it as a lifeline to Mitch, bracing himself against the tombstone, trying to pull Mitch out without being pulled in himself. It didn't seem to be working well, judging from Mitch's shouted obscenities. Apparently, he had sprained or broken an ankle in the fall. Eric tried grabbing hold of his clothing and hauling him up, but this also failed—he lost his grip on Mitch's muddy clothing, and dropped him for a second dunking.

I tried desperately to think of a way to draw Ian's attention away from Ethan, without getting caught myself.

I searched along the chain-link fence as quietly as I could and found a place where someone or something had previously burrowed in or out. The gap between the ground and the bottom of the fence was narrow, but I lowered myself to my belly and began to snake my way through the opening. Metal prongs of broken fencing caught at my skin and clothes, but I made it through. I came clumsily to my feet. I ran to the Jeep and slammed myself against it.

The car alarm went off.

Over its din, I heard Eric and Ian shouting that we were getting away.

"Never mind!" Mitch yelled. "Just get me the hell out of here."

I hurried back through the fence, but stayed hidden within the oleander. Ethan might have made his way free by now, but I couldn't be sure, and I didn't want to abandon him. I decided I'd wait where I was a little longer. With any luck, the car alarm might attract the attention of a passing patrol car.

I watched as Ian stumbled his way toward his brother and uncle. With his assistance, Mitch was freed from his trap. "Eric, go shut that damned alarm off. Bring the car in here," Mitch said. "We need the headlights."

Ian handed the keys over to him. Eric moved with surprising speed back to the Jeep, eventually coming close enough to turn the alarm off with the key-chain remote. He paused, in the quiet that followed, and seemed to look back toward the oleander. I hunkered down, hoping I wasn't more visible to him than I thought I was.

I heard Ian say, "Maybe I should call the helicopter."

"Yes, yes . . . that's even better," Mitch said. "The chopper will see them. We'll leave from here."

When Eric pulled the car in, he said, "I think there's someone hiding in those bushes, by the back fence."

Hell.

"You and Ian, search along that back fence," Mitch ordered. "You hear me, Ian?"

"Who's going to watch the gate?" Ian protested.

"I'll watch the gate. Leave the Jeep lights on."

"I need my gun," Eric said. "Give it back."

"I'm not going to sit here crippled and unarmed, you dunce! They don't have guns. Take a stick."

"Give me the flashlight, at least."

Mitch conceded that this would aid in the search and handed it to him. "Now hurry! By now the bastard's over the fence and halfway to Hong Kong."

"He's going to Hong Kong?" Eric asked, distracted.

"Damn you, Eric, get over to that fence!"

From the moment I had heard Eric mention the oleander, I began easing out from my hiding place. One flashlight, I told myself. The car was providing light in one line of sight, but Mitch wouldn't be able to maneuver that source of light. That was to my advantage. Staying as low as I could, I hurried out of the oleander and toward a nearby tomb.

Ian moved down the outside of the cemetery; Eric used the flashlight and a large stick to poke and prod at the bushes. I could stay hidden from them where I was, but not from Mitch, who was focused on shouting instructions to them, but at any moment might start to look around him. It was only a matter of time before he saw the silver of the duct tape reflected on my wrists in the moonlight.

The one place none of them seemed to be watching was the cemetery's front gates. I started to make my way toward them, thinking that if I didn't find a way through the entrance before the helicopter arrived, at least I might be able to hide under the equipment.

If the helicopter was going to carry all of the Yeagers and a crew for a distance that would allow them to escape law enforcement, it would probably be a big one. Landing it in other parts of the city might have attracted too much attention. But here? As Mitch Yeager had noted, no one in here was going to complain.

I wondered if the helicopter might be too big to land in the cemetery. No, I decided—I could see an area of more modern graves that was flat and open. That area was not near the front gates, though.

Mitch Yeager sat between me and the area I wanted to reach. I'd have to pass fairly close to him if I wanted to reach the gate. If the helicopter arrived before I made it, well—I decided I'd run back and kill him, if I had to do it by pushing him into the grave again, jumping in after him, and head-butting him to death.

I was really hoping against having to try that.

I crept along until I drew just about even with him, only a few yards away, but obscured from his view by tombstones and equipment, and watched him sit in the moonlight. His attention was fully absorbed by the hunt in the oleander. The expression on his face was smug.

Rage rose within me. The arrogant asshole was confident that once again he'd escape justice. He had every reason to believe that, of course. Maureen O'Connor and her family, the Ducanes, Rose Hannon, Baby Max, Corrigan, even his own adopted son—what price had he ever paid for the pain and death he had caused? None. He had become wealthy and more respectable. Why should he fear capture?

For a moment, the idea of killing him by any means I could didn't seem so bad.

I had taken one creeping step toward him when there was sudden shouting and wrestling in the bushes.

"Don't shoot him!" Mitch shouted.

I saw Ethan being dragged from the bushes as he and Eric fought. Eric used his size and weight to tackle Ethan to the ground. He raised the flashlight, ready to strike him, when Mitch's shout stopped him mid-swing.

"No! Bring him to me!"

68

"I SAID, BRING HIM TO ME, YOU MORONS!"

Eric stood slowly. In the past twenty minutes or so, we had probably given him the biggest workout he'd had in twenty years. As Ian hauled Ethan up between them, Eric shined his flashlight beam over the ground. "There!" he shouted. "What the fuck is that?"

He picked up an object that I couldn't make out from where I stood.

They brought Ethan to the edge of the grave where Mitch sat.

Eric tossed something shiny down before Mitch.

"A tape recorder?" Mitch said, outraged. "Eric, get rid of it."

Eric stomped on it with a heavy booted heel, then picked it up and made as if to hurl it away.

"No," Mitch said. "In the grave."

I heard it hit with a splash.

"You don't have shit, do you?" Mitch said.

Ethan, still out of breath from his struggle with Eric, smiled. "Risk it, if you think I don't."

Mitch stared at him, rubbing his ankle. "I might."

He turned to Ian. "Shoot him in the kneecap."

One flashlight, I told myself, and shouted, from behind a tombstone, "Bad bet, Yeager."

"Irene!" Ethan shouted. "No!"

"Get her! Get that bitch! No, Ian, give me your gun first."

As usual, his troops needed direction, and while he shouted orders, I ran like hell, ducking and dodging behind marble monuments and concrete vaults, and then in and around the equipment.

Eric had that one flashlight, which might be why he caught up with me first, but he was tired from his previous battles, and I was able to land a hard kick on his knee before he had a good grip on me. He let loose and gave a howl of pain as he stumbled to the ground. Before he could get up again, I was set upon by Ian, who handed me a little payback before hauling me to my feet and over to Mitch. Eric slowly limped after us.

Ian left me next to Ethan. Mitch Yeager looked between us. "You know, until just now, I thought the love story was just one more lie." Ethan put an arm around my shoulders. He was shaking. Or I was.

"Separate them. Stand her up by the grave," Mitch commanded, indicating the one I had pushed him into earlier.

When they had done so, Mitch said, "Thanks to you, I have had a trying evening, Ms. Kelly." He paused, then smiled. "Do you hear that sound?"

It was faint, but distinct. A helicopter.

"I'm going to leave, and take the smart boy with me, because something tells me his sense of self-preservation is stronger than yours. He has guts, but he's not so caught up in sacrifice as you are, is he? His generation is ultimately more pragmatic. They don't see the sense in struggling. If there is an easy way, they take it."

"That's bullshit," I said.

"Oh no. I'll offer him an easy way out of this mess you've obviously lured him into, and he'll take it." He paused again, listening to the helicopter coming closer. "I wonder if you have the locket at all?"

"Your gamble," I said.

"Your loss," he said. "Shoot her."

I saw what Ethan was going to do just a moment before he moved.

"No!" I shouted, but he stepped in front of me.

I waited for the sound of gunfire. Instead, I heard, "Which one of us do you want to do it?"

The helicopter was roaring closer now. In the distance, I thought I heard sirens.

Too late. Too late.

"God damn it," Mitch said, and raised the gun he held.

I bent slightly to the side to hook my ankle around Ethan's, to try to move him out of harm's way, but like the sirens, I was too late. Mitch fired.

I felt the jolt of Ethan's reaction as he was hit. He pitched backward, and I was helpless to stop my own backward fall into the grave as his weight came against me.

I landed hard, splashing foul water everywhere. Ethan landed on top of me. The double impact knocked the wind out of me. For a moment, I could not breathe or seem to catch my breath.

Beneath my back, I felt ooze. My hands, still painfully trapped behind me, and something hard—the tape recorder?—digging into my back.

Ethan's blood, wet and warm, began to soak from his back onto my chest. Mitch Yeager looked down on us and raised his pistol again.

I heard someone shout in panic, "Uncle Mitch!"

A sudden great noise and light filled the grave from overhead. A wind that stirred dirt and water into a spray that forced me to close my eyes.

There was noise, and more noise, a clamor that only increased and made no sense from my world of the grave.

Ethan was dying.

I didn't even care that Mitch was escaping.

I don't know how long it was, exactly, before I realized that Mitch's helicopter was shouting orders at the Yeagers. And claiming to be the police.

69

ETHAN HAD ALREADY BEEN AIRLIFTED TO ST. ANNE'S, THE TRAUMA CENTER nearest the cemetery, by the time my hands were cut free of duct tape and I had been helped up onto the grass. I had been taken to St. Anne's, too, but mostly just to get cleaned up a bit and loaded up with antibiotics. Something about soaking cuts and scrapes in bacteria-filled water that smelled of decomposition tended to alarm medical people. I had my face stitched from the encounter with the bit of angel wing. I was bruised.

That was nothing. The real ache wasn't physical.

Frank's presence eased some of that. He hadn't let me out of his sight from the moment I had been hauled up out of the grave. Since I reeked of blood and dead bodies at that point, that was brave of him. Lydia had brought a change of clothes for me and I had showered, but I could swear I still smelled the cemetery. I tried not to take that as an omen.

The police had questions. They had to wait a little while to get answers. I saw Zeke Brennan for the second time in twenty-four hours, but this time, he was working for Ethan and me. Zeke didn't prevent me from being fully cooperative. My patience nearly did—I couldn't concentrate well, given my anxiety over Ethan. As a favor to Frank, one of the officers who had accompanied us to the hospital continually checked on Ethan's progress and let us know when there was any news. There wasn't much other than, "Still in surgery."

Mitch and his nephews had been taken to Las Piernas General. I suppose someone was afraid that the entire staff of the *Express*, which seemed to be at St. Anne's, might attack them if they were brought to the same facility.

Frank told me that Max Ducane was waiting to see me, to verify for himself that I was all right. He told me that Max had called him earlier that evening—officially yesterday evening, now—to tell him that the people who had been tailing Eric and Ian for him had lost them. "I was already worried about you, and had just tried your cell phone. Max said the Yeagers had parked on Maple, gone into a building, and never come back to their car. After a while, they realized the Yeagers had ditched them by walking through an alley to Chestnut or Polson."

When he heard that they were near where I was, Frank had found Ethan's address in the phone book and called to ask for a unit to go by the apartment. They found the door unlatched and my purse still in the living room. "So we had the Jeep's LoJack traced, and brought out the cavalry."

"Thank you isn't enough, but—thank you."

"As long as you're okay, and Ethan's okay, we're good."

Frank had warned me that the waiting room was crowded. I keep forgetting that he has a master's degree in understatement.

I halted in the hospital hallway. Frank stopped beside me. "Too much for you right now?" he asked.

"No, I won't be able to sleep if we go home. But it bothers me a little, because—"

"Because you can't help but wonder if they're here out of guilt. Who cares? They're here. They could be feeling just as guilty in comfort at home."

"You're right," I said.

Max spotted me. He was with Helen and my aunt Mary. I caught a glimpse of Barbara and Kenny just before the newspaper staff noticed my presence. There was a near riot while I was surrounded by them. I was alive, I could talk. They asked if I was all right. They winced at the sight of the bandages and bruises. They asked if I knew anything about Ethan's condition.

But then the crowd moved a little, and my sister was saying that there was someone here who was anxious to see me, and on a night I had lain in a grave, I suddenly saw a ghost.

O'Connor. O'Connor was here. I must have called his name aloud.

When he turned toward me and smiled, I felt faint. Frank put an arm around me, and whether anyone else was aware of it or not, that was all that kept me on my feet.

The ghost spoke. "Yes, I'm O'Connor—and you must be Irene," he said, in O'Connor's voice, but sweetened with a gorgeous Irish accent. "Conn was forever talking of you to me. I'm his brother Dermot."

He extended a hand. I took it in mine and promptly burst into tears.

"There now," he said, "it's all right. It's all right now." Somehow we were maneuvered to some chairs, and I managed to regain some semblance of composure.

"It's the devil's own day you've had, isn't it?" he said. "But I'm told you and this fellow they're operating on have caught the one who murdered poor Maureen, all those years ago?"

"Yes."

"Well done, child. Well done. That would please Conn so, and please him more to know you had done it. And if you need a good cry, you go right ahead and cry."

We talked for a time, and I said, "You're here for the DNA tests?"

"Yes, but I'm thinkin' it will be a waste of good money by Kenny, here."

"Oh." I felt let down. Poor Kenny . . .

"He's the image of my mother's eldest brother, you see."

"What?"

"Me and Conn, we had the look of the O'Connors. Kenny here favors the O'Haras, my mother's family." He paused and said, "I'm still glad I came, for many reasons. It's good to know your family and friends, isn't it? You'll have to tell me all about your life, since I haven't had a report in years now. Frank, don't be jealous, but Conn always thought she'd end up with a policeman from Bakersfield."

We explained that Conn was right. We made Dermot promise he'd come to dinner soon, so we could tell him the whole tale.

John Walters interrupted with an announcement that Ethan's blood type was type O, and he invited anyone else who was type O to join him in donating blood. "Or any other type," he said. "Because what Ethan can't use, someone else will."

"Has anyone contacted his family?" I asked.

"He doesn't seem to have any," John said. "His father died while he was in college, and his mother died years ago. No siblings."

Max and Helen had stood up together when he made the first part of this announcement. When they saw that quite a few others were already on their way, they stayed back long enough to talk to me for a few minutes. "I'm so glad you're all right," Max said, "and that the Yeagers are finally being made to pay for some of their sins. Maybe we'll finally find out what happened to the baby."

I looked at Helen and said, "I think I know."

She met my gaze. "Do you?"

"Yes. But perhaps you'd like to be somewhere more private?"

"No," she said with a smile. "I think I've been private long enough, don't you? But for Max's sake, let's ask the nurse if there is somewhere we can talk."

We were ushered into a small conference room.

"Max," I said, "you're the real Max Ducane."

"I don't know what the two of you were talking about just now, or what this is all about, but it's okay, I'm really okay now knowing I'm not Max. DNA doesn't lie."

"No, it doesn't. Which is why, if Helen's blood were tested, you'd know you were sitting next to your maternal grandmother."

"What?"

"Do you tell this, or do I?" I asked Helen.

"Allow me to at least technically keep my word to Lillian," she said.

I nodded and went on. "Sometime around 1936, a rather adventurous young woman who had a job at a newspaper fell in love with Handsome Jack Corrigan. He settled down later, but at the time, she knew that it was hopeless to expect him to make much of a husband. He was probably seeing Lillian Vanderveer when the newspaperwoman learned she was pregnant with his child."

"The newspaperwoman was not virtuous, I'm afraid," Helen said.

"Oh, I don't think it's likely she would have given herself to anyone else. But at that time, in her situation, unmarried and pregnant, her alternatives weren't many. She loved her career, in a way that perhaps only someone else who has ink in her veins can understand, but this pregnancy would mean she would lose her job. Abortion would have been an illegal and dangerous back-alley matter, and she was a Catholic girl as well."

"Again, not a very good one."

"She wanted the child to live, but what choices did she have? If she gave birth out of wedlock, she and the child would be subject to constant ridicule. There was no chance on earth that her conservative employer would allow her to continue to work for the newspaper. If she tried to support the child through any of the other few jobs that were available to women, she would be consigning both of them to a life of poverty."

"She was willing to do that for herself, but it was such a hard thing to choose for the child."

"I'm not so sure about this next part, because I only have the observations of another child to go on—an eight- or nine-year-old boy."

"A great observer. Just didn't know what he was seeing."

"I'm much older than he was then, and although it was there before me, I didn't see it either, not until we had our talk the other day." I turned to Max. "Conn O'Connor was a nosy child, dedicated to Jack Corrigan, and not overly fond of Lillian—although he later became her friend. He spied on his hero one night and learned that he was going on a date with Lillian, a married woman.

He probably didn't know that Lillian was in the early stages of a pregnancy. There was a car accident—a horrible accident, one that left Jack partially lame the rest of his life. But what few others know—what O'Connor didn't know until many years later himself—was that Lillian was injured in that same accident. She miscarried."

"I'll let you ask Lillian about her part of this story," Helen said.

"Perhaps the injury was worse, because she never conceived another child. And there was the possibility, if her husband returned from Europe, that he would ask questions about when and how the pregnancy ended."

"He was an ass," was all that Helen would say on that subject.

"Helen liked Lillian, and perhaps she even wondered if Lillian's child might have been a half brother or half sister of her own. Whatever the case, Helen and Lillian comforted each other, and somewhere in all this time of worry and woe, they came up with a solution. Helen would quit the paper, ostensibly to help Lillian with her new project. They would live in the mountains, away from the prying eyes of local society. Lillian's name would be on the child's birth certificate, and she would raise him or her in a life of privilege. She swore, in exchange for Helen's secrecy—and her child—that she would never deny Helen access to the little girl who was born up in the mountains that winter."

Max was staring at her, obviously having trouble taking it all in.

"You'd probably like to hate me," Helen said to him. "Maybe you do. I won't blame you at all. The promises I made to Lillian were the hardest I've ever had to keep. But they were promises."

He shook his head, saying, "I don't hate you, but . . . my God, Helen . . ."

She began to cry. I wanted to go to her, but Frank put a hand on my shoulder.

Max hesitated only briefly, then embraced her.

"You have questions, I'm sure," she said, still crying. "I can't answer all of them, but I'm sure I can get Lillian to see the wisdom of letting some part of these secrets out now."

"Did Jack Corrigan ever know?" he asked.

"Yes. I think at first he suspected—well, I'll leave that part of the story to Lillian. One day O'Connor announced that he was marrying a woman he'd only bedded once, because she was pregnant, and Jack was a horse's ass about it. So I confronted him, and in turn he confronted me, and after calling Lillian and threatening her with all sorts of ridiculous things, he learned the truth from us."

Max sat silently, then said, "Can we test to make sure, just so we know I'm the child who . . ."

"Of course."

"And Lillian—do you think she'll help me bring this out in public? Some of it, anyway?"

"We'll work on that together. I think if she realizes that the Yeagers can finally be punished for what they did to Katy, and our lives, then . . . yes." She smiled. "She really isn't one tenth as selfish as she pretends to be."

We left them to talk together. I went out to check on Ethan again. We arrived just in time to hear a doctor express cautious optimism about his survival. We learned that he was out of surgery and about to be moved to ICU. "No visitors for a while, please—except—is there someone named Irene here?" I came forward. "If you can keep it very brief, I think it would be good for him to see you're alive." He smiled. "He thinks we're lying to him."

Frank came with me. Ethan was pale, connected to a lot of machinery, obviously full of painkillers. He smiled at us and said, "Thought I'd lost you."

"No. Rest and recover. We'll get a room ready for you at home."

He looked toward Frank. "You sure you want me there?"

"You saved her," Frank said. "You're family now, like it or not."

"Family," he said. "Sounds good."

ABOUT THE AUTHOR

JAN BURKE is the recipient of the Mystery Writers of America's Edgar Award® for Best Novel, the Agatha Award, the Macavity Award, and the Ellery Queen Mystery Magazine Readers Award. She lives in Southern California with her husband, Tim, and her dogs, Cappy and Britches.